the
hard
way

Other books by Michael Lassell

Poems for Lost and Un-lost Boys
Decade Dance

A RICHARD KASAK BOOK

the hard way

MICHAEL LASSELL

The Hard Way
Copyright © 1995 Michael Lassell
Acknowledgments on page 317

All Rights Reserved

No part of this book may be reproduced, stored in a retrieval system, or transmitted in any form, by any means, including mechanical, electronic, photocopying, recording or otherwise, without prior written permission of the publishers.

First Richard Kasak Book Edition 1995

First Printing January 1995

ISBN 1-56333-231-0

Cover Art ©1995 Judy Simonian

Cover Design by Kurt Griffith

Manufactured in the United States of America
Published by Masquerade Books, Inc.
801 Second Avenue
New York, N.Y. 10017

• the hard way •

Foreword   3

PART ONE: The Cradle of Civilization

Hometowns: Brooklyn/Long Island/Los Angeles/New York   17
A Child's Garden Of Verses   37
   Cold heat
   What was meant by heredity
   Brother snow
   Scab, the Teeth, and Tongues (watch TV)
   Daddy
   His mother's incest
   Grandfather's robe
Pancho Villa And A Fear Of Crocodiles   49

PART TWO: For Better or Worse

This Is The Story Of Kay   61
Willie   67
On The Game   97
   Personal foibles #1
   Hustling
   Stars
   Stroke of midnight
   Tim
   Monday
   Uptown local
   Making a mark

PART THREE: Our Bodies and Our Blood

Confessions Of A Clothes Whore   111
25 Reasons To Hate Heterosexuals   117
Writ Of Habeas Corpus: Tennessee Williams/Truman Capote   125
When Death Is Too Much With Us   133
Heart In San Francisco   141
The Way Of All Flesh   151
   Even the actor dies
   Saturday night in New York City
   Keepsake
   Prism
   What it means to live alone again
   Indiana Gary
   Kissing Ramón
   The day that Adrien didn't come to New York
   Shuttle, 9:00 A.M

• the hard way •

Poems For Roberto — 165
   Passing through
   Andrew, son of James
   How to visit your ex
   Brady Street, San Francisco
   Another pang of Roberto
   Eighteen years
   Our town
A Simple Matter Of Conversion — 183

PART FOUR: My Life in Art

Skyfires — 191
Negative Image — 225
How To Be A Poet — 235
   How to be a hedonist
   How to watch your brother die
   How to go to the theater
   How to write a poem
   How to choose life

PART FIVE: New Frontiers

PRIDE — 257
Lovesick — 261
A New York State Of Mind — 267
Two Poems For New York City — 285
   Return to the Naked City
   Open windows
Near The Fire: The March On Washington, 1993 — 289
Amateur Night: On Masks, Gender And The Hellacious
      Halloween Hoedown Of 1970 — 299
Oh, God! Not Again! Confessions Of A Reluctant Agnostic — 309

Foreword

So, what the hell is this?

Think back, if you were born, to 1976—that much-ballyhooed American Bicentennial Year in which the U.S. turned 200 and I just felt it (red with shame, white with rage, blue with depression) and I had just completed my third college degree (this one from the Yale School of Drama) and broken up—largely because of the time-consuming pursuit of the aforesaid—with my first lover, Roberto (not to be confused with my dear college friend Robert, both of them now dead and both appearing herein. Robert was a lawyer).

I had recently moved to L.A. for the second—but perhaps not final—time, when I happened upon Christopher Isherwood's *Christopher and His Kind: 1929–1939*, a name-naming, truth-telling, nonfiction reflection on his *Berlin Stories*, the source of John van Druten's *I Am A Camera* (the 1951 play, which I read at Yale, of course, and subsequent 1955 film) musicalized into *Cabaret*, to which original stage version my parents took me as a twentieth birthday gift in 1967, and which 1972 film version appealed to me mightily, not only because of its flirtatious and ambiguous sexuality, but because I had been working a terrific long-distance crush on Michael York ever since the first of seventeen times I saw Franco Zeffirelli's *Romeo and Juliet* while living in London in 1968 and 1969, and because Liza Minnelli was dating Desi Arnaz, Jr., who was going to CalArts at the same time I was, so we sometimes saw them in the cafeteria eating lunch together. Nice sentence, eh?

That same year—back to 1976, now—I had written a review for *Yale/theater* of Tennessee Williams's *Memoirs,* in which—ever the dilettante—I quoted Oscar Wilde's 1890 essay "The Critic as Artist" to the effect that the trouble with memoirs is that they are too often written by people with faulty memories or by those to whom nothing particularly remarkable has ever happened. In fact, Gore Vidal attacked his old drinking buddy in the *New York Review of Books* for the drama queen's poetically realistic manipulation of the far-from-flattering facts of his quixotic life.

In assembling this collection of (mostly) already published fiction, nonfiction, and poetry, all these names and events came back to me like badly dressed tourists to Capistrano, although, naturally, I had to look up all the dates just to make sure my memory was working within a plus-or-minus range of five years or so. It was, I am happy to report—senility running in my family as it does (and starting at shockingly early ages).

By 1976 I had already met Tennessee Williams, once and briefly, when he was appearing in his own *Small Craft Warnings* with Candy Darling, a transvestite icon of the early 1970s in New York. You remember that scene, or have heard tell: drugs and Holly Woodlawn at the Chelsea Hotel, drugs and Holly Woodlawn at The Factory, drugs and Holly Woodlawn in *After Dark* (soft-core arts-and-entertainment porn).

After 1976 I managed to meet both Isherwood and Vidal (whom I interviewed for *L.A. Style* magazine when he published *Hollywood* in 1990), and he inscribed my first edition of *The City and the Plain* (published in 1948, the year after I was born) with the lovely words: "To Michael, this manual from Gore Vidal," which you have to know to the book to appreciate, which I did and I do.

| *The Hard Way* |

I met Isherwood by writing him a fan letter after being moved by the courage of *Christopher and His Kind* (although, of course, times had changed a weeny tad between 1929 and 1976; so the revelations of the book, while still tantalizing, were far from career-kaputing for those who were stripped of their borrowed *à clef* costumes, appearing for the first time, as it were, in their now-wrinkled, nonfiction birthday suits.

The gay eminence invited me to tea, and off I went to the beach in the little red Audi, puffing away on little white Marlboro cigarettes while the backseat puddled up with gasoline from a leak in the fuel line. I was, as all were, charmed and conquered by Chris's graciousness, generosity, and the view from his deck of the Santa Monica Mountains, where the whole of the expatriate Brit clique seemed to live.

Fond as I am of what my friend Clark Henley (author of the hilarious *Butch Manual)* and I used to call "festive gay exaggeration," I occasionally overstate the intimacy of my relationship with the master prose stylist and soothsayer (he told the truth and told it soothingly). I tell you my truth now: We knew each other; we were not friends. I did sit nude for painter Don Bachardy, Isherwood's life partner of several decades, while the mild-mannered English novelist, then quite ill with the cancer that would kill him, sat in a rocking chair, and I tried to decide whether the erection I was having was embarrassing me or not. I wrote about this experience for a now-defunct gay glossy called *In Touch* in 1986.

When Isherwood died that same year, I was invited to participate in a memorial reading at the Los Angeles Theater Center, although Isherwood wanted no such public event. This is, however, where I first actually got to talk to Julie Harris, I believe—unless it was that Thanksgiving party at Don Freed's when Ed Asner brought his new wife and Julie Harris made fruitcake from Emily Dickinson's recipe. Harris, of course, played Sally Bowles in both stage and screen versions of *I Am a Camera,* though I never saw her perform live until my Colgate University roommate, John Francis Neville III, and I drove to his hometown of Syracuse and stood through a road-company production of Tennessee Williams's *A Streetcar Named Desire* (we were such dedicated little thespians in 1966). So, you see, it's true: Everything relates and all paths cross. I am also an inveterate name-dropper. Forgive me. It's a symptom of low self-esteem, which is kind of another story, but you can read between the lines.

Like Williams, like Vidal, like Isherwood, I have plundered this life of mine for incident and offered it up to scrutiny in fiction and nonfiction settings at varying degrees of distance to fact. (My dear friend Kenny Moore used to say that I'd lie when the truth would do me more good, which is another way of saying I'm a born writer.)

I do not compare myself to these three queer giants of letters to borrow their prestige, or attempt to justify myself to the critic of memoirs in Wilde's 1890 essay through the quality of my writing or the inherent sway my life might hold on the imagination of my peers. I have been flattered, gratified, and always surprised to find out that I have had some impact on some people, and that some readers, at least, find something in my writing amusing, inspiring, or, at least, familiar. Nothing makes me happier than knowing from their teachers' reports that high-school students are finding courage, compassion, and relief from persecution by reading my poem "How to watch your brother die" or a silly little essay I dashed off for the *L.A. Weekly* called "25 Reasons to Hate Heterosexuals."

Nevertheless, I still have a hard time telling the truth; not only because the truth—the language of reality—is hard to hear when your ears are pointedly full of the music of fantasy, but because it's hard to know per se…and even harder to remember long after the fact. I have so mixed my fiction and nonfiction media (even in my poetry) that I am not even exactly sure sometimes whether something happened or whether I have simply accepted as fact some fabrication I had intended as a mythopoetic or camouflaging embellishment ("festive gay exaggeration").

Anyway, if you read through this book, you will find some incidents reported as fact and some offered up as fiction which seem downright identical. This is the nature of writing, and of fiction in particular: to spin the empirically factual with the aesthetically real like pigment on one of those twirling $1 paintings

| The Hard Way |

you can make yourself at county fairs. Since all facts take on a veneer of fiction by virtue of having been written (yes, even in newspapers), all writing is to some degree fiction. Even when I have not meant to mislead, I have—by using the first-person singular pronoun *I*. Here's a helpful reading hint: Just because I use the word "I" does not mean *I* have ever done the things I say "I" has done. (This "I" is very similar to the "you" I seem to find myself talking to, as if my twin were in the room with me instead of dead. P. S. There was no twin, it's just a feeling I've had all my life—that I'm the surviving member of a set of doubles. I think it has to do with psychosis.)

So, which is Ella Fitzgerald and which is Memorex? I can't even always tell you. The bottom line, of course, is that it just doesn't matter; which is why, dear reader, I have not bothered to label the prose "fiction" and "nonfiction." In some cases, I wouldn't even know how. Try not to make the mistake a *Boston Globe* book critic made in reviewing *Poets for Life: 76 Poets Respond to AIDS*, when he wrote that not all the poems were written by gay people, that "How to watch your brother die" was written by a heterosexual man about the death of his gay brother. "How to watch your brother die" was written about the death of a gay man, by a gay man, from the point of view of his straight brother. This is why they call it "art." And the reviewer, who answered my subsequent letter with a heartfelt apology, was himself homosexual. So what's a queer to do?

Henrik Ibsen, another thespic northern light I read about in drama school, and a decidedly nonqueer one at that, once said that every word he had written was autobiographical in the sense that he had lived through it *inwardly*—from the folk magic of *Peer Gynt* to the protorealist introspection of *A Doll's House*. (It was Ibsen who, when his work was criticized as "not poetry," wrote heroically that if his writing was not poetry, then the definition of poetry would have to change to accommodate it. Sing it, girl! There was a time, and let us not forget it, that a book as erotic as this one is in part—as downright *pornygrafic* was not only considered "not art" (the battle cry of every bitter brain-dead journalist who ever wrote a word of criticism, myself included), but not publishable, and this was as recently as my adolescence:

– 7 –

Henry Miller's *Tropic of Cancer* could not be published in this country until 1961!

Virtually all of the material in this book was written and published between 1983 and 1993, although it covers all the years I can remember. The focus, of course, is on the post-Stonewall Liberation Years (although I was, avant-gardiste that I am and have been, out—or out-ish—before 1969). I am, like most writers, horrified to read work written as recently as ten days ago, much less ten years ago, but I have bitten the bullet and made few changes, except when some reference is so out of cultural currency as to obscure my own obscure point, or when I can't remember what the hell I meant by something. But what you see here is pretty much the way it was the first time it appeared in black and white.

Each book is a gift, not to its readers, but to its author. Writers live—or at least work—to see their words in print; and yet that is, for most of us, the elusive, often seemingly unattainable goal. I have been fortunate to have seen my own efforts typeset many times: in my own previous collections of poetry; in numerous anthologies of poetry, fiction, and nonfiction; and in scores of magazines, newspapers, and literary journals all over this country and abroad (sometimes translated into languages I do not speak).

In every case, my writing has become public because someone, or some several ones, have deemed the work worthy despite the considerable risk, both financial and otherwise, of letting out into the world minority sentiments that have little favor in the world in which we find ourselves living—particularly minority sentiments often expressed in the vernacular of sailors and truck drivers, and, more often as not, involving the conjoined genitalia of such archetypes—or various other more uptown homosexual beings. For those of us who write about being gay—and about the sexual part of being gay—being published is still difficult, particularly when the content of the writing is neither entertaining in the MTV sense of the word, or uplifting, in the *700 Club* sense.

During his tortured lifetime, Tennessee Williams was accused frequently of intending to shock. He replied that he simply told

| *The Hard Way* |

the truth, and that the truth was shocking. Now, more than ever, the truth shocks. Partly because few people know it, fewer are willing to speak it, and fewer still are willing to distribute it. My own highly subjective and far from codified truth is that of a sometimes sad, always angry American queer poet ca. 1994. Trust me: colorful as it has been from time to time, you don't want to be me. Occasionally, this causes severe distress. In the summer of 1993, that distress had transmogrified into depression, then despair. I felt irrelevant and so disenfranchised that I found it difficult to function. A therapist asked if there was anything at all in my life I could point to as a success. My first reaction was my friends. I have been richly blessed with loving accomplices in this misdemeanor of life. Since I had nothing to lose but pain, I reached out to them, and they responded with such an outpouring of support that it changed me in some paradigmatic way.

John Preston engineered this book—his last and greatest gift to me—and I am eternally grateful, not only for this collection, but for his having sought me out time and again to participate in his own anthologies. Richard Kasak agreed to publish it sight unseen, so he is to be thanked most profusely, too. May his bookkeepers speak kindly of him in the aftermath.

I am always grateful to the people who have published my work, and some of them deserve mention here: Sasha Alyson, who swallowed his great reluctance to publish poetry, then gave me *Decade Dance* and claims never to have regretted it even though it hasn't profited him a penny; and David Kalmansohn of *Frontiers* in Los Angeles, who lets me rave and ramble, stew and spew on the pages of his magazine, much to my creative profit; and Richard Rouilard, as supportive now that he is at the *Los Angeles Times Magazine* as he always was in the good years of the *Advocate*, when he was editor there.

And, as always, but this time with special affection: Howard Junker of ZYZZYVA, Bob Hershon and Ron Schreiber of *Hanging Loose,* Frederick Raborg of *Amelia* (who published my first book, *Poems for Lost and Un-lost Boys*), Phil Willkie and the gang at the *James White Review* in Minneapolis, Rudy Kikel at *Bay Windows* in Boston, Amy Scholder and Ira Silverberg of *High Risk* renown, Carl Morse and Joan Larkin for including me in *Gay & Lesbian Poetry in Our Time,* and Michael Denneny of St. Martin's Press for for his constant support and friendship.

I have also to thank, in no particular order whatsoever (so please don't anyone be offended): Eric Latzky, for the handy pocket-sized *Tao Te Ching;* Alan B. Coleman and John Krider, for nonstop invitations to Key West; Linda Ekblad for having been my best friend since the day I was born (by which natal act I usurped her role as the only baby in our extended circle of family and friends); Joie Davidow, for her energetic, high-spirited participation in the world we share; Tim Miller and Doug Sadownick for being so utterly different and so perennially a pair of madcap coconspirators; Gavin Dillard, for letting me plunder our shared history for my work; Paul Monette, still angry after all these years; Barry Sandler, for his constant subversion of the American Lie.... Susan LaTempa and Danny Milder and the girls... Eileen Rosaly and Peter Jason... Jim and Johnna McHugh (and Chloé, of course)... Joe DeCola... Ralph Brooks... Felice Picano... Eve Ensler... Andrew Berner... Norman Laurila... Richard Labonte... A. K. Salz... Mark Thompson and Malcolm Boyd... the late and greatly mourned Asotto Saint... Sarah Pettit... Betty Berzon and Terry DeCrescenzo... Michael Nava... Bill Pryor and Michael Zachary... Barnet Kellman and Nancy Mette and Kate and Eliza... Julia Cameron...and Ben Mah—always and again, because he wakes up my heart every time it breaks.

Greenwich Village
Yom Kippur, 1994

For Roy Cameron

Nothing in the world
is as soft and yielding as water.
Yet for dissolving the hard and inflexible,
nothing can surpass it.

The soft overcomes the hard;
the gentle overcomes the rigid.
Everyone knows this is true,
but few can put it into practice.

—Lao-Tzu (born ca. 604 B.C.)
Tao Te Ching
Translated by Stephen Mitchell (1988)

Part One

THE CRADLE OF CIVILIZATION

Hometowns:
Brooklyn/Long Island/Los Angeles/New York

Do I have a hometown? I never thought so. I know where I was born: Flower Fifth Avenue Hospital in New York City. My parents lived in Brooklyn at the time, in Greenpoint, in one of two identical railroad flats over a shop where the pickle-making business founded by my maternal grandfather still turned out Old Reliable dills. My mother grew up at 8 Lombardy Street, and in its unglamorous confines my earliest memories took form: my father tightening barrel hoops with a rubber mallet, the small desk under the girlie calendar where my beloved Aunt Helene kept the books, the sour smell of brine seeping through oak staves. My grandfather had died of bleeding ulcers at the Mayo Clinic during the war while my father was off with General Eisenhower invading Normandy (ancestral home, it is supposed, of the Lassell family). My maternal grandmother, a sofa-sized, sad-faced woman in every photograph, followed her husband within months, dead of a broken heart—or bone cancer, depending on who's telling the story, how much alcohol has been consumed, and how much sentiment is wafting through the room. Cancer was considered shameful in those days, so my mother's not really sure how her mother died, a statement that embodies a sorrow all its own.

In any case, I was a postwar Brooklyn Boom baby, and my father, Purple Heart in hand, was working for his brother-in-law making pickles and horseradish and selling them to places in Manhattan, some of which still exist, and a few of which—like the Empire Diner on Tenth Avenue—I've patronized just for the sake of continuity. From 1947 to 1950, we lived in one of the 8 Lombardy Street flats, across the landing (where our bathroom was) from my mother's brother Jack, his wife (my godmother, Helene), and their daughter Gloria, fourteen years my senior and my first baby-sitter. At 6 Lombardy Street lived Helen and Alex (known then, before balding, as Whitey) and their daughter Linda, my first playmate and the only "sibling" I would ever know (remember her name: it recurs).

Alex and my father worked in the same machine shop after high school and met their future wives at their employer's vacation compound in Rocky Point, then the antipodal outpost of Long Island. My parents and Helen and Alex dated together in the late 1930s, while the women were stenographers in Rockefeller Center and the men cranked out tools for Martin Swanson, patriarch of a tribe of Swedes (and Helen's uncle). There are pictures of the two couples at the 1938 World's Fair in Flushing, all decked out, the women in fox-collared coats and broad-brimmed hats; the men in suits and fedoras, carrying walking sticks (a momentary rage). Both couples married in 1940; Linda was born during the war, I after.

So there were countless relatives and near-relatives around me in my early years, and scores of Greenpoint photographs to document the emotions my parents rarely spoke of: Michael in his highchair pulling his uncle's tie, bundled in a sled in snow, chasing pigeons in a spring park, with Uncle Doug's blue-ribbon rabbits. They are photographs of contentment and love, and I hold them as proof positive that I was happy once, although it was many years ago.

These friends-and-relations, each of whom was referred to as aunt or uncle in one Northern European language or another, came together in my maternal grandparents' summer house in the

| *The Hard Way* |

Catskills: my father's parents (American-born father, English immigrant mother); his three sisters—my aunts Carrie, Lottie, and Rose—and their families; my aunt Helene, her Polish mother (Granny, the knitting genius who bruised cheeks with two-fisted kisses), her sister (Auntie Anne), brother Joey, their spouses and children; and all the Swedes. My first trip to Palenville was in August 1947. I was three weeks old. My first birthday party, shared with my cousin Gloria's fifteenth (duly reported in the local newspaper), took place on the lawn by the huge blue hydrangeas.

To a toddler let loose from the confines of Brooklyn, this immersion in the countryside, every need attended to, was Eden. On Lombardy Street, you could smell the gasworks, where Uncle Jimmy worked, just down the block. The view from our front window was the Trunz meat-packing plant, now only recently demolished. And Linda, who is just enough older to remember, tells me there was a slaughterhouse where the animals were skinned for furs, but I don't remember it. I don't exactly *remember* the happiness of Palenville, either, but the photographic record of those days is, for me, an absolute truth. Potbellied and flaxen-haired, new at walking but running through sprinklers in diapers or less, surrounded by strong young men in T-shirts and shorts, by benign seniors lounging in the shade, by laughing women in flowered cotton sundresses with enormous buttons and pockets that held scented handkerchiefs embroidered with violets or strawberries—how could a child not be happy? There was even a swimmin' hole nearby—icy creek water coursing through a natural rock formation we called The Tub.

In the huge trees were birdhouses carved like cuckoo clocks by my grandfather before he died with half a stomach, the best doctors in the country helpless to save him, his long-suffering wife keeping a diary of her accumulating grief, a document my mother saved and intends to dig out of a trunk to read again. It will find its way into my hands one day, and I will pass it along to my cousin's daughter, or to a child of hers (the first, a boy named Justin, made his debut the week after my parents' fiftieth anniversary). My father's mother was born in London, I think, to a Jewish upholsterer and a concert singer who had given a command performance before Queen Victoria. She died shortly after

I was born. There are pictures of my grandmother's last Easter: She's gaunt, wasting, holding an infant me in her arms, trying to smile, undoubtedly delighted to be cradling the first child of her younger son, the last of her five surviving children to reproduce. I look at those pictures and wonder whether she ever got over the stigma of being half-Jewish in the Ellis Island days of New York, a biographical detail alluded to obliquely all my life, but never stated until I was nearly forty and my father was telling stories about his own Depression boyhood: skipping out on the rent month after month at night, playing hooky and sneaking into Broadway theaters to see Fanny Brice. The things my parents leave unsaid say more about them than most of the things they proclaim.

In many ways, the selling of the house in Palenville after my German grandmother's lonely death—"She just reached behind her to zip up her dress," my mother told me, "and her arm broke; she died a few months later"—marked the end of a certain innocence in my life, and the beginning of a profound feeling of restlessness, a spiritual homelessness that has always dogged me, a mutt you can't discourage by kindness or cruelty.

In 1950, just shy of my third birthday, my family joined the great exodus from the tenements of Brooklyn and the Bronx to the tract homes of Long Island, to the "developments," the "bedroom communities." With visions of middle-class materialism dancing in their heads, the children of the immigrant working class, aided and abetted by the G.I. Bill, poured whatever money they had managed to put aside (or inherit) on five-room Cape Cods on streets of nearly identical addresses. (Our street was named Campbell, I've been told, as a bribe to a sewer official who subsequently reversed his refusal to approve the builder's proposal for this new neighborhood.) Futures secure, and photo albums bursting with snapshots of their houses in each stage of construction, they went about the business of raising lawns and children.

For the next fifteen years—there are photos galore: Michael with a snowman, a puppy, a crew cut, a swimming pool, a tuxedo, and a girl—I lived in that unincorporated and altogether undistinguished section of Nassau County's New Hyde Park, on land that only shortly before had been occupied by gracious estate farms (one of the local manor houses still survives, choked by a sprawling "recreational facility"). Our fellow homesteaders came from similar metropolitan backgrounds and shared dreams of peaceful nights, safe streets, and Wonder Bread kids protected from epidemics like the influenza one in 1917 that took my mother's bookish brother George and pudgy sister Anna—the only member of my family I've ever resembled, a fact I know from the only surviving photograph of the sad-faced little girl. And I'm told by my parents that I took to suburbia like a duck to water (the suburbs are a repository of clichés, maxims, platitudes, and aphorisms) and struck out on my own to create whatever three-year-old excitement I could muster. I was shielded from life's disasters by a back-stoop mother network, a kind of over-the-hedges telegraph system of "I've got your kids, have you got mine?" If Mrs. LoPresti had made stuffed shells and sausage for dinner, she had me.

The cyclone fence in my parents' yard was meant, my father tells me now, not to keep anyone out, but to keep me in. "It didn't work," he adds with a chuckle, sipping his salt-free seltzer and flipping the filets mignons on his gas-fueled grill (sprayed with Pam to cut down on cleanup). Along the fence his roses grow, some of the bushes almost as old as I am. "Your mother gets such a kick out of those roses," he says with pride. There are hundreds of snapshots of this yard, of the roses, and family barbecues on Memorial Day, Labor Day, and my birthday, when I'd always ask for hot dogs and hamburgers, corn-on-the-cob, and watermelon—photos that record the decline of the Brooklyn/Catskills crowd and the gradual reduction of their number.

But for all the good times, the singing around the patio, I always felt that I did not fit in. I was one of the only "only children" I knew. Except for Linda, whose family soon moved into the house that kitty-cornered our yard, next to the LoPrestis. All my cousins—in places like Seaford, Plainview, Westbury—had brothers and sisters, none of them remotely like me. My mother had a second pregnancy, in 1949, but submitted to what was then called a "therapeutic" abortion after she came down with German measles at a critical phase of gestation. Since this was *never* spoken of, I do not know the details to this day, but she held me tighter than any mother in the neighborhood while I ached for freedom and for a younger brother with a passion that was almost lyrical. As late as high school, I stealthily poked holes in my father's condoms, hoping to induce an "accidental" pregnancy.

By the time I was five, before I started school, I had become an inward, moody child, suddenly unphysical, given to crippling headaches, obviously bright, even precocious, but fat, self-conscious, awkward, and neurotically dependent, a crybaby, an embarrassment.

At a neighborhood wedding when I was in my twenties, a woman who had lived down the block the whole time we were growing up together, said to me, "I've known you all my life, but I still think of you as someone from someplace else." She could not have put it better. I was so convinced that I was adopted, I stayed home from school one day to look for the adoption papers. Even now, no matter where I am, I seem to be from someplace else, looking at the world from a minority perspective, and I've had to rethink the concept of "home" over and over again. Is it a place or an attitude, a feeling of well-being, serenity, an ease of self? Hideous as Oz could be, I couldn't for the life of me figure out why Dorothy ever wanted to go back to Kansas (particularly after the Wicked Witch fizzled), yet I was plagued by nightmares in which my mother died or disappeared, leaving me abandoned.

Like many people, when I hear the word *hometown*, I conjure the kind of place where middle-aged men don comical uniforms and play *oompah* songs in gingerbread gazebos on the Fourth of July. A place where everyone is known and cared for, and the common good is not only good but common, a tangible thing universally agreed upon; where the smell of fresh sawdust means a barn is going up, and once a year a circus sets up a big top and boys leave off baseball to stare at the tattooed bosoms of the hootchie-cootchie bearded fat lady.

Where this idealized image of small towns comes from, of

course, is literature, films, and TV. Before *Twin Peaks,* it is to be remembered, there was *Peyton Place,* the book before the movie, the movie before the series. The claustrophobic stagnation of small towns was exposed, along with the seamier belly of small-town indiscretions, but Main Street, USA, is a powerful myth—like that of your immigrant ancestors' bucolic village in Alsace, where great-grandparents sat in their vineyard for an itinerant photographer, not really knowing what was happening to them. To me a "hometown" is a place where family feelings extend to neighbors and friends, a place where families allow their children breathing room to become themselves instead of carbon copies of imperfect elders, and where no child ever grows up quivering with anxiety for becoming something the common good has decided is uncommonly bad: for example, a communist, a serial killer, or a homosexual.

And a "hometown" should look like Litchfield, Connecticut, a whitewashed, wood-framed, eighteenth-century hamlet complete with potpourri-scented Christmas shop and steepled church on a central green. Litchfield is well known, but my parents and I discovered it by accident one tight-jawed afternoon driving through the flame-leafed autumn, ignoring the presence of my lover beside me in the backseat, a lover who would surely have been fiercely doted on, had he not been both male and Latino.

Neither Brooklyn nor New Hyde Park look like Litchfield, but the truth is that the naïve virtues we associate with towns that look like Hallmark cards were more than amply evident inside my family. We had enormous Christmases of abundant gifts (my parents were generous, my godparents outrageous). Every holiday was spent with the clan, which was moving family by family across the county line. Auntie might dance on the table in her underwear on New Year's Eve, and Uncle Jack's jokes might be crude and corny ("Eat every carrot and pee in the bowl"), but Uncle Roy sent postage stamps from all over the world in his Coast Guard travels—from Papua, New Guinea, to Antarctica—and Aunt Mildred was overcome with emotion trying to read me *Black Beauty.* And if a firecracker went off in a boy's hand or a pack of matches ignited in his pocket, he would be circled by a crowd of caring women who would rub ice on his blistering skin and wipe away tears with kisses. But this was the age of innocence, and the innocence seemed to dwindle to a trickle before I was ready. I took its loss personally.

Even places that look like back lots for the kinds of movies no one has made since the death of Louis B. Mayer are far from guileless. And New Hyde Park, as I came into my school years, proved neither innocent nor particularly wicked, neither picturesque nor ugly in the way that people who hate cities think cities are ugly. It is just a narrow place (an isthmus of the imagination) without a single distinguishing feature. Aesthetically void, New Hyde Park was—and is—a grid of boxy houses lived in by white, mostly Christian, mostly Republican families living mostly unexamined lives and not being bothered about it one bit. There was a wooded section once where we played Tarzan and Indians, but they tore it out to build the dullest shopping center ever erected on Long Island. There was a Currier and Ives–like skating pond, too, on the old Ritter farm, but it's been paved over, fenced in, and made into a county park that's always empty because it's been claimed by Canada geese—which no longer migrate—and it's full of their finger-sized droppings.

It's near the house where my friend Ralph lived. The summer of my senior year in high school, I would wait up for him until he came back from his night job at the airport. He was four years older, and although we had known each other since childhood, we'd only recently become friends. He was a former state track champion and the first heterosexual I ever told I was gay. He expressed no shock or disgust, but became a closer friend than ever. I spent my eighteenth birthday getting drunk with Ralph and Linda. He was shot down in Vietnam, and all that I have of him now is a photograph of his name on the Vietnam War Memorial taken by Linda on a recent trip to Washington.

Whatever needs New Hyde Park may have filled for my parents' generation, it met few of mine. And the more like an outsider I became, the fewer hungers were satisfied. Whatever decencies New Hyde Park and my loving extended family might have possessed, they had no tolerance whatever for eccentricity or difference, for contradiction or deviation. For these, my formative years, my unsensationally unhappy childhood, unfolded at the height of the Eisenhower-McCarthy era, and well-behaved children of upstanding citizens were fed a steady diet of conformity salad and what-will-the-Joneses-think? stew. We were the good people, and values were absolute (like the black-and-white television of the time: *Lassie, Howdy Doody, The Lone Ranger)*. People who were like us (white, Protestant, Republican) were good people; people who were different (you name it) were not.

And it was not considered a good thing for a male child to be a lisping sissy who hated baseball; who got good grades and loved eating, drawing, and Jesus; who managed to charm parents and teachers with his mastery of manners, but who was afraid to go outside for recess; who was threatened by bullies and teased by everyone else; who spent his leisure hours designing gowns for Brenda Starr's trousseau and hiding them because he managed to intuit that he was a transgressor every time he exercised his free will. And the lengths to which New Hyde Park, Trinity Lutheran Church, and the Parkville School went to normalize me, which felt humiliating every time, were astounding. Even more astounding, I suppose, was their complete failure to saddle and bridle me with their outworn assumptions of appropriate behavior. Nowadays we might talk about exceptional children of unexceptional parents. Then I was just a tormented kid who could not obey but who was forced to obey, and the only way I could handle the expectations was to split into two halves: the angelic cherub who sang in the choir and did what he was told, and the willful anarchist who took suicidal risks on bicycles, who smashed and broke and set fire to things, who stole flagrantly from the time he was eight years old. Well, that's the suburbs for you: decor by Disney, script by Stephen King.

Even the happiest hometown memories hold sadness now, like fossils in amber. I think of my life sometimes as Ingmar Bergman's *Fanny and Alexander:* the beginning a wild and loving Christmas feast; and a sudden change, without warning, to the strict, unloving fanaticism of fundamentalist Lutherans, which, by the way, my parents are. And almost nothing has been able to depress me faster than a visit to my parents, who are retired now, my mother from Sperry Rand, my father from the

Pepsi-Cola Corporation. They live in the same house they purchased with the money they inherited from my grandparents. Many of their neighbors have died or moved away—to Florida mostly (another K Mart dream)—but the tempest-in-a-teapot world of suburban life goes on. My father and his next-door neighbor are no longer speaking after sharing a property line for four decades because of a contretemps over a hedge and a garden fence. Alexander Pope could have had a field day with these characters ("The Rape of the Locked Gate"), not to mention Jonathan Swift. It all seems so illusory, so fantastical.

We had our share of reality in New Hyde Park: infidelities, teenage pregnancies, unmarried motherhood, even a little Mafia action—my best friend's uncle was shot through the head, gangland style, in the parking lot of the Sterling Lanes, the underground bowling alley on Union Turnpike (the opening of which, complete with the town's first public elevator, was the highlight of my long-delayed puberty). We were, of course, dying to seeing if Johnny's uncle had left any bloodstains behind, but we were dutifully forbidden to go near the scene of the crime, just as we were prohibited from attending any movie displeasing to or unflattering of Pope Pius XII (who had turned his jewel-laden back on the Holocaust), even though my family was not Catholic. This Romanizing of my mother's sensibilities can be traced to her relentlessly hygienic circle of kaffeeklatsching canasta pals—Lucy, Joan, and Santa—all of them addicted to the League of Decency. Which is what led to the fight when I was barred from seeing *The World of Suzie Wong* in 1960, an injustice I rectified by flying to Hong Kong in 1989 to visit the kinds of bars where girls like Suzie led unsuspecting artists like William Holden astray—only there weren't any girls.

Sex, like everything else in the suburbs, was a secret. The overt racism was a secret, the anti-Semitism, the physical maladies of children: the boy with epilepsy, the girl with "blue-baby syndrome," even my own cousin Ginny, who died—a saint—of an increasingly debilitating disease the name of which I don't think I ever knew. (Was it polio, the bone-twisting specter of our early summers? Or cerebral palsy, which would make sense, since my mother became, briefly, a CP volunteer?) I was not even told when Ginny died, my closest cousin in age and a friend by virtue of her frailty. She was simply disappeared, like Mrs. Roche, who hanged herself in the basement one fine day, only to be discovered by her ten-year-old daughter Paula, when she scampered across the street from school for lunch. None of this was ever spoken of over dinner on Formica kitchen tables.

I was thirteen years old in 1960 (yes, I remember exactly where I was when Kennedy died, and yes, I saw Jack Ruby kill Lee Harvey Oswald on live television, and yes, the funeral was the first occasion my parents and I had to weep together for the same reason). My father had left my uncle's inept employ, and my mother went back to work to save money for my college education. And I was to leave the relative security of a grade school right down the block to be bused to Great Neck, two miles and a galaxy away. If I hadn't felt enough like an outsider before, I was now an alien. Clearly over my head academically, I was a social outcast by virtue of modest family means and Christian heritage (I wasn't exactly from the wrong side of the tracks, but I was definitely from the wrong side of the Long Island Expressway, which divides the haves from the haves-a-lot). Seemingly all of my well-to-do classmates had lost their grandparents in Nazi concentration camps—undoubtedly at the hands of my own relatives, I was assured. I became *personally* guilty in their eyes after the release of *Judgment at Nuremberg* in 1961.

I entered high school a paranoid, introverted kid afraid of everything, but most terrified of being excluded. I had been raised to think I had no right to express an opinion that differed from my parents'. And here I was awash in a sea of kids who had been trained that rugged individualism, fierce competition, and outspokenness might be the keys to their very survival in a hostile world. I started to crack. For the first time in my life, I started to cause trouble. I will be full of remorse until my dying day for the extortion, or attempted extortion, of money from a smaller classmate named Lenny Katz. I was nearly expelled for a term, but I was that desperate for attention, for power, for some arena in which I did not feel entirely inferior. A failure at criminal behavior, I settled, at the suggestion of Mr. Lipari (a gruff but caring social studies teacher) on academic prowess, which was within my grasp. Largely to impress Emily Miller, I started to get straight As. I did not stop hating myself. And it wouldn't be long before the As became harder to get: I was starting to drink, more and more often, more and more heavily.

By the time I was in high school, I knew I was homosexual. I had a massive crush on the school's star actor, Ray Singer (who was to become a friend years later in Los Angeles), and I had had an immediate and unequivocal physical reaction—a body gasp—when a fellow student stripped down to postpubescent nudity in gym class. The combination of his fully developed genitalia, his clearly defined adult musculature, and his radiant black skin (for he was one of the dozen non-Caucasians in this student body of three thousand) made an impression that duplicated in my mind and groin what Columbus must have felt like when the *Niña, Pinta,* and *Santa Maria* dropped anchor off the shore of Hispañola. Like Archimedes in his tub, I had found it. But I had no idea what "it" was, what it meant to be a homosexual, or how one went about becoming one. It would take years of mistakes to find out, years in which lovers of both genders would be left behind, quizzical looks on their faces, wondering what they had done to drive me away. Years in which I became convinced that I was incapable of love, that I was undeserving of love, that love did not exist. Years in which I downed more than my share of double Scotch boilermakers, my jump-start cocktail of choice.

I visited my old high school recently, on a beautiful early autumn day, and walked around its wooded campus. I felt almost nothing for those interminable years of pain and panic, which I take as a good sign. Ultimately, I'm grateful to Great Neck, though it is one of the most loathsome places I've ever been. If I'd lived just a few blocks farther south or east, I would have gone to New Hyde Park Memorial, home of football champions and prom queens of legendary pert-nosed beauty. Sister-person Linda thinks she would have been better off there, among those unobsessed by wealth and achievement; I would have been crushed. For among the crowds of popular kids who needled me incessantly for not being rich, for not being Jewish, for being fat and ill-at-ease, were a group of Great Neck students—a loose federation of thinkers—who had inherited from their grandparents that rich and poignant tradition of Jewish humanitarianism, a love of music and literature and justice. A tradition that inspired many of my classmates to spend their summers in Mississippi on the now-famous but then quite dangerous freedom rides that eventually broke the spine of legal segregation.

It was in this subculture of Great Neck South High School in the early 1960s that I began to see myself as one of the underdogs, one of the wronged, a lover of truth and beauty, a creature possessed of the will and talent to move others by word and deed to greater understanding and compassion for the downtrodden of this, our imperfect earth. It was in high school, too, that I first began to spend time in Greenwich Village, where I took guitar lessons at a Sixth Avenue place (above the Waverly Theater) where Joan Baez and Bob Dylan hung out, though I saw them only once. And that's when I began to find some kind of spiritual home: not New York per se, not the district known affectionately as The Village, although that's where I live today, but a metaphoric place, a cosmopolitan bohemian enclave of kindred souls. Without ever having really lived in one, I had become a city kid. Before I knew what was happening, I fulfilled all the demographic criteria to call myself an urban gay male.

I owe it to my early idyllic summers in the Catskills, I suppose, and four intensely angry undergraduate years at Colgate University (a lovely, vile place, with the exception of a handful of visionary teachers, most of them now dead, a bastion of the worst in bourgeois thought, word, and deed) that I am moved to tears today by nature in all its glory: sunsets in the Canary Islands, the tumultuous gray of a storm off the coast of Normandy, the once-nightly collective howl of the coyotes of Yosemite, a sound so close, so enormous, you feel it rather than hear it. Despite the cynicism of years, I can believe in God when I am so congruent with nature. But it is in cities, the biggest ones, that you meet people from all over the world, that you abut the myriad traditions of society, of the many societies. In Los Angeles, where I lived for fourteen years, I was drawn to the Latin tradition of Mexico, of Central and South America, although I am clearly a stranger in that "Spanish-surnamed" world. But *outside* is a place that is comfortable to me because it is, finally, familiar territory (despite my constant, pathetic attempts to fit in). If I were to identify my "hometown" as a concept rather than a place, it would be "The City, Outside."

In the last twenty-two years, I have lived for the most part in New Haven (as poor an excuse for a city as has ever been beset by the urban redevelopment cartel) and Los Angeles, with briefer stints in San Francisco and New York. I lived in London for the better part of a college year and have visited cities in Europe and Asia. In all of them it is the city of night, the city of throwaways, of runaways and the damned, the city of night, to borrow dear John Rechy's penetrating phrase, that holds my imagination; the city of the neglected, abused, and misunderstood, the city of those who sleep through banking hours and emerge from their crippling ostracism to find simpatico fellow travelers in the portion of the day abandoned by the respectable and the condemning majority.

They have their ludicrous pretensions, God knows (just thumb through the *New York Times,* or the *New York Review of Books,* or drop in on any underground club any night of the week), but to me cities are still places where you can be yourself, whether or not you'd kill for attention. You don't have to explain yourself to anyone. And because I was smothered as a child for being a nonconformist in the making, I enjoy breathing through both my nostrils now wherever I go, filling my lungs with the air of permission cities manufacture with their smog. On Long Island I constantly found myself on the verge of an apology: I am sorry I'm not more normal, sorry my hair's too long, sorry I'm not a Christian, a Republican, sorry I couldn't produce grandchildren for the days dwindling down. The suburbs induce an asthma of the psyche, wit, and soul. In New York, London, Paris, I begin to hear the poetry of my life as some kind of liturgy offered to an elusive but bounteous God. It is in cities that, in Whitman's definitive words, I can sing the song of myself. No rural poet of the nineteenth century came close to Whitman's unrestrained, raw, pulsing authenticity, which I admire and respect. Barbaric yawp? Amen!

In the Bible, of course, cities are associated with sin. And I like that aspect, too, of the universal metropolis, since the Bible seems to define as sin everything that is most natural in human behavior. Maybe it's the suburban obsession with aerosol cleansers that makes sex seem so filthy there—all those odors, those sticky and potentially hazardous fluids! But sex doesn't seem nearly as dirty to me in cities, just more vital. I've had sex with porn stars for cash that was as virginal in its way as one of my earliest encounters: in a field at dawn, along the banks of the Mohawk River, in the shadow of a ruined mill. (It wasn't until a fighter jet took off about ten feet over our heads that we realized we were making love at the weedy end of a military airstrip.) Cities are not spotless; they are not orderly or polite. However, they possess sensual charms: I have been overwhelmed by the scent of a cabdriver's leather jacket, his heavily lidded gaze in the rearview mirror, by a whiff of pungent aftershave on a young waiter in a Greek coffee shop on a blustery day, by the pull of spandex across a bicycle messenger's rock-hard thighs. This is the stuff of cities. On a recent Saturday night I was walking down Eighth Avenue near 42nd Street (where I had just seen a Pulitzer Prize–winning playwright in a "boy-lesque" joint where nude Puerto Ricans let you touch their dicks for a dollar). A gay little person (that's *dwarf* in the vernacular) walked up to me, put his hand on my over-ample belly, and tried to pick me up. Literally. Cities are full of such adventures. Maybe they don't spill out of *Huckleberry Finn,* but they're not always out of *Salo,* either. There's always a hit of Fellini evident in cities, but there's a dose of Fellini anywhere there's a jolt of life.

Nowadays I do my nocturnal prowling clean and sober. It's been fifteen years since my last drink. I'm proud of the longevity, but the original decision was not a moral one. In the beginning my choice was between drinking and suicide; later life offered the options of sobriety or death.

I have had to surrender a lot of old ideas in order to preserve my sobriety, and one of the first to go was my need to condescend to anyone. Although my male thirst for competition never seems to wane, I prefer to see commonality rather than difference, inclusion rather than exclusion. I have found that "bottom-of-the-barrel" people can be among the sweetest, most loving, and most generous people on earth, far kinder and gentler than any government officials I've ever met. The hustlers, strippers, and other denizens of the night who frequent my writing are sometimes dangerous and often untrustworthy, but they have their own dignity, their own dreams and needs, their own limits and frustrations. Certainly they have their own pain, and it is to be respected rather than belittled. In any case, it is not these soulmates of my id who manifest themselves in nightmares as the dark, pursuing "other." These men are what I am: prodigal sons who never went home to dinner.

But I have not always been sober, and the last and worst of my drinking was so associated with New York that I had to flee. Los Angeles, last refuge of people on the run, seemed a perfect place to go. I suffered through one more family barbecue (a disastrous Bicentennial Fourth of July) and the loneliest birthday of them all (my twenty-ninth) and touched down at LAX on July 28, 1976. It was raining.

I arrived in Los Angeles physically, mentally, emotionally, spiritually, morally bankrupt. I know in my heart that I'd be dead by now if an old school friend hadn't opened a door for me into a healing way of life that requires no artificial stimulation, no sedation. In a very real sense, the home I found in Los Angeles was not a *place* to live, but a way to live, and a group of peers to do it with—an eclectic group that included pimps and prostitutes, doctors and deejays from Southland Jesus stations. In little more than two years, I had a lover and a clique of friends whom I admired and, in some cases, adored. I got thin in Los Angeles, and tan. My hair crept back toward childhood platinum. I danced all night in the hottest discos, paced the halls of the preferred bathhouses, pumped iron in the coolest gym, basking in the occasional lustful glance. Men approached me on the street and invited me home for sex. I had become everything I had ever dreamed of or prayed for: accepted, inside, in demand.

And yet, of all my memories of L.A. my happiest is of a Christmas spent with a collection of sober gay alcoholic friends. A full turkey dinner with all the gourmet trimmings, the event was hosted by my closet friend Kenny and his lover Roy; and prepared by them along with Michael and Bill (another interracial couple) and other members of our circle. It must have been around 1980, and it was the first time in my life that I was fully relaxed for a holiday, the first time I was entirely comfortable, even serene, in a group of equals, judging no one, feeling no pressure to assert myself. I was a man among men, a friend among friends. The pictures from that day are as silly as we were, all of us dressed in red and green and all of us in love with each other and with life. I am tempted to say that this group of good men was, for years, the "hometown" I had always felt I'd missed. It would be very close to the truth. There was nothing I couldn't say to these men, nothing I wouldn't have done for them or asked them to do if I needed help. I had regained Eden, rediscovered laughter and innocence; I had been reborn.

And then my friends began to get sick. And then they began to die.

And I began to notice that L.A. was very much like suburban Long Island. My tan started to fade; the sun started giving me cancer. My hair started to darken. I stopped going to the gym and began putting on weight. My lover and I started to bicker over nothing. There didn't seem to be much energy for dancing. We hung on, but that was not the same thing as celebrating our existence. When Kenny died in 1987 (a week after my return from Spain) and my best friend, Clark Henley, died in 1988 (a week before my trip to France), and my lover called it quits somewhere between the two, taking up with a flashy programmer for PBS (which will never see another dime from me), I saw no more reason to stay in a city I had come to detest, though it's hard to imagine that any city could have withstood the enormity of my unvented rage.

I have nothing original to say about Los Angeles. I hated all the same trite things other New Yorkers hate who tried to make it in L.A. and failed (although this summation might be a bit self-deprecating). I tried to stay neutral, but I threw in the towel; I couldn't take the driving anymore, the relentless redundancy of the weather (hot, white, hazy, dry), the earthquakes in ascending numbers on the Richter scale. Perhaps it was the rampant racism and the vigorous suppression of the Asian, Latin, and African-American majority. Maybe it was just the stiffening redneck heart that beats beneath the public persona of Hollywood or the "cultural renaissance" that failed to materialize. At root was a pervasive discontent with the citywide solemnization of lowest-common-denominator mediocrity; this ritualized anti-intellectualism made the City of Angels seem too much like New Hyde Park with its homogenized traditional American values contradicting every humanistic principle of my own. It didn't help that the gay community was growing increasingly Republican (I called it the Rise of the Limp-Wristed Right).

I miss my friends in L.A., my "family," the headstones that mark the graves of some of the closest, the T-cell charts that record the precipitous decline of others. I was deeply attached to those men. The grief has been deep and the mourning long. But in the end, after fourteen years, L.A. was easier to leave than a decent party you drop in on between more-important engagements.

I returned to New York in April. My parents picked me up at the airport—as they had done many times (it's a nod to family feeling that reminds me of happiness). I stayed with Linda for a while, then moved into a second-story apartment on Grove Street in Greenwich Village. There were pink geraniums in a window box down the street, and a cherry tree in full bloom. The bright spring green of the new ginkgo, sycamore, and ailanthus leaves—almost chartreuse in the sunlight—was a pleasant contrast with the natural red brick and the painted Chinese red of the town houses that date from the early 1820s down by P.S. 3. The history of New York is one of the things I love most about it. Cities are like that: they have histories.

Here's another corner of New York: the orchestra of the Metropolitan Opera House at Lincoln Center. Beside me is a young dancer named Julio (pronounce the J—he's from Brazil). The American Ballet Theater is dancing up there onstage. It's the fourth time in two weeks I've been here. I love the ballet. I felt starved for it in L.A. without even realizing it. Julio's an excellent dancer. I've seen him, at one of those Times Square dives where young men strip between fuck movies. They don't earn a lot of money dancing, but they meet the men there who pay them for sex—either on the premises or off. Julio (as in Juliet)—whose birthday, not coincidentally, is, like mine, in July—cut his foot today during an audition for a new company he wants to study with. He's tiny, looks sometimes like a child. I'm crazy about him. During the Gay Pride parade in June, he struts from Central Park to Christopher Street, a distance of several miles, in Carnival-inspired Carmen Miranda drag: lots of headdress, lots of beads and crimson flounces, black spike heels. I took a photograph, which came out beautifully. I keep it in the mock-wood cardboard box with all the others.

For my birthday this year, Linda gave me Terry Miller's history of The Village *(Greenwich Village and How It Got That Way)*. She inscribed it: "Always your spiritual home, now your physical home as well." And maybe it's as simple, as unmysterious as that: I'm finally living where I belong, where I've wanted to live all the time. "It's what you've wanted for twenty years," my mother said as she inspected my apartment, having had to see it herself to approve of the wisdom of my extravagance (I'll pay more in rent for eight months than she and my father paid for their house in 1950).

Greenwich Village isn't a symbolic place for me anymore, a kind of Rive Gauche Gotham where suburban kids go to take guitar lessons. It's real now, a place where unimaginative people come to sin. It has broken water pipes, noisy heterosexual neighbors, obnoxious tourists, homeless panhandlers. But it's a place where the neighborhood drunks know you by name and wave as you walk home from another insane day at work or a night at the Philharmonic or a hotel roll in the hay with a dazzling new boy from the Gaiety, or a dinner with a dozen sober gay and lesbian poet friends—a birthday dinner, as it happens, for two of you (the other Moon Child, a friend from L.A. who lives in SoHo now). It's a place where dogs know each other's trees, where you can see the Empire State Building, the Chrysler Building, the World Trade Center, the Hudson River, and the Macy's Fourth-of-July fireworks from your own tarry roof, or sit on the stoop and watch the New Kids on the Block catapult from a pair of limos into the Pink Teacup, the local soul-food place across the street.

It's a place where "hometown" seems like a reality, a place immune to nothing, a city place with all its organs intact, all its juices flowing, and all its emotions available for use, a place where I don't feel robbed of ethnicity but part of a multiethnic whole. It's a place where strangers seem like family because of a wink or a smile, a shared ironic take on life's little absurdities, a place where weather changes every day, and every day is an excursion into the unknown. A place where nothing is resolved, but everything might be resolved. Where anything's possible, nothing unlikely. A place like Oz and Kansas rolled into one—at least for me.

I was forty-three in July. I'm fat again, balding, alone—without even a fern or a goldfish to distract me from my work, from myself. And if that sounds hideously self-obsessed, you'll have to forgive me. I have never felt more complete in my life. Even New Hyde Park has lost its power to undermine my equanimity. And maybe that's why coming back to New York feels so much like coming home.

Quick! Somebody take a picture.

A Child's Garden Of Verses

Cold heat
For Rose Lassell (née Meyers)

Baking in the hot sun of
California July, I
stare at a photo of
England in the snow.
These are the things I think of:

Waiting for Robert in a cold so cold
the frozen sap of the towering pines
cracked like an angry glacier;

Walking in the London rain with Kay
looking for her birth house the morning
after raw sex for the first time;

Wishing that my grandmother had not
died before I knew her, the one from
England who was half a Jew.

That says it all: a man, a woman,
a death—and my own death, as
certain as that lingering pain in my
left thigh, the chest heaviness that
grows with every breath, every poem,
every sigh, and the constant longing
for one unspecified *you*.

What was meant by heredity

Imogene Coca lived with my Uncle Doug for almost thirty years, the one who raised prize rabbits in the backyard of his house in Astoria, Queens, the one his mother left him when she died at ninety. He would show up once a year late at night, looking boiled red and Irish happy, and keep everyone up too late for a work night. And you had to like Doug—he was just such an unpretentious, happy-go-lucky kind of guy—but some people had to get up early in the morning, which was something our Doug could never get through his thick Mick skull. Imogene Coca, whose real name was Carol something-or-other, wore petticoats and nail polish every day of her life. She smoked unfiltered Luckies and waved the smoke from her enormous red mouth, her hands made heavy by costume rings and plastic bracelets. And she would drink one rye-and-ginger after another and laugh and laugh at his silly jokes until Uncle Doug dropped dead one day and Imogene Coca found out she hadn't even been named beneficiary of his lousy insurance policy. Which may have been an oversight or superstition, or it might just have been because Doug thought rules were for saps—which is why he never felt the nip of Catholic guilt when he rowed into the commercial fishing beds to hook a dozen fluke an hour, which Imogene would clean and fry with a laugh and a Lucky dangling from her fat lower lip. Anyway, there were no more prize rabbits and no insurance money. And not long thereafter, Imogene Coca got lung cancer and coughed herself to bloody death, and no one went to visit her at Mercy Hospital because, after all, she had never actually managed to *marry* Doug, who was not, it turned out, officially related to us anyway, so no one had to worry about bursting a blood vessel in his brain, since Uncle Doug was, in fact, only a friend left over from high school before the war.

And that's what was meant by heredity at our house.

Brother snow

You are as cold as the
thumb of flesh they
flushed from my mother's
womb, as white and wet—
her blood the color of
cardinals caught off guard
by winter, the scarlet of
guilt and fevers. If you'd
been a girl, we would have
named you Rose, Rubella
Rose, after our grandmother
resting in peace. You were
a bunting of silence to
wrap a family secret in,
hushed as frost falling
between the black and
empty branches of trees—
three trees: father, son,
and mother ghost. You were
not an ideal playmate,
melting away again and
again, even after I'd
shaped from newborn you
an albino menagerie the
neighbors came visiting
all week long, but
you were loyal, as
true a blue as shadows:
bony fingers cast on ice-
encrusted mammals by a
manless moon.

Scab, the Teeth, and Tongues (watch TV)

I remember Howdy Doody and Buffalo Bob.
Princess Summer Fall kept getting killed
in crashes and being replaced. Clarabel
became Cap'n Kangaroo right after Miss
Frances, and the Teeth actually knew him
(the Merry Mailman, too) but never said so.

I remember watching *The Lone Ranger* one
Saturday noon with Tongues and the Teeth
in front of the mahogany console I wasn't
allowed to touch (it smelled of cedar and
Ella Fitzgerald 78s). Tonto kneeled and
cradled the wounded *kemo sabe* in his arms.

Lassie always came to the rescue, and so
did Rin Tin Tin. I never had a dog, and
when Trigger died he was stuffed by Roy
and Dale. I got a parakeet instead called
Happy, but he wasn't. He kept flying into
the mirror and getting stuck behind the TV.

Loretta Young's husband was always killed
in Korea. Gertrude Berg was someone's mom,
and there was a flood. She was afraid of
the rescue line, but she finally got on it.
It snapped; she was swept away in the file
footage. I got hysterical and went to bed.

We watched Ed Sullivan, but Tongues and the
Teeth talked all the way through it. Tongues
was in love with Perry Como and sang along
to the tunes she knew. The Teeth liked crime
stories and long, boring things that turned
out to be the McCarthy hearings and wars.

There was a drama in black and white. A man and woman were fighting in their car, then stopped at a café. The woman went to the bathroom and was never seen again. The man was distraught, the mystery never solved.
I never let Tongues out of my sight again.

Daddy

Oh Daddy,
I'm far away and miss you
so much. The bogeyman is on the
prowl again, draped in last year's
judgment. Things go bump
in the cold sweaty night,
growl in the swelling neck and
sunken groin where men have danced
on points of pins
and Sabu rode his elephant
all the morning long in rain.

Kiss me quiet the in
moonless room. Tell me about
Heaven and good boys turn
to angels when they die;
how you'll be there to meet me—
like that dream of disembarking
in the Land of Dead and
Grandpa's Airedale Mickey
lumbered up to lick my hand—
how you played hooky from school and
snuck off to Broadway to
steal a piece of Fanny Brice;
and how God loved His only son
so much He killed him.

Remember the time we went to
Radio City and saw
Ben Hur from the first and only
row? You ate popcorn and were
Charlton Heston with
your arm around my chair,
your shoulder straining on the
reins. I was happy as Haya

| *The Hard Way* |

Harareet to ride your chariot
anywhere.

I dreamed I was crucified once
but felt nothing, was shot
as many times as St. Sebastian
but did not complain, was
hoisted by a hook around my
breastbone—eyes skyward like
a saint or martyr—but
it did not hurt. That's how
pain is in dreams: all concave
terror, but pain in life is
terror and agony too. No wonder
passion can have two meanings.

And God whispered:
This is my beloved son in whom I am well pleased.
And Jesus was so moved
he gladly gave his life
for a stranger.

Oh Daddy,
all I ever wanted was to
crawl into your arms, as firm
as hairless Samson's buttock cheeks.
Naked and enslaved, he grunts the
prison treadmill round, trapezius muscles
rising to the task. You bought me that
beefcake Bible for my confirmation
and it more or less confirmed
what you feared.
I was grateful for Samson's he-man flesh, for
Jesus' long untangled hair
and angels gentle as
bathing or Hedy Lamarr.

| MICHAEL LASSELL |

Oh Daddy,
wherever you are, I still want to
suck your chest hair, sink
into your skin like the
painless dream lashings of
a leather scourge, spread
tattoos across your stung trunk
like oil from Hedy's cruet
rubbed into the sore and
musk Semitic meat of Victor Mature
as John the Baptist—no!
that's not right (that was Rita
Hayworth dropping veils)—
as *Samson,* rather, pulling down
the temple by its columns,
loincloth stiff on glistening limbs
anointed by angry desire.

Secrets spill in the dark aisles
of theaters and churches
like blood from test tubes spreading
contagion. All I wanted was to
touch your cock that time
in the shower once when
I was small. Shame feels like
déjà vu these days, but still
I love a shower room full of
nude men dripping water through
marble swirls of hair.

Oh Daddy,
it was you all the time in those
backroom bars and bathhouse crannies
at four A.M.,
all those men who
filled me with the
Holy Spirit. I was
speaking in tongues. And when the

| *The Hard Way* |

profane angel death comes
flapping down with winks and
wings akimbo, I will
recognize his sultry and
engendering breath, will
look into his bedroom eyes,
and see you there:
the dusky idol of my
'50s matinee,
strong and silent,
sullen as Gregory Peck's
lower lip lusting after
Bathsheba in a Technicolor dream.

His mother's incest

His mother's incest was a bird.
It had no beak, no claw,
and yet it scarred.
It fluttered in the dark like
feathers and made the sound her
satin nightgowns made when they
slept in the same bed—
How long? How long?

His mother's incest wove a nest
of tangled need. It cooed
above Q-Tips in waxy ears,
peeped at early erections in
baths she gave him—
How long? How long?

His mother's incest was a bird.
He has no wing. He has no song.

Grandfather's robe
For Armwell Wesley Lassell

It was warm, wool, and maroon.
The matching belt had silky
fringe I managed to tangle
whenever I wore it for measles

or mumps. Mostly it was Dad's,
though he never wore it much.
You can see one just like it
in any number of '30s films

because it's a classy item.
Even during the Depression, Pop
worked in the men's department
of a swank Fifth Avenue store.

Now it's the annex of the public
library, where my name comes up
on screen if you punch the right
buttons. I was going to be named

after Pop (Armwell Wesley), but
Mom named me for Dad instead. I
would have been a 3d. The robe
was rough on hairless boy skin,

but it held the scent of men:
the shaving cream my father
used, Grandpa's sweet Prince
Albert tobacco. It survived the

'70s, even though Pop had died
already of a second stroke a week
after my Uncle Sonny (Army 2d).
It got moth holes, so my mother

worked her magic on it. By the
time that robe hit the Goodwill
bag, I was in all kinds of robes—
from cotton and terry to satin—

and had outgrown the diseases
comfort and a moldy robe could
cure. These days, Dad has a red
robe, and I prefer to be naked.

Pancho Villa
And A Fear Of Crocodiles

Of course. I understand. You think I'm crazy. Well, who can blame you? Surely not I. If I had seen what you saw, if I had seen it more than once, I'd think me crazy, too. Quite moon-howling lunatic, bedlam of bedlams, mad Tom of the wind-blown heath picking at imaginary what-gnats and scattering sexual innuendos like a dog scratching fleas.

It's certainly not the first time I've screamed at the walls until my throat ached, cried in a ball on the floor until I fell asleep and slept until the drunks came cursing home. But those are not the maddest days. Not by a…long shot. Those are nothing more than eruptions, violent outbursts, the gnashing of teeth in need of root canal work. Those are just the days the parts of speech—the larynx and palate, the diaphragm and lungs—consort with one another, and the monumental anger lying dormant underneath the latest bout of tranquillity flexes like the muscle of a giant clam. And the rage that comes pouring out like a hurricane through the eye of a needle is focused in a single obscenity, and your lips are stretched as tight around the sound as vaginal labia around the skull of a large child and a difficult birth.

On days like these even I think I'm going insane, but I still feel a kinship with sanity.

But there are other days, too. Days of mere weariness, of indolent snow falling silently on a small pond in the early hours of morning. Days of endless time, of hours before lunch followed by hours until dinner, hours to sleeping, to dreaming, to death. Day upon day like unwashed women waiting for rescue. And on days like these, I think I'd better...I'd *best* be locked up to preserve the common weal.

The world is full enough of martyrs. There aren't enough deaths for them all.

But I'm not mad. That's only the nightmare talking. The mad boy drowned years ago under the ice. It was too cold to go in after him, too cold for the descent into the dark indifference of water the color of dove feathers, of the eyebrows on old Romanians playing checkers in the park. Going in after him would have been suicide, plain and simple. They all said so. There was no question of blame, though some say he was pushed under the ice by other boys jealous of his madness and the skates his parents bought him by way of...compensation? Did I get that right? Words can kill, you know. So can the absence of words. Words and the absence of words are a madness, too, of sorts.

The mad boy's name was Julian, or so they say, for this was years before my time began to run. And he was a fat sweet chatterbox as mad as a hatter. He would...crow like a rooster, pick up insects and turn them back in the direction from which they had crawled, follow the paperboy all over town and fetch each newspaper thrown on a porch like some kind of retriever or spaniel, then return it to the newsboy, who, once Julian had learned this trick, had to knock on every door and hand the paper to each customer or never get his route done. Because the paper boy spent so much time every day with Julian, he became the mad boy's best friend. But who could not resent that? Or the endless stream of non sequiturs to which Julian, ignorant of the laws of either grammar or logic, was more than annoyingly given? And the newsboy did resent it and took it out on Julian mercilessly in word and deed. But, like a beaten dog,

Julian was loyal to his young master and would never leave his side.

All of this was common knowledge, which is the kind of knowledge our town had been supplied in great abundance.

Julian wore red clothing exclusively and lied even when the truth would have done him more good. Some say this was because he was too stupid to know the truth, or had forgotten it; but others think it was just Julian's way of making sense of the world, which apparently made very little sense to him on its own terms. They say the truth will set you free. But maybe Julian didn't like the idea of freedom. I tell the truth all the time, and it hasn't freed me.

Eventually, Julian *became* the paperboy—after his friend the paperboy won a place on the high-school football team—and everyone was glad he had found something he could do, and everyone assumed he would just keep right on doing it until he was old enough to retire. Some thought he might make a decent mailman, except that Julian couldn't read, because he couldn't sit still long enough to learn. He just kept jumping up and down and running his red crayon back and forth across any piece of paper that was set in front of him. Of course, he could not color in the usual sense; he had no concept whatever of staying inside the lines. On the other hand, he never, never colored off the edge of the page.

After the tragedy, Julian's parents went quite mad themselves—only later, much later, in their...declining years. The first hints of their own dementia was their attempt—each of them—to file a joint income-tax return to make up for the boy they lost when the ice thinned in that one crucial place. But ice is like that, and so is love.

The IRS caught on almost at once, of course—five or six years, something like that—but it didn't stop the old couple from going out to the middle of that tiny man-made lake and jumping up and down on the frozen place their only son had fallen through one February day before his new red sweater had even been paid for.

What I remember most about them was that they were kind, and that is *not* a fabrication or a memory in benevolent retreat from the truth. Kindness ran in that family. Everyone says it, even now. And even when the old people were getting more than one year older with each passing year, people in town kept remarking how kind they were, how well they wore their grief, their lifelong grief. At Halloween they always gave out the best candy—boxes of Red Hots—and delicious apples, and once they gave me a dollar after I rang their bell and shouted, "Trick or treat." It was the red sweater I was wearing, they said, the red sweater that made them think I was the boy who drowned under ice the color of quiet neglect.

But that was eons before my Halloween bonanza, the Pleistocene to the Atomic Age. The frozen body of Julian the witless newsboy must have been washed out to sea three decades before I was born, although I sometimes...I *often* dream—or imagine—that I am there that day, looking on in horror while fear spreads across Julian's usually smiling face, and the sound of ice cracking underfoot splits the muffled silence like dry lightning.

The authorities eventually put the old folks away. She kept waking up screaming about crocodiles and porcupines, and he couldn't get it out of his head that he was still in the 69th Cavalry chasing Pancho Villa along the banks of the Rio Grande. That's madness for you. A reality all its own. It was sad to watch them putting two old people like that into separate wings of the same asylum when their only crime was to have survived, to have survived their one offspring. They couldn't see each other from their windows, but they could both see *out* of their windows, could both see the same spot of grass under a lopsided tree and a bench that was weathered and gray as an old farm horse.

I used to go there and sit on that bench. When the old woman waved from her window on the sixth floor of the west tower, I waved back and ate jelly sandwiches I'd packed in the army-surplus knapsack my father had given me, although the canteen that came with it...

What was I saying? I lost my train of thought. Silly saying, that. *Train* of thought. I was saying, saying, swaying, swearing, wearing...wearing an old red sweater, yes, that was it—and when the old man saluted from the ninth floor of the east tower, I waved at him, and they'd both know that the other was safe and sound in a private little world I held the keys to.

I was sitting in a bar once—in Connecticut, of course—when a not-unpleasant-looking young man sat down at the table without any formalities whatsoever. He seemed extremely agitated about something, as though his animal self had grown too big for the skin of his reason. In very short order he proposed that we rob the bar and then run off to California, a place I knew only from films and by reputation. I tried to decline as graciously as possible, knowing that the scheme would never net enough cash to keep us both ahead of the law from sea to shining sea, but he had taken quite an irrational liking to me and grew rather insistent, explaining that he had just escaped from the state mental institution, was carrying a gun, and would kill me if I crossed him. Suddenly a moat opened up around our table. The jukebox music grew as loud and distant as a sonic boom filtered through memory. Suddenly my fear for my life stranded me inside his pathological plot, his brain-fever fantasy, and—just as suddenly—the walls of the bar turned to cotton batting and absorbed everything I had ever known about myself. I began to think seriously of going along with him, at least until we got to Chicago, which I'd always wanted to see, wind notwithstanding. There I would get in touch with the police and be done with it all. Say I was kidnapped. Get famous for a day or two.

Eventually the bartender noticed the mental defective spitting on the floor and hauled him out of the bar by his collar. There was, in fact, no gun. Only a white metal comb and felonious intent. The story about the mental institution turned out to be true, I was informed by the local police, to whom I complained of the assault.

By comparison, my own "madness" is hardly more than an eccentricity, the eccentricity of a frightened male.

Did you know that Nathaniel Hawthorne's only son was named Julian? Julian Hawthorne. If I ever have a son myself, I'm going to name him Julian Hawthorne and read to him from Nathaniel Hawthorne's books and hold him after I frighten him and tell him, "There, there, don't cry. It's only a story. There's nothing to be afraid of."

But I guess I never will have a son. Not now. Too late by years. No son to sit under a crooked tree and wave as I salute out the window of my locked ward. My parents never had children, either. Except me.

And what do *I* know about the price of rice in China?

Cheap, I'll bet.

"The family name dies with you," my mother said time after time. But names don't die. Just dreams and mad newsboys.

I remember walking on the low-tide beach past the breakwater of a small town on the Cornish coast of England. It was fall. Autumn. I met a man dressed all in tweeds. I was crouched over a tide pool watching the animal life. Tweeds just appeared out of nowhere, stood over me and asked if I were a marine biologist. I said no, but only because I was afraid I'd be caught in a lie if he were a marine biologist himself. I needn't have worried. He was not a marine biologist. He was an old pervert. What he wanted, which he announced with few of the preliminaries experience had taught me to expect from the British, was for me to drive with him to a neighboring cove, to strip off our clothing, and to beat his jellied flesh with the seaweed that had washed up on shore, a hoselike variety that grows in yard-long tubes the color of uniforms and animal excrement. Later, in the pub, he introduced me to a retired Nazi pornographer, a lady potter with a hat like pink lettuce, and her homosexual son from the London School of Economics.

There's madness in this, but was it his or mine?

The economist's name was Julian, too, although his mother named him Albert. He changed his name to Julian to honor the apostate Roman emperor who attempted to eradicate Christianity and to restore the classical pagan deities. His hands were as long and thin as a girl's. His nose was as long and thin as a whippet's. His breath smelled of kippers.

In the summer, before they took him away, the old man sat in a small inflatable wading pool and thought he was rinsing himself clean of the dust of Mexican bandits in the tepid Rio Grande. This I remember, for I was the paperboy by then. The old woman would look up from hanging wet clothes on a slackened line and remind her husband to be wary of crocodiles, which, she insisted, were indigenous to Southwest Texas. "It's not the crocs I'm worried about," the old man would say, "but the rattlers and the rats." And one fine day—after the fire in the cardboard-box factory—a possum-sized rat did appear, and the old man beat it to death with a broom shouting, "Take that, Pancho Villa, take that!" And I shouldn't have to tell you that boys in the neighborhood shouted, "Take that, Pancho Villa, take that" forever after.

One day I went to the asylum, at the corner of Union Turnpike and Confederate Avenue, and they told me that the old man had died. At first they just told me he had a heart attack; but, when I started asking questions, they told the whole truth. Apparently, a brick fell off the roof of the recreation pavilion—no one knew what a brick was doing up there, but up there it apparently was—and the brick hit a man on the finger while he was tapping his initials into an aluminum ashtray on the table below. The man, naturally, jumped to his feet, which made the bench he was sitting on flip up because there was a fat man sitting on the other end of it. The fat men went sprawling, and the old man, who thought he was still in the 69th Cavalry, bent over to help the fat man, had a heart attack, and died. Just like that.

And would you believe me if I told you that it was June 9, and the old man's sixty-ninth birthday?

(If not, I can change some details.)

So you see, it hardly makes any sense at all to accuse me of insanity. I have almost total recall. I remember the past and am, therefore, condemned not to repeat it.

I stopped going to the asylum because the old woman stopped showing up at her window after they told her that her husband had died and was being buried in Potter's Field, which she thought was the asylum baseball diamond, so she was pretty upset, what with the crocodiles that lived in the creek near the scoreboard. She died, too, after that, but I didn't hear about it for years, since I was away myself by that time.

I had a dream once—a waking dream—and that's when I died the first time.

Ordinarily I don't like talking about my dreams, which

strangers are always trying to get me to do. Refusing irritates them, so I usually make something up. I do a lot of that. Anyway, as I was saying, I don't generally like to talk about dreams—I don't even like to have them—but waking dreams are different, somehow, since you're awake and can keep them from becoming too threatening.

In any event, it was a hot night, and I was lying on my back under just a sheet. A red bedspread was folded at the foot of the bed, which was pointed due west. Suddenly, and without opening my eyes, I could see an orange light, and I knew that the nearby city had been hit by a nuclear bomb. I knew that the room I was in was consumed by flames that were too hot to feel. I knew that as long as I kept my eyes closed I would experience no pain, only a slight pressure, like a breeze. I knew the flesh was charring off my bones and turning to ashes, and that the moisture was being fried out of my body, leaving nothing in the burning bed but a blackened skeleton.

And then—just as suddenly—I knew the dream was over. I could open my eyes, and everything would be all right.

Life is like that, and so is drowning under ice. If you keep your eyes closed long enough, eventually the madness passes.

Part Two

FOR BETTER OR WORSE

This Is The Story Of Kay

It is not the beginning, but as good a place to start as any: a small hotel in London, the swinging London of 1969, of Twiggy, "Hey, Jude," and Lord Kitchener's Valet, a bed-and-breakfast near the Earl's Court Exhibition Hall. It is January twenty-second. You have checked in under assumed names as a couple. Ironically, your names are the same as the names of your parents—*your* parents, not hers—whose wedding anniversary is the twenty-second of September. You have brought a small valise and wear rings turned backward to convince the woman at the desk that you are married. Have you fooled her?

The decision was a reasoned one. You met Kay through a friend she dated several times, a friend named Robert who had moved on to men leaving a virgin in his wake. You become friends, visit museums, hold hands in parks. You develop a bond of trust. She tells you she has never slept with your mutual friend. You do not tell her that you have. You say only that you have never slept with a woman before. Even this is a kind of lie. You make arrangements to meet the following Saturday night.

She has packed champagne and a silk nightgown. You go to

dinner, attend *Jules et Jim* at an art cinema near a stone bridge and walk home in a slow cold rain. During the film, you fondle her breasts, rest your hand high on her thigh. You return to the York House hotel. It is in the same crescent street where you live with Robert, the man who did not become her first lover or your own. It is a small room. The walls are papered, of course, in flowers: pink and maroon. The heavy Victorian armoire with the oval mirrors in its doors would hold ten times what you have brought with you.

You lie on the floor in front of a gas fire. You drink the Moët. The cork hits the ceiling and lands somewhere on the threadbare carpet. (When did you learn to uncork champagne, decant it into crystal flutes?) There is no light but the blue light from the gas fire. You have chosen a romantic metaphor for this cool and calculated night of husbandry. Were it your honeymoon, the moment could not be more seductive, more innocent.

The removal of clothing begins slowly, but accelerates. You are soon naked on the floor. She seems very much more naked than you. Your foreplay is slow and sensual, your repertoire limited by inexperience and a characteristic reluctance to explore unknown territory. But you are unwilling for the evening to fail. Unschooled in such matters, you are certain in advance that lack of consummation would constitute a failure. It will be, *must* be a benchmark in your lives. There is much invested, and many unanswered questions.

You move gracelessly to the bed at her suggestion. Soon you agree you are both ready to attempt penetration. She is on the pill, she tells you. You are relieved and take an appropriate position. She guides you with her hand...

But wait. Another moment from the vault of time is pecking on the inside of its shell, a nearer memory by twenty years:

It is Hong Kong and you are very nearly old. It is hot this time of year, late spring. Typhoons gather in the South China Sea. Everything is on alert. Sampans and junks in Aberdeen Harbor are lashed together in readiness. The air is thick, damp, still—island weather.... You wish for nakedness and beaches, idleness. Last night

| The Hard Way |

you slept soundly in the arms of the Orient, waking before dawn to find the sun coming up over China, the sky ablaze in orange, yellow, crimson. You ate litchi fruit pried from its spiny skin and sui mai *served in a bamboo basket, then visited a temple to honor Buddha's birthday. The scent of burning joss still clings to your nostrils. The monks—their shaven heads wrinkled with age or smooth as youth—have been captured, exposed in your Japanese camera to Japanese film.*

As the air-conditioned tourist coach climbs the hill past the racetrack and the military compound where the fearsome ghurkas do calisthenics in full uniform, you pass a man in a white Lacoste shirt, black shorts, a boy/man. Your eyes meet. As the coach inches through traffic toward Victoria Peak, you turn your head to the left. He stops, stops his companion, never lets your eyes out of his eyes. He is small, muscular, Chinese, of course, with blue-black hair worn longer than usual in Central District. He is on his way to play tennis. Both he and his companion carry racquets covered in leather. He smiles, waves, beckons, takes several steps toward the bus, which lurches forward now into second gear. You are conscious of heat on your face, of the sun in your red and graying beard, of desire and missed opportunities, ironies, the early deaths of men you coveted and never possessed, of never having been young and beautiful simultaneously, of never having known the admiration of older men.

Soon you will stand alone in the mist at the top of the island, invisible to city and harbor alike, but you no longer care about rebuilt temples, luxury hotels, or brothels in streets narrow as hallways, as brothels under banners of laundry and lantern lights, The World of Suzie Wong *forbidden you in your adolescence. It is all the same to you, all but the face of this boy/man on his way to play tennis, who stops to smile and covet you through the tinted window of an air-cooled bus stalled in the Happy Valley on its way up a hill to nowhere.*

But you come back, as you come back often, to Kay, again and again. Perhaps you loved her more than she knows. Yes. You are naked in a London bed, a rainy winter day at the front end of a year:

…She guides you with her hand. You push. She groans. There is a moment of hesitation. Should you withdraw? She answers the unasked question with the upward pressure of her hips against the downward pressure of your own.

And so it goes. For four hours you try to break her membrane. You have rubbed yourself raw in the attempt. You never once soften, but you have gotten no further at 4:00 A.M. than you were at midnight. You are willing to abandon the attempt altogether rather than assert your power to cause her pain. She is not; she will not leave this room intact. You push again and again. It is nearly dawn before you realize the time has come. Whatever she must feel is hers to feel. For yourself, you must...and you will...and you do. And she lets out a sharp moan, holds her breath for a startled moment like a wrong note in the clarinet line of a jazz symphony, and pulls you tight around the shoulders. You push your way inside.

You feel the warm wet entrance of her like a promise you want to believe, a muscled haven that takes your sex in its caress and pulls you inside. You withdraw. It clutches. You enter. It loosens to greet you, tightens. You push, withdraw. You hear the lapping of water on the rocks at low tide. You push again, pump faster. Then slow. You pull out the shaft, then the head, until her lips close and nothing holds you but a thread of viscous fluid. She is panting now. You drive.

The bed creaks beneath you. The fire still flickers in the grate. You thrust harder and harder until you know you will explode. You clench the muscles of your face, the muscles of your thighs and hips and legs, the muscles that begin in the buttocks and sink into the bowels, and then you let the muscles go and make a sound and pour into her, over and over.

She groans in pleasure, the uncensored sound your mother made when you were a boy and ran into her room one night to see if she was hurt. This sound in the night haunts you like a fox pursued by hounds, the sound you utter at the news of a death you cannot bear, the news of one more death. It is not death you are thinking of now, but life, your life, hers, the life of the child you have not created, but might have created. The lives of others you may someday make together or apart...

But the unknown future in which you had such faith does not, as it happens, father children.

The slowing is gradual, as you expected. The silence is long, its meter the whisper of gas jets, the unspecified sibilance of rain on streets, pavement, windows.

You have finally finished. You are covered in a hot, sticky liquid it is too dark to see. As you drift off to sleep in each other's arms, you see the shadows of trees on the sheer white curtains.

It can't be more than an hour later when there is a knock on the door, and the door swings open. The two of you pull the flowered bed cover to your chins. The maid has brought your breakfast on a tray. She stands in the room. You survey the landscape. Your clothing is strewn over chairs, her bra hangs from the armoire by a strap.

The maid says, "Tea," registers nothing, goes. You drift back to sleep and wake only minutes before noon. The house is in full gear. A vacuum is making its way down the hall. It is a noise you have despised since childhood. You pull back the covers and leap to standing. Your cock is chafed and sore but still erect.

The sheets are drenched in blood, as if a balloon of it the size of a melon had burst, as if a pig had been slaughtered in the bed. Your legs, her legs are caked with dried blood, blood the color of clay in ravines. Your pubic hair is stiff with it. You smell it on your hands. It is smeared on her breasts and belly, your ass. It is a world of blood in a room full of fabrics and flowers. The empty champagne bottle lies on its side, its open mouth pointed in your direction, a cherub taken off guard by debauchery.

You say nothing but are secretly pleased. You wash. You leave, hoping not to hear screams behind you when the char pulls back the blankets and discovers the mark you have left on her mattress.

The day is unseasonably warm. It rains softly. You walk a long way. You are both unusually silent. You take the underground near the Victoria and Albert Museum to the neighborhood where she was born, before moving to the States. Her father has given her the address, but the building no longer exists. In the place of her birth house is a block-long row of shops, a concrete bunker offering inferior goods for working-class consumption. A derrick towers above an excavation in the road like a mechanical giraffe deciding whether to proceed. It is the end of England.

Later she tells you she did not know whether it was your blood or her own.

Later, in a Fifth Avenue apartment overlooking Washington Square, she tells you she does not know whether she loves you, or just likes you a lot, and that she knows it does not matter because you do not love her. You are not certain she is right, but it is likely, so you take her word for it.

Later you move on to men, but do not forget the blood of this woman, this bed, this first and hardest time, this woman who will keep your letters for two decades, your letters and the ink drawings you did at Oxford in the fall.

Later you know what love is and whose blood is whose, and how to keep the two apart forever.

But the sound of a new death in your throat, *that* stays with you. *That* is a sound you will need again, will make use of again. Again and again, ad infinitum.

Willie

Willie was black and sixteen, but he lied about his age. You can't get laid when you're sixteen, or at least you couldn't back in stinking 1970. Now it's all the kids do. Smoke dope. Get laid. Things haven't changed. It's just the kids get younger, more careful if they're smart, and they are smart. Willie was sixteen, I was twenty-two, twenty-three, something like that. And I was black and blue from falling down the night before at The Pub, but underneath the bruises I was white. More or less.

I'll tell you right now I talk too much and I need a lot of attention. A shrink told me that. Sometimes I tell bad jokes. It annoys people sometimes. Some people. I'm no saint at a party—when I used to go to parties.

"Speaking with authority is no mean thing," I said when I met him. First words out of my mouth when somebody finally introduced us. I remember it like it was yesterday. Only it wasn't yesterday. It was nearly twenty years ago. It was Berk who introduced us, in a way. We had been staring at each other for an hour, Willie and me, so I finally walked over to where he was standing with old Berkeley, and Berk said to Willie, "Talk to

Gar while I roll some joints," and off he walked without a word to me, the rude prick. Willie said something I don't remember—paid me some compliment, I think it was—and out came "Speaking with authority is no mean thing." I have no idea what I meant by that, and it was a hell of a thing to lay on a street kid for no reason at all. "No mean thing," I actually said, "though it doesn't take any particular expertise." I used to talk like that all the time, even though it makes me sick to think about it, and it kind of nauseated me even then. I don't remember what he said next or what I said by way of reply. Sometimes when you're drunk, you don't remember everything that happens. Sometimes nothing. I remember plenty from those days, but not much good.

I remember at one point I said, "What's your name?" and he said, "Willie," and I said, "Like willy-nilly," and he said, "Oh, yeah." He didn't ask questions much, just kept answering mine, not giving away one piece of information that wasn't strictly required to be polite. And Willie was polite. He just wasn't a conversationalist, that's all. And when I run out of questions, I start talking about myself. It pisses some people off, and I guess it's a defense. What can I say? Anyway, that's what I did. Willie didn't interrupt, and he seemed interested. Sexually, that is. More interested than I'd be, or than was necessary, which was his way of indicating that he was waiting for me to ask the Big Question, which he would then be happy to answer in the affirmative.

"Besides," he said later, "what did I have to say? That I go to high school and had a great geometry lesson that day? I didn't know anything you'd care about." He was wrong. He could have said anything.

Even if I wasn't drawn to him like a magnet, which I was, even if I didn't have instant designs on his body, which I did, even if I wasn't more than slightly mellow, about which there was no question, I would still have been interested. That's the thing about people. They underestimate how much they have in common. They underestimate how fascinating someone else might find the smallest piece of information about them, particularly if the person in question is a sucker for eyes the size of plums.

| *The Hard Way* |

Suppose Willie *had* said, "I had a great geometry lesson." Suppose I said, "Tell me about it." Suppose he then said that he finally grasped the concept of—I don't know, what?—congruent angles, for example. Then I could drop back on my own experience with congruent angles, and then we'd have something in common. Geometry was a bitch. All those axioms and theorems. Thank God I had a good memory. I hated geometry, but I loved my teacher, until she went off and got married in the middle of tenth grade. People were going off and leaving a lot in those days. There, you see? A whole world opens up the minute the slightest detail is revealed. I would have respected Willie if he had told me about congruent angles. And I would have felt an instant kinship with him as people that was more than just wanting to hold him in my arms. Because all he had to do was say "congruent angles" and he would have been part of my world. But people don't do that. They hide.

Anyway, Willie was big for his age. Too big for his own good, I used to tell him. He was big and black and had muscles from his neck to his calves, though most of his bulk was in his upper body from working out so hard on his chest, back, and arms with a set of weights he found that somebody was throwing out. His skin was dark. Not some medium-brown color, like most black people two or three hundred years out of Africa. Willie's skin was dark, dark black, the kind with blue and purple tones in it, not the reds and greens and yellows that go into brown. A person could spend a lifetime lost in the colors of black men's skins and never see them all. It was one of the first things I liked about him, that skin darker than anyone I had ever seen. It was smooth and warm over hard muscle and bone. Like a panther's skin. But that would come later.

Willie had big eyes and a broad nose, thick lips and a wide-open smile (pretty much the opposite of me). But it was hard to look at him sometimes because of those shit teeth he had, all rotted away from too much macaroni and Coca-Cola instead of milk and meat. Like everybody else, he looked his best when he was smiling, except for those teeth, and he always held his lips tight when he felt a laugh coming on and then shoved a hand up in front of his face if he couldn't stifle it. Naturally, I couldn't resist trying to crack him up. It was fun, but it was sad, knowing how much pain there must have been in those teeth at his age and nobody around to do a damn thing for him. Willie liked white men and smart men, which was all right with me, because fairly white and reasonably quick on the uptake were about all I had to offer. Willie liked getting fucked, too, a fact he slipped into the conversation about my army career in case I couldn't tell. And that was fine with me, because that is just my style of making myself known.

Berk, by the way, was this hippie friend who kept his long red hair perfume-clean with handmade herbal shampoo he bought in a Greenwich Village health-food store, to which he would go every now and again by a train they used to call the Pennsylvania Railroad. He was an assistant librarian at the college, so he wore thick, rimless glasses and had a scrawny little moustache. He was pretty dumb for a librarian, which you would have thought was pretty smart, but he was having these parties all the time so the local fags could meet each other. Berkeley, whose real name was Howard, was goofy-looking in what everybody said was an odd, kind of cute sort of way if you liked them like that. He had a huge cock that never really got hard, at least not in my experience. Anyway, that's how I met Willie.

Berk lived in a black neighborhood in those days. But that was nothing special. We all lived in one of the black neighborhoods, or else in scummy downtown. Who could afford to live anyplace else? The university was buying up all the good property for laboratories and dormitories for spoiled rich kids, and the Puerto Ricans were moving up from the harbor, where they had already displaced the Italians, who were making it big enough on the docks to finally move to the suburbs, taking all the good restaurants with them. Berk liked to be called Berkeley, but I called him Berk or Berkshire (after the mountains), and he used to come home from the library carrying a few hundred books, and there'd be this hefty black teenager cruising him all the time. So one day Berk just said, "I'm having a party tonight for some gay friends"—Berk felt that it was his political duty to use the word *gay* at least once in every sentence—"and you're welcome to join us." And the kid, who was Willie, said sure. Later Berk told

Bud that he thought he was going to get Willie in bed after the party, but Bud had the same idea for himself as soon as he saw the kid, because Bud was the most radical of all of us, by his own estimation, and Bud thought sleeping with a black teenager was politically avant-garde. Bud was an asshole. But Willie liked tall men and thin men and blond men with beards, so I lucked out. Bud had cut his off because beards were a sexist oppression of women. Gary said it was Bud had crabs.

The others were surprised, too, that I put the make on Willie. I thought Chris Wood and Ira Rubin, who were into three-ways, were going to keel over, and Miguel was being a pain in the butt about it, but he was a pain in the butt about everything, particularly when he wasn't getting what he wanted, and he was most decidedly not getting me, at least not again. So everyone was being a dickhead. Didn't know I was into "dark meat," they said, didn't know I was a "dinge queen." Fucking assholes, all of them. No wonder there's racism all over this fucking country. Nothing pisses me off more than hearing members of one oppressed group ragging on people they feel superior to. What goddamn pointless no-dick nerve.

Anyway, the whole thing was a joke to me. I mean, I know it might sound weird to the goons in Mississippi underneath their white sheets—and I knew plenty of them in the army—but there's a lot of things about a lot of people, a lot of *groups* of people that I find more than a little objectionable, but skin color just isn't one of them. Maybe it was that book about George Washington Carver I read when I was eight years old, I don't know. Because there were zero black kids around where I grew up, or my old man would have moved, which was when it was polite to say "Negro" instead of "colored," which is the word my old man always used when he wasn't saying "nigger."

So I met Willie at Berkeley the librarian's Halloween party and fell over an ugly rag rug Berk's sister made on a feminist commune in Vermont, because it takes a few good drinks to invite anybody home for the night, especially if the answer is likely to be yes, so I was showing off a little. After I came to, just slightly dazed from the bong on the head, Berk told everybody that his sister had to tell the other commune women that she was giving the rug to a woman or else they wouldn't let her use the loom or whatever it was. Bud thought this was right on, Gary thought it was sexist, and Chris Wood said he liked the colors. Anyway, we left, Willie and me, and everybody else was pissed off. About us or something else. I don't know.

Willie wasn't wearing a costume, thank God. In fact, nobody at this Halloween party was wearing a costume except the transvestites, but that wasn't because it was Halloween. But Willie wasn't wearing a coat either, just a turtleneck sweater. And it was cold. Real cold. The way it can be in New England when it takes a mind to it. I kept asking him if he was warm enough and should we walk faster, but he kept saying, "I'm fine," which I did not believe for a minute, because he looked like every inch of his skin must be covered with goose bumps. He kept pulling his head as far as it would go into the neck of his sweater.

"My grandmother used to live here," Willie said between his chattering brown teeth as we crossed the highway spur they stopped building right in the middle of this shit city. It was the first personal thing he ever said about himself. At least that I can remember.

"Where?" I said. "Here?"

"Yup," he said with a slight sideways dip of his head. "Right here." But not like he was sad. Just cold.

What people told me was that it used to be a nice neighborhood before it got rundown and became a black neighborhood and got rundown some more. So they bulldozed it, except for the block where the old Jewish bakery was on Sunday morning, and they started to build this highway that was going to bypass downtown. But they ran out of money, like they always do. So now they had this hundred burned-out acres of ruined city like Germany after World War II and a highway that came to a dead end with a medical school on the ghetto side of it and the telephone company on the university side. It was a certified fucking U.S. government urban-redevelopment mess.

I tried to get Willie to tell me some of this over again, just to hear him talk, but he was too cold.

"Was it a nice old house?" I asked him.

"No," he said. "Just a dump, like all the others."
We kept walking.

I lived in one room of a dive that looked like a dead Swiss chalet squeezed behind an old garage where they still took cars upstairs on a huge elevator. That was on one side. A rabbi lived on the other side in a old town house that had cream-colored paint peeling off the red bricks underneath. He had the only decent patch of yard on the block. Behind us it was all parking lots and the backs of dirty brick buildings, most of which were abandoned, thanks to the master redevelopment scheme, or is that scam? But one of them had the Arthur Murray Dance Studio in it, so every Tuesday night or so you could see six or eight old people waltzing around and stepping out onto the fire escape for a smoke.

Anyway, we got to my place and snuck past the old witch who stood guard at the door, although nobody was asking her to, and managed to get safe inside the upper back room, which is where I lived, if you can call it that. I called it "hanging up my jeans." Willie didn't want to take his clothes off for a while. I thought he was being shy or something, and I knew he was jailbait no matter how old he said he was, but only if anyone cared about him enough to press charges, which obviously no one did, or they would have fixed his teeth. It was a real shame to be as beautiful a kid as Willie and not have anyone care if your teeth rotted out of your mouth. I mean, I hated my old man for a lot of things, but at least he kept me fed until I got out of high school. Willie lived with his mother, but he was on his own in all the ways that matter.

"You've done this before, haven't you?" I asked him. I am not interested in anyone's virginity.

"Hundreds of times," he said and took off his sweater like that proved it. If you ever want somebody out of their clothes, just accuse them of being a prude. It works every time.

I was right about his being cold. His skin was as cold as the bare wood floor under the sink. I stripped him down and ran my hands over him so there wouldn't be any mistake about what I had in mind, and he let me know that what I had in mind was fine with him. Then I made him get into bed, under all the covers I could find, including my coat. I turned the radiator up full, which sent loud knocking sounds through the pipes. Then I stripped myself and climbed in with him.

I had to just hold him for about a half hour, he was so cold, just hold him and warm him up. Myself, I'm always warm, even though I tend to be skinny. I'm lucky about that. It's something I got from my mother, and it's something people like about me. Once somebody told me that people had healing in the warmth of their hands. I don't think I ever healed anybody of anything, but I've warmed up some hands and feet in my time; and before long Willie was warm, and we were doing what came naturally. I could tell by the way I slipped into him without trouble that he'd done it before. More than once. Or else he was ready. Those sounds he was making into my one thin pillow were not pain sounds. And it was love in his eyes when he kissed me good night and said thanks. I was drunk, sure, but I remember thinking, "What kind of world is this when one roll in the hay with a stranger can inspire such gratitude? What kind of a situation do we have here when a kid with as much beauty as Willie had pouring out of him feels a need to thank people for just touching him?" I didn't know the answer, but I felt the same way. "Don't thank me," I told him, but not out loud, "I'm not worth it."

We fell asleep, but before I finally dozed off, I could see stars through the branches of the tree in the rabbi's yard next door. The tree had an old truck tire on it that the rabbi's children swung on like a swing. The children all had names from the Old Testament, which I recognized from Sunday school, which my mother made me go to against my will. I remember thinking, "That's nice," when their mother called them inside for lunch one day. She sounded like a smart kid rattling off the answers to a Bible quiz. She was younger than her husband, who had a gray beard and worked for the university. Her hair was still dark under her pale cotton kerchiefs, and her hands always looked clean, cool, and pale when she was tending her garden, which was full of purple irises. Nothing but. Sometimes I'd watch her just sit and stare at them for hours. But it was cold now, and the irises were not in bloom.

| *The Hard Way* |

I woke up a few hours later. It was already getting to be light in the gray kind of way it gets when there are too many clouds for a sunrise. Willie was curled up in my arms, his butt up against my crotch, and he was now warm enough that there was a layer of sweat between us. I had a hard-on, as usual, and I didn't have to shift myself around much to get back inside him. I just held myself there until we were breathing together, inhaling and exhaling, in and out, and he woke up and we fucked again before he even turned around.

Willie had the kind of eyes that said "I love you" even when what he was really saying was, "I gotta pee." So I let him use the sink, which I hated for anyone to do, but I didn't want him to have to walk down the hall to the head. It was too cold for a kid who had such a hard time getting warm.

I remember later when his skin got dry and chalky sometimes that it reminded me of the frost on the dark earth of the rabbi's iris garden that first morning while I watched him piss in my sink. He was embarrassed, sure, and kept trying to hide that big thing of his from sight; but I just lay there smiling my face off and watching his chunky ass flex while he got the last drops of piss out and ran steaming water into the sink to kill the smell of it. That was our first morning. All Saints' Day, it was, the morning after Halloween. We took a shower together down the hall while the old ladies banged on the door and I sucked Willie off. Then I loaned him a jacket and took him out for a hot breakfast. I walked him to his school bus, but I didn't kiss him.

"Thanks," he said again.

I said, "I'll see you later," and I did.

Anyway, Berkeley, Bud, Chris, and Ira might have been surprised, and Miguel was still being a pain in the ass that I got to take Willie home and that I kept doing it all the time they were standing around waiting for me to get tired of the kid so they could have a shot. Only they didn't know everything. And one of the things they didn't know was how I felt about Willie and that Willie wasn't the first black man in my life. By 1970 I'd already balled every color of the rainbow—men and women—so the race thing was not the Big Issue they all thought it was. Miguel in particular was hard to figure, since he was always trying to get into my pants. I didn't get it, but why should I tell them everything? They didn't tell me everything I wanted to know, not even the things I asked them to tell me. For some reason, whenever I was around them, I felt like a kid begging for more food.

I don't know when our unconsciouses all got together and agreed that they were going to have authority over me, but they had it, or we all thought they did, which is pretty much the same thing. Anyway, they thought the way to keep an upper hand was not telling me things, which is exactly the same way I kept them from having more control than I wanted them to have. It's what they call a symbiosis in biology. And I learned about it in basic, not at some cocksucking Ivy League school.

Anyway, Willie was not the first.

The first black guy I'd ever known was named George. I had seen others before, but I actually knew Georgie, at least to talk to. His father was a janitor out in the boonies, so he wound up going to our school. The first time I saw him was in the first week of junior high, at gym glass. He had a locker down the row from me, and when he was peeling off his clothes I just kept wondering whether his color changed anywhere, or what. But when he stood there naked, he was the same color on the tip of his dick that he was on his nose, and that was a lesson to me. Georgie was dark, but not as dark as Willie. And he was small—small, smooth, and muscular, a gymnast, in fact, in the days when a black gymnast had about as good a shot as a black doctor on Park Avenue.

I used to watch Georgie on the high bar and on the rings and wonder what it was like to touch flesh like that, which seemed more real than my own. I had no definition in those days, and my ribs stuck out everywhere—like a broomstick with TB, my old man used to say. I'd watch Georgie sail around that gym horse switching hands, and watch Coach Hesse, his eyes twinkling with reflected fluorescent light as Georgie went through his turns, feet pointed, legs parallel, always perfect and always ready to improve, Hesse standing right under him during his dismount to make sure nothing ever happened to his prize pupil, Georgie just trusting the mean fuck like mad. And I'd watch them together and think, old Coach Hesse comes alive when Georgie's around. Old Coach Hesse thinks he's got some purpose in life when he lucks onto a kid like George. Old Coach Hesse acts more like Georgie's father than he does to his own fat kids, certainly more than my old man ever acted toward me. I don't ever remember seeing that kind of light in my old man's eyes, like he suddenly saw in me the reason to be alive he'd been waiting to see for years, like old Simeon and Anna in the temple who God said could live until they saw the Messiah. Maybe I was wrong to be looking for it. Maybe the only reason we're each alive is just to be alive. But I kept searching for some hint that my father saw in me his own immortality. I never saw it, never saw much from him but anger and boredom. But I saw it in Hesse's eyes with Georgie, and it was more than his usual horny leer when he was trying to get some tennis fruit to suck him off, which everybody knew was going on, so it probably wasn't.

I'd watch Georgie in the halls at school laughing with the other jocks and with his girlfriend, who was the only black cheerleader (her mother was a maid, the whole thing was completely degrading, but they seemed happy anyway). And I'd watch him in class with his broad smile whether he knew the answer or not. And I'd watch him in that locker room and in that shower rubbing white foam all over that dark skin, getting his dick half-hard soaping it, me getting half-hard watching him until I had to turn away. And him always real intense on whatever he did, history or floor exercises, and always smiling in between. And the only time I ever touched him was by accident, like, passing in and out of the shower. Our arms would glance off each other, and I'd say, "Sorry, George," and he'd smile wide off his face and say, "Hey, Gar, how're you doing?"

And that's as physical as we ever got, but I still think of Georgie as the first man I ever had sex with. Because after school when I'd be moping around the house being bored with nothing to do because I didn't feel like cooking dinner for the old man or whatever, I'd slip out of my clothes and pull my pud and think of licking the sweat off Georgie's chest and legs and of wrapping my mouth around that cute little wiener of his and of working my dick into his smooth, hard butt and kneading those cheeks with my hands. And I'd dream about me and Georgie and Coach Hesse and that smile and that twinkle in his eye.

After I got out of high school, my old man called me a fag one day for no particular reason, so I enlisted in the army to prove he was wrong.

I knew all kinds of guys in the army, from all over the country, most of them poor and most of them young, like me. Most of them assholes, too. There were these two particular black guys in basic in godforsaken Texas. Peckerman was from Indiana and must have been only part black because he had nearly blond hair and light skin with freckles, and eyes that shifted from gray to green, and how else would he get a name like Peckerman?—which is what everybody called him: Pecker-Man. He was a typist by trade, and he didn't care who knew what. He'd go walking down the barracks and some wise honky would say, "There goes one nelly nigger," and then some black dude would say, "That ain't no nigger, that there's a faggot." And Pecker-Man would say, "You don't know shit from chocklit puddin' 'bout me till I got my dick up your ass, white bitch." Or sometimes "black cunt," whichever he thought more appropriate. Some guys thought he was just angling for a discharge, but nobody wanted to talk to Pecker-Man anyway—not blacks and not whites—at least until Leroy came along. Leroy was being a badass dude from D.C., and had the scars to prove it. Leroy was black as the ace of spades and enlisted to beat some heavy felony rap. He'd already done grand-larceny time and wanted no more part of prison. Everybody called him Big Leroy, and nobody—big or small—crossed Leroy anyhow.

Anyway, everybody used to say that Leroy was putting it to Pecker-Man in a big way, like he got used to in jail, because they were always together, but I never saw them doing anything, and I was watching. "I fuck what I want to fuck," Big Leroy used to say to anybody who said anything to him about Pecker-Man, "and it's gonna be your mouth if I hear one more jiveass word out of it." But he told me one time that he hung around Peckerman because he couldn't stand everybody picking on the guy like he was some kind of disease. "Peckerman's a brother,

| The Hard Way |

man," he told me, "and I stick by my brothers 'til they do me wrong." I liked that "brother" stuff, you know? 'Cause there was nothing like that where I was coming from.

I don't remember much about what happened after that, except me and Leroy used to raise hell a lot, drinking our guts out whenever we got a chance to blow the camp, and one morning me and Leroy woke up in the barracks all beat up. It made us feel closer than we ever did before, but we didn't talk much after that, after we figured out neither of us remembered anything. We didn't want anybody to know we couldn't remember, and I'm not sure even we really wanted to know, either.

Then we were shipped out, even Pecker-Man. To Vietnam, of course. "Nam," the geeks back home always called it. I always called it "Vietnam," like it deserved enough respect at least to say its whole name out loud. We were there about a year and Peckerman and Leroy got sent out on patrol one time, which Peckerman wasn't even really trained for, but he was being punished by some chopper-jock louie for something, and Big Leroy bought the VC ambush and went down. One guy who came back—there were only two, both of them brothers—said Pecker-Man screamed like a drunken mammy when he saw Big Leroy go down and ran into the jungle blasting his ammo away at rotten bamboo. They never found either of them, but guessed they were both dead when they found some VC kids playing with two human dicks, both of them black. They skewered the VC with their bayonets for Leroy and Pecker-Man. I got a lot to be sorry for. I never killed any kids, but I never stopped the others who did, but that was when it was still cool to be stoned and what they called merciless. That was before. It wasn't until after that everybody got uptight about the dope and the whores and killing VC brats. As for me, I fucked any hole that stood still long enough to drop a load in it. I never expected to live long enough to get a disease. It was a bitch. Before and after.

After the war everybody was saying that I ought to be glad I was alive and I ought to do something with my life. Well, I was glad to be alive, more or less, but I figured I'd already done with my life what had to be done, what with having defended democracy on foreign soil and all, and I didn't have the slightest idea what the hell else I was supposed to do with it now. So I went to college courtesy of Uncle Sam and met Willie in Collegetown, USA. Under ordinary circumstances, I couldn't have gotten a job raking leaves at this place, but because this was like 1969 and I was a vet, and the vets were getting fucked over royally everywhere you looked, I couldn't get into the shit colleges I had the high-school grades for; only the ones with terrific reputations, lots of money, and liberal enough politics to set up special programs for those of us who qualified as underprivileged. I didn't fit any of the major groups, but I slipped in because of my Purple Heart and my limp and because I told them my grandfather was full-blooded Cherokee.

So there I was at old alma mater, too old and too smashed up to play ball, which I never really liked anyway, learning how to talk about things I didn't understand in a way that was guaranteed to keep anybody else from understanding them, either. That's when I met Willie. Right after I dropped out. And I was just bumming around town, taking drugs and getting laid when I could, just like everybody else, in school or out. I even got it on with the Vassar dyke who was going to cure me of being a fairy for some reason that seemed important at the time, but then I got into acid, so she was the last.

I was so bored sometimes I couldn't even keep walking down the street. I'd just slow down to a halt and stand on the sidewalk like I was having an epileptic fit of the petit mal variety until somebody or something made me move. I wasn't even going to go to Berk's fucking Halloween party, but I knew nobody would be at The Pub until it was over. As it turned out, I'm glad I went.

So Willie moved in with me, and at least I had somebody to go home to and talk to and warm his feet.

I was walking down the street one night in a snowstorm, and I met this jerk Albert I knew. He was a psychiatrist at the university hospital, but he was a fruit, just like everybody else. I'd been with Willie about two months at the time. Albert was a nerdy kind of Brooklyn type, and we were chatting about this and that in the snow in front of the mental-health center. Albert had been at some of Berk's parties, too. So we were talking, and one thing leads to another, and he says, "Tell me about this thing you have for black men." And I say, "I don't have 'a thing' for black men." And he said, "What about Willie?" And I say, "Willie is a person, not a thing."

So Albert lays out this theory how white guys who like black guys secretly hate themselves and so they choose sex objects as different from themselves as possible. And then he says that white guys who like fucking black guys—I don't know who was talking to him about Willie and me, but it could have been anybody—were as racist as the Ku Klux Klan, and were all into domination of oppressed people because they feel so oppressed themselves by their own self-hatred. Well, I already knew what I thought about guys whose lovers looked exactly like themselves, and what I thought was that those people hated themselves so much the only "relationship" they could stand was essentially masturbatory because they couldn't begin to inflict themselves on anyone but a narcissistic surrogate, which was pretty twisted. And I told him so. Which probably pissed him off, since his own cretinous boyfriend, a notorious slut everybody'd had at least twice, looked so much like him they had to sew name tags in their boxer shorts to tell themselves apart. Which I also told him.

Besides, I told him, warming up now in the cold, I had no *political* objections to being fucked myself, which he implied. I just didn't like the way it felt. And besides, I told him, it wasn't about *race*, which is something I would have thought a big deal psycho-whatever-he-was would know, but about class and the economic basis of oppression based on race, which is something else I did not learn in hallowed halls of ivy but in the grunt corps, and which was one of the last things I ever said to my old man before he died (but not before he told me that VC weed turned me into a Commie and that I was solely responsible for my mother's death, for which I would willingly have killed him if he wasn't doing so admirable a job himself).

Sometimes I'm not sure what fight I'm fighting, which is why I seem to be fighting some things too hard, but I may also have told old Albert that I did not limit my fucking escapades to members of my own sex or to people whose skin colors differed from my own, and I probably wound up my little lecture in the snow by suggesting that it was probably a breach of professional ethics to drop two cents worth of free, unasked-for psychiatric evaluation in my lap unless he was going to offer the whole long-haul analysis on similar terms and that I could tell him more about self-hatred by reading any one of his own journals than he could tell about mine from some casual observations at a party or some thirdhand cut-rate gossip. And then I told him his lover was shitty at sex and that if he had any self-esteem he'd dump the twerp.

By this time my ears were nearly frozen off, since earmuffs are so goddamn dorky, even if you need them, and so we parted company that night on Park Street, which never did have a park on it to anyone's certain knowledge. For once in my life, I didn't feel as if my brief college career was wasted, and I don't even think I wanted a drink.

I went home and asked Willie if he felt oppressed by my wanting to ball him, and he looked kind of odd and said no. And I asked him if he would feel better if he got to ball me occasionally or to have psychiatric counseling, and he said only if I wanted him to, and I told him that I was glad he was seventeen now because it made me feel like less of a child molester, and he said that if I wanted to feel like a child molester he would dress up in a diaper, as long as I didn't make him leave. Then I kissed him and helped him write a book report on *Ivanhoe*.

But times were shitty. And then they got worse.

Education was what we argued about mostly. Why it was all right for me to quit college but not for him to quit high school, and him with only one full year to go after next September?

"They just make fun of me, for being black and being gay and for being stupid and having shit teeth, Willie would say."

"So you stay in school until you're not stupid. And you get a decent job and fix your teeth, and then that's two less things to be made fun of. Then they can make fun of your skin color and the men you sleep with—and then we'll both know there's nothing you can do about that, so they're the dickheads." I've never met anyone yet who didn't have at least one thing you could make fun of if you were the kind of asshole so low to the ground you couldn't shit unless it was on the head of somebody you brought down by kicking them in the nuts. "You're a gay black man, Willie-boy," I said, "and there's nothing to be ashamed of in that unless you choose to be. If God had wanted you white and straight, that's how you would have come down the chute."

There was a pause while he thought about it and decided if he was going to let me in or close me out.

"Calling a nigger 'boy' is politically incorrect," he said and started to grin, holding up his hand so I wouldn't have to look at his teeth. He smoked a joint, and I wished I had enough money to fix his teeth. But my job running the garage elevator next door barely kept us dressed and fed. So I just kissed him, over and over again. It was all I knew how to do.

Willie stayed in school and with me in the leftover dive on High Street, which was actually the name of the street, if you can believe it. And once he told me his mother never even asked him why he wasn't staying home anymore, and that burst my bubble about how much better life would have been if it had been my old man who died of cancer and my mother who hit the bottle from grief.

Willie had this cousin Tina, who was a drag queen, which is how everybody wound up finding out Willie was queer, because Tina had a mouth on her like a hand grenade: dangerous before it went off and ugly after. That was Tina: a cunt with a prick. I made a habit of never fucking with her, literally and otherwise. Tina used to hang around the downtown White Castle, smoking cigarettes and drinking coffee and trying to pick up the lowlife. She must have given a lot of blow jobs in her day, Miss Tina, just to pay the rent, because I can't imagine paying much for a skinny-ass transvestite hooker who didn't even shave before she went out for the night in a red wool dress she'd wash in the bathroom sink and dry in the oven. "You want a man, you don't want one in a dress," I said whenever I saw Tina coming down the street, swinging her hips from wall to curb. "You want a dress, get a real woman."

I hated Tina because she gave Willie such a hard time and

was always hitting on him for the cash I had given him for his lunch and such. I hated Tina, but I try not to be too hard on people just because I don't agree with them. My fellow students, as my teachers at the college used to call them, seemed to belong to a secret club that agreed on how to think about something, and everybody else was always wrong and took the heat for disagreeing. I always figure if I disagree with someone, I'm fifty percent responsible for the controversy even if I'm sure I'm right, which was less often than I let on to Willie at the time. He was too young to have to listen to me talking out loud about whether he was too young to be in a relationship with me and whether I was doing the right thing. He's too young to get too dependent on me, I used to think, because I'm too unreliable; but it's hard to train somebody to be independent of you when you love them, at least if you think of it as love, even if it *is* the right thing. At least for them.

Anyway, I saw parts of a lot of soldiers in the service who were so sure they were right, they forgot there might be consequences to insisting. Just like a belligerent drunk. I should know. I'm nasty when I've been drinking. That's why I started smoking dope. "Stick to your principles," I say, "but if you get mowed down, be sure to remember you could have stepped aside." Weigh the cost. Decide and change your mind if you have to, but the V.C. heading south were just as right in their own minds as the U.S. infantry heading north. All that bloodshed was people being right in two different languages, drowning each other out because both sides were too fucking stupid to look in each other's eyes and figure out another way. So their side won. And we were still right, according to the daily news, and a lot of beautiful people got blown away in the process.

"Try to believe in a God who would allow that," I'd say to Willie on those cold winter mornings when he said he wanted to go to church. Usually he just went to the bakery out in no-man's-land and came back with cinnamon rolls and prune danish, and we'd sit and read the paper and rename the cat while we ate them and the rabbi's children built a snowman in the yard. You could tell he was Jewish because they gave him a little beanie and a beard made out of the string mop.

It was on these Sunday mornings I'd be the most unsure about Willie, him just sitting there naked, not saying much, feeling more than he was letting on. I mean, a good father would encourage a kid to believe in something more than the stinking world. Not like my old man. "Life sucks, kid," he'd tell me, "and so do you." I know he was just bitter because of my mother dying and having a weird kid he didn't know what to do with. I knew it was all horseshit, but it still hurt like hell, you know? Before I got tough enough to turn it off.

I wasn't Willie's father, though. I was his lover. But he was too young and needed to know so much that I kept thinking like a father. I wanted his teeth fixed, and I wanted him to finish school and get a good job and be happy. I wanted to protect him from what was coming down, and I wanted to teach him how to take care of himself for the times when I wasn't around. Sometimes on Sunday mornings I'd be hung over and full of remorse and feeling much older than I usually felt, which was older than I was, and I'd feel like I let him down. Then he'd take my throbbing head in his soft, sweet lap and massage my forehead and temples with his cool, long fingers and sing along with the radio. I could feel his stomach going in and out when he breathed and hear the vibrations of his singing through his abdomen wall, and I wished that he could put into words how he was feeling and just vibrate them into my ear through his stomach like that and stop being afraid.

And that was when this Black Panther cousin of Willie's got arrested for murder and the city went berserk. The only evidence against the blood was the lunatic testimony of an old wino even Tina thought was too fucking crazy for trade. But the FBI and the CIA and the Secret Service and the National Guard and God knows who else were all over the place, and things were starting to stack up as white against black, same as everywhere else. And everybody was pissed off, and it was not a good time for a pair of black and white faggots to be walking down the street hand in hand. Whoever said Love Conquers All never had the shit kicked out of them by a dozen punks with baseball bats.

So I went to this party with Willie one night way over in the deep black part of town. Tina was there with a few of her Puerto Rican cohorts and their tattooed boyfriends. The Panthers weren't there because Huey Newton hadn't met Jean Genet yet, the French fag writer thief who was being a bald-headed revolutionary, so the Panther *Gazette* or whatever it was called hadn't said it was cool for queers to be revolutionaries yet. (You get what kind of times these were, right?) Anyway, none of the Panthers were hanging around with the pansies yet, the way they did later, because it was still uncool to be gay, much less black and gay, much less black and gay and being balled on a regular basis by a honky. So I was taking a lot of heat at this party, even though I'd known some of the people there for ages, and most of them knew Willie and me. Unfortunately, the day of this party the federal court had ruled to admit the lunatic's testimony and denied Willie's cousin bail. Now, the suspect was Tina's baby brother, and she had her tits in a wringer and her ass way up on her back. And she was poking her poison tongue into the ear of this real pretty man named Randall J. I had a hard-on for Randall J. for as long as I could remember, but he showed no signs of interest in me, which Miguel told me was because Randall was hip and didn't suck no white dick. It was a disappointment, sure, but one thing I learned was, there's no limit to prejudice. So when Randall J. walked into the kitchen where I was leaning against the fridge and said, "What the fuck you doin' here, no-dick white motherfucker?" I got mad. Okay, I admit I was three sheets to the wind, and so were some of the brothers who started taking up Randall J.'s persecution, and Willie was trying to keep them off me, but I was just so fucking angry that I started to cry.

It must have been the quality of the weed we'd been doing, but I just broke down altogether, which threw everybody for a loop. They had to sit me down on the bed on top of everybody's coats and just let me sob it out, which I did, harder than I cried even when my mother died and left me alone with my old man. Well, I felt like a fool, blubbering on a pile of coats in a tiny bedroom off a smaller kitchen, even though some of my black friends told Randall J. off right to one of his faces, but I knew then and there that Willie and I were headed for a nosedive, because something inside me said, "Gar, you have let them see too much of the wrong thing at the wrong time," and when we got home, Willie was pissed.

"Man, you can't never, you can't *never* cry," he steamed.

You'd have thought he had dog shit in his mouth the way he said it.

"You cry and they'll stomp all over your white ass."

Another five years of shoving down the hate, and Willie would understand that sometimes there's no controlling how anger comes spilling out. Could be murder. Could be suicide. You never knew.

"Men don't fucking cry," Willie was saying, slamming the closet door and opening it to slam it again. Which is just what my old man told me at my mother's funeral.

But I was wishing he could have cried, was wishing he could have cried green puke and barfed up every time somebody had called him nigger or faggot or moron or shit-for-teeth and he couldn't do a thing about it. I knew he'd cry sooner or later if he lived long enough, but I knew that I scared him too bad by letting him look too deep inside too soon. And the chink I'd been making in his armor was now welded shut. And the sound of it was the sound of a cell door slamming. Him in. Me out. *Sayonara*. Good-bye.

So I blew it. Or life blew it. Whatever. Maybe I was wrong all the time to be with such a kid. I don't know. The older I get, the less I know.

Shortly after this party fiasco, some heavy Panther types told Tina to tell Willie to tell me to lay my dick off the brotherhood, and pretty soon after that Willie and I were a dead item. Willie had never been in a war, but I had.

We blamed it on politics, on the Panthers, on the trial that was finally thrown out of court years later, and on the stinking shit times we were all living in. There wasn't any big scene, we just stopped being with each other all the time. Willie started staying overnight at Tina's house, and I started seeing Miguel, but he said I was fucking him so hard I must be thinking I was getting even with Randall J. So that didn't last too long, either.

Miguel's got a mouth that lands him in jail, and I was spending a lot of time holding my guts over a toilet bowl while Miguel screamed Spanish obscenities at the local constabulary.

    The Panthers got Tina out of her dress for a while, and she was running around the streets in a safari jacket and aviator sunglasses with a .357 Magnum strapped to her bony ribs, and I knew *that* was lethal. I also knew that if the Panthers weren't letting Tina give head, she would never make it in the new order, and I wasn't surprised to hear she split for Philadelphia with a hog jock. Willie was carrying a gun, too, which I didn't like, but maybe he needed the protection. I saw him one day, which is how I found out about Tina, and he told me that the Panthers had talked him into quitting booze and drugs and he was studying the wisdom of Allah through the writings of Mohammed. I told him, "Good," because that's what he wanted to do. He was looking for something, and I wanted him to find it. So his escort Panther was giving him the nod to go and he said, "Well, I gotta go," and I said, "I hope you're happy," and he said, "Yeah, well." Then he threw his arms around me and hugged me (which is how I found out about the gun), and his eyes were flashing "I love you" all over the street, but his uptight soul brother was flashing a different message, so I let him drag Willie off to the revolution without so much as a good-bye kiss.

Some years later, sometime in the seventies, it must have been—after Canada, anyway—I was living in a green stucco dive under the Hollywood Freeway when I met Orfeo, the next great love of my life. I used to go to this disco and watch the Mexican kids dance with their sisters and sometimes their sisters' husbands. This one night a pasty-white pock-faced pansy who looked like he'd been drawn for a bad Saturday-morning cartoon show was coming on to me, which was flattering in a way, except he was such a turd. He kept lisping and drooling through the braces on his teeth, and if I'd had more to drink I'd probably have set him back a few grand by ripping my knuckles apart on his face. But I just turned away and asked whoever it was standing there to dance. (I could still dance until about eleven if I didn't start drinking before nine.) Anyway, the guy turned out to be cute, cute and

| *The Hard Way* |

Latin, and he said sure. He turned out to be a terrific dancer, too, so we danced for two hours nonstop while the geek drooled at us from the losers' part of the stag line waiting for us to be done so he could ask me to dance, so I led Orfeo off the dance floor in the opposite direction.

"I live about half a block from here," he said, and I said, "I always wanted to visit that part of the world," and about twenty minutes later my dick was inching happily into his asshole.

In the morning I found out there were two things about Orfeo that surprised me: One, he had two children; two, he had never let another man fuck him before. "Why me?" I asked.

"I don't know," he said. "You just seemed right."

I liked little Orfeo. For our second date, I brought him a can of dark cherries in sweet syrup as a kind of joke present, 'cause I was his first, and he was my first virgin. He laughed right away and threw his arms around my neck, and twenty minutes later he had a dick up his ass for the second time.

I was falling in love. I could feel it. I liked him. I liked the kids. I thought, "Maybe there's hope after all." But I was wrong.

"Who's Willie?" he asked when I came to one morning.

"I don't know," I lied. "Why?"

You kept talking about him in your sleep," he said, which I didn't think was odd, but I didn't tell him who Willie was. There would be plenty of time for that later if everything worked out.

We used to take his kids around with us a lot. Ursula was seven and Brandon was five. We went to the zoo and Knott's Berry Farm. We went to the park and to the circus, where we sat so close to the action that the clowns handed each of them a balloon, Ursula on Orfeo's lap, Brandon on mine.

The thing was, their mother was white. A strung-out white junkie who just took off one day and left Orfeo with the kids, which was fine with him. And me, because when the four of us were together, it was just like we were made for each other. In the first place, he'd gotten married only to shut up his mother. After his wife split, Orfeo took his kids to live in Hawaii because his mother, an old Catholic battle-ax, told him that if she found out he was screwing men, she'd go to the authorities and have the kids taken away. And she would have done it too, since he didn't have legal custody. You only had to look at the acid-green dress she wore to church to know she didn't know the meaning of the word *bluff*.

I used to love holding hands with Orfeo and the kids, all four of us, walking down the street. Of course, it shocked hell out of people, but we didn't care. Most people need shocking, and we were a family in love. Except Orfeo, who wasn't in love with me (not that I could blame him). He was in love with the man who kicked them out of the house in Honolulu because the kids were getting on his nerves, and Orfeo was back in L.A. only to dispose of the kids in the most socially acceptable way, leaving them at his sister's place in the Simi Valley. I was a monkey wrench in this well-oiled, unspoken scheme of his, and so one fine day after I hadn't seen him for a while because that whole day we spent shopping for tropical fish drove me nuts, I knocked on Orfeo's front door, and his sister opened it.

"Hey, Gar," she said. "Uh, Orfeo's gone. Didn't he tell you?"

Well, no, he hadn't told me. And now he was already back in Honolulu with the German pilot who hated kids, so there wasn't much I could do about it.

"Orfeo doesn't like to get hit," his sister said, and I kind of remembered the last night I saw him, the night of the tropical fish.

The kids were in a bad mood that day, and it was too hot, and I was drinking beer to cool off. Then I yelled at Brandon when he pissed in his pants in the car, and Ursula started crying and never really stopped the whole day except to down her burger and fries; but then her paper crown broke and she started all over again. I went out by myself that night because Orfeo didn't want to leave the kids alone, or so he said. When I got back, he was sitting there. I remember it clear as day. And I remember that something happened, and I said, "Well, what has that Nazi got that I don't have?" And I remember taking a swing at him, but I don't remember if I hit him or not. I remember he threw the can of dark cherries at me and that both kids woke up screaming. But I don't exactly remember what he was he was saying while he was throwing it. It was the closest I ever came to forgiving my father.

It turned out to be the last time I saw Orfeo. About a year later, he sent me school pictures of the two kids in Hawaiian shirts, but he didn't say where they were or what his plans were. He just thought I'd like to see the pictures. There was no return address, but the postmark looked like it said California. I headed East.

I fell in with a bunch of artists when I finally got to New York. Don't ask me how. We'd just pal around being friends and they'd be talking about this show and that show, and what gallery owner was the biggest pig, whatever. And when somebody got horny, we'd just get it on. Sometimes it would be one, sometimes another. Nobody was getting married. We were all drinking and smoking and fucking around, and they were doing paintings and sculptures and shit, and I was selling tokens in a subway booth in Queens and wondering what would be happening at The Factory later that night, as if I couldn't guess.

I was living in the Chelsea Hotel, where there was dog shit in the hall from some famous composer who'd gone off his nut after his boyfriend died, and I used to fuck this transvestite actress named Candy Darling now and again on the bathroom floor. I was living with a nasty midget lesbian named Dora, dealing drugs a little, turning the odd trick, just to make the rent most months. But I got busted and did some time upstate. No big thing. No big maximum-security scene. But I got fucked enough times by black men and white and brown and even one red man to shut anyone up about Willie. I never got to liking it, just putting up with it, like life. Unfortunately, I never really got back on my feet again after that and was sort of bumming around the Village trying to get by on spare change to augment my disability check thanks to some goon deciding I had chronic alcoholism as a result of Vietnam-era combat stress, which was a true hoot, but I cashed the checks just the same.

I didn't dare get caught around drugs or I'd wind up back in jail, or at least that's what the probation fruit told me at our first-and-only session. So I was hanging around Sheridan Square one time, trying to hit up the out-of-towners for the price of a bottle when they got off the subway, and I hear someone yell, "Gar!"

Well, I hadn't used "Gar" since I left California, and I've had a few names since. Lately it's been Marco for no reason I can remember except that whatever I was telling people my name was, "Marco" is what they were hearing. Anyway, I turn around and there's this real handsome black man standing there like a model out of *GQ* fucking magazine. The suit is five…seven hundred bucks, minimum. He's got a pocket hanky that matches his tie and another half-thou worth of attaché case and a bunch of flowers in the other. He's got on thin horn-rimmed glasses with tinted lenses and this huge smile under a broad nose. He's got the most beautiful teeth I've ever seen.

"Hey, man. It's me, Willie," he says. "Don't you remember?"

And my memory starts to chug and churn, and my head is shaking back and forth, like no-no-no. Only something pleasant is rising on my spine, and I say, "Holy shit, Willie, what happened to your teeth?" And he puts down the briefcase and throws his arms around me, and he starts to cry and keeps crying and hugging and laughing until maybe I'm crying a little bit, too.

"God, Willie, you look terrific," I say. "What're you doing with yourself?"

"I'm a dentist," Willie says, and I just about fall out.

"No shit," I say, like it's a question.

"No shit," Willie says. "I'm in private practice with an oral surgeon who's also gay. Our office is on Fifth Avenue, just north of Washington Square."

"You went to college," I say, so proud I can hardly stand it.

"Had to," he says. "And dental school."

"You look fucking fabulous, Willie," I say, and he does. Fucking fabulous. Like an angel.

"And I owe it to you, Gar. For making me stay in school."

"Shit," I say. "If you stayed after I took off for parts unknown, you stayed because you wanted to stay. You wanted an education. I knew that. You just weren't sure. I'm sorry I didn't stay in myself long enough to get a decent job."

"Things are pretty rough with you, aren't they, Gar?" I never could put one over on Willie.

"Well, I cannot tell a lie," I say, "as the namesake of Washington Square once said. Now the pigeons shit on his statue."

"I've got plenty of money, Gar. Here—"

And then the little asshole goes for his wallet.

"What are you, crazy?" I say like the cabbies taught me. "I'm gonna take money from you?"

"I took money from you."

"You were just a kid."

"Well," he hesitates, now that I remind him about who is who, "how about a drink or dinner, at least, just to catch up on old times?"

"Shit, Willie," I say, "I'm in a little bit of a hurry right this minute. I'll tell you what. You give me your card—you got a card, don't you? You got to have a card if you're a dentist—"

"I've got a card."

"Well," I continue, "I'll give you a call, and you can look at my teeth, or what's left of them. How's that?"

Willie grins just like old Georgie used to do in junior high, only now he doesn't put his hand in front of his face. Now he reaches into his pocket and pulls out his card, which has on it: WILMINGTON D. HAMMOND, D.D.S.

"I never knew it was Wilmington," I say, and he laughs. I never knew he needed glasses, either. "I'm proud of you, Willie," I manage to squeeze out. "I'm glad things worked out for you."

"Because of you. Because of everything you did," he says, just as polite as ever.

"Whatever," I say, because I know he's wrong.

"You'll call me," he says. "You've got to promise, or I won't let you go."

"Don't worry, Willie," I say. "You were the best piece of ass I ever had, and I've had a few."

And he smiles again and hands me the flowers. "You take these," he says, just like he bought them for me. "You always liked them."

Purple irises, the whole bunch.

So he hugs me again and steps into the street, hailing a cab, which screeches to a halt on a dime.

"Call me," he shouts as he gets into the taxi.

"I will," I say. "Don't worry."

Only I don't, of course. It's not good to call in situations like these. Besides, times change, and so do people. A bunch of white goons offed a black kid in Bensonhurst last week. There's been a lot of progress in a lot of years, but we're all still pigs in a jungle. "It's not race," I keep saying. "It's class." But people don't listen, not to me anyway. I'm just a madman ranting like a fool on the street and cradling myself to sleep with memories of shittier times than these, and of pretty Willie sleeping in my arms on a cold and bitter Halloween.

I'm trying to stay off the booze for good now. Most of my friends are dead, or I've lost track of them. Some V.A. quack says my liver's shot and it's my only chance, which is probably bullshit scare tactics, but I got half a lung missing from the cigarettes, and they warned me about that too, so maybe they're right. It's hard to be dry and clean, too, 'cause all these feelings and memories keep coming up and catching in my throat, like they'll choke me to death if I don't have a drink. Then somebody suggested that I might have a better chance if I sat down and thought about all this Willie stuff and cleared away the wreckage of my past, he called it.

What did I have to lose?

One thing's to be clear about, though. I never thought of Willie as wreckage. I wouldn't be surprised to be told that's what he thinks about me, which is why I never phoned him, though he seemed really glad to see me. His life is fine without me, at least for now. I like to feel needed, you know?

But I felt happier than a fly on shit standing there in the dusk with two dozen hothouse irises in one hand and Willie's calling card in the other. And I stood there while the sun went down and knew that whatever anybody says about Willie, the two of us were never wrong. And I knew if anybody looked in my eye, they'd have seen what I saw when old Coach Hesse was watching Georgie on the high bar, that twinkle of something I never saw in my old man's eye, that one drop of salt water and pride in the corner of an eye that lets me know that God's in His heaven and all's right with the stinking world.

And who knows? My teeth really do need some attention. I

always figured I'd be dead before they wore out. And maybe sometime I'll get myself together and give Willie a jingle—strictly for professional reasons, of course—and maybe we'll see what happens if I stay sober long enough.

I just wish thinking about all this stuff didn't make me so damn thirsty, which is another long story altogether.

On The Game

Personal foibles #1

I like to sleep with the smell
of a man's cock on my hands,
maybe the smell of cock and
lightly scented oil,
maybe the smell of my own
cock, maybe not, maybe
the cock of a Thai boy at the
Gaiety Burlesk (his hips
politely tilted at the last
moment to take my finger)
or a dark-skinned Caribbean
from the Show Palace:
uncut, semihard, hoselike,
dripping discount baby lotion.
I'm a perfectionist,
so I can't afford to be
fussy. Not just any
Tom dick or Harry cock will do,
but cock that has
lingered in my hands while
a stranger's eye fixes hard
on mine and doesn't know if
I want him to cum or if I'm
going to cut if off with a
 razor hidden somewhere about
my nudity, a cock that
has smelled fear, or ambiguity
at least, a cock that went
looking for a hand with
cash in it and
found mine in
my pocket. The smell of
cock on my hands makes me
sleep soundly and dream
of beauty.

Hustling

Queer, fat, and crippled, old Billy Gage limps into Hunter's on a leg and a half, and a couple of b-builders hoist him on a stool. "How's it hanging, Ace?" he asks pro forma, and the Ace—thinking to be insightful—answers, "Life's a bitch, you know?" "Not as bad as death," Bill replies shrilly, tweaking the Ace's leftmost tit, having a laugh and a drink at everyone else's expense.

Floating in a downer haze, he orbs the new kid at eight ball with a crisp first fifty in his jeans and elaborate plums for the future tucked in his brain cells. Billy smiles at the greed in the green kid's dewy eye and sniffs the street dreams bouncing off the ceiling rafters.

"Four in the corner," the peach fuzz says like a foregone conclusion, and his second fifty trick rubs his cue on the table rim, sneering out his need through a sweat-sweet beard just itching for the rich libations of a young man's thigh-hold.

"So what's up *your* hairy ass these days?" the b-tender asks, filling a glass, and Billy lets out a screech like an owl goat. "Something rubber a dodo laid," says old Billy Gage, slapping black Ace on his bloated shoulder and settling in for a long winter night of serious nostalgia.

Stars

Pissed about something, I get in the car, pick out this kid on Hustler Street and offer him fifty to fuck him. "Okay," he says, simple as dimples and hops right in. Tells me the story of his life, how he sang in a choir till the fruitnik who runs it starts sucking him off and his voice changes overnight. Hits the b-vard four years back. Sings in a neo-punk band when they get a gig. Draws the line at horse but has a bad case of forearm curiosity.

"So what are you into?" he wants to know and I want to show him.

We drive to the top of the park and climb the observatory scaffold. He's looking for the Pleiades, a cluster in Taurus he remembers from school, and I am reminded by the new moon of my old youth, when God lived in the full phase. Then the kid, whose name is Brett, throws his arm around my neck for no discernible reason and puts a kiss on my left cheek. I feel a chill like a lost thing found. I look in his eyes and see stars.

Stroke of midnight

Love after dark is a complex
illusion: lunacy or lust,
a simple discharge of the
day's disappointments,
a certain nostalgia for
bathhouse abandon,
miscellaneous need.

Midnight is often mistaken.

Brazilian boy of
twenty-two,
slim-hipped boy
who studies ballet and
strips in a Times Square
dive between clients:

In the wee hours,
my hands tied to his hair,
my rubber-coated cock
buried inside him, I
call this intercourse of
commerce forever diamonds
and know it's as real as
the scar on his belly,
the money he craves
on his tongue.

Tim

He was adopted, grew up
on a reservation in west
Idaho, eyes were winter

moons in negative, lashes
were owls in the topmost
branches of tree fathers.

His nose could have been
on nickels. He was twenty,
would not kiss me, though

Grandpa always said there
was Cree inside us. He
was Shoshone and cynical.

He cost seventy dollars.
My fingers on his spine
reminded me of bicycles.

He wore a long ponytail,
three earrings. I sucked
his cock until he came.

The patch of dark hair
on his stomach was like
a thin scalp at the Indian

museum on One Fifty-
Fifth St. "Well," he said,
leaving, "life is awkward."

The towel he used after a
shower was dark dark red,
his scent woody crimson.

Monday
*For Marsha P. Johnson,
drag queen and revolutionary*

*"And may flights of angels
attend thee to thy dress…"*

It's hot and slow in New York City.
The air has slowed to a standstill;
the uptown local is slower than
the clerk who sold the token, slowly.
Even the track rats are slow in their chewing.
The news, too, is traveling in
slow motion, the news that
Malcolm Michaels, Jr.—son of Elizabeth,
New Jersey, and known to friends as Marsha,
the tall black drag queen of Greenwich Village,
the in-your-face, no-nonsense street
hustler who fired the first shot at Stonewall
when she hurled a garbage can—
or was it her size 12 heels?—through the
dark bar window and let in the light of
the world, yes, *that* Marsha, the one who
panhandled and took drugs and slept
in doorways and got depressed and
never apologized or even thanked you
for quarters, *our* Marsha—
is dead, and not just plain old dead or
plague dead or the usual sort of New York City
summer squabble dead, but mysteriously drowned—
jumped, fell, or was pushed—in the mighty,
muddy Hudson, bloating up real slow
underneath the pier at the end
of Christopher Street, the pier where
the Pride Day dance is held each year and
where the Dutch prison used to be, as in
"Up the River," the lazy, hazy river

| *The Hard Way* |

where boys in bikinis and men in less
bask in the slow Sunday sun not knowing
it was Mother Marsha who gave us all life
or that the old queen with the bad makeup
is finally dead. And nobody even asking,
fast or slow, who killed her.

Uptown local

Fine hair in long unplaited
tendrils, a Flemish painting but
wet black, someone Dürer might have

etched.

Black shoes and shorts, white
socks and shirt. Skin with history
in its pigment and equatorial

attitude.

Seated, knees together like a girl.
It is the fuller upper lip that
makes his mouth seem carved,

totemic.

He looks up, beatific, directly
into my unsated gaze, without
haste, hesitation, or altered

aspect.

An insect, frightened by noise,
scuttles below the bench he
sits on, his book a study of

Bauhaus.

| *The Hard Way* |

Aboard, I scribble. He rests his
eyes, opens heavy lids once, to
smile at a youngster's insistent

simplicity.

At Times Square we get off, single
file. He is yards ahead in the
heat. Even his easy speed is

charged.

Slowly, he merges with the crowd,
a mystical boy who appears, then
slips into the hungry urban

ether.

Making a mark

In the stainless steel sink,
the water goblet gleams
without a trace of the Puerto
Rican hustler's mouth that
drank from it so greedily after
a hot oil massage that slid
 without coaxing into a wordless
release.

In the subway station
under Times Square, six
Ecuadoran men in black hats
play panpipes.
Strangers nod and smile.
Gold teeth glisten.
They leave the imprint of their
lips on the hot summer night.

Part Three

OUR BODIES AND OUR BLOOD

Confessions Of A Clothes Whore

It was my tenth year, when my cousin Gloria decided to marry her husband Tom the first of three times, that I became acquainted with the notion that dressing up was humiliating as well as uncomfortable. The folks decided I ought to have my first real suit, so off we trucked in our gray-and-beige Chrysler coupe to Seventh Avenue and Seventeenth Street in New York City to select from the Barney's Boys Town's "Fat, Chubby, or Otherwise Too Rotund for Childhood" rack the only suit that fit. It was a tweedish, grayish thing with a "muted" maroon stripe you could see across town (in a fog). It was made of wool the consistency of raw hemp. "I just don't know what we're going to do if he gets any bigger," my mother trilled sensitively to the harried haberdasher (who was, I swear, *Barney* himself). The requirement that I wear this iron maiden to church every Sunday did more for my conversion to agnosticism than the combined hypocrisy of every fanatic who ever lived, and most of them lived in my neighborhood.

    My earliest recollection of dressing for acceptance was in junior high school after an aborted attempt to pass off my mother's penny loafers as my own. (How was I supposed to know shoes had sex? I *still* don't know what virgin wool means.) I was in the habit of hanging out with a group of kids whose parents knew my parents, so they *had* to invite me to parties. At the center of this group was an outgoing, handsome, talented, athletic youth named Donald who dated every girl in school. I'd known him since kindergarten and, hoping to ape his popularity, began mimicking his duds: gray and black suits, tab-collar shirts and skinny acetate ties (with matching Ban-Lon socks), and shoes that are now called Beatle boots, but which we called "Puerto Rican fence-climbers" (cultural stereotyping through fashion).

In high school my fickle fancy turned away from Donald and his ilk when Suzanne Reid would not let me put my hand on her robin's-egg blue, beaded taffeta bosom. The new object of my unrequited crush was one Ray Singer, a dark and smoky actor with long hair and fingers who played guitar in a Greenwich Village coffeehouse on weekends. I was walking behind the auditorium one day in my rock-'n'-roll slicked hair and shoes when Ray's unofficial best friend, Alex, approached from the opposite direction. A scruffy little slug of a thing who smoked Gauloise cigarettes, Alex decided for some reason to fabricate a Mr. Blackwell's "One Worst Dressed Male in the Environs of the Auditorium List." I won, hands down. After listening to Alex's fashion advice, I ran to the nearest mall and bought a turtleneck sweater and tan suede desert boots, washed the Alberto VO5 out of my hair for the last time and declared myself "ethnic" (a beatnik in transition from bongo-drum poetry to folk music).

I was happy in this guise until I was accepted at the college of my guidance counselor's ill-informed choice, a school exclusively populated by preppies who couldn't get into Yale. Taking a quick look around Joe College Town, I hied me out to acquire a pair of Bass Weejuns and a trunk full of crewneck sweaters. This wardrobe was worn with pride (white adhesive tape wound dutifully around the front of the Weejuns in the best Beta Theta Pi manner, without socks, even in two feet of snow) until I was refused admittance to the fraternity of my own ill-informed choice (I couldn't have been *that* drunk—I mean, how many fraternities do you know who *won't* let you in because you drink too much?) and discovered clothing as a form of social protest. Out I went to buy a pea jacket, work boots, and a pair of wire-rimmed glasses. I maintained my Ivy League wardrobe, including the blue blazer with the junior-honor-society pocket patch, for such festivities as funerals, visiting parents, directing guest parking at football games (a real spine-tickler, that), and crashing faculty parties with my friend Marc Goldman, who is now a doctor somewhere.

Now, it happened that I hated Colgate University (oops, it slipped out) more than any other right-wing repressive place on earth, so I undertook several treks abroad, during which I collected clothing to wow 'em back in the States, which helped me to become the center of every conversation: "Oh, this old double-breasted-gray-flannel-with-the-pewter-buttons thing? Berlin, I think. Did I ever tell you how I was arrested at the Brandenburg Gate because of my flawless German?"

Somewhere in there I went on a scotch and cottage cheese diet and lost a hundred pounds, discovering the joys and glory of loose clothing for the first time in my life. I took this discovery with me to London for a year. First I ravaged Carnaby Street ("I am cool"), then—thanks to a favorable exchange rate and low-interest student loans, not to mention my father's indulgence—I moved up the social ladder to Knightsbridge and Harrods ("I am an American exchange student pretending to be rich"). I bought Cardin suits made to order for $65 ("I am in-the-know"), an Empire-style greatcoat from Sweden ("I am trendy with a natural appreciation of sartorial history"), and sweaters from Scotland ("I am nonetheless pragmatic"). I wore tails to the opening of the opera and International Youth Hiker attire on trips to the Lake Country and Cornwall. "Sartorial schizophrenia" could not begin to describe the condition of my closet. (No wonder there was no room in it for me!)

When I got back to the States, I was dubbed "Gorgeous George" by my clearly envious as well as narrow-minded younger peers, which forced me to reevaluate gender-appropriate attire. I took to wearing love beads, strung by myself and my girlfriend Judy. When I pierced my ear as an act o' defiance, it was not to look like a woman, but like a pirate ("I am butch...sort of...well, androgynous, maybe"). During my stint as a design student, I started making my own clothes ("I am an *artiste*") the designs of which harkened back to previous centuries in which pirates were permitted certain excess yardage in the sleeve and flounce.

For my first stab at "California Living" in the early 1970s, I slipped into the popular genderfuck mode, wearing my long hair in pigtails and mother-of-pearl polish on my fingernails. I attended classes in long skirts of my own devising. Fortunately, this was a very, very avant-gardy arty-farty grassy-sassy graduate school, where teachers swam naked, trombonists performed in nightgowns, and one of my best friends would show up in the cafeteria in Carmen Miranda drag. But the upkeep was killer. I finally said "fuck genderfuck," gained a couple hundred pounds and lived in a pair of industrial-strength Levi's and two shirts (thrift-shop Hawaiian for summer and plaid flannel for winter), under a yard-sale overcoat that belted under the nipples and hung to the ground. I did my best mid-'70s slumming in this garb.

When I returned to California for a new life in 1976, I cast off my old ideas about life, lost a few tons of East Coast flab and got back into clothes. And back into clothes. And back into clothes, discovering for the first time the reckless joys of negligible self-esteem in concert with compulsive shopping. I would put on a brand new outfit, get in the car for a social event, discover some minuscule imperfection (a cat hair on my shorts, for example), then dash to the mall, flashing the plastic around until I was totally re-dressed from top to toe and could breathe easier. I was stepping up my shopping to Rodeo Drive against all sane financial advice, when a good friend said to me one day, "The trouble with $200 cotton shirts is that nobody tells the truth to someone who's wearing one" (façade as fortress).

This was rather startling news, since I was now along into my thirties, past my aging disco-bunny phase, and into caring about what went on underneath other people's clothing in more ways than one. Fortunately for my spiritual development, I ran out of money, declared bankruptcy, threw away the charge cards, and learned to make do with the wardrobe at hand.

As an oversized and undersubsidized middle-aged male, I now have a few rules about the clothing I wear. I dress for comfort, economy, and convenience of care (loose and cotton blend). I wear what *I* think is appropriate for the milieu (playing against the unnecessary attraction of attention, since I am unwilling to put up with the garbage that goes along with it). This means I do not wear suits to the track or T-shirts with the sleeves ripped off to black-tie openings at the Music Center (nor do I wear black tie, of course, which qualifies as oppressor-male business-class drag).

I don't dress for success or to win or for social or economic status. I am not usually found in the current fashion trends. I'm too big, too broke, and too busy to keep up, and I feel ridiculous in what the trendies are usually wearing even if it looks great on them or in the abstract. Except on rare occasions, I don't wear ties since I no longer go to funerals, visit my parents, or direct guest parking at college football games. I think clothing should show an individual off to his or her own notion of his or her best advantage, and I think it's time to blow the lid off "gender appropriate" clothing.

Which is not to say that I'm immune to manipulating an image or that I don't have a sartorial ideal. If I had a lot of money, I'd have a lot of clothing, as long as someone else was taking care of it. Fashion may be shallow, but it's also fun. For now, what I like to say with my clothing is: "Yes, I know, but I used to be as big as a house, so this is a true improvement. I'm actually quite hip and fairly well off, but essentially shy, and I'm having trouble adjusting to fame, so I find baggy clothing more comfortable. I am so busy being interesting and running from one fabulous social event to another that I don't have time to shop, so I just dress in whatever my last gorgeous lover dropped on the bedroom floor between planes—or whatever the army of the last festive country I visited was wearing." I like to appear in the kind of artfully chosen rags that say I'm honest, knowledgeable in all things, and available for certain kinds of sexual encounters, as long as I am in control, which I usually am.

I also like to give my daily ensemble an edge that says, "He might be swell, he might be nuts, so tread carefully until given permission to dive in."

I will also do nearly anything to make myself look taller or thinner, including surrounding myself with short, dumpy friends. Whom I love as people, of course.

25 Reasons To Hate Heterosexuals

Having been identifiably homosexual for twenty years or more, I have spent a good deal of time and energy attempting to root out exactly what it is about us faggots and dykes that so upsets all those misery-mongering heteros who write venomous letters to the editors of publications liberal enough to espouse hatred in the name of free speech. Just what is it heterosexuals hate so much, and exactly what logic can be applied to life as we know it to justify that hatred?

I have come to the rather unsurprising conclusion that when one applies heterosexual logic to heterosexual behavior, it is perfectly reasonable to hate heterosexuals. In fact, given the evidence, it is nearly required.

Now, to be fair, not all heterosexuals are alike. Some of you may even hold one or two of them dear because of some past service rendered. But though you may be tempted to generalize from the particular, remember not to make sweeping allowances based on their occasional decency. Do not allow yourself the dubious, romanticized luxury of exempting extraordinary individuals from the invidious antisocial force they have become.

| Michael LASSELL |

In the spirit of civic-mindedness, therefore, I have prepared the following list of justifications for hating those I shall refer to as "grims," Gore Vidal's clever invocation, to differentiate them from "gays," the current socially responsible term for homosexuals (referring always, unless otherwise indicated, to both males and females).

1. *Grims cause war.* Gays are not even allowed in the armed forces, and are summarily discharged if they somehow slither past the cleverly worded psychological screening test: "Are you homosexual?" It may be noted that not only do grims start wars, they also lose them. The last homosexual who had an armada at his disposal was Alexander the Great. He conquered the world.
2. *Grims cause famine.* Famine occurs when the food supply fails to meet the needs of the population. Because agriculture is, by and large, a grim pursuit, and because the vast majority of the population is produced by grims, it is only logical to conclude that it is grims who cause famine by eating more than they should and having too many babies.
3. *Grims are responsible for the economic decline of the Western world.* Since gays are pretty much prevented from participating in world economic institutions—those being bastions of very grim white heterosexual males (WHMs, pronounced "whams")—it is clear that heterosexuals have caused inflation, the devaluation of the dollar on the world market, and the collapse of American industry (which is not only owned by grims but controlled by labor unions led by fag-hating grim union officials). It is grims who are laying off auto workers in Detroit, not gays.
4. *Grims are responsible for crime.* Grims, having invented not only all of the seven deadly sins, but also murder, armed robbery, and rape, commit more felonies per square inch than gays in this and every other country. This more-than-ten-to-one ratio is so embarrassing to grim chiefs of police (WHMs almost without exception) and grim legislators that the category of "crimes against nature" was invented so that being homosexual became in itself a crime. ("Sodomy" is

the name for a "crime against nature" committed by persons of either sex; it is, however, prosecuted where it is illegal only when those therein engaged are of the same sex.) Still, even if every single gay man, woman, child, cat, and dog on earth is committing a crime by breathing, more crimes are caused by grims than gays. This seems to prove that grims have a predilection for crime.

5. *Grims spread disease.* Not only are heterosexuals responsible for transmitting the majority of *all diseases*, they are responsible for the recent proliferation of *sexually transmitted diseases*. Furthermore, they are single-handedly responsible for the spread of such hetero-only maladies as congenital birth defects. One theory gaining widespread acceptance is that phenomena such as autism, Downs syndrome, dyslexia, imbecility and withered limbs are God's retribution for original sin, an irrefutably grim faux pas.
6. *Nearly all child-abusing parents are grim.* Period.
7. *Grims molest children.* Because the statistics are so unilaterally damning, grims usually do not quote them. But the fact is that anywhere from 95 to 98 percent of all sex crimes against children and adults are committed by *adult male heterosexuals* against *female children* (and that even when the victims are male, the perpetrators consider themselves to be hets). Clearly then, all adult male heterosexuals must be enjoined from any profession in which they are likely to come into contact with young girls.
8. *All Communists are grim.* The Communist Party does not accept gays. (They call *that* a party?)
9. *Adolf Hitler was heterosexual.* If it can happen once, it can happen again.
10. *Grims are sinful and godless.* It is worth noting that in America nearly all grims are Christians, Jews, or illegal aliens. Illegal alien grims may be hated ipso facto; if they don't like it here, let them stay home in the countries American WHM generals have turned into war zones. In theory, Christians practice the teachings of Jesus Christ. Jesus taught that one should love one's neighbor as oneself, to do for the least as one would for the Messiah, and to eschew judging one's fellows.

In fact, as any scanning of TV missionaries proves, Christians preach love of money and doing to the least of the Father's children whatever you can get away with under cover of the Constitution. As a look into the lives of any political Christian—the Jerry Falwell/Pat Robertson ilk—teaches, Christianity is a thinly veiled movement under cover of which an international conspiracy works to acquire all wealth, capital, and land for secular purposes.

Then there are grim Jews. To hear them tell it, all Jews are grim. However, the established Jewish orthodoxy, recognizing that there is an outside chance that a Jewish homosexual might spring sui generis from the radical left, has organized itself against the principle of equality. In New York, for example, home to more homosexuals per square inch than any other state in the Union, the combined organized resistance of the Christian and Jewish religions have thus far prevented passage of the merest token of gay-rights law: i.e., protection from discrimination in jobs, housing, and public accommodations. At public hearings in New York, busloads of quaintly dressed rabbis have screamed hatred at homosexuals, just the way the Nazis and the Ku Klux Klan scream hatred at them. Don't you just love religion?

11. *Idi Amin was heterosexual.* So was *Family Feud.*
12. *Grims are sometimes members of racial and/or ethnic minorities.* This is not a reason to hate them per se, but this situation does bear some examination. White grims invented the concept of racial minorities and of economic enslavement based on race and are therefore hoist on their own petard, as it were. White gays may hate grim members of racial minorities for passing hatred down the pecking order; gays, however, may not hate any gay member of any group (this is self-defeating and nasty). Gays also may not hate grim members of racial minorities as much as they hate white grims. (This would be politically incorrect, according to the San Francisco caucus.) I grant you this gets complicated. Sometimes the hierarchy of oppression must be arbitrated. Who has the right to hate most: A white woman with a speech impediment, or a black man in a wheelchair? A gay

white male Republican (I know, there's no end of shamelessness when it comes to internalized homophobia) or a grim black male Republican (you see, it gets worse)? A black lesbian poet or a Latina octogenarian on welfare? Well, that's what the Supreme Court is for.

13. *Grims may be hated on the basis of sex alone.* Grims are either male or female. Grim males may be hated for causing wars, causing inflation, inventing rape, and undermining the integrity of the American family with the sexual double standard. Grim females may be hated for committing the act of motherhood, and are thereby responsible for the misery of the world.

14. *Grims flaunt their sexuality.* If they would keep it in their own bedrooms it would be marginally tolerable, but they do it right on the street, kissing and holding hands and showing blatant affection for each other in shops and in parks and playgrounds. They are doing irreparable, *irreversible psychological damage* to innocent gay children and impressionable gay teenagers, who ought to have the right to be protected from these odious displays of so-called affection. Furthermore, *grims recruit minors* by brainwashing them into thinking that heterosexuality is actually an acceptable alternative lifestyle. Bunk!

15. *Grims are different.* Not only are they different from pansies and diesel dykes, they are different from one another, too. This is too confusing, and confusion is acceptable justification for hatred.

16. *Grims lack adventure and breadth.* Many gays once were grim; most grims have never been gay.

17. *Grims have no moral fortitude.* As pushy as they are about the supremacy of heterosexuality, none of them believe it. In fact, each grim is so convinced of the superiority of *homo*-sexuality that grims are absolutely forbidden to try it (the implication being that once you go gay, you can never be the other way). I mean, if homosexuality is so horrid, why don't all the grims just try it once, see for themselves, and go on about their business?

18. *Grims are not as smart as gays.* To corroborate this obvious

fact, you can consult any number of surveys and studies conducted by grims that prove beyond a shadow of a doubt that education is in the hands of a homosexual elite that grants top academic honors only to homos.
19. *Grims are expendable*. With the advent of genetic engineering, grims are no longer needed for the one function they were created to fulfill: producing gay babies. Starting on January 1, 2000, all grims will be directed to sex-reassignment camps for reevaluation and reeducation the very minute they touch the genitals of the opposite sex. Future children will be made by artificially inseminating lesbian ova with donated male homosexual sperm.
20. *Grims are not attractive*. Spend a day at the local zoo. Spend an evening at the local grim disco. You'll need no further evidence. Note further that because all male models are gay, any good-looking grim male is considered so only because of his resemblance to a gay ideal.
21. *Grims are not well dressed*. Ask any fashion-conscious grim what he's wearing this year, and you can bet it's something he picked up at a gay garage sale.
22. *Grims have no taste and no sense of humor*. Watch three consecutive hours of prime-time network television. This is the best thing grims can come up with to earn a buck. Have you see ten good movies this year? Grims control the entertainment industry. This is why it is not entertaining. Grims are responsible for Tidy Bowl, Ronald McDonald, Massengill Douche, *The Love Boat*, and *The Dating Game*. A note about grim humor: There is no such thing (Bob Hope is grim).
23. *Beverly Hills is grim*. So is *Beverly Hills 90210*.
24. *Grims are boring*. "If you're bored, you're boring," my highly grim mother used to say. Grims are boring because they are not smart or attractive and have no taste or sense of humor. They have too much time on their hands. They are lazy, and because it is easier to hate people than to do anything else ("to curse the darkness than to light a candle), grims fill the gaps in their empty, tawdry lives by hating. Homos are their hate target of choice these days, but it has been blacks and Jews and, of course, could be again.

25. *Grims preach hatred.* Grims invented it, patented it, packaged, advertised, and offered it for sale worldwide with poisoned baby formula. If the grims are not stopped soon, Russians will bomb Korean airplanes; Arabs will terrorize Israeli schoolchildren; England will continue its genocide in Ireland and will declare war on Argentina; the United States will invite the United Nations to find a home elsewhere; Salvadorans will kill their Salvadoran brothers; American-born Mexican-Americans will form gangs and institute violent rivalries with their Mexican-born cousins; Chinese youths will kill each other in San Francisco over Communist or Nationalist ties to Asia; Hindus and Moslems will continue to kill over imaginary lines in the name of the Vedas and Koran; we will all lose the energy to oppose nuclear armament and world hunger; greed will overcome even the churches and synagogues; and profligacy will take all. Believe me, if we don't stop all this grim behavior, the future will be bleak: It will be just like the past.

Writ Of Habeas Corpus:
Tennessee Williams/Truman Capote

"Time rushes toward us with its hospital tray of varied narcotics, even while it is preparing us for its inevitably fatal operation."
—Tennessee Williams

"I came to understand that death is the central factor of life. And the simple comprehension of this fact alters your entire perspective."
—Truman Capote

The Kindness of Strangers by Donald Spoto (Little, Brown).
Tennessee: Cry of the Heart by Dotson Rader (Doubleday).
Conversations with Capote by Lawrence Grobel (New American Library).

In the early morning hours of February 25, 1983, an old man woke from a troubled sleep and edged his age-spotted hand to a bedside table strewn with legally acquired pharmaceuticals. But instead of one more sleeping pill, one more ticket to ride the railway of escape, the old man grabbed a bottle top and, instead of sliding down his gullet to bring narcotic relief, the wad of plastic stuck in his throat, and Tennessee Williams—perhaps the most important voice the American theater has ever known—choked to death, alone in the night. Dying alone had been his greatest fear.

The following year, in August 1984, another burnt-out genius, another alcoholic homosexual, another notorious penman whose truth terrified the tame masses, kicked the slop bucket that his life had become. Truman Capote, precocious youth, poisonous adult and prefect of the "novel of fact," dropped stone dead in the home of Beautiful Person Joanna Carson, ex-wife of Johnny-talk-lately, the man who brought Capote into the living rooms and bedrooms of America, made him a media star, let him do his court-jester routine on network television.

"More tears are shed over answered than unanswered prayers," Capote quoted, plundering the aphorism for the title of his masterpiece, *Answered Prayers*—the work of undisputed greatness that would install him in the pantheon with Hawthorne, Melville, and Whitman, the book he held out like a cross to the vampiric press (desperate to despise him but afraid to sink in its teeth until all the galleys were bound).

In life, the two dead men were no strangers. Capote dedicated his *Music for Chameleons* to Williams and claimed that the playwright met the great love of his life (Frank Merlo) only after Capote was done with him. But that's the way of the literary establishment and its gay demimonde: small, incestuous, fragile—a world of shifting alliances and manufactured events. Gore Vidal, the man Capote said "has never written anything anybody will remember," got his nose in there, too, befriending both Williams and Capote, feuding with both, obsessed with Capote's success, condescending to Williams's ambivalent attitudes about his own sexuality, writing nasty screeds about America's preeminent playwright from the moldy, homophobic pages of the *New York Review of Books,* first when Williams published his *Memoirs* in 1976 and again in 1985 after two Williams biographies hit the stalls, horses of two very different colors.

First off the presses in the posthumous biographies' derby was *The Kindness of Strangers* by Donald Spoto, the man who strapped the bloated body of Alfred Hitchcock to the mainmast and flogged him with the fat man's dirty off-screen linen in *The Dark Side of Genius*. The Williams book is different—it's boring. Oh, it's thorough, all right. Spoto needed some respectability, so he turned his sights on one of the more gothic and tortured souls of a generation, passed it through the academic process of verification and annotation, and delivered a Williams so lifeless it's as if the playwright fell dead out of his mother's womb.

Spoto tells the truth about Williams, but it's the truth of an after-the-fact observer, not that of a participant; and his prose flows like a calculus text, all symbols and formulas and no body fluids, no tears behind the talk of loss, no sweat behind the learned discussion of anguish, no blood in the genitals despite all the prodding fingers. Worst of all, Spoto's got it into his head that he's more than a chronicler, more than a scribe. It's not enough for him to index the minutiae of a life that was given entirely to grand themes, human passions, and theatrical gestures. Spoto feels a need to analyze the great Williams dramas—*Glass Menagerie, A Streetcar Named Desire, Cat on a Hot Tin Roof, Night of the Iguana* and others—and his analyses are about as deep as an oil slick on a damp road.

But Spoto's pop-psychological insights into Williams's unconscious are even less penetrating. All in all, Spoto's book is just what your average scared-witless junior-college teacher would want it to be: an unreadable collection of facts, about as much like Williams as the outline of a snow angel is like the flaming seraphim described in the Book of Revelation.

So who should appear on the scene but Dotson Rader, an intimate of Williams in the years of bad plays, bad drugs, and bad decisions, of violent madness, helplessness, and horror, of all those years in the shit-strewn halls of the Chelsea Hotel, of the amphetamine eyes of the Warhol Factory gamins, of bars without names in SoHo, and of boys without names and—for the right price—without limits. Rader's agenda is to save his fellow fairy from respectability in "an intimate memoir," a post-*Midnight Cowboy* film noir narrative called *Tennessee: Cry of the Heart*.

Rader's thesis is that art in this culture is produced only by the disaffected—specifically homosexuals or Jews, or both—and that the aesthetic impulse is an alienated individual's mode of survival. And, of course, he's taken a lot of flak from heterosexual Christians, and from gay Jews who don't want their covers pulled. In fact, Rader—who scored drugs and drugged-out hustlers for his elder friend and shared more than a few of both—paints the finished canvas that Spoto has sketched clumsily. But Rader's a writer, and Spoto's a typist.

(If you don't know that that line is snatched from Capote, you probably don't give a rat's ass about any of this.)

Rader and Spoto agree on most things. Williams's great loves were his maternal grandparents, his sister Rose, Frank Merlo, writing, swimming, and sex. The central event in his life was the primitive lobotomy performed on his beloved sister in the 1930s at his mother's insistence, a lobotomy that left the sweet Rose with the grin of an idiot and the psyche of a child. He hated his parents for different reasons, as he did his bureaucrat brother Dakin, who had the writer incarcerated in a snake pit of a mental institution. By the time the heavy drug addiction took over—after the cancer death of Merlo, the lover of some fourteen years, already estranged at the time of his death—Williams was paranoid, willful, selfish, manipulative, and hypochondriacal. But he was also warm, loving, generous, deeply afraid, and in need of protection.

He was the best of friends; he was the worst of friends. Rader stuck with him through the lean years when great plays and glowing reviews did not come, when humiliations arrived as frequently as bad dreams, when "house guests" were stealing original manuscripts for souvenirs. It was squalid. But Rader *loved the man* and knew that Williams's courage was in the reality, not in the hype, that Williams's greatness blared like a trumpet in this age of latter-day hypocrisy *because* of his entire personality, not in spite of its less-heroic aspects.

Naturally, the mildewed critical establishment has taken the public position that it had never before been aware that Williams was unhappy, homosexual, or a drug addict, and clasped the neutered Williams of Spoto's hollow book to its collective family-newspaper bosom. Just as naturally, these same critics have dumped their derisive verbiage all over Rader's book, and from sea to shining sea the official word has gone out that Rader is to Spoto what the *National Enquirer* is to the *Encyclopedia Britannica*.

In fact, Rader's book—despite occasional sentences that would make Edwin Newman cringe—is so full of life and so full of love that I could not put it down. When I got to the death scene in Spoto's book, I heaved a sigh of relief, the kind associated with the completion of a particularly odious physics assignment in college. At the end of Rader's book, I cried. I had lost a friend.

Williams was fond of saying that he never meant to shock people: that he told the truth and people found the truth shocking. Rader's book is neither shocking nor repulsive. It's the truth, and most people hate the truth as much as they love *Dynasty*.

What Spoto and Rader both miss, however, is that Williams's complex, seemingly inscrutable personality is quite prosaic if you know the first thing about the alcoholic personality profile. It is characterized not only by the intake of unmanageable quantities of alcohol and drugs but, more importantly, by pathological self-centeredness, a desperate need for approval, and alternating flights of grandiosity and vortical nose-dives of self-loathing. Williams to a tee—and Capote, *and* most other American writers of note (Faulkner and Fitzgerald, for example). Among playwrights, O'Neill certainly, and William Inge, that master of American normalcy who gave the world *Picnic, Bus Stop,* and *Come Back, Little Sheba,* a lush who was once Williams's lover (according to Rader) and who, after years of drunkenness, managed to do himself officially and finally in.

It's enough to give credence to the antique Greek notion that there ain't no free lunch: The gods give you a gift, you pay through the nose. It's almost as if the psyche, in a desperate attempt to maintain some sort of balance in a society that despises genius and rewards notoriety per se, manufactures some ugly self-destructive tic to compensate for the special talent, as if the concept of talent residing in a happy individual is hubris beyond the gods' endurance. Men must come to terms with an uneasy marriage of the creative *(eros)* and destructive *(thanatos),* of love and death.

But Williams's output during the period of his addiction is inferior work, and Capote's drug-influenced writing—the work following *In Cold Blood,* let's say, to be generous—is too sparse to be definitive. Maybe the failure is fear in the face of success. Maybe it's the Jonah of art being swallowed by the insatiable whale of celebrity, only to be spewed out as ultimately indigestible. Maybe living as an outsider simply exacts too high a toll. It's hard enough to be a celebrity in this country of lost ideals. Maybe it's impossible to be a celebrity outlaw.

Lawrence Grobel, who is known primarily for interviews with actors for *Playboy* magazine, has in *Conversations with Capote* thrown together a postmortem of a book, nothing more than a series of interviews he conducted with Capote while the valiant little fart got slowly stewed in a bar on Long Island. Aside from being incredibly entertaining in the same camp way Capote could be on TV, the book is nearly worthless. It's different from a magazine interview only in breadth, not depth. As an interviewer, Grobel is remarkably well informed, but he's about as successful at getting Capote to say anything meaningful or incisive as Norman Mailer has been in winning the Nobel Prize. He lets Capote off so many hooks, you'd think Capote was a roe-fatted salmon that Grobel, the sympathetic angler, was helping upstream to spawn. Grobel is far too respectful of Capote, who, God knows, could brook no criticism unless he was its source.

In fact, Capote emerges from his conversations such a big-city braggart that it's hard to believe he actually created the mellifluous prose of *Other Voices, Other Rooms*, the heartland horror of *In Cold Blood*, the wrenching sentiment of *A Christmas Memory*, the quiet compassion of *Breakfast at Tiffany's*. Is this old souse lapping up the fawning attention of a self-serving journalist really the Truman Capote who dazzles with style and loosens fillings with the perfection of emotional nuance?

It couldn't be. It's just the booze talking. *Conversations with Capote* is about as reliable a document as Tennessee Williams's *Memoirs*, much of which was censored by editors at Doubleday, at least according to Williams himself. Williams had axes to grind, and he ground them down to their handles on well-oiled wheels of self-defensive wit. Capote grinds them with literary lasers, but the conversations do not burn with the rigor of journalistic truth, of which Capote himself set the standard. They are petty, mean, and vain. What emerges from this collection of drunken ruminations is that Capote is a much lesser figure than he believed, particularly since *Answered Prayers*, aside from the ruinous excerpts published in *Esquire*, seems never to have existed. It was a Flying Dutchman of a book, as insubstantial as that blank-paged novel Jack Nicholson was writing in *The Shining*.

If I sound bitter or disrespectful, it's not in regard to Capote's *work,* which I greatly admire, and some of which clearly ranks among the best in English. But he had such a potent talent, and it was largely wasted. He should have written more. *In Cold Blood* should have been only the prelude. He might have been a genius, but he gave in to his need for drugs and robbed us all of the fruits of his gift. How much closer to authentic tragedy do we ever get?

Literary biography is of limited value, and two of these books prove it. The essence of the Williams oeuvre is the struggle of the complex individual to find expression in a world of limits and absolutes. Spoto's book doesn't come close to that mark; Rader's is right on the money, presenting a Williams that Williams himself could have created—and probably did. In Capote's work we see the creation of order from the chaos of violence via the imposition of structure and style. In Grobel's *Conversations,* although we pick up some nifty facts and anecdotes, we see only a petulant ego doing as much damage as it can, a mischievous child who never tires of negative attention. Lucky for us, we've got the plays, short stories, poems, novels, and articles the two left behind. They were unhappy boys who made magic while they grew into unhappy men. And, like prom queens, they were so popular. For a time.

When Death Is Too Much With Us

"My eyes filled with tears, but I was trembling with joy. For the boy wasn't dead, Chopin and Wilde weren't dead; they were alive...within the wave of love. Within the wave, every action had its own sanction and beauty.... As long as I myself was within the wave, I should always know this. And it seemed to me, then, that I should be able to reenter it whenever I pleased, throughout the rest of my life."
—Christopher Isherwood

It's a beautiful, *cool* Friday in Los Angeles—the weather as much like San Francisco as an adult might reasonably expect. I've been passing the day with no cash in my pocket, praying the sort of prayers I've been trained to forgo: "Dear God: Send Money. Love, Michael." By late afternoon, an adorable pink check has found its way into my hands and, dressed in my best gay summer shorts, I head to the gay bank to cash/deposit my newfound gay wealth. An acquaintance happens to drive up, and we do gay chitchat for a minute: "How-are-you-what-are-you-doing-so-and-so-says-hi-are-you-still-with-your-lover-etc." Then he lets me have it:

"Do you know anyone who died from AIDS?" *Oh, no,* I say to myself, but, trying to be responsible, I reply: "Yes," hoping a terse answer will divert him from further inquiry. Fat chance!

"How many?"

I say: "Four. Is this a contest?" (*That should shame his mouth shut,* I think.)

But he is undaunted: "Do you know anybody who has it now?"

"Yes," I say squirming, but the subject is once again on the floor. Mortality is once again too much with me, and once again on an all-too-rare idyllic L.A. day, I am talking about gay death and gay dying and the Meaning of It All. Only this time I'm trying to do it without dying a little myself, and this time you get to listen.

When my political friend Ken died, it was still GRID: Gay Related Immune Deficiency. He died from a series of opportunistic infections: hepatitis, pneumonia, amoebic dysentery, shingles. He wasted away to nothing in the days before we knew *it* was often fatal. Ken maintained a cheerful optimism; then he was dead. Our political club planted a tree in his memory. It was as nice a gesture as any, I suppose; I did not attend the ceremony, since I am allergic to gestures.

Then a former boss of mine died. By this time it was already AIDS. One, two, three, zip: felt like shit, was diagnosed, and died. Three weeks.

Yeah, I know all too many people, men, friends, acquaintances. I know three people who were diagnosed as having AIDS *by mistake!* It seems they had CMV. Ooops, sorry, guys, our mistake. The straight doctors were...well, "insensitive," to be charitable— "incompetent butchers" when I'm in a bad mood. (If someone tells me I have AIDS, he'd better be right if he wants to see sunrise.)

Yet men like me are dying. And I'm in a high-risk group, as they say: gay white male, thirty-six, resident of L.A. and a fan of frequent if not unlimited sex (sorry, honey: remember it's you I love). I've cut down my sex life, but I may be carrying a disease I caught two years ago from a stranger or a friend, even from my lover, who may be infectious without knowing it. A year from now I could be among the gay dead—and my parents are still actively avoiding coming to terms with my homosexuality. It's the end of their second decade trying, bless their resistant Republican hearts.

Now, I've never been dead and have no after-death experiences to relate. I'm just an urban gay male trying to get through the day the best I can. But there's been a lot of death in my life, and I guess it's time to look at it.

The first wave of deaths was family. It was the 1960s, and I was a teenager, and those deaths marked the end of innocence for me. Family members died. The family died. My family—my "larger" family of aunts and uncles and cousins by the (literal) dozens—was never rich, never artistic, just full of life. We sang and danced and drank and told jokes around a Christmas groaning board, showing off our shirts and ties and sweaters and toys. And then they started dying. The worst was my Aunt Helene, my godmother, protector, friend. She never withheld her love to manipulate my behavior; she faced my every caprice with unconditional acceptance. Like the death of the father in Bergman's Fanny and Alexander, that death shattered reality for me. Only little pieces of reality made sense after that. Family was over. I ate. I drank. I was not merry.

The '70s came along and I was "out." By this time the second wave of deaths hit, the Vietnam deaths. My friend Ralph, the first person I ever told I was gay, was missing in action and presumed dead. The church we grew up in erected a flagpole in honor of "Lieutenant" somebody—the same person I called Ralph, the man who accepted my sexuality while my parents were busy rejecting it. We used to talk about God, Ralph and I, and the path from brain-dead fundamental Protestantism to a personal spiritual path that we could follow with a straight face. Then Ralph slammed his jet fighter into the Southeast Asian jungle and, as far as I was concerned, God died with him.

I drank some more, got into drugs. By this time I hated everything about myself, most particularly my sexuality, having for some reason believed all the lies everyone had ever told me. I was obsessed with suicide, I wanted to be dead. After two rounds of deaths, that's how I was dealing with it: "Fuck Life!"

And there were other deaths: suicides, motorcycle and automobile accidents, bone-splitting cancers, a drowning. Deaths near and far. I participated in them all; and each man's death diminished my life, but no man's life enhanced it. I went to a memorial service at Grace Cathedral in San Francisco for a stranger who had been fag-bashed to death. Like Brecht, I felt that if all humanity were jammed into the hold of a ship, each man and woman would freeze to death from loneliness.

By 1976 I was as tired as I could get. I stopped drinking, stopped taking drugs, lost weight, started feeling good. Encouraged by others who were trying sobriety as a way of life, I started talking about God; tentatively at first, thinking that some "personal relationship with God" was beginning to happen in my life, as Ralph used to say it would. I had friends—good, loving, supportive, positive, endorsing friends.

I was included. I was in good health. I was relatively unscathed by my self-destruction, my obsession with death. I met Ben in 1978 and have been increasingly in love with him on a daily basis ever since. The first two years, he did the relationship part of the relationship alone. All I could do was show up. He waited until I knew what love was. I felt good about being gay for the first time in my life. I felt good about being alive. I was a productive member of society, a contributing member of the gay community.

And then they started dying again—from AIDS, from alcoholism, whatever. Ken and I got hepatitis at the same time. I got mine instead of going to law school. He never recovered. I wanted to think, like the spiritual positivists, that I could choose to live, that I could want to live so badly that nothing need affect me adversely. Then my best friend Clark's T-cell ratio inverted and we gave serious (and silly) consideration to the possibility that he might die. That I might die.

We joked about it, gay humor being our forte. We cried about it, gay drama running a close second. We talked about dead friends whose deaths were sad or inspirational. We hoped that if it came to it, we could die with grace, even though we had often lived as bumbling fools. I prayed that, no matter what, I would die sober and that it would not be too hard on Ben. It was a by-product of my own new love of life, caring about people. I cared about people. I was surprised. Kenny (as opposed to Ken), a man I call a "spiritual advisor" (really just a friendly former drunk with a direct line to a power that keeps him happy all the time) tried to get me to redefine my attitudes toward death: Death as " graduation"; passing over; there is no death, there is only moving to another plane of spirituality, a new level; and so on.

In *Fanny and Alexander*, which I saw with Kenny (not Ken, who was already dead) in San Francisco, the people who die do not go away. "I lived my whole life with you. Where else should

I go in death?" one characters asks. I want to believe that. It would make it so easy to accept loss, death. Another friend in San Francisco, Manuel, is rotting piece by piece. He has half a hip left, he's missing several spinal vertebrae, has a blood disease and is considered terminal, but clean for now. His reaction is "I've done everything—and everything pretty much I wanted to do. I had great friends and great times with them. If I die tomorrow, it's okay with me."

You know what my reaction is? Holy shit! I haven't done a goddamn thing. I haven't won a Nobel Peace Prize or an Olympic gold medal. I haven't written a best-selling book or sold a screenplay or stolen a piece of the Acropolis, prayed in a Buddhist temple in Kyoto, walked the Taj Mahal by moonlight, or even returned my library books!!!

Most interesting to me about that list is that there's no sex in it. Here I am, a homosexual, and the things I would die regretting have nothing whatever to do with sex. I mean, I have *done* sex. Sex with dignity and sex-as-humiliation. I've done sex in a field at dawn and in the back rooms of 42nd Street. The things I want to do before I die that I have not yet done involve the experience of the beauty of life, the joy of life, and the communication of that beauty and joy to friends and strangers, to "those who come after."

All this death, all this impending middle-age, is changing me. It's moving, shifting me away from the center of a hedonistic universe and toward some spiritual pantheism in which we all take part. It's matriarchal, healing, Yin, flowing, intuitive, female, water, all that stuff. It's round and circular and cyclical and complete in and of itself, and we are all a part of it, and we all get to feel it if we want. All we need to do is choose it.

All this thinking about death makes me think what a powerful people we are, we faggots and dykes. They called us sinful, and we made monuments to the beauty of God. They called us insane, and we healed ourselves and go merrily along feeling whole and healing our fellows. They make us illegal, and we change the laws. They beat us; encamp us; murder us, one at a time and in groups; they lie about us with impunity and without conscience;

but we keep surviving as a people. Because for every one who has died, there are gay people somewhere determined to live.

People loving each other, or three or four, however haltingly, however hesitantly—that is Community in the making. It is survival, perseverance. It is the beginning of…well, immortality of a kind, a step on a spiritual path we may not even know exists.

You see, I don't quite yet believe that after I leave here, I'm going to go somewhere else, some other level or spiritual plane. I don't believe that I have a soul that is going to outlive my body. I'd like to believe it, but I don't. So I'm just going to have to make it from one day to the next with some sort of principle that makes sense to me, even though I am not rich and famous, my mother is not marching with Parents and Friends of Lesbians and Gays, my lover and I can never agree on a movie or a restaurant, and my friends still die from time to time. Even though the gay and lesbian community is facing its latest greatest crisis. And that principle is easy and simple. I'm going to be myself: happy, joyous, free, and gay. And I'm going to make myself available to help the living and the dying any way I can.

There is a scene in the movie *Gandhi* when Gandhi starts out on the "Salt March" declaring, "A journey of a thousand miles begins with the first step." He is marching to the sea in a symbolic gesture of reclaiming the right of free access to salt, to reclaim control of India for the Indian people. A young boy climbs a dead tree for a better view; and what he sees makes him smile. This scrawny little cherub has just had an experience that would change his life, etched on his consciousness in the guise of a small smile: the first revelation that he is Indian, proud to be Indian, and happy to participate in the making and shaping of his country.

And that's my principle. One step at a time on a journey of a thousand miles, as one among many, so that no gay or lesbian child, no teenager, youth adolescent, young adult, middle-aged parent, or senior citizen need ever again feel what I felt when I was ashamed and alone and embarrassed, when I hated life and was trying my damnedest to obliterate myself. I'm going to be sober for the millions who are still drinking. I'm going to be as

| *The Hard Way* |

fully alive today as I can because many are dying. I'm going to be happy today so the unhappy can see it's possible, that it's a matter of choice. I don't need any credit for it. I probably won't do it at large public gatherings, but I'm going to do it. And whenever I can, I'm going to make every other person's experience with me a moment of joy, whenever our paths cross, whether for an instant or for many years.

When all is said and done, if I find out I have "*it*" (or any of the other "its" out there), I guess I could forgo the piece of the Acropolis, the temple at Kyoto, the Taj Mahal in the moonlight to go as gentle into the night as I can, because I will know that the love I have engendered will survive me. I am just now thinking the least-possible original thought: that love is God, God is love. And that's just fine with me.[1]

---

[1] Shortly after this piece appeared, a package arrived in the mail. It contained a small clear-plastic box. Inside, wrapped in blue tissue paper, was, the accompanying note explained, a white marble piece of the Acropolis. Stolen by a friend of the friend who sent it to me, he had treasured it, then passed it along to the man who was now passing it on to me. I've treasured it, too, purloined though it be, and it sits now on a table beside a piece of the Mayan city of Tulum. Okay, I'm ashamed of myself. So maybe someday I'll give them back (or maybe I'll swipe a chip of the Sphinx to go with them).

Heart In San Francisco

Corbett Avenue in San Francisco winds down one of the Twin Peaks like a Mediterranean byway sloping to the sea. Walking up the hill from a lucky parking space, I am made painfully aware of how much weight I'd have to lose to get around this city comfortably. It's worse for my friend Clark, a bodybuilder possessed of legendary pecs and biceps: Clark has AIDS, the pneumonia kind. By the time we get to the top of the second flight of stairs to his room with a view, he sounds like Camille on her deathbed.

But Clark, a writer who is something like thirty-five, isn't doing tragedy. Instead, he's making a heart-shaped card for his friend Larry back in L.A. It's still a month until St. Valentine's Day, but Larry might not live that long; he's one of a half-dozen people with AIDS Clark helped tend before his own diagnosis. Of them, only Larry is still alive, but he's in some San Fernando Valley hospital he checked into because, as Clark puts it, "he's decided to die." The valentine is Clark's way of making sure Larry knows he's loved.

Clark, whose last name is Henley (as in the Henley Regatta, my dears) and who wrote a book called *The Butch Manual*, which was a hilarious satire of that Castro Street clone thing, sits his stuffed Babar the Elephant King doll in his still-decorated Christmas tree and shoots off a Polaroid, then takes another—of the now-faded Curious George I bought him Back East five or six years ago (the same Curious George we rescued from Clark's blazing Peugeot when it burned to the ground in that bank parking lot in Palm Springs, which is how George faded in the first place, from riding around with Clark in the backseat). Clark and I go way back, and the painful possibility of losing him is with me every day. He's not the first man with AIDS I've known. He's not even the hundred and first. It's just that he's as close to me as skin.

Fort Mason is a former military installation down in San Francisco's Marina district. The masts of the local mini-yachts bobble in the choppy water; the lights blaze at the Safeway where Armistead Maupin's much-beloved *Tales of the City* series began five wondrous volumes ago, before the epidemic. Fort Mason's a community and arts center now, and tonight the parking lot is filling up fast. Louise Hay, a metaphysician/healer is offering one of her "hay rides," a healing session specifically for PWAs and their lovers and friends. Like alcoholism, AIDS is a family disease.

There are maybe three hundred people in the room, most of them men. Many are clearly ill, or, as the Louise Hay jargon goes, "dis-eased." Some haven't the strength to sit upright. Some are marked by the purple lesions of Kaposi's sarcoma. One bright and beautiful redhead seems healthy enough until he grins a greeting at an arriving blond—his KS lesions suddenly visible on his gums. The room is thick with mortality.

I'm sitting between my two best friends, Clark and Kenny, a psychological counselor in his forties who's known affectionately as "The Silver Fox." Until they both got AIDS and both wound up living in San Francisco (home to Clark, a dream to Kenny), neither of them could stand the other, even while listening to me chatter on about how wonderful the other was. I don't think it was mere jealousy over my split attention. Kenny was on one path, Clark another. They diverged.

People wander in and come over to chat. I recognize a dozen

people from previous trips north and earlier days in other American cities. Over there by the door is Jason Serinus, a professional whistler (yes, that's right, *whistler*) and healer, and the editor of a book called *Psychoimmunity and the Healing Process: A Holistic Approach to Immunity and AIDS*. Back East in the heady post-Stonewall, pre–Bobby Seale days, Jason was Guy Nassberg from Rockville Center, Long Island. He was the first man I knew who talked about the politics of being gay. He introduced me to the principles that gave me a fighting chance. It was also Guy Nassberg (later known by the less-offensively-sexist moniker *Jay* Nassberg) who, while wearing a tight red dress, gallantly threw the evil René (in the Halloween guise of Joan Bennett) down the stairs after the movie star manqué insulted the RadicaLesbians from Boston, which was no easy task—but that's another story.

Five years ago, you could see this many men butt-naked in the darkened corridors of any number of popular San Francisco bathhouses. Then they were learning how to celebrate their bodies; some got lost in them. Now they come together to share their experience, some positive energy and, perhaps, a bit of hope. They are looking, most of them, for some elusive spiritual *something*—anything, maybe—that will help see them through.

Louise Hay is hard to take if you live in your head, easy to dismiss if you're a skeptic. And I do, and I am. But in the next three hours she'll have her audience chanting, singing, meditating, talking, listening, touching, hugging. She doesn't promise to cure AIDS or its symptoms (although, as a survivor of vaginal cancer, she believes AIDS, and all other physical dis-eases, to be curable). She does purport to heal. For some this means learning to live without anger, guilt, or fear; for others it means being willing to die at peace with life and everyone in it.

Clark is trying to hide it, but he's scared. What is unspoken between us is that his pneumocystis is creeping back. His blood counts are worsening and, consequently, his doctor is reducing his dosage of AZT. He's been advised not to go on his planned trip to Hawaii. The statisticians measure his life expectancy in months.

| Michael LASSELL |

The wilier of San Francisco's thousands of downtown homeless check into the main branch of the public library when the weather gets cold. As long as they're reading, as long as they're not bothering anyone, they can stay. For many, the children's room is a haven from the streets as well as a source of books they can handle; some are only semiliterate. Right now a pair of particularly eager readers, dressed in the hallmark layered tatters of life on the streets, sit under a photo exhibit I've walked through the chilling midday rain to see: "The Children of the Tenderloin." Many of the children are in rags. Some laugh; many weep. Their penetrating eyes drink in a world that frightens them. We are allies in this.

For most San Franciscans, the Tenderloin is a high-crime district where every kind of sleazy reject and castoff can be found in abundance. For the Bay Area Women's Resource Center, which organized the photo exhibit and publishes its catalog, the Tenderloin (where policemen were once bribed from prosecuting crimes of the flesh with slabs of prime beef) is "evolving turf." Once abandoned to strays, derelicts, and burned-out flower children, the area is populated now by recent immigrants, many of them Southeast Asians and Central Americans with small children. They're poor, but ambitious. There's a tentative feeling of neighborhood in the area now, even of community in the making.

It's nearly impossible to avoid the Tenderloin if you walk from the Civic Center, with its imposing Beaux Arts government buildings, to Union Square, a shopping district at the highest end of consumer capitalism. On the way from Market to the impending comfort of the sleek Hotel Diva, my home away from home, I get to see the Children of the Tenderloin in action coming home from school. They look just like kids in any city, most of them unaware that another kind of world exists. This is both heartening, and terribly poignant.

I also see a drug buy in an alley, and a filthy drunk of indeterminate age and reeking of indeterminate beverage asks, then begs me to go home with him. I'm not flattered—I've had better offers—but I'm not offended or repulsed, either. Street people frighten me less than ever. I'm farther up the scale financially from these people than I've ever been before, and yet I've never identified more closely. There's a kinship, I guess, in the thin threads by which we all hang onto life, us disenfranchised types, by which we survive, when we do survive. When asked for quarters, I hand over dollars. I don't resent it. I don't think about the morality or efficiency of it or whether I can afford it or whether I am only doing it to assert my superiority or assuage my guilt. I just do it. It doesn't make me feel anything except grateful to be part of something bigger than most of what I am and do most of the time.

Clark's been driving out of our way on each of our outings this week so he can point out parts of the city he thinks I may not know about yet. He's a native, and in spite of very democratic proclivities, he's sometimes as reactionary a hometown chauvinist as columnist Herb Caen, the leading apologist for prebeatnik San Francisco, who thinks the city's going to hell in a jet-propelled handbasket. Clark grew up rich in chichi Hillsborough; his sister came out (in the Society sense) with Patty Hearst, and his parents live in a spectacular building at the top of crookedy Lombard Street. From their panoramic penthouse apartment, they can look down on everything. If Clark does die, I'll have a lot of San Francisco landmarks to remind me of him.

One is the Sheraton Palace Hotel, a Grand Guignol behemoth that survived the 1906 earthquake (referred to always in insider jargon as *the* earthquake). The hotel's Garden Room (where the debs are presented at each year's ball) has a leaded glass skylight the size of a basketball court, marble pillars, potted palms and—on Sunday afternoon at least—a harpist to ease diners' digestion and distract them from the prices. Half a block down the carpeted lobby, I discover a wood-paneled room called the Pied Piper Bar. Over the bar is a Maxfield Parrish mural of the Pied Piper and the children of Hamelin Town, dancing to their demise.

How many gay men do you think flocked to San Francisco in the '70s to find something they could never find in Indiana (where the Super Shuttle driver from the airport is from) or Iowa (where the waiter at the Zuni Café is from) or from Santa Monica, even (the home of the bellman at the Hotel Diva) or from New York City, the hometown I left behind? We came to San Francisco to find freedom. Many of us found it. It has made the AIDS epidemic even more tragic. And if AIDS did come home to Idaho or Illinois to die, forcing Middle America to confront unnecessary grief, then it is because those "I" states that don't have oceans attached to them sent their gay sons away, sometimes with shotguns at our backs.

It's a principle, even a *law* of metaphysics—insofar as metaphysics has laws—that we each manufacture or manifest the problems in our lives because of the "gifts" or lessons that these problems hold for us when we surrender to and accept them. How could we have known that there would be a "gift" like death in the process of liberation from the self-hatred we learned at the starched, pressed apron hems of the mothers of the "I" states we fled?

If you think you've seen personal courage in your life, take a walk down to Fort Mason the second Thursday of each month, when Louise Hay visits, and watch men with AIDS speak into a microphone to explain what gifts they have found because they have AIDS. Hear from men—beautiful *young* men most of them—who found unconditional love for the first time, about children reunited with parents, about agnostics reunited with a nurturing God, about lovers happy to nurse one another through the ultimate crisis, who would rather face the same death alone than watch the ones they love suffer needlessly longer.

Wonder, when it is over, why you have been spared, and why you feel more like singing than weeping.

The old guy at the Post Street bus stop off Geary near Polk is a character out of Dashiell Hammett (butch local literary hero), the kind of foil you'd expect to find in a prison movie taking the rap for Mr. Big. I'd guess him to be of Italian extraction, but who knows? He's on his way to the track just to get out of the neighborhood: "What could I lose, twenty-eight bucks?" He laments the scarcity of bookies, who used to thrive on every corner. He won so frequently in his salad days that he didn't have to work a regular job until he came out of the service after World War II; now he's a retired dockworker—crusty, salty.

"And Polk Street?" he says with a thumb over his shoulder toward San Francisco's first centralized gay neighborhood, where I bought the rings Roberto and I wore when we were "married," now sadly debased. "Forget about it. You wouldn't believe what walks around here at night. My God! And I don't mean the gays, either. People got something against the gays, I got nothing to do with. It's these petty punks who walk around waiting to rob them when they come out of a bar, whatever. Gays in San Francisco? They got more class than anybody."

Two Asian policemen are holding guns in the faces of two young Latin men who have attempted to rob the American Airlines ticket agency in the St. Francis Hotel on Union Square (across the street from Saks). A San Francisco friend suggests this encounter's a harbinger of San Francisco's future. It certainly plays into current cultural stereotypes.

The police in San Francisco aren't any better or worse than the police anywhere else. They're trained to protect property, and that's what they do. The SFPD tends to enforce the city's many laws with some reasonable notion of human priorities, however. Naturally they'll arrest two hapless guys who have broken into a closed office, and they won't take any chances doing it. But they won't roust an exhausted wino because he's sitting on a municipal planter next to a sign that puts him on notice that municipal planters are off-limits to the derriere.

And San Francisco is the only city I've ever been where the cop who slips you a sly wink may actually be offering shelter from the darkening storm.

Clark's uncle is probably around seventy. He's retired from whatever branch of the money-moving profession he was engaged in all his almost perfectly proper life. A few years ago, his lover of some three or four decades died, leaving the preppie old Mr. Chips with nothing much to do. He took a master's degree in history at San Francisco State, teaching himself French in the process. Now he longs to go live in London for a while to do some research there and in Paris on the French Revolution. The irony of his specialty apparently eludes him.

| Michael LASSELL |

At the moment, he's treating his nephew and me to a lunch at the Hayes Street Grill, an overrated eatery in one of San Francisco's numerous gentrifying neighborhoods that is owned by one of the city's major restaurant critics. (Conflict of interest, anyone?) Clark and I are wearing sports coats instead of our usual leather jackets. Clark's coughing a lot; I'm eating a lot of greasy fries. Like most of the old guard, Unc loves the opera, and he speaks knowledgeably about all the arts. No aspiring gay writer could possibly ask for a better nanny. There was no such tutorial role model in my life when I was growing up all tortured and alone.

By the end of the afternoon, Clark will have been diagnosed with a recurrence of *pneumocystis* pneumonia. For the next two weeks he will be given daily intravenous three-hour doses of a drug so toxic that he will be incapacitated by headaches, nausea, and fatigue for the remainder of each day. In between he'll cry. He'll sleep a lot in his tiny $700-a-month apartment on one of the scenic Twin Peaks, just up the hill from the formerly fabulous Castro District, where gay America found its Main Street. He'll practice the principles of Louise Hay and others like her. He'll make drawings for his beloved nieces and nephews while his uncle keeps an eye on him, and he'll keep on trying to help others, sicker and more lonely than he is. As long as he can. And we'll all go on pretending to believe in miracles.

Up on Nob Hill, where the Fairmont and Mark Hopkins and Huntington hotels book rooms for major bucks, is a little park on California Street between the ultraconservative Pacific Union Club and Grace Cathedral, where my boyfriend Andy and I once sat with a thousand other gay people mourning the loss of a man who was a stranger to most of us. He had been beaten to death for being homosexual. It was 1977, when we could all still afford the time and energy to weep for every member of our community who died unfairly and prematurely. Lately, there's a new death every day, and friends don't ask each other about friends because the number of AIDS cases keeps on growing exponentially with no end in sight.

There's a fountain in the middle of the park, a large cement dish held aloft by four nude bronze youths. A great deal of cruising used to go on here, I'm told—and, for all I know, it may still go on. At the moment, it's a park for old men to feed pigeons in, for young mothers to take the kids to play in, and for art students to sketch in. A place for weary visitors to sit and recoup.

It's too cold to be sitting outside, but a dozen adolescents are playing a game of football that seems to be a combination of touch and tackle with rules that shift oftener than the wind off the distant water. Two of the kids are black; another looks part black. There's an Asian kid, a couple of Latinos, some Caucasians, a pair of Middle Easterners. Before the deluge, San Francisco was mecca to a movement that held at its center the concept of universal brotherhood and love. Watching that football game in the cool afternoon, smelling the wet grass and mud, it's hard not to feel some of that old idealism churn up again, hard not to think that maybe we children of the sixties made *some* difference after all, made it just a little easier for this pack of roughneck city brats, with their sailor's lexicon of imaginative profanity and angels' locks, to play a kind of football on a brisk winter's day without having to think of race between attempted downs.

At the end of Louise Hay's evening, everyone is encouraged to embrace as many other people in the room as they can stand. No one's a wallflower here, not the four-hundred pound woman with the teddy bear or the man with cerebral palsy who sits in his wheelchair and clumsily but earnestly hugs all comers.

I embrace a man with blond hair, then make eye contact. There's a fear in his eyes that says he's found the exhilaration of life too late and that he will die before he can experience enough of it. "You're beautiful," I say uncharacteristically. His eyes start to panic. I raise my hand to his face and draw my fingers over a KS lesion on his cheek. I want him to know I think he's beautiful even with his lesions—not in spite of them or separate from them. He gets the unspoken message and smiles.

The cable car on Powell Street ends at Market in a plaza where all kinds of people come together. There's a busker playing great guitar to an appreciative crowd as the sun dips behind the hills and cold day starts inching toward colder night. The tourists are there, of course, even out of season, and the commuters on their way to the BART lines for the East Bay and beyond. Middle-class folk from the city shop across the street at the Emporium. Teenagers in various outfits of studded leather and rags cluster together to be surly. A small band of Indians stands together in an alcoholic haze. A black woman preaches the Gospel with gusto. A one-legged Vietnam vet sits quietly on a bench. The variously needy wander back and forth asking for money or favors. The Asian kids from the Tenderloin skateboards among the legs of the adults, past a blind accordion player and a homeless man with his homeless dog.

San Francisco is a beautiful place with clean air, but I don't go there for that. I go to San Francisco—cut loose of the expectations and demands that regularly weigh me down—to get in touch with who I am, and the city never fails to gift me with insight. I go because, at many levels, San Francisco has become again an incredibly vulnerable city, and because of its vulnerability, it's become again a city full of hope. And hope, I have come to know, is where the heart is.[2]

---

[2] My friend Kenny Moore died in Lake Tahoe in October 1987, in the home of Clark's cousin Dan, who nursed him in is last months. Clark died in August 1988. I have been there since, but I find that San Francisco died with them, in the first decade of the plague.

The Way Of All Flesh

Even the actor dies
For Franklyn Seales

It was not a mutual friend who
told me you had joined the disappeared
but Mitzi Gaynor, the cleaning woman
where I work (the hours so long I
never heard you were dying
six blocks
up Seventh Avenue).

"I know someone from your island,"
I said in passing and told her
your name. "The actor?" she
responded, fussing with a
can of trash; "Someone told me
he died."

Mitzi is heavy and has a few teeth
missing. There is nothing in her
of your patrician control
as you rode the arc of each role like
a wave that would surely reach shore
despite the disturbance of oceans.

Days after the news
I caught your face in a
TV sitcom rerun,
dialed your number, and heard
in your mother's cool contralto
a slice of your sweet music,
the sorrow of owls.
She had just returned from
claiming your ashes;

your sisters and brothers will
scatter them over the soft, clean water
of your boyhood bay. After
forty-one days in the AIDS ward of
St. Vincent's, you return to
the St. Vincent of your wistful
aqua dreams.

If I were a praying man,
which I no longer am, I'd pray that you
rest easy, my hard-driven friend of
sound arm and round laughter,
fifth child of ten in heartsick Olive's brood.
Your long estrangement in this land is over;
your last wishes head southward
in a burnished urn like
Cleopatra's barge, and you
astride, triumphant Antony,
bronze of skin and wrapped in leather,
lover eternal
bringing victory home.

Saturday night in New York City
For Irare

Pork Lo Mein for one, please,
No Smoking section, and chopsticks.

An Italian film with subtitles,
the emotion thick as saddle butter.
I'll take the one on the aisle and
put my coat on the one beside;
territory's a hard thing to come by,
the boy so beautiful I cried.

The bookstore closing, but a kind
word from the clerk on her way to the
crosstown bus, maybe a Diet Coke
from the deli for later at home while
I work the figures I'll bring
to the meeting Monday.

This must be what they mean by
survival, and what I mean by *Fine*
when friends call to see how I'm
doing, single again and gay in
New York City.

Keepsake
For Clark

The ebony elephant stares through ivory eyes
on the top shelf of memory,
under the dust of age and
quiet as the slow decline of
bodies over forty.
The precious stones embedded in its
silver blanket are my thoughts of one
as ruby red as tainted blood in hospital vials,
the dying slow as Spain and haunting as a
snake spine.

If one
could have lived, he would have.
His tango at the tea dance of death was not
a lark,
though the rhythm of his heartbeat was
a Latin inspiration to the chorus,
waltzing in despair.

 And now the hand-carved pachyderm needs Elmer's glue
to keep his whittled tusks in place
and frequent brushings to free him from
spider silk.
And every time the sun catches a gem facet,
something glistens
sharp as a hypodermic needle,
something aches
like a routine immunization
gone painfully awry.

Prism
For Kenny again
—after two years

The dark enclosure
of your absence
is a congress of colors,
a file of neckties
in a father's closet
forbidden to children.
The mysterious '50s were
curious gray and lost
maroon—the morose day we
skimmed the Pacific and
the sky went blaring
trumpets of a Telemann
fanfare (and the blood-red
sauce we poured on our
shellfish in an enclave of
silent seaside).
The thought of you is
Mary Todd, your turquoise
Lincoln; the empty yellow
of Palm Springs lust
(me all moon-eyed greed,
a black leather gauntlet
flung down in the oleander
crickets call from).
And you are shirts of
primary rainbow panes
(kelly, lemon, royal)
and the autumn moods of
beige and brown—
you know a buck from a
roan doe, the feather of
a peregrine from a roosting
quail. You are silver hair

| Michael LASSELL |

and eggshell flesh,
sheets white as ash-worm,
lesions violet as the mark
of hard kisses on Latin skin.
And your slow going in the
cold night is pine forest
green in rain,
marooned and gray
on a lake as periwinkle deep
as blue jays; you are clouded
from view, calm as cream,
mute as umber. And I am
a prism of ice
to refract your light
(teal, sienna, persimmon,
gold)
to keep you glowing
in the present tense,
a sepia tint
to log the indigo memory
of necessary you.

What it means to live alone again
For Stephen Greco

The rising steps on the stairs are never
his boots; he is not the one who has
swung the rusted gate shut under the fuchsia bougainvillea.
The oily clack of a gold key in an old lock is always a
neighbor staggering home after being rejected at one more
Vine Street dive. Nothing appears or disappears
from the refrigerator. No one's ever lying.
The phone is always for you.
There are no recriminations.
No surprises.
Lit candles never greet you as you walk through a door
after yet another lousy day working yourself into a lather.
You do a lot of reading.
Little explaining.
There are never flowers.
There is no one to disturb you when you're working late,
no one to brew a cup of tea.
The waking cough in the middle of a windy night is
the sound of your own snoring.
There is no hand nearby to cool your forehead when you
start from an angry dream.
The warmth of the bed beside you is the heat from a new
electric blanket.
You could care less what anyone thinks.
You suddenly can't recall his face.
You wonder who will call the hospital
should the need again arise.
You survive the first solo earthquake without panic.
Your lips cannot remember kissing.
You never dream of dying.

Indiana Gary

At the Sixties Café on Santa Monica
a wheat-white
blue-eyed Gary tells you
the story of his Indiana life:
a farm,
a father who
shot him when he said
he was gay, a mother who
quoted damnation from the Bible. The usual.

Hair is playing on the VCR,
Jim Morrison's stoned stallion beauty
posters the wall. Gary wears
love beads—
the kind you spent the summer of '69
stringing with Judy
in Rome, New York.

He lives outside West Hollywood
with a cockatiel
and dreams.
You order dessert, hoping to
smell lust brewing with your coffee but
Jonathan walks in
with a friend from
Chicago. Talk turns, as it does,
to death—
and it does.
It does.

The dying makes your head swim—
and you are on the move from
hamburger and ketchup chat of
terminal disease.
You're off like a shot of scotch

The Hard Way

down the parched streets
of Boys Town while
Gary fires questions at your back.
You know by now you can't outrun the sprint-
er death
but you seek a day's reprieve,
some sanctuary from this deafening angel's
name. You throw yourself at the mercy
of a twinkie bar
called Rage.

Kissing Ramón

One kisses Ramón goodnight on Bank Street in the Village.

At the corner, the bank is expanding into the bookstore, and Ramón tells you about the poet laureate of the Philippines, who lives right down the street, on Greenwich.

Sometimes the kisses are long and deep, and there are passersby.

Sometimes one grows hard almost instantly.

"Shut off your fucking engine," the policewoman bellows through her bullhorn.

Bullets.

Sirens.

Sometimes his ear is ice on one's flushed cheek.

A fat man in a tight jacket turns the lights of his van on from a block away.

Masculine Principle No. 1 (Urban):
All men must own a car. All cars must have alarm systems. All alarm systems must make intrusive electronic noises whenever activated or deactivated, no matter how obnoxious this may be to one who is trying to cheat the dark of its tariff (insomnia) by falling asleep before midnight realizes what's happened.

Masculine Principle No. 1 (Rural):
Insert the words "pickup truck" in place of the word "car" above.

Masculine Principle No. 2:
One kisses Ramón and wonders about the moisture that lingers on one's lips and in one's moustache, despite all published evi-

| *The Hard Way* |

dence that kissing, even deep wet sloppy kissing, is relatively safe, but what is safety? Not even Larry Kramer knows for sure.

One wipes away the saliva, feels guilty, brushes one's teeth, feels guilty, masturbates, feels unfulfilled, falls to sleep, is wakened by:

Men's voices, angry shouting.
Women's voices, hurt, weeping.

Intrusive electronic noises.

Mice running in the walls; rats warring in the walls.

Shouting in masculine Spanish.
Screaming in feminine French.

"Shut off your fucking engine," the policewoman bellows through her bullhorn.

You'd think you'd like to swallow bullets: soft, sweet, deadly.

Sometimes one touches Ramón's ass just for luck, like Buddha's belly.

Masculine Principle No. 3:
Ramón buys baklava at a deli on Ninth Avenue. One waits with Ramón in the cold for the Abingdon Square bus. One mentions the death of a friend. Ramón explains his life on Planet Positive, his fear of death, his anger and denial. Speechless and without experience, one still feels a need to respond.

Sometimes one feels Ramón's cheek and it's soft as sifted flour.

Kisses.

Bullets.

Sirens.

The day that Adrien didn't come to New York

The day that Adrien didn't come to New York
was new May green. Jane,
the woman from Ohio who lives upstairs, was
dancing flamenco in lead
boots at six a.m. or whatever it is she does
up there. Soft rain,
pretending to be wind, tripped the chimes
of a neighbor's weed tree.
Anticipation lay in my lap like a cool pillow.

The day that Adrien didn't come to New York
the phone rang early.
His voice quivered. Words that didn't sound
right filtered through
my refusing to hear, words like: a friend,
AIDS emergency, and
I canceled my flight. Sometimes, I thought,
the well suffer, too,
sudden setbacks from which we don't recover.

The day that Adrien didn't come to New York
I admired his loyalty.
Disappointment and relief were wrestling for
my undivided attention.
Despair, as usual, won—and naked immobility.
I took a nap in the
leather recliner, but didn't have a dream. The
rain stopped pretending
 to be wind and became a metaphor for slow aging.

The day that Adrien didn't come to New York
I tried to beat the
loneliness out of my limbs at the gym, but
forgot why I even bother.
A tall, blond, muscled love god was staring

| *The Hard Way* |

his reproach at my
imperfection in the whirlpool. I never knew he
was flirting until later,
when the elevator door snapped shut between us.

The day that Adrien didn't come to New York
I said, I'm giving up
love forever. And no one said, *Yeah, sure*. I
went to the SoHo opening
of a gallery show about self and identity. The
white room was full
of strangers. I looked for myself in the art
and saw a blurred black
shadow in a steel diptych I didn't understand.

The day that Adrien didn't come to New York
was as unsurprising as
the news last week of Patrick's death, sadder
than the end of long
enduring passions. This aching day in spring
was nothing at all,
not rain or mail or running into Matthew. It
was nothing but Adrien,
and the day he never made it to New York.

Shuttle, 9 A.M.
For Yves/Assotto

She was reading a romance novel
by the white light of a Marky Mark
ad for Calvin Klein cotton underwear in the Times Square subway
station—near the first track of the
crosstown shuttle to Grand Central.

She was wearing a long gray coat
and leaned into Marky with her
left shoulder, the better to see the
pages of her half-finished paperback
while I waited on the stalled train
thinking wet-wool commuter thoughts.

She was reminding me of something
but I couldn't remember what.
How beyond my arms love seemed now?
How elusive youth? Or that I needed
to buy a new jar of Metamucil from
the Duane Reade on my lunch hour?

Or was it that beauty is everywhere?
In her padded houndstooth shoulder
leaning into fat-free fluorescent
Marky the way Yves leans into AIDS:
nonchalantly, giving his weight to it,
turning the pages slowly, curious,

waiting.

Poems For Roberto

I met Roberto Muñoz at a bar called Gold Street in San Francisco on, as I remember it, the seventeenth of May, 1973. It was St. Patrick's Day. I had spent the morning alone watching the parade from the corner of Polk Street where the Mitchell brothers' porn theater was (incredibly painted with sea creatures, including a whale nearly as big as the one suspended from the ceiling of the Museum of Natural History in New York City). This was two decades before one of the brothers killed the other, although the blue building still stands. I had determined, while watching the gay couples hand-in-hand watching the high-school flag twirlers and kilted bagpipers parade by, that what I needed, at the age of twenty-five, was a male lover. I had had three long-term relationships with women that were complex, emotional, and sexual. I had had crushes, affairs, one-night stands, and anonymous sex with dozens of men. And so I set out that night to find the lover who would change my life.

Roberto, who was twenty-one at the time, was on the balcony of Gold Street, I was at the bar. Charles Pierce, preeminent female impersonator, was doing his show on the small stage. I looked up and saw the largest pair of dark eyes I had ever seen, surrounded by masses of dark hair. He was peering over the rim of a huge goblet of foaming green liquid (which turned out to be some kind of holiday daiquiri). He was watching me. I was held by his eyes until he tipped down his drink enough for me to see his smile. We were together for three years.

They were not idyllic. For one thing, I was in drama school at Yale, Roberto was working as a teller in a bank on the New Haven green. I was up to my eyeballs in work, he had nothing to do. I was a WASP in WASP country, he was the only Chicano north of El Paso. Both of us were new at love, and although we felt it deeply, we were not up to the task of loving past our differences or the abuses we had been taught by life to heap upon ourselves. We split, with some rancor, in 1976, and I moved back to California, leaving Roberto in a town he never meant to live in, 3,000 miles from his family. We reconciled the following year—not that we ever became lovers again, but we resumed acknowledging our feelings of love for one another.

When Roberto called that October to tell me his father died, I was about six weeks clean and sober—and nearly as distraught as he was. Although Ed spoke little English and had only the haziest knowledge of my relationship with his youngest son, he opened his home and family to me. I was a pallbearer at the emotionally effusive wake and grim burial, in a sunbaked, treeless cemetery somewhere in the hill country east of San Francisco—near Concord, I think, or Walnut Creek.

Roberto and I kept up over the years, even saw each other from time to time, even had sex once for old time's sake, as the poetry describes. Then he stopped sending postcards from his trips to Europe—alone, it always seemed, though he wrote of a lover. By the time I moved back to New York in 1990, Roberto was no longer listed in the New Haven telephone book. The phone company, for which he had worked for years, had no employee by his name. I assumed he was living in New Haven with a lover and working elsewhere.

While writing out my Christmas cards that year, I decided to try to find Roberto through his family. There was, however, no more listing for any Muñoz in Pittsburg, California, where they had always, as far as I knew, lived. I thought to call Bobby's sister, Lolly, whose husband Jim had been in the navy. They were living in Oceanside, outside San Diego, the last I knew. I called information, and got Jim on the phone. He didn't remember me from the family vacation to Lake Tahoe in August of 1973, or from Ed's funeral. I called when he said Lolly would be home.

Since Roberto's mother and sisters were privy to our relationship, and since I was Roberto's first "friend," she remembered me immediately. And seemed actually glad to hear my voice. We were chatting, Lolly and I, about her three kids—J.D., Peggy Sue, and Andrew—when she said, almost in passing, "You know, Bobby died." I told her I had actually had a premonition he might have, although I didn't know. I hadn't wanted to know. She couldn't remember what year. There was a lover, whose name she could not recall, and he and the Muñoz family were at war, the way families and lovers all over this country are at war, sharing nothing but a corpse and a few precious photos. A mark of how far the world has changed: The issue of homosexuality was never raised. She seemed to accept it totally, with no embarrassment or difficulty. Of course, Bobby was dead, and so was Ed. What would have been the point? I told her I would call again. But I never have. The link in that chain is gone.

The anger was almost immediate. How could he have been sick and not told me? Did he think I no longer cared what happened to him? Did it not occur to him? Was he trying to spare me, or hurt me? It hadn't been quick. Lolly and her family, even Mary, their mother (by now past senility in a nursing home), had flown to the East Coast, visited Roberto in New Haven, gone to the one and only Broadway show of their lives (Lolly didn't remember which one). "You wouldn't have wanted to see him the way he looked at the end," Lolly said in a voice that told me she'd said it many times before. "It's better that you remember him the way he was."

The way he was. With that cascading hair, the smile that was mischief itself in the first photo he sent me, ironing in the kitchen of the Brady Street apartment. Eventually we would come to share this place with his sister, Rosemary, a nursing student, and her lover, Jewel, a tattooed Pueblo Indian who worked as an electrician in San Francisco because, apparently, there weren't any more jobs on her reservation doing what she liked best: breaking horses.

There is little left now of Roberto. The snapshots, of course—one I dreamed of recently: Roberto in gray slacks and the gray corduroy jacket he bought at Macy's when he was working at the bank, beside our Christmas tree in the first New Haven apartment, and beside my grandfather's rocker, which I abandoned when I moved back to California. And there is, of course, the gold and silver crucifix, the one he bought me in those long, long weeks between our first meeting in March and the day we began to live together in May of 1973. It's a small and delicate charm, on a chain so thin it broke over and over again—and over and over again we had it fixed. When he gave it to me, he said it was to protect me when he was not there to do it himself. It hangs now in my bedroom, as it has hung in every bedroom I have had since we lived together in 1976. To remind me of Roberto, the first great love of my life. Every now and again, I read the words etched on the back: (MIKE LOVE BOB), a direct order as well as an inscription. And at times when I come to doubt it—though this is surely an indulgence—I hold it as proof that I was loved in those mad years of drinking and drugs and politics and opening nights at the theater where I performed so often, so long ago.

These poems, written between about 1980 and 1992, chronicle my relationship with Roberto. They were meant as a testament to him—and to preserve his memory—even before I knew of his death, sometime before his fortieth birthday. I spent my first Fourth of July in San Francisco with Roberto in 1973, but I travel there often for a convention that happens over Independence Day weekend each year. The holiday as well as the city figure prominently as emotional triggers for that lost time of fading innocence. And, of course, I never go to San Francisco without paying a visit to Brady Street, a tiny two-block byway across Market Street from the Zuni Café.

Roberto is buried alongside his father in a place I will never see. His mother, too, may be there by now, the always befuddled, always loving Mary, who insisted on calling me son, who took me by the hand at the funeral of her long-suffering husband, an d introduced me to every member of the family, every grieving friend and sympathetic neighbor, as *el compadre de mi hijo, Roberto.*

He deserved better. They all deserved better, my temporary family of illegal immigrant farm workers. I will always miss him, and wish I had been asked to help carry this small, large man to his grave, as I did his sweet and much-wronged father. May they all rest in peace. And may we, too, find peace.

Passing through

The old oaks were heavy in the wake of a hurricane.
The power was out all over New England.
Brick buildings stood closer together than
I remembered, hoarding their hollows: Peter's basement,
Stephen's second floor, an attic window in ivy where
a nameless boy led strangers to a fool's paradise
night after night for years.

The towers were still Gothic, the carillon slightly
off key; slick streets still recalled men who
did not fall in love when they had the chance
and the heart-pounding presence of things, as if
they mattered.

Arthur has married; Alan died of AIDS.
The bookstore's gone downhill; the hotel's improved.
Larry still drinks in the corner bar where
a young man dances like you used to walk—
 stepping between puddles on high-heeled platform shoes.
I could have called you on the phone but
sat opposite the door hoping you'd sail in,
burst into song at the sight of me and fold into my arms.
I waited for you in Boston, too, where you've never been
and mourned the boats the high tide washed onto the
train tracks when the storm turned everything on end.

The Holiday Inn was full of octogenarian tourists
trying to get some experience in under the wire.

I wondered why they hadn't learned any better
and why the reception was still all snow in the room I
ran to the night of the suitcase and door frame in
splinters.

| *The Hard Way* |

In the dark I waited for you to slip into bed beside me,
but you never came. In the morning there was breakfast
and a taxi rush to the train. There were cigarettes
and newspapers and the memory of your lashes,
the angle of your starlight, eyes.

Andrew, son of James

Andrew was no
ordinary child as he
sat on my lap in the
backseat of a souped-up
TransAm gunning it
out of the Alameda naval
station toward Concord
and his grandmother.
I was no
ordinary child, either,
his uncle's lover,
him not understanding,
me no longer able to
hold it together. He
sat on my lap and
clung to my beard for
fear of speed and
cried at the airport when I
finally left for good.
Youngest of three,
it was Andrew it was
hardest to leave,
not the man I was
mad to love.

I cried in the plane as it
flew over the
Grand Canyon at dusk. The
stewardess offered a third
drink free by way of
consolation and asked
in the course of things
if I had any
children.

How to visit your ex

Travel seventy-five miles out of your way to
visit a city you hated when you lived there.
Tell yourself it's just for old time's sake.
Tell yourself you'd go
even if he weren't still living there.

Stand bewildered in a vacant lot
where your favorite luncheonette used to be.
Find the city
depressingly small, dirtier than you remembered,
cold.
Walk the old streets and think the old thoughts,
feel again the sadness of long winters,
hot wet summers. Shop
someplace you couldn't afford before. Buy something
you wanted then, just to get
even with life.

Sit in the college library with nothing to do,
use the same chair you sat in
when you wrote your
oral report on Jacobean tragedy.

Look up his name in the phone book, just to see
if he's listed. Dial the number, just to see
if he's home. Let it ring a long time.
Call the bank
where he used to work. They will tell you
he doesn't work there anymore.
They give you a name.
Call information. Dial the number.
Then say,
"Hi" when he comes to the phone. He'll know
who it is.
"Come by at eight."

| Michael LASSELL |

Take off your boots or you'll wet his floor.
He will be
shorter than you remembered,
and will have grown a beard.
Hide how disappointed you are his new place is so
small. Feel responsible for him. Look around
for this and that,
things you once shared, things
he remembers you by whenever he dusts them.
Refuse a drink. Stare into his
eyes. Kiss him
at the first opportunity. Kiss him
over and over again.

Surprise yourself that you are so passionate.
Devour him.
Remember the reasons
you first fell in love. Forget all the reasons
love died. Pretend that it wasn't so bad—
the fights, the doctors, the nights you spent
in jail.
Find his body warm
in more ways than you knew existed. Know
his mouth is someplace you'll always remember,
his mouth, and the bar where you first
laid eyes on him, a dark nimbus of hair
behind a goblet of green foam.

"I'm surprised you agreed to see me," you'll tell him.
"Why?" he'll ask.
Shake your head as if you have no answer.
Say, "I'm surprised to be in bed again
after all this time."
He'll say, "Anytime you want to, just call."
Think that three thousand miles is a long way to travel
for good sex, but it might be worth it.
"Why did you want to?" he'll ask, expecting a
compliment. Tell him the truth. Say,

| *The Hard Way* |

"Because so many people are dying. People I love.
 Because every death makes the disappointment with life
a little more complete. Because
the end of a relationship is like
an unnecessary death."
Smile when he says,
"You always were full of shit."

Drive to the top of an empty mountain.
Stare into the sky. Appreciate the stars.
Remember how much you love snow.
Think that it's come to an end after all,
but do not think of death.

Brady Street, San Francisco

The apartment
is still standing, still about to fall.
It's circled now in Technicolors of
competing graffiti
more artful than we were to
stay in love.
Our names in cement are long gone.
It's my first time back since the news.

From the street
nothing seems to have changed.
My mind too has trapped the action in mid-flight:
how I hid in the closet (naked) the
first morning your family descended unannounced
and told your father we'd had
balls for breakfast when my Spanish slipped on
eggs. You shot your
one-note nasal laugh and spun on your heel,
but I'd cracked the shell of tension.
Your mother sat on the couch—
a miniature goddess of plenty, her feet
not touching the floor—and adopted me
in her knowing smile.

Here's a junk drawer more of memories:
an orange cat that lived through an airshaft fall;
the Twin Peaks fog from our bedroom window bay;
snacking on Stevie Wonder and your skin;
the double mattress we had to carry home
on our backs because
it cost every cent we'd saved.

After the first fight over nothing you
slammed into the street. I screamed
from the third floor into the dark I'd

The Hard Way

die if
you didn't love me; you cried and
crept back up the stairs creak by
indolent creak.
We stayed together.
That time.
And when the loving was over—
three years, two apártments,
and a continent later—
no one died. Not
altogether. At least not
right away.

We left behind the odor of queers in the carpet,
the grease from our last
cooked meal,
a hole I punched in the plaster with my anger
and covered with the Desiderata so
the landlord wouldn't howl.

You see, it takes only a score of years
to make the bitter memories sweet,
like lemons in a sugar glaze.
I'd eat an orchard of them for you now
if you could be alive again to see me try.

Another pang of Roberto

A late winter day in April called me back to New Haven
on business.
All right—
I admit it: I came to feel
your absence—and did:
on Davenport, where our building looks
the same as always, the hospital uglier, the Hill
even more run-down. Music in Spanish was
blaring from the open fire-escape door to our apartment.

Across town,
I couldn't find our last address, the old
Victorian off Whitney Avenue, and stared at the wrong house
for ages trying to make it home:
our two-bedroom palace where we fried the
tortillas your mother air-freighted from California
when you were the
only Mexican north
of Atlanta—this stolen plant-and-fern farm we shook
with swearing, cooking chicken for Calvin and Miguel,
drinking ourselves into jail and
proving our love by drawing blood,
kissing the wounds clean again,
four arms loamy to the elbow with potting soil.

I stood on the town green, too,
empty of demonstrations now,
and replayed a newsreel of
your grated window at the bank,
your smiling and counting,
all business and blushing at once, handing over your
keys to my car with an endearment whispered
just loud enough to be overheard.

| The Hard Way |

Why did you die without telling me you were ill?
Did you want to protect me or think I wouldn't care
just because we'd both moved on?
Or did you think I'd find out somehow?
Was it even, perhaps, revenge?
And why does the grieving never end?

Just the other day in the Village,
I was walking down Christopher and thought,
I'll have to tell Roberto that that lousy Mexican restaurant
is a Puerto Rican drag bar now, and realized again
how dead you are.

You wouldn't have wanted to see him like that, your sister said.
But she was wrong.
Your death, a cruel enigma, is
the end of New Haven for me, this hate-filled town
of scholarship and folly where you died, your death
more potent here than
any place on earth, your having been
so angry here, so young and muscled, so
dancing brown and Latin, and alive.

Eighteen years

Flying into San Francisco on the third of July
I remember our first Fourth, eighteen years gone,
in the sun-dried suburbs due east of the East Bay.

I never felt whiter as the green enchiladas were
passed 'round the back patio—but *tu padre* limped
over on swollen feet to give me a beer and a hand.

Your brothers could have killed us with an unkind
word. Instead, we played football in the street
and set off Chinatown fireworks for Lolly's kids.

We watched roller derby from Fresno on TV and
pulled walnuts from a tree by the garage. "So,
you're a picker, too," your teenaged *tia* beamed.

When your silent father died, we two were living
on opposite coasts of a wide country. You wept so
loud I flew to you and bore his body to its grave.

Now you are buried beside him under the dry brown
grass; your mother is locked in a room, drifting
like a wisp of cloud with no rainstorm to attend.

J.D., Peggy Sue, and dearest Andrew are all grown,
(older now than you were when we met): married,
parents, divorced, engaged. I get news, somehow.

Eighteen years is a long time for a small dog
to run circles in a yard barking, drawing blood
from ankle bones. And yet it runs. It runs…

Our town

On vacation from New York,
I ran into John
on the Fourth of July
in San Francisco—
near the jewelry store
where you bought me a crucifix
on time.
You remember, from Connecticut?
He lives in Los Angeles now.
We called him Blinky,
all the drugs he took
as a teenager dancing
in his helpless eyes
like a straight man at a disco.
He's clean and sober now a
dozen hard-won years.
It shows.
No longer a beautiful boy,
he isn't yet the handsome man
he'll someday be (like me,
he's received an indefinite stay
of execution).
He hadn't heard you were dead,
and was of all the people I know
the only one left who'd truly
miss you.
He told me
Miss Bea had died,
who so annoyed me
with his pudgy mincing waddle,
saddle-sized bags and Elton John-like
goggles, an affront to
the kind of queer I wanted to be.
John didn't remember
throwing up in the back of the Olds
the night you were arrested for
arrogance, either, or Italian

black-eyed Sue
and the party at the Chicken
when we all wound up in a
jail cell.
He doesn't know what became of
Calvin or Miguel,
but remembers Fred, who
kept half New Haven high
before he lost his job
at the hospital pharmacy—
I mean,
how many pills have to be missing before
they suspect a competitive enterprise?
He tried to get me to remember
Hank,
but I never got further than the name.
Of Dennis, nothing.
We didn't know him well, but
John is all the you I've got.
And my anger at your dying
without saying good-bye
makes sense in all this world only
to him.
It's a small town, America,
for which I'm grateful:
Someday, I suppose,
we'll all hook up in the gay bar on
the hill, recounting past glories and
lost loves
(your raven mane carried home
on the bus in a Baggie),
the joys of being boys together,
the torments of men. And
our eternal gossip will float
over the wet cemetery grass like
a mist,
a San Francisco morning fog that
disperses in the high noon
of a new sun.

A Simple Matter Of Conversion

It is ten years into plague. I am walking down a street in the East Village. It is early night and I am full of desire. He is leaning against a building that is covered in graffiti. He is wearing: faded black denim cutoffs, small and tight, held together by safety pins and fastened around his narrow waist by a fat studded belt. His torn-off T-shirt is white with a SILENCIO = MUERTE button on it in pink on black. There is a heavy silver chain around his neck, from which something that looks like a bone is suspended.

His body is marble sculpted by a Renaissance idolater. The flesh of his torso flows around his navel like a stream around a hidden hollow. His head is shaved. On the left side, from which I approach, he has had an elaborate eagle tattooed over his ear, which is pierced at least a dozen times and glistens with silver rings. The wings of the eagle are splayed, erect; the beak is gaping; open talons reach for the meal of his frightened eye, which turns slightly to the left to meet my need. It is a mouth I remember from before, from decades before. It swallows time.

It is long-lost Rob's mouth that this tattooed boy in the East

Village has turned in my direction with his eye of prey, and it is through Rob's over-red lips that he says, "My name is Luke," and invites me home, up six filthy flights in a nearby tenement. The room, like his imagination, has been furnished from the street.

As soon as the locks are secure, he turns to face me. I put my hands on his bare waist, which is hot and dry. I touch my lips to his lips, push them into a kiss. He kisses back. He opens his lips slightly; I insert my tongue. He moans and pushes the front of his shorts into my cock, which is filling with blood. I fumble with his belt, get it open, put one hand down the back and caress his ass. His shorts drop over his boots to the floor. We do not stop kissing. I feel his hard cock on my belly. I stretch my hand down the crack of his ass and feel the coarse, sparse growth of hair. I pull up with my middle finger on the bull's-eye of his asshole. He moans again. Blood surges into my cock. I pull the T-shirt up over his head, his arms suspended in the air like the arms of a praying mantis or Sebastian becoming a saint. His body is a minefield of surprises. His hard boy's chest is white. It is the pale and neutral flesh canvas for another tattoo that covers his breastbone: an elaborate heart, a flaming heart that drips blood the color of stage light through cellophane. It holds my eye like an animal one comes across by accident in the wilderness. Beyond it I am conscious of his dark, thick cock pointed straight at the ceiling, but I sink only as far as this heart and lick the drops of blood.

He is lying on the bed while I undress quickly. Naked, I bend to pull the boots off him, first one, then the second. There is another tattoo around his right ankle, a neatly symmetrical chain, somewhat stylized but cleanly rendered. I lift his leg and put the toes of his right foot into my mouth. I begin to suck. He purrs, his torso rippling like a tide, the heart floating on the crest of it in a vessel of fire. I slip my shoulders underneath his thighs and move down until his asshole is positioned directly in front of my cock.

"Do you have a rubber?" I ask, and he turns slightly on an axis, each of his ribs a perfect ridge below his arm, and turns back with a lubricant in his hand. I do not react. He rubs my cock, and I wonder whether I will come before I even get inside him. Then he stops.

"Do it," he says.
"But…"
"Do it."

I hesitate but slip inside him and realize I have forgotten what sex is, what my cock feels like buried to the hilt in the ass of a beautiful stranger, the red of my pubic hair meeting the black of his asshair. He stares into my eyes and puts his arms around my shoulders.

How many years, how many years has it been? I wonder.

I feel an odd sensation in my neck. I put my hand to the spot. My fingers are covered with blood.

"Don't worry," he says, looking up at me. He holds a razor blade in his hand. "It isn't deep. It's only a symbolic gesture." Then he pulls me down and takes my neck in his mouth, sucking, sucking, pulling the blood out of me into his throat. And all the while I am pumping. It is as if I have never had sex before in my life. I am pumping and he takes the razor and makes a small incision on his own neck. His blood begins to dribble down his long hard neck like a leak through a crack in marble.

"Blood brothers?" he asks.

And I explode into his asshole, shot after shot of semen. I am groaning, and he is howling with pleasure as he shoots onto his own stomach, the milky stuff splattering the tattoo on his hairless chest, and every inch of me is finally alive as I bite down on his neck and taste the blood of him on my tongue.

Part Four

MY LIFE IN ART

Skyfires

*For Icarus, still a boy,
and a fledgling poet, now a man*

I. DAWN

(On the publication of his first book of poems)

*The thing that hath been, it is that which shall be;
and that which is done is that which shall be done;
and there is nothing new under the sun.*

—ECCLESIASTES 1:9

On the back of the book is a photo of the poet (all lips and eyelids, shoulders, forearms). I could quote him in the sighing of a thigh, a hand hovering over a waist and never lighting, like a thrush or mockingbird. His eyes sink into me, into the muscle and bone. I loved him once ten years and am furious he has seen fit to live so fully and so long without me on his breath. His words tear into my chest like his lovemaking teeth into the hearts of other men than me. His face has aged and styles have changed over the years, but the eyes still have it; they conceal still whether his life is sin or blessing, a metaphor of unimagined depravity or a simile of unquenchable spirit. He looks into the center of things; what drops into him spills out in a dozen words arranged on paper—or in the arch of an eyebrow, shadow of a dimple, ironic glance in a mirror, or the lens of an antique camera he bought at auction in Singapore.

I stare into the photo, and Gavin is in my eyes again as he has been, all these years, wrapped tightly in my heart and mind.

2. SUNRISE
(The first inkling)

> *More worship the rising than the setting sun.*
> —Plutarch, *Lives* (Pompey to Sulla)

Icarus woke earlier than his father. Incarceration had taught him that: wake up earlier or fall asleep later; it was the only way to have any privacy, any time alone. It was his father's fault, after all. Icarus had had nothing to do with it, really. He had just carried his father's message to the king's daughter, Ariadne, in love with the Athenian traitor, Theseus. How was Icarus to know the old man and the princess were in league to fashion the foreigner's escape from the labyrinth his father had designed, had designed so cleverly that even the inventor could no longer contrive to escape it without a ruse? But Daedalus, always the thinker, had come up with a solution, pressed into a tablet of flattened red wax and given it to his son.

Daedalus had warned Icarus to keep the tablet out of the heat of the sun until after Ariadne had decoded it. Then they would let the wax melt, the plan ran, the message lost for all time with the evidence. It was a perfect scheme, at least for the lustful Ariadne and her suitor Theseus. For Daedalus and Icarus, however, the result was catastrophic.

Ariadne—vain, pampered, and shallow as she was most of the time—could be a tigress when she got her mind set on something she wanted; she had carried out his father's plan with the fortitude of a warrior. Theseus had escaped and abducted the self-centered princess along with, rumor had it, her younger and far more agreeable sisters as well. As for Theseus' crime, the slaying of the bull/man Minotaur, well, King Minos was so furious about the death, the escape, *and* the abduction, that there was little hope either Icarus or Daedalus would ever be freed. They were the only ones left in Crete who had had anything to do with it. Ariadne's handmaidens, it was said, had been sold into slavery in Thrace, just to assuage the king's humiliation.

And so, morning after morning, Icarus sat in the crude open-

| *The Hard Way* |

ing that served as their only window and stared out at the sky and the sea, going over it all again and again, blaming his father, ancient Daedalus, who sat up night after night until nearly dawn racking his brain for a means of escape, an escape Icarus knew would never come. The stone tower was too high to jump from; they were never given enough of anything to construct a ladder; there were armed guards encamped all around the base of the tower; and the tower itself was set on a minute island miles from land, boats being absolutely forbidden to dock except under the most stringent security conditions. But, futile as it seemed, the old man pored over his papers and perused his books and ruminated night after lonely night in the shadow of the moon and stars or the stingy supply of candles their captors allowed.

Icarus woke each morning just after his father nodded off on his pallet for a few hours of fitful sleep. He stood each morning at the window at dawn going over it in his unforgiving mind. His body had just begun to mature, and something he did not understand was growing inside him, swelling, demanding to explode from his body as urgently, as violently as he longed to break from his confinement, to be free to walk and run, to engage the boys of his childhood in contests and sports, to lie naked by a cool stream in an olive grove, to listen to the sweet panpipes of a precocious shepherd. The pressures of his body were enormous, and the discovery of temporary physical release, which his father absolutely forbade (on the premise that the habit sapped intellectual curiosity), only made him long for freedom more actively.

Morning after morning he would stand in the large window and feel the sea breeze on his face—a handsome face, his father had said. "Yes, you have a handsome and a pleasing face," he said, "But a handsome and a pleasing face is nothing compared to a quick and agile mind." Well, Icarus thought, everyone in Greece knew where a quick and agile mind had gotten Daedalus, and Icarus along with him.

Morning after morning he would stand in the window, his hands on his thin bare hips, and watch the soldiers below pouring urns of seawater over one another. The shock of the icy water in the cold dawn cascaded over the tanned backs and flanks of two dozen hard men, soldiers who were sworn to the death to maintain his imprisonment. All those men for one old man and a boy, he thought contemptuously as he watched them in their exercise and horseplay, as they sharpened spears, polished armor, slept together in their dark blankets, coarse as unshaved faces, their heads on leather shields, swords always ready.

Icarus aped their exercises with the resources at hand. He would push against the floor and the walls, stand on his hands, lift his father's heaviest books again and again over his head, until his adolescent body began to show signs of muscle. "Yes, you have a good and a strong body," his father had conceded when Icarus asked him (often more than once each day), "but a good and a strong body is of value only when it is the temple of a quick and agile mind." Daedalus had tried to shape and hone that mind as the soldiers did their weapons, but Icarus, as well proportioned as any youngster he'd ever seen, was easily bored by his lessons, constantly distracted by the sounds of the raucous men below, by the patterns of the clouds above them, by the great expanse of sea around them, and by the birds that swooped within inches of his son's outstretched, imploring arms.

And so Icarus stood at the window in the dawn before Daedalus woke and gave his body the only respite he could manage from his long aching to be free. And he gathered the feathers the birds dropped on the window ledge and drew them across his face and chest to feel their flight on his skin. He sat in the window and soaked in the sun that came through the opening and felt its warmth penetrate his flesh, felt the warmth as it turned to sweat that wet him, the cool breeze that chilled his skin as the prickly perspiration turned into air, cool sea air, leaving hard human salt on his unblemished limbs. "Old Minos may control the land and sea," his father would say as Icarus stood idly by the window, "but he will never control the sky…that is Apollo's realm."

And Icarus would sigh, knowing that he would now be called from his musings for yet another tutorial in the complex lexicon of his father's gods. If they were so powerful, Icarus thought, why did they not carry him off to freedom? Why did no ravishing swan or eagle descend to carry him off to liberation?

And one hot morning in the third year of their imprisonment, on a day that Daedalus had said was to be the fourteenth anniversary of his youngest son's birth, Icarus stood in the dawn window and waited for the sun to come up over the horizon. He thought, with an ironic smirk in his eye, of the charioteer god, Apollo, whose horses were hitched to the sun... Apollo, the sun god, the god of music and the lyre, his father's personal favorite because of the god's particular affinity for a quick and agile mind. And as he stared into the sun that morning, he had to rub his eyes, then again. He looked down at the soldiers still sleeping at the base of the tower, their night fires nothing more now than cinders. Because as Icarus looked to the horizon that morning, he thought he could make out a team of blazing horses, a fiery chariot of burnished gold, and a charioteer of such magnificent face and form that Icarus held his breath. He looked at his father, slumped as usual over his workbench, his scrolls undone before him. And then he looked back into the sun and into the smiling face of a man unlike any he had ever seen, a man whose perfection dazzled young Icarus, a man who held his chariot team in check with one bulging forearm, and who held the other forward in an invitation, it seemed, for Icarus to take hold of it.

3. MORNING

(On the arrival of the young man in academy)

The greater the love, the more false to its object,
Not to be born is the best for man;
After the kiss comes the impulse to throttle,
Break the embraces, dance while you can.
—W. H. Auden, "O Who Can Ever Gaze His Fill?"

By the time Gavin woke up, the desert sun was already blazing down on his second-floor dorm room and in through the wide open windows. His body was covered with perspiration. He kicked back the sheet and pulled his long brown hair from underneath him and laid it on the pillow to his right. He ran a hand down his flat chest and stomach and wrapped his fingers around his erect penis. He closed his eyes against the sunshine and could see red through his eyelids, translucent as papyrus. He thought of Winston and came almost immediately, the semen puddling in his navel like a belly-dancer's jewel. He noticed that he came in greater quantity later in the day than in the morning and wondered why that was. Something about tension, he guessed.

It was too hot and too early for much, but it was too late for his first class.

He rubbed the come around his stomach and squeezed the last of it out of his balls, and then got out of the bottom bunk and stood wet and naked in the middle of the room. Now that his roommate had dropped out of school, he would have the room to himself for the reset of the semester. He looked around for a hint of what to do next. The clock gave him a clue. It read 10:31. That meant his 9:00 was over, his 10:00 already begun, and getting to 11:00 would mean going without breakfast. He would be free until poetry at 2:00.

Gavin walked into the bathroom and stepped into the shower, letting the tepid water gush over him while it heated up. He soaped away the sweat, the semen, the fatigue of the night, let the refreshing water drain through his yard-long hair, rubbed the blue soap bar over his body, drawing it hard across the tight pucker of his ass, which made him arch his back and sigh.

Downstairs in the graduate wing, Marshall looked around the dark room and wondered why he felt like a failure. He looked at Eric's bed and wondered where he'd been keeping himself. Eric hadn't been around the dorm for weeks, although he showed up in class now and then, never telling anyone where he was sleeping. Marshall wondered if he had done something to drive Eric away and let his eyes wander over the photographs he had pasted all over the cinder-block walls in Eric's absence. Almost every inch was covered with them, black and white mostly, these images he had cut out of magazines and library books—at great peril to his immortal soul, of course, but it was that important for him to possess these strangers and to surround himself with long shadows in which to live. He had painted the room first, a mute dark green, the color of a leather-bound photo album he had once prized and long ago lost. The pictures were taped neatly behind, showing no evidence of attachment and were meticulously arranged by size, shape, and content, fanning out from several thematic centers: here a writers' cluster, there a dancers' wall easing into movie stars and great stage personages of the past century.

Finding a new and wonderful photograph of, say, Emile Zola, could mean hours of rearranging. He had spent whole days, from morning to night, standing on ladders, beds, and chairs, making the juxtapositions perfect—lining up Paul Robeson's eyes with those of Hedy Lamarr, Charles Laughton with Gertrude Stein—evaluating the infinite number of possible relationships between subjects, dimensions, and shadings of emotion before affixing each picture to is new place in the pantheon of his idols. "If the three of Rudolf Nureyev from *La dame aux camélias* go on the top," he might say out loud, "then Maria Tallchief will have to move a row to the left because her attitude is the same as the Antoinette Sibley, in which case the Tony Dowell and Judith Jamison, so symmetrical, can go where Fred and Ginger were, and they can go over her to the movie stars...." He could go on for days immersed in his thousand faces, his celebrities and unknown, monumental nudes—mostly male.

He was restless this morning, but no one in his garden of faces needed tending. He hadn't finished his paper on the origins of the Chinese theater and hadn't learned all of the *Julius Caesar* monologue, but he didn't feel like studying. Maybe he would type out a poem from his handwritten version to read in class this afternoon.

He took out a sheet of blank paper and rolled it into his portable Olympic. He typed from his chicken scrawl.

> *Silence always silence;*
> *What makes it all so dread?*
> *So cold/so frightened/so all alone—*
> *when the silence moon and stars*
> *are animate in the heavens...*

Upstairs, in the hot desert silence, Gavin could hear the faint clutter of keys hitting Marshall's typewriter platen. He could hear some music somewhere, too, and tried to figure out if it was recorded or just some music students in rehearsal. Naked and wet, he looked around the room, fixing his eyes on the desk. He took it as a sign, and sat down in front of it. He drew a fine-toothed comb through his heavily conditioned, fragrant hair and looked at a piece of paper on which he had written nine words the night before.

He stared at them for a moment, the comb in one hand, an old-fashioned fountain pen in the other. He put down the comb and added a second stanza of six words to the nine that comprised the first. He smiled. It was perfect. Then he wrote his name and the date on the paper and slipped on his white muslin drawstring pants.

Marshall was typing when the door cracked open. He never locked it, but most people knocked.

"Yeah?" he said.

Gavin opened the door. "Hi," he said.

"Hi." Marshall was noncommittal, but Gavin was used to it.

"What are you doing?"

"Typing a poem. You?"

"I just finished one."

"Sit down," Marshall said, and Gavin looked around the dark room, its thick green curtains still drawn against the sun, the air conditioner purring above their heads. He sat on Eric's bed under Leonard Bernstein and Anna Magnani, their faces and arms contorted in identical attitudes of hysteria. Marshall stayed behind his desk, Tennessee Williams grinning from a large wicker chair just behind his shoulder.

"Hot," Gavin said.

"Yeah." Marshall looked into Gavin's eyes and wondered how anyone could allow such unguarded access to the inner depths.

"You wanna hear my poem?" Gavin asked. "It's short."

"Sure." Marshall decided Gavin's unchecked vulnerability was in fact safe enough, since what the eyes allowed access to was so mysterious that they revealed nothing at all.

And Gavin read the poem while Marshall paid no attention. He was too intent on the smooth curves of Gavin's torso, his legs behind thin muslin, the sculpture of his beautiful bare feet.

"I like it better than the last one," he said when Gavin's voice finished reading.

Gavin looked at him as he sat behind his desk and wondered why Marshall seemed to hide behind everything—clothes, the dark, his desk and books, words, the feelings he wrote about that Gavin, barely out of high school, felt but did not yet understand, his beard and suntan, his wavy hair and the eyeglasses he always wore: clear plastic frames with pink plastic lenses.

When Marshall looked at Gavin, he thought of sunny days on a Greek beach, Mykonos, perhaps, riding nude and barebacked together on a black Arabian, Gavin's smooth white-boy's ass pushing into his own groin.

Gavin stared at Marshall for a while and wondered why he never made a move to touch him. It was obvious Marshall was crazy about him. Gavin had no idea why, and couldn't figure it out. Men seemed to go for him, older men in particular, but Marshall wasn't that much older—five or six years, maybe. Marshall was saying nothing. He just stared.

"You want to read me your poem?" Gavin asked.

"Um, no. I'll read it in class later if I get it done. It's pretty long."

"Oh," Gavin said, not having anything else to say. "Well, I guess I'll go get something to eat. You want something?"

"No, thanks," Marshall answered too quickly, "I've got some food here."

And Gavin left, without an invitation having been tendered, closing the door softly behind him. And Marshall sat at his desk watching the door close on beauty and the white muslin draped across Gavin's perfect boy's ass, and he wished he had asked for something, anything, just so he could have eaten out of Gavin's hand.

Downstairs, Gavin pushed fully open the already-partly-open door to Winston, the Chinese puppeteer's, room.

He wasn't there.

"Where's Win?" Gavin asked.

"Not here," answered Michael, roommate, actor, and doll maker who was calling himself Max these days.

Gavin stood in the middle of the room. Max tried his best to ignore him. He was crocheting a flamingo to appliqué onto a teddy bear's bolero jacket.

Gavin sat on Winston's bed, a kind of harem couch covered with pillows and hung with hand-dyed Indian fabrics. He could smell the cloves in oranges Winston kept as natural scent. Apples with faces cut into them were drying on strings. He picked up one of the puppets.

"Winnie doesn't like people touching the puppets," Michael/Max said without looking up.

Gavin continued playing with it, one hand up the princess's feathered dress to her head, the other manipulating the two sticks that carried her expressive hands. Gavin put on a princess's voice and said: "So tell me, Max, how come you don't like Gavin?"

"I'm really kind of busy right now," Max replied, but Gavin tossed his waist-long, dark chestnut hair, whipped the princess's miniature carved hands up to her face in alarm, and persisted:

"Please, Maxie-waxie, please tell me why you don't like Gavin."

Max continued crocheting his 'mingo.

"Pretty please with sugar on it...?"

"Because...," Max managed after Gavin had already decided he wasn't going to answer.

"Because...?" the princess prompted.

Max dropped his hands into his lap and exposed his sweet moon face to Gavin's eyes. "Because you can always get what you want."

Gavin put the puppet down and dropped the princess voice. "And what do I want?" he asked. He didn't have the slightest idea what Max's answer might be, or what his own answer might be to the same question.

Max's chin started to quiver. Then he looked into Hurricane Gavin's eyes and said, "Winston...and Marshall." Then he picked up the black thread and angrily bit a length of it off with his crooked teeth.

"And what does Gavin get?" Gavin asked, amused and saddened at the same time, as he was about most things.

"Winston," Max said, threading a tiny needle without apparent effort.

There was a silence while Max tied a knot in the end of the thread. "And Marshall," he continued, concentrating on his work.

"And what do you want, Max?" Gavin asked, genuinely curious.

Max was sewing a minuscule black jet of an eye onto the flamingo's head. He put in a stitch and looked up. "Same as you, Gavin. Only you get it. Because you're beautiful. And I'm not."

"You think I'm beautiful?" Gavin asked. He had no idea what beauty was, and no sense of his own except the reactions of others.

"Everyone thinks you're beautiful, Gavin."

"Winston?"

"Winston does not sleep with people he doesn't think are beautiful."

"Marshall?"

"Him most of all."

"You think Marshall wants to sleep with me because I'm beautiful?"

"Christ, Gavin! Yes. Yes, I do. Can't you tell? I can tell. He *told* Winston."

"Marshall's slept with you," Gavin said.

"Once. It took ten minutes, and there was somebody else in the room."

"Don't you think he finds you beautiful?"

"No, I don't."

"The first time I had sex with Winston was in the back of a van."

"I know. I was there. I kept watching Marshall watching you and wanting you because you're so fucking beautiful."

"Marshall thinks everything is beautiful," Gavin said.

Max stared at him.

"Except himself," Gavin corrected.

Then he got up and walked toward the door.

"Oh," Gavin said before he closed the door on Max's doll

making. "I never get what I want. Because I don't want anything. Nothing. I don't care."

Max didn't know what to make of Gavin.

"And, Max," Gavin said, "I've never slept with Marshall."

Then Gavin closed the door and tossed his mane of hair and wondered what everyone was also so upset about.

4. NOON

(On waking, the father finds his heir engaged in immoral congress with the sun)

> *And the scene on my helmet tells the true story: a chariot, eight*
> *naked boys, wingèd ones,*
> *and the wine, the mirror, the parasol—my triumph*
> *inherits me. He holds my sword. He is what I see,*
> *that is why you see him: the naked boy without wings.*
> —Richard Howard, "The Giant on Giant-Killing"

It was noon on the fifteenth anniversary of his son's birth, in the fourth year of their captivity, when Daedalus opened his feebling eyes and saw the child of his old age standing stark naked in the window of their tower prison.

"What in the name of the gods are you doing?" old Daedalus grumbled as he unhinged himself from a sleeping position.

"Looking for Apollo," the boy said. "He's right overhead, and I can't see him unless I stand like this."

"Well, be careful," the old man warned. "I don't want you falling out the window." But the fact of the matter was that the old man was proud of the boy, and quite surprised that the little one had taken up his ancestors' religion so earnestly. He had shown no such predilection as a child.

The boy's hair was long now, long and golden, as his mother's had been in her youth. Daedalus thought of his dead wife and was grateful that she had not lived to see the ignominy of his incarceration. How proud she had been of the honors heaped upon her ancient husband when he laid the last brick of the labyrinth, King Minos's crowning glory and deadly lair of the bull/man Minotaur. And how sensitive she was; she could not even watch the spring ceremony when seven Athenian youths and seven Athenian maidens were tossed to the Minotaur for sacrifice...but that was how it all began, and Daedalus could not bear going over it again.

How he hated this stupid little room in its ridiculous tower, its dangerously gaping window nearly daring them to plunge from it to their own destruction. Daedalus sat at his table and looked at the books he knew now by heart. They had not suggested any way of escape. Nor had they suggested a convenient path to greater patience or acceptance. He did not want to rot here watching this fine young strip of a son growing old and useless before his eyes, his all-too-rapidly-diminishing eyes. Daedalus scraped the candle wax off an old tome of Egyptian alchemy and rolled it into a ball. He tossed the ball onto the floor. It rolled into the corner where Icarus kept his pile of feathers. Well, collecting feathers was a harmless enough occupation, Daedalus thought. Daedalus passed on to the boy what he knew of each species' habits, and the boy listened with rapt attention, constantly wanting to know the patterns of flight—did they soar or glide, take off from a standstill or a run, land on ground or water? Yes, thanks be to the gods, the boy was finally showing an admirably agile mind about some things, in any event, though he seemed a bit touched in the head sometimes, too.

Daedalus looked up and saw his naked son standing spread-eagled in the window, the sun blazing white on his long yellow curls, burnished copper on the shoulders the child had built up lifting books over his head. Daedalus was sorry to have mixed his son up in his own hubristic plot to outwit Minos, but the king was notoriously unjust, even for a barbarian, which he surely was, and would probably have destroyed both of them on the spot if the boy had not been so patently innocent and Daedalus himself so well known and so highly respected. The aged architect rose slowly and shuffled nearer to the window, a bit off to the side of the boy, where he could see quite clearly that Icarus, head back, basking in the sun, was fully adult and fully erect, his manly rod jutting straight out from a shock of golden hair.

"Come down off there like that," Daedalus croaked, but Icarus just rolled his head back and forth behind him, trailing his long woman's hair down his tan muscled back. "The soldiers will be having a fine time looking at you like that," Daedalus nagged, but Icarus stood there holding the window frame until his knees began to sag and his arms began to contract, and the hot fluid of his sex spurted like lava out the window toward the ground. Daedalus was amazed at the volume of it, and that the boy could carry it off without even touching himself, but he was more than a little annoyed when he heard the cheers of the guards below.

Daedalus strode to the window, grabbed the boy around the waist, and, surprisingly strong when he needed to be, dropped his son to the floor. Then he leaned out the window and glared down at the soldiers below. A small knot of them was standing under the window licking the boy's liquid off each other, manipulating their own and each other's organs. Daedalus was furious. "Get away from there!" he sputtered, but the soldiers just laughed at him and pointed. He shook his fist, but they laughed the heartier. Beside himself, Daedalus lifted up his robe, pulled out his own ancient, sagging member, and let loose a jet of piss. The soldiers howled curses at him and scattered like birds from a stone hurled into their midst.

Daedalus pulled himself back into the room, where Icarus was sitting in the corner braiding feathers into his hair, singing under his breath. The sun glistened off the moisture of his new moustache. He was a beauty; no doubt about it.

Perhaps, Daedalus thought, we could lure one of the guards up here on a sexual premise—Hemner seemed to favor the boy—then knock him senseless and get out of the tower. That this was considerably dangerous did not cross the old man's mind. What did was that being on the ground among the other soldiers would put them no closer to freedom. It might, however, turn them both into the whores of the camp. The prospect was too odious for the risk. He would never turn his son over to apprentice for a soldier. No, a strong and healthy body such as Icarus quite clearly boasted was important only as the temple of a quick and agile mind, a tenuous quality in his son, though Daedalus was not going to give up nourishing it without a fight.

It had been the diligent father's plan, before the catastrophe, to present the boy to a statesman, a philosopher, teacher, or mathematician. These men were gentler with their young lovers and taught them disciplines that would serve the boys all their lives—not battle skills, but the skills of the mind—those smiled on by Apollo. But now there was no one but himself to teach the boy, and so his education would, of necessity, be incomplete, incest being out of the question, at least in Daedalus's mind.

The old ponderer sat again at his books and watched Icarus, who was at the moment sitting cross-legged, exposing the soles of his dirty feet, moving a cormorant feather back and forth in the air with one delicate hand and wiggling the long, tapered finger of the other.

"What are you doing?" Daedalus asked.

"Playing the lyre," Icarus answered.

"What lyre is that?" Daedalus asked.

"Yes," Icarus sighed, "he said you wouldn't be able to see it. Only those he has chosen can see it."

Well, Daedalus thought, it was inevitable. If he himself had been imprisoned at the boy's age, he would be somewhat out off his head, too. But, being a doting parent old enough to be his son's grandfather, he gave in to the caprice: "*Who* said?"

"Apollo," Icarus replied, as if the answer were the most obvious thing in the world, as if the name were the most precious in the world.

"Apollo speaks to you?" Daedalus asked. This was bad.

"Of course he speaks. He sings, he teaches me to play the lyre. The strings are made of his hair, you know…that's why I have to use a feather. They're so delicate even a virgin's fingers would snap them. He says only the chosen may play the lyre of Apollo."

Daedalus was becoming concerned. "And what else does he say?"

"That I am the most beautiful of all mortal boys. That Ganymede has raged jealously against my beauty to all the gods of Olympus. That Zeus and Hera have fought openly…about me. But that Apollo has claimed the right to be my…protector."

He certainly is a coy child, Daedalus thought. "Icarus—," he began.

"He says he has never before seen such beauty as mine—eyes

that pour my soul into his like rain into the holy vessels of Delphi. He says my neck is the perfection of his temple. When he puts his mouth on my neck, I can feel the wind of the south on his breath. When his mouth is on my nipples, I shiver as though the wind of the north has slid down my back through my hair. And when he puts his mouth on my sex, I feel the center of a vortex in my heart, and my love for him pours out of me. And the warmth of him dries me as he pauses just at noon above the tower. He can't stay, but he watches over his shoulder at me as he drives his chariot away. He calls me sacred and says my flesh is softer than a god's, my fluid in his mouth sweet as nectar. I love to feel the thistle of his beard between my legs and his tongue…his tongue— He is so gentle, Father, like no man I have ever seen."

"Er, yes…," Daedalus managed to say, staring for a moment into the open sky-blue eyes of his youngest son. "Very…poetic."

Icarus smiled and continued to play his invisible instrument.

Daedalus went back to his workbench and remembered his teacher, Akmanadoros, who had taken him from his own father many years before. And suddenly Akmanadoros came to him in a small gust of warm wind and played with the old man's cheek the way he had done when Daedalus was merely a curious and not altogether conscientious schoolboy.

And Daedalus watched as Icarus in his corner began to work several owl feathers into the ball of candle wax he had found. Daedalus watched as his enterprising son flattened the wax in the palm of his hand and began to layer feather upon feather into the wax, weaving strands of his hair between the stems like golden thread.

"What are you making, my son?" Daedalus asked cautiously.

"A fan," Icarus answered, "a gift for my lover to cool his face as he races the course of the sun…a fan in the shape of a bird's wing—because my lover's freedom is his flight."

Daedalus looked at the small wing Icarus had fashioned from wax, feathers, and hair. Then he stood and went to the window and watched the sea birds soar and glide and dive down over the shore. And Daedalus remembered his own voice saying: "Minos may control the sea and land, but the sky is free."

And Daedalus had an idea.

5. DAY

(After poetry...passion or the apocalypse)

> *The beauty I saw in him was a cross between Marilyn Monroe and shade.*   —Dennis Cooper, "Boys I've Wanted"

Marshall stood in the window watching the red glow and black smoke of the hill fires that had been raging for weeks. They looked like news films he had seen from hills overlooking the Vietnamese terrain, blazing with war and hatred, napalm, ignorance, futility.

The school was out of danger for now, which is to say it was not in danger *yet*, but everyone had been instructed to pack one *small* suitcase in case the college had to be evacuated on sudden notice. Marshall had packed the pictures. All of them. The room looked like a tenement deserted before demolition. Hunks of tape hung from the wall, some with corners of pictures still clinging to them. In some places patches of the green paint had come off on the tape and left scars on the wall where white showed through. Well, he thought, if this dump doesn't burn down, I'm going to have a hell of a time cleaning up.

The red sky in the middle of the day gave an eerie look of sunset to the scrub-covered landscape. The black smoke from the fire and the white steam from the water pumped onto it from helicopters and airplanes swirled together in the sky, forming a bank of gray clouds over the mountains that included every shade from snow to coal. He wondered whether a nuclear holocaust would be similar or different.

Gavin had been breathtaking in class. Marshall's own poem had been only modestly received, if immodestly delivered; he was that sure of himself. Kramer said he thought it was "outstanding"—that was true—but Kramer was a jerk. Gavin had nodded sagely and, without saying a thing, let it be known that he approved. But Dr. Paulson thought it...overlong and perhaps a bit repetitious, even though the repetitions had been intentional, a way of invoking the incantatory quality of Paulson's own poetry, of his wildly rhythmic *Bacchae* translation. One woman couldn't understand why his poetry was so sad and so intense all the time. "No one's life could be *that* bad," she snorted through an enormous nose, as if in twenty years she had never encountered pain. "Mine is," Gavin had said as simple as the Last Judgment, offering no further explication or assurance.

Dr. Paulson loved Gavin's new poem, although Marshall had not heard a word of it because he could not keep his mind and eyes off the poet. It was a poem he did not really understand. If he were being honest about it, which he would not be, at least not aloud, he thought the poem had too little in it to be much of anything, too few words that spoke to the soul. What was it Paulson had said? Oh, yes: "Simplicity speaks to the soul." But Marshall had no soul, at least none that he could identify, and so he envied Gavin's words that sank into his thorax liked barbed weapons even when they made no sense to his mind.

Marshall looked at the fire blazing over the hills, looked at the parched desert landscape, and rubbed a hand across a forehead, drawing a fine layer of silt across his furrows. He looked at the blank space near his desk where the picture of Picasso had hung and announced to its ghost: "I'm going for a walk."

There wasn't much place to walk, at least not on campus. There wasn't much place to do anything. If he strolled the perimeter of the college, all the paths and every hall, stopping at the cafeteria and the main gallery, it might take an hour. Just beyond the school grounds was the freeway, cutting through the gap in the mountains like an escape chute, providing access to automobiles and automobile exhaust, city smog, and, all too possibly, a monstrous fire raging out of control just behind the southern ridge. If the evacuation order came, the exodus would be toward the cool green hills of the north.

All over the county hot cinders borne on desert winds had set off satellite fires, and the pessimistic evaluation was that millions of acres and several billion dollars' worth of real estate could be gone within hours if there were not some break in the weather—hot, dry, windy. The glow over the mountain seemed to heat the valley by degrees.

When Marshall turned his back on the impending conflagration, he saw Gavin, sitting on the roof outside his window. He was naked except for minuscule shorts and his voluminous hair.

Marshall looked up and felt envy and lust, realizing he probably managed to commit all seven of the deadly sins on a daily basis. Gavin waved and shouted.

As they sat on the roof, watching the glow of fire, Marshall could not keep his eyes off Gavin's lap, where his balls had slipped out of the loose legs of his nylon shorts.

"How old are you?" he asked Gavin.

"Eighteen. Why?"

"Just wondering."

Seven years, Marshall thought. Seven years. Could Gavin possibly be as immune to life seven years from now as Marshall already felt himself to be, so bitter, so entrenched and lonely? And what would they each be like in seven more years? Would there even be seven more years?

Gavin turned his eyes on Marshall, and Marshall sensed a rush of Gavin crawling up the hair of his thighs, could feel himself engorging.

"I liked your poem in class," Marshall said.

"I liked yours, too," Gavin responded and shook his hair like a horse in a good temper. Some of the long hairs stuck to his hot wet chest and curled around a dark nipple. A small gust blew a good strand of it into his mouth. He spit it out, then pulled off the hairs that remained stuck to his face with saliva. He'd done it before. With his eyes closed.

"What are you going to do when you get out of school?" Marshall asked, embarrassed by his own banality and not caring at all what was going to happen any further into the future than the next hour. After all, hadn't he already decided that he had reached the point of no more meaningful experience? From now on all the rest was decline and speculation, reflection and reinvention. Isn't that what he had decided one night in contemplation of his human photo menagerie?

"I don't know," Gavin said. "Go to San Francisco."

"What'll you do?"

Gavin shrugged silently. "Live off some old broad. That's what I did last summer." He turned back and dropped his eyes into Marshall's eyes. "Or maybe some old guy."

"It's hot," Marshall said.
"We could go in and cool off."

They climbed back through the window. Gavin slid the glass window shut, drew the curtains closed, and turned on the air conditioner. The room was immediately cooler. And more isolated. Gavin smiled into his dimples and nodded. Then he walked to a mirror, sat down, and took a brush to his hair.

"Let me do that," Marshall said. And he took the long, silky hair with the sun-red highlights and brushed it.

"Should I do it a hundred times?" he asked, not seriously.

"Do it as much as you want," Gavin said. "It feels great."

By the time they were both tired of the brushing, Marshall was hard in his jeans. Gavin stood and walked to the bed.

"I think I'll lie down for a while," he said, looking at Marshall.

Marshall walked closer, then looked as deep as he could into the ambiguous vacuum of Gavin's black eyes. He waited for some sign; none came that he could decipher. He put his hand up to Gavin's face and touched a cheek, touched his hair.

"So beautiful," he said.

Gavin leaned his head into the hand, then tossed his hair once and turned his back.

Marshall put his hand on the crown of Gavin's head and drew it down the length of his hair to its ends, letting it settle in a friendly way on the black nylon of Gavin's narrow hips. He leaned in toward the perfect boy poet of his imagination and kissed him chastely on the shoulder. He smelled of skin.

"I think I'll go lie down, too," Marshall said.

Gavin never forced anyone to do anything they didn't want to do. He was not yet clear about the mechanics of secret desire—not only because he wanted nothing himself, but because it was only beginning to dawn on him that other people did not do exactly as they pleased.

"Oh," he said, surprised. "Okay. 'Bye."

Marshall knew the decisive moment had come, and he hated himself for letting it pass, when the slightest gesture would have meant fulfillment. It was one thing to fall for someone who couldn't love you back; he was an old hand at unrequited love and lust. It was another not to reach out and take what was offered so clearly. It meant his loneliness was more important to him than love, or at least more necessary. Was it better, somehow, was it even *noble*, to abstain from sex when the bruised heart was so confused it could not tell infatuation from appetite or romance? And what was suddenly so wrong with sex for its own sake? He'd had sex with a dozen men without any agony at all—beautiful, muscled men: dancers, gymnasts—men whose bodies could have validated his own desirability as easily as Gavin's willing embrace, if he had given them as much power, if their lack of interest could have crushed him as completely as Gavin's rejecting him would have. Why was everything so complicated, so difficult for him? And what did any of it matter?

"See you later," he said, and turned his back on all the possibilities of his mind.

Gavin pushed fully open the already-partly-open door to Winston, the Chinese puppeteer's, room. It was dark. There was incense burning in a small bronze burner shaped like a heron. In front of the window was an enormous packed suitcase with Winston's puppets in it, but the room was empty. Gavin turned to go as Winston stepped into the room from his bathroom with a small red towel around his middle. His indigo hair was a mass of curls that relaxed almost as far down his back as Gavin's straighter, lighter mane.

"Hi," Winston said, his face lighting up like a Renaissance woodblock sun.

"Hi," Gavin said.

Winston unwrapped the red towel and stood naked. He walked up to Gavin, close enough to feel the heat, inclined his head slightly to one side, and kissed him. He was already hard as he took Gavin's hand gently and walked toward the bed. Winston sat down and looked through obsidian eyes into the perplexed expression on the face of his occasional lover. He pulled the thin black nylon shorts off Gavin's hips and put his mouth around his cock.

Gavin sighed and stepped out of the shorts. Winston sank back into his dozen pillows and pulled his right knee to the side as an invitation. Gavin took a long look at Winston, beautiful by any standard, and felt his desire drain out of him. He wanted Marshall, and no substitute, even one as lovely as Winston, could ease that thought from his mind.

"Um… I guess I'm not in the mood," he said.

Winston sat up and leaned forward to take Gavin's hand, a look of panicked failure filling his eyes.

"I can't right now," Gavin said, "that's all. I'm sorry, okay?"

Marshall closed the drapes, turned on the cold air, and looked at the empty damaged walls where his pictures had hung so neatly, and he wondered where Eric was these days. Then he stripped off his closes and stretched out on the cool green cover of his narrow bed.

He closed his eyes and tried to picture himself holding Gavin naked in his arms, as he had pictured them together so many times before. He could see himself taking that face with those equine eyes into his hands and holding the face still and leaning into it and putting his mouth on Gavin's mouth, could feel his tongue touch the slight opening between the two fleshy lips of the younger poet, could feel the jawbones of the poet press into his palms. And he could feel his hands sliding down the small chest and sculpted torso of this North Carolina teenager and slipping them under the waistband of the thin black nylon shorts—

There was a loud knock on the door that echoed in Marshall's solar plexus. Was it the evacuation order? He held his breath, but didn't answer.

"Marshall, it's Max. Are you in there?"

He didn't answer.

"Shit," he heard from the other side of the door. Then silence.

He closed his eyes again and tried to pick up his fantasy where it had been interrupted but found he had to start again from the beginning: the face in his hand, the hands sliding down over the skin, smooth as chamois…

But the third dimension had gone out of it. No longer a wish to be fulfilled, it read to his own mind like a mediocre script he had read once before without liking it much the first time.

| *The Hard Way* |

He grabbed his cock and jerked off fast and hard, thinking of the soft, pained question of Gavin's face when he left him standing alone in his room. Marshall hated himself for his cowardice, hated his body and his desire and those who desired him, and he came in gushing spurts, the come hitting him in the face, in his hair and eyes. There had never been so much of it.

In the accumulating silence, he could hear the hum of the air conditioner. Then a door slammed somewhere, a voice was raised, and another door hit its frame too hard. Then he dozed off and dreamed of nothing he could remember.

When he woke up, it was raining.

6. AFTERNOON
("And yet for all his wings, the fowl was drowned")

Give me the splendid silent sun, with all his beams full-dazzling!
—Walt Whitman, *Leaves of Grass*

It was the summer of the fifth year of our captivity, and I was bored with the project my father had been working on for nearly a year. It was in the afternoon, I remember, and old Daedalus was saying we might make our flight that very day if I would condescend to help him. I had helped him—for months!—but right that minute I was restless, *preoccupied* I guess the word should be. I stepped up into the window ledge and let the hot breath of the air surround me. My hair was past my waist now, golden yellow and twined with all the smaller feathers we had gathered, the ones Daedalus said were too small for his use. I had fashioned a necklace of falcon feathers and a wristlet of raven. My beard had grown in gold and red. Father trimmed it with a sharpened stone. I was tanned darker than Hemner's horse, and I could tell from the way he looked up at me that Hemner would have loved the chance to ride me the way he rode that stallion he was so proud of. And I might have let him, were I not faithful to Apollo—and enjoyed it, too.

I was standing in the window, I remember, my hands above my head, feet together, one knee bent. I felt as if I might dive upward into the sky. I dropped my arms slowly, as gracefully as I remembered the bull dancers doing in the years before our captivity. I wondered what my cousin Perdix might be doing at home. Learning masonry, in all likelihood. It's what he always wanted, to build and make things, like my father. I never had much aptitude for the sort of thing he reveled in. Daedalus always liked him, although I think my father might have been a little embarrassed to have such a bright child around, one who outshone me—that's for certain—particularly in those areas that meant so much to the old man, for Perdix has a quick and agile mind. But Perdix is not beautiful. Perdix was not chosen by Apollo, cannot sing as I can sing, play as my lover has taught me to play, write the lyrics and the odes I compose nearly extempore.

Poetry drives my father mad. He calls it immoral, artificial, deceitful, wasteful, a *caprice*—as if a labyrinth so complex that no one can find his way out of it was not capricious.

I smile and say, "Of course—that's just the point."

He sputters and glowers and drives back into his wing-making. Oh, yes, Daedalus is making wings for us both. He got the idea from me, he says, though I can't think how; and he's convinced, based on his endless calculations, that he can construct wings strong enough to carry us out of this foul place, though where we'd go I have no idea. Certainly not back to Crete, where Minos would have us shot down like to many terns for his supper.

I told him I'd fly if he did. After all, if the wings work, we'll be free. If they don't...well, Hemner will catch me. I know he will.

It's taken ten months nearly to the day to get as far as we've gotten—Father's kept a record of our time here, which, of course, he will have to leave behind. He's finished three of the wings already, made them out of feathers, candle wax, strands of my hair and his beard, and threads from carefully unraveling my garments. I never need them anymore. Apollo prefers me naked. Just as I prefer him. Of his own cloak, Father has made strips of cloth with which he intends to fasten the wings to our shoulders and arms. It could work. After all, he was reputed to be a genius in his day. It's hard to see what Mother saw in him, though she told me once he was ravishingly beautiful and that she envied

Akmanadoros my father's youth. It seems odd that my father's lover was a mere mortal when mine is a god. Just as it seems odd he would leave his lover for a woman, even one as level-tempered as my mother was. I would miss her terribly if it weren't for Apollo and his daily visits—and the way he bows down and worships me.

"Icarus!"

"Yes, Father?"

"You're preening like a peacock. Come down from there. The proud are often brought low. Do not forget...moderation in all things."

"Oh, Father, moderation is for mortals."

"And you are not mortal, then?"

"Yes, for now. But Apollo promises me immortality, which means I shall someday be a god, doesn't it? I will be very happy to be a god and live eternally. I've even asked to retain my youth. He agreed."

"Exactly what did Apollo say?"

"He said that in generations to come—in eons to come, thousands and thousands of years from now—I will be known as the youth who found immortality in the love of Apollo."

"Well, your Apollo is certainly a fine wordsmith."

"I thought you didn't believe in Apollo."

"Of course I believe in Apollo. I just do not believe that you are his lover, pretty as you may be, or that he comes to you every day in the beams of the sun and all of that, or that he's taught you all you know."

"How else have I learned it then, Father?"

"You always were a dreamer. Perhaps it's inborn. Your mother always said that an artistic temperament was an inborn thing. But be careful, my son. The words of the gods are not always what they seem."

"Are you nearly finished?"

"Yes, come here and let me tie these on your arms."

Daedalus tried to look at his son for the last time. "Remember," he said, "you must fly directly away from the setting sun. Do not fly too near the water or the wax will become too hard and the feathers will fall out. Do not fly too high or the heat of the sun will melt the wax and the feathers will fall out. Do you have the courage?"

"Of course," Icarus replied. And Daedalus embraced his son for the last time, placed one kiss on each cheek, stepped up to the window, and dove out into the air, plummeting nearly to the ground before he caught the first updraft.

"Come, Icarus, follow me," he heard his father shout, and outside on the ground there was chaos as the soldiers ran in all directions at once at the sight of the old captive soaring above them on the giant wings of an albatross.

Icarus stood in his window and watched his father glide. He was so absorbed in Daedalus's comical attempt to master flight that he almost did not hear the door of the cell open. Just as he turned to face the scraping sound, Hemner stormed into the room naked and aroused.

"Do not go, Icarus," Hemner said. "I am your slave. I must have you."

I smiled as gently as I could, for I actually had quite an affection for Hemner and that hard body of his encased in coiled black hair. And although we'd never even touched, the sight of him in high blood convinced me I couldn't have held out much longer. After all, I was only human.

"Hemner," I said, "I am the lover of another, of Apollo, the sun."

I could hear my father calling me from outside, over and over again. My name in his throat sounded like the cackling of crows. I stared deep into Hemner's eyes, which were, I had never before noticed, as green as the sea in summer and deep in pain knowing he would never hold me in his arms. I might have dawdled a bit longer, but Hemner made a lunge for me—quite understandable, given his long-unsated lust—and I had to jump just to get out of the way.

The feeling was miraculous. It was as liberating as the pony races Perdix and I had along the shore as boys, the cool ocean breeze whipping our boyish hair. The strain on my arms was wonderful as I managed to float on air currents over the sea.

The Hard Way

The cool wind on my face was as welcome as the warmth of morning. The sensation of absolute power in my loins made my head light as spent passion.

"Not too high and not too low," my father caw-cawed at me from over the waves. "Follow me!"

I watched him for a moment, ever the dutiful son, and traced the arc of a graceful tern over the breakers. I watched him and the astonished affection in his prunish face. Then I shouted, "Farewell, my good father, and may the gods of your enterprise speed you to safety. Apollo waits!"

And I turned and set my sights on the muscled back of my lover as his sun chariot raced across the sky. "Come, Icarus," I longed for him to say, "Come and find eternal youth in my embrace."

I heard nothing. But my heart smiled because of the love I felt for him and the surge I felt in my loins. I started upward after him.

I heard him calling my name, but I pretended not to. I found his insolence more than a little overbearing. When I finally turned around to get a look at him, he was flapping his absurd little wings like a lunatic. He had the most pathetic look of determination on his face, which was dripping with sweat, his hair sticking to it and to his neck and chest, shoulders and back. In fact, his wet hair was clinging all over him. He looked like Aphrodite rising from the foam. He was dripping feathers, too, which reeked and came unwound from the many plaits he had woven into what I must say myself was quite an ingenious design.

Well, it was near the end of the day, and I thought no one would notice if I just stopped and hovered over the horizon for a moment before sinking into the night. When he finally reached me, he slowed to a near stop, using his wings like the fins of a fish to hold himself steady.

"Didn't you hear me?" he demanded. He might have tried a humbler approach, at least for openers.

"Yes," I said. "I heard you."

"Then why didn't you come to me?"

"My dear young friend," I said, every inch the indignant master, "it is for you to come to me. When have you ever heard it said that the sun reversed itself in its course to accommodate a pigeon?"

He looked hurt. I had succeeded.

Oh, he was a beauty, all right. One of the prettiest little men in Greece. Of course, he was much prettier two years ago, when I first noticed him standing in that window shaking his tight hips at me, luring me with the twin knobs of his pelvis and that sparse soft hair just beginning to sprout like moss. That was before he started all the nonsense with the chicken feathers. Yes, he was, in his day, the prettiest boy in southern Crete. But he was not the first, and I had no intention of his being the last. There were others even during the time I was visiting him. He was special, it's true, and perhaps I did lead him on mercilessly, but none of the others took it so seriously. And I went out of my way to tell him that Hemner would make a fine lover in my stead.

It flattered me that Icarus wanted to be faithful. But I knew it was because he had not seen enough mortal men to make a reasoned comparison. He should have gone with Hemner and forgotten about me. After all, I am a god. He wanted to be immortal (they all do), but only Zeus can do that. When I suggested it, my father nearly roared the pillars of heaven down. "Just what I need," the old man cried. "What do you think my life with Ganymede would be like with another adorable adolescent traipsing around for the rest of time, not to mention Hera with that temper of hers."

Yes, Icarus had chosen badly by choosing me. Like Zeus, I have an eye for young men. And for women, too, as far as that goes. He should have flown off to Sicily with his father. Italians are obsessed with feathers.

"Well," he said petulantly, "you could at least have waited." The gentle thunder in the distance was Zeus laughing and warning at the same time.

"My dear Icarus," I said, "gods do not wait for small boys with feathers glued to their arms."

The look on his face told me he had just learned a lesson all mortals learn sooner or later, a lesson so fundamental that they try to protect one another from it.

"You said I would be immortal."

"Well," I said, "strictly speaking, I said your reputation would last forever."

"And that I would stay young forever."

"Yes," I said as gently as I could without, I hoped, giving in to sentiment. "Those who die in youth shall remain forever young."

"But I *love* you," he said as sadly as I'd ever heard it said before—or since, for that matter.

I was going to suggest he turn tail and flap off to his father—or at least to Hemner—when a look of coy serenity came over his face.

"What is it?" I asked, thinking he was up to something.

"Nothing," he said. "Nothing at all."

And then he reached both arms gracefully over his head, letting his feet dangle before him. The position displayed him at his fullest length, his skin pulled tight across his trunk, his belly hollowed between his ribs and hips, his organ filling with blood. Oh, it was an appealing attitude, make no mistake. And I was sorely tempted. But then he looked into my eyes with those gorgeous orbs of his like lacquered robins' eggs, and he smiled. I was stiffening rapidly myself, he looked so extremely vulnerable and at the same time voluptuous beyond endurance. He looked as if he could dive upward to Olympus on his own power.

I heard a louder groan of thunder, which undoubtedly meant that Zeus was calling for some paramour to relieve his excitement.

"Don't you want me anymore?" Icarus asked.

By now I was in a state of great agitation, and I did want him—more than I had ever wanted him or any mortal before him.

"Yes," I said, "I do want you."

Then he bent his knees ever so slightly and rotated them outward just enough so that I could see the sack under his hard sex tighten with his own pleasure.

"Then come to me," he said.

I knew I shouldn't, but I could not help myself. A louder roar of thunder was Zeus's anger or pleasure—I could not tell one from the other. I tied the reins to the chariot and dropped my tunic, standing naked before him in all my glory. He arched his back, rolling his shoulders and pushing his hips forward slightly.

I stepped from the chariot to approach him as he broke into a broad, childish grin. I reached out to grab him around the tender middle when he slipped out of his wings and, laughing giddily, dropped like a pelican into the ocean, never to be seen again.

I knew the sky-splitting thunder was Zeus's wrath at having lost the boy to his brother, the sea. And although both Zeus and I begged Poseidon for his return, the King of the Ocean was adamant. And quite, quite sated, I am sure.

Daedalus watched with horror as his son flew higher and higher toward the sun to disaster, the disaster that was certain to follow so foolish a prank. What was the boy thinking of? Had he not warned him again and again of the danger of melting wax? He watched until he could no longer see his son in the glare of the sun.

He could see Hemner on shore. The handsome captain held a hand over his eyes to shield them, staring into the sun. Suddenly Hemner let out a moan, and Daedalus looked up to see the boy plummeting into the liquid arms of the sea.

And Daedalus knew that Icarus was drowned by his own device and had met his fate because they had both been guilty of striving beyond mortal propriety.

And Daedalus wept, as he flew alone toward Sicily, but in his weeping the order of the gods was confirmed in his mind.

7. SUNSET
(The blind poet returns to Los Angeles)

Looking back I think he must have been an angel.
—David Trinidad, *Pavane*

Yes, there is Gavin dancing at Studio One, all the hair off his head and all the magic drained out of him except for the pomegranate mouth and wellspring eyes—still dark, as rich with their inscrutable vulnerability—that pained look of never knowing what will hurt, or who, or for how long.

He smiles and waves and looks at me after all these years as if we shared lunch just yesterday, not seven years ago in another world and time. He waves as if he is glad to see me, his gestures the stage directions for an unwritten play.

He dances in Levi's, shirtless, like a hundred or so others, identical. All the muscle must have come from so much flying so close to the sun. Dark hair sprouts between the mounds of his hard and handsome premeditated flesh.

I watch him from behind a beer. I think: Here is Gavin again like the moon through barbed wire.

He waves again, bent at the middle, dancing to the floor, his partner his double.

It was the year a planeload of undocumented farm workers slammed into a mountain in Mexico and set the valley on fire. It was the year the December sunsets over Santa Monica were so extraordinary from the towers of Century City. I had already been back in town—what?—four years after a three-year absence?

And here is Gavin again, as he had been in San Francisco when I walked down the street and saw his picture on a pornhouse wall. And went into the dark and musty place and watched with longing as Gavin engaged in a series of encounters that paled beside my own past fantasies. I watched the engorging of organs, tongues in mouths, sweat sliding between tumescent nipples, and thought of his white boy back and loose geisha hair and bareback ponies on the Aegean shore, my hand floating over the concave curve of his boy back, hovering.

I sat in the mildewed darkness with my hand through the open fly of my jeans and watched a black man on the screen put his cock up Gavin's lubricated ass. I clutched my own cock and felt the heat rising in my ears. I turned my head in the dark and saw the yearning eyes of a boy who had moved closer to me twice. I buttoned one button of my jeans and walked past him, nearly rubbing my crotch in his face as I went by.

I stood in the lobby and watched as he came out of the auditorium. He was older than I had been in the early Gavin days— older than I thought in the dark—and was wearing a red sweater. Our eyes locked and the boy/man walked into the ladies' room, the only bathroom that had not been boarded up by the management. I followed. There were two men combing their hair at each other in a large, smudged mirror. The kid—I wanted and needed him to be a *kid*—was just disappearing into the last stall. I followed, stood outside the booth, its door partly open, then pushed it open all the way.

He was sitting on the porcelain stool with his red sweater pulled off and his pants down at his ankles. He held his dick in his hand. I turned and looked at the two men in the mirror. They brought their glances around to mine and started walking in my direction. I stepped inside the stall with my heart pounding the way it was when I almost touched Gavin. I slid the small chrome bolt into its caddy and moved between the kid's knees. He looked up through long eyelashes and, without saying a word, pulled my belt open. He pulled my jeans down off my hips and let out a flattering sigh at the sight of my stiff prick and the thick blond hair of my thighs. He took me in his mouth and massaged my ass while I pinched his right nipple with the tongue-moistened fingers of my right hand and held a handful of his hair in my left.

And I felt the warm wet abyss of this gray-eyed no-name close on my cock, and I pushed my hips into and out of his kindly stranger's face, shutting my eyes and thinking of the perfection of Gavin and his pony hair, his unshy mouth and lubricated ass filled with a stranger's cock. And I pulled the boy/man to his feet and turned him around and bent him over the bowl so his hands were flat against the cold white tile of the back wall. Then I slipped my saliva-slickened cock into his smooth hot ass without effort and thought about my hand hovering above the warmth of Gavin's waist, afraid to touch him.

And I walked my fingers up the knobs of the nameless red sweater's spine and grabbed his hips and thrust a little harder and deeper and faster than I might have, because I no longer saw beauty as unattainable. I no longer saw beauty at all. And I came so hard and so far into this small stranger, who no longer wore a red sweater, or anything at all, that I could feel the muscles of his abdomen clench, could feel the muscles of his asshole holding onto me for dear life, the same as my heart muscle clenched as I walked from Gavin's dorm room so many years ago without having tasted his body and its boy-sweet fluids.

| *The Hard Way* |

And now here is Gavin again, dancing. Gavin like the moon through the barbed wire of Dachau, Gavin seeming to be glad to see me while he dances for the floor.

What year was it, exactly?

The year of the electrical storms and lightning, the fireballs ravaging Kansas, the solar eclipse that lasted three days, sinking the world into a pink miasma of fear. It was the year of the explosions in Pennsylvania, the Canadian meteor showers, Indiana mine disasters, the sub-Saharan drought, the chemical fires that raged for four days in Texas, gas fires in Missouri, oil fires in the hulls of ships at sea, the volcanic eruption in Colombia, the burning of Atlanta and Hanoi, the bombing of Cambodia, the annihilation of Nagasaki, and the drowning of Atlantis, lost continent of philosophers' dreams.

Because all those years were all of him: so far, so much an eyeful, so willingly available had I but known, so much a Gavin in an eye like a hollow. How much I could have loved him, poet and alone.

Negative Image

The city had been beastly—hot and humid, the way it always is in New York in August. You could feel the fever of the pavement come up at your feet through the soles of your shoes. Racial tension was running high, as usual, but everyone was equally miserable, complaining ad nauseam about the relentless tropical weather and saying how it wasn't the heat but the humidity that made summers so unbearable. I thought if I heard one more person drop that irritating cliché into a conversation with a stranger, I'd have to kill them both. I understood why the murder rate soared with the temperature.

I'd gone up to Times Square to see if I could snag a seat in an air-conditioned theater at the half-price TKTS booth, but I was too early to get on line and had to waste some time. I was watching a group of German tourists, all blond and rosy, the boys with their muscular hiking legs bulging through thin blue shorts, and I bumped into a cute little black guy.

He had his T-shirt tucked like a towel into the back of cut-off Levi's. His skin was gleaming from sunlight on sweat. We exchanged apologies and more than casual eye contact, but he moved on down Broadway without breaking stride. He wasn't even a block away when I noticed that this slight, accidental human contact had triggered a hard-on in my jeans. It had been days since I'd had sex. Something about the heat was making me angry, and something about the anger was making me horny. I was primed.

I looked around to see what was up and found myself standing in front of a small "all-male cinema." I could hardly believe my eyes. There on the poster, under sooty rain-streaked glass, was good old Ray Asher. I'd have recognized that face anywhere, it was so burned into my brain. After all, Ray was the first guy I'd ever gotten it on with. The first guy I'd ever smoked dope with, too, which made him pretty memorable. And he *was* pretty. At least to my way of thinking.

I'd known Ray a little around our college campus, but we'd never talked much. Then one night we found ourselves sitting next to each other at my favorite Brando flick, *On the Waterfront*, which the film society was showing in the science lecture hall on the main quad. It's one of those brutal black-and-white films that makes you feel depressed and really good at the same time, kind of morose but ready to kick ass. When the movie was over and Ray asked me if I wanted to come up to his dorm room to sample some pot he swore was Hawaiian, I said, "Sure." But it wasn't the weed I was hot for.

I don't know what his ancestry was, but Ray looked like what I thought an Italian should be, or a Sicilian anyway. He was shorter than me, about five-seven or -eight, and had dark skin and curly black hair. Which made him pretty much my opposite. If he had been a magnet, I'd have been a billion iron filings clinging to his poles.

His nose was typically aquiline, and he had a thick beard stubble that always looked like it needed shaving. He had full fleshy lips that were most comfortable when slightly open in a kind of pout and the bluest eyes I'd ever seen in so dark a face. He was like a boy with a man mask on, an acolyte pretending to be priest for the Festival of Fools. I'd never managed to catch him in the shower, but I'd seen him in shorts. His arms and legs were covered with hair. He had a compact little butt and a basket that looked like it held more than you'd expect from a man his size.

When we got to his room, he peeled off his jacket, shoes, and socks and opened the top button of his jeans. He was wearing a loose sweater that hung nicely across his hard chest. Since we were making ourselves at home, I took off my boots and sat on one of the two beds. Ray sat on the other. His roommate had dropped out mid-semester, so he had the room to himself for the rest of the year. I leaned forward, my elbows on my knees, my eyes glued to every move he made.

He rolled a couple of reefers and lit one, taking a deep toke, squinting his Mediterranean-blue eyes. When he handed me the joint, I had to tell him I'd never smoked marijuana before, but he told me what to do, then showed me. He stared at me intently as I tried to follow his lead. At one point, our eyes locked into the kind of open invitation that would have spooked both of us—if we weren't so stoned. He broke the tension with a wink.

I don't know what was in that shit we smoked, but I blasted off, higher than I was prepared for, certainly as high as I've ever been on grass since. It was *great* stuff.

Well, Ray stretched out on one bed and I stretched out on the other and we started groovin' on the ganja, each of us in our own private world. It wasn't long before I was getting that nice warm feeling in my lap that meant an erection was coming up...like daffodils in spring. I had no idea how horny grass would make me. I looked over at Ray on the other bed. He had kicked off his jeans and was lying there in his Jockey shorts and sweater, which was pulled up to his chin. He was stroking his nipples with one hand and rubbing his hairy stomach with the other. He had achieved an enormous piss-hard boner that was peeking over the waistband of his briefs.

I came to immediate full attention. My balls were pinched against the crotch of my jeans, so I stripped them off. I took my shirt off, too, so I wasn't wearing anything but my underpants and socks. When Ray happened to look my way, he saw me propped up against the wall staring at him, my own bloodswollen cock strained against the fly of my B.V.D.s, oozing a drop or two of slippery juice into the absorbing cotton. Ray slid his hand down to his groin, stuck his hand under the elastic, and started massaging his cock and balls. He kept his intense blue eyes riveted on me. I thought I would come just looking at him.

He was tugging on his prick now, and the Jockeys were slipping farther and farther off it with every motion of his hand. I was getting a better and better look at the thing. I'd never seen one so big and dark. The veins were enormous. I liked what I was seeing. A silent voice inside my head was screaming at me to do something when Ray said, "You ever done it with a guy before?"

I was embarrassed by the question, but I was more shamed by the truth, which was that I'd wanted to—God, I'd wanted to!—but I never had. So I dropped my hand into my lap, took hold of my throbbing tool, and said, "Yeah."

Ray shifted his weight onto his shoulders, lifted his knees into the air, and with one motion slid the Jockey shorts down his hips and kicked them off with his feet. He spread his legs—one knee up, one leg extended—exposing two huge balls totally covered with curly black fur. They looked like two goose eggs in a hair nest. His thick, uncut dick tapered to a hot purple head that pointed up past his navel. He lifted the sweater over his head and posed there on the bed, totally naked and ready to be had.

"Well," he finally said, "then what are you doing way over there?"

Now, I said I'd never done it before, and I hadn't, but I'd read some choice books and had a vivid imagination when I wanted one. I had a pretty good idea about the basics going in, and I managed to finesse the more sophisticated moves without too much fumbling. I stood up and dropped my drawers. My cock was sticking straight out across the room—right at Ray's eye level. I was smaller than him, but I came to a full round head, so I figured we were about even. He sat up on the bed as I walked toward him and opened his mouth. I popped in without so much as an implied hesitation. I thought I'd shoot the minute that warm, wet mouth of his took me inside it, but Ray had other ideas.

After sucking me to the brink of bursting, he pulled his head

| *The Hard Way* |

off me and started to tongue my balls, by this time as tight up inside me with pleasure as they get before I shoot. I could feel him pulling at the hairs behind my nuts with his teeth. Then he turned me around, bent me over, and started lapping my ass like a thirsty dog.

I'd never felt anything like it, and I didn't know how much I could take before my skin split its seams. He zeroed in on my virgin hole, prying it open with his thumbs, and stuck his tongue as far into it as he could, his hands spread across my buttcheeks. "I'm going to come," I moaned. Ray wheeled me around and took my cock in his mouth so he could drink the hot milk that was gushing out of me. I thought I'd squirt a gallon, but he kept taking it, gulping it, crooning as he swallowed, each contraction of his throat coaxing more liquid out of me.

When I was finally done jerking, he took my pecker in his hand and licked the end of it, like a kid with a Popsicle, then he scratched that hard black beard stubble of his across the tops of my legs. I thought I'd collapse with satisfaction.

Ray looked up at me with those fabulous eyes of his and leaned back on the pillow, offering his big, dark hunk of meat. It was already dripping into the raven hair of his taut abdomen. He had his knees pulled up and wide, and I could see the white hemispheres of his lower ass between his thighs. It shone like an oasis in the dessert. He put his hands behind his head, showing off two tufts of moist, glistening hair, then smiled and said, "Go to it, man. You're the best."

I'd never gone down on a guy before, especially one hung as big as Ray, but I took to cocksucking like my mouth had been made for it. I started with the small pointed head of his cock and took as much of the shaft as I could. I had a little trouble at first, but as I relaxed into it—excited by Ray's obvious increasing pleasure and the man smell of him—I was able to take most of the hot rod into my mouth. I started to lick his come-heavy balls and his musky asshole, but before I could get into it, Ray let out a loud, guttural cry, and his stomach muscles clenched violently. His scrotum tightened and a huge wad of hot come landed on my left shoulder. I straightened up and let the rest of the semen spurt into my face. I was trying to lick it off as fast as possible, but he was shooting the stuff all over. I was dripping with it.

When his spasms finally subsided, he licked the rest of his come off my face, and stuck his tongue, which was loaded with it, into my mouth. I loved the salty taste of his rigid tongue. It made me hard all over again. I asked Ray if I could fuck him. He said he wasn't into that, so he had me straddle his hips, the great bulk of his semihard cock now nestled in the crack of my ass.

As he rocked his hips gently and stroked my thighs with his hands, I jerked myself off, shooting onto his hairy chest almost immediately. I stayed like that, running my hands around in the sticky hair, until it started to dry. Then we stepped into a steaming shower. It took us nearly an hour, we spent so much time soaping each other's privates and sucking each other's tongues, and Ray wanted to get off again. It was a night to remember, and I've done my best to retain every particular.

Naturally, I wanted to get it on with Ray again as soon as possible, but he said that he didn't like to mess around with the same guy twice, and that he preferred women in any case. I was pissed off, but by then I'd found another dark little man to play with, this one a Panamanian. His ass wasn't quite as perfect as Ray's, but he liked it stuffed regularly, so I wasn't complaining. Then I heard that Ray knocked up one of his girlfriends and they both got tossed out of school. I never saw him again—until that day in Times Square when I happened to spot his picture on a porn-movie lobby card.

I paid my money and sat down in the small, dark theater. There were twenty or so other guys in there, spread out. The air conditioner was turned up full blast, but nobody was shivering, at least not from the cold. One guy in front had his pants around his ankles, and another was diving into the lap of a fat man in the back. I sat down near the middle of the auditorium.

It was a pretty standard flick as these things go: sucking, fucking, and a lot of moaning on the sound track. There wasn't any plot to speak of, but it was Ray, all right. He was playing this supposedly straight guy who keeps getting involved with impossibly perfect blond studs. Each scene became a contest to see who could be hotter and hunkier than the other.

Ray had obviously done some serious bodybuilding since that night I first sucked dick. And whatever experiences he had had or not had before I met him, he was giving his paying customers the full range of the male repertoire—from jerking off to getting fucked fore and aft by a pair of look-alike muscleheads. The scene reminded me of Chinese handcuffs, those woven bamboo tubes you can't get off until you stop pulling and start to push.

I sat in the mildewed darkness with my hand through the open fly of my 501s and watched the engagement of lubricated organs, tongues in mouths and assholes, sweat sliding between nipples rubbed raw by admiring partners, and I thought about that flash of white ass I caught a glimpse of that first night with Ray all those years ago. By the time the scene came where a huge black man was slamming himself up Ray's chute, I was frigging my own cock so hard I was about to come in my pants.

I turned my head and caught the eyes of a Latin-looking kid who had moved closer to me twice. He didn't look old enough to be in here, but I figured he probably knew what he was doing—even if he didn't speak the language. I closed one button of my jeans and walked past him, nearly rubbing my crotch in his face as I went by. I could feel his desire, his heat. I could feel a drop of moisture leaking out of my dick into my knotted pubic hair.

I walked through the draped-off "lobby" and downstairs into the toilet. There were two older guys in there with their hands in each other's pockets. They stopped when I walked in, but got back to business within seconds. There weren't many places to go in this theater, so I knew the kid—and I wanted him to be a kid—would show up here if he was going to follow at all. He did.

Our eyes did a quick inventory. He was older than I thought in the dark, but more attractive, like a saint being tortured by the Inquisition in some Spanish Renaissance painting. In fact, he looked a lot like Ray, as Ray looked upstairs on screen: on the short and solid side, dark, hairy, overdeveloped. He was wearing tight black jeans with a tantalizing basket and a red tank top that showed volcanic nipples. You could almost see them pulsing they were so big, so full of themselves. He walked past me into the stall at the far end of the bathroom. The two old guys stopped again to see if there was a chance on them getting in on some new action. There wasn't, and they knew it.

The kid was hidden inside the stall, but he hadn't shut the door. I could see his feet under the partition. Then I heard a zipper, and he dropped his pants to his ankles. The hook was baited, and I was ready to be reeled in. It would have been plain rude to ignore so direct an offer, especially since I had started this little fishing expedition myself.

He was sitting on the porcelain stool with his shirt off, nude down to his high tops. His tits were the size of quarters and protruded what must have been half an inch. They were wreathed in jet black hair. His dick wasn't the biggest I've ever seen, but it had a terrific shape to it and was nearly classic in proportion and detail. The head was dark red and was stretching the skin on the underside of the shaft to its limit, he was so hot.

I turned and looked at the two old men, wondering how soon it would be before I stopped being a contender and stepped out of the ring for good. My heart started pounding in my chest, the way it did when I walked across the room with my hard-on pointed at Ray's mouth that first time. I shut the door and slid the bolt into its slot and moved between the kid's thighs.

He looked up through long eyelashes and, without a word, pulled my belt open. He unbuttoned the one I had closed and pulled my jeans down to my knees, brushing his long curly hair against my stiffening cock. When he sat back up to get a good look at what he'd gone after, he let out an audible "Oh…" I was glad he was pleased. I licked my fingers and took one of his tits between the thumb and middle finger of each hand and started squeezing, pulling, twisting, until his mouth was open with promise of things to come and he wrapped his lips around my dick, massaging my butt as I pinched and tweaked. He was making so much noise, I thought he'd go crazy and I was having a fine time, too.

I dropped my head back and started rocking my hips, pushing farther and farther into his throat. I could see in my mind's eye that patch of white ass from all those years ago, the same patch of ass that was splayed across a movie screen somewhere above my head. I pulled out of the kid's mouth and, before he could offer an objection, I flipped him around. He bent over the bowl with his hands on the back wall for balance and offered me his ass with a demure upward tilt of his hips.

I reached around and stuck the middle finger of my right hand into his mouth. When it was slick with spit, I pulled it out and tried his asshole, a loose pucker surrounded by dark moss. My finger slid in without resistance, so I rubbed some saliva onto my cock and pushed into his asshole, which opened to take me. The kid smelled like a workingman wearing perfume. He was letting out little *ay...ay...ay*s every time I lunged, and he took his hands off the wall to spread his cheeks farther apart. I was thrusting into him, in and out, in and out, like a popular tune you can't get out of your mind. I was sweating like a horse in the homestretch.

I grabbed hold of the horns of the kid's pelvis, ramming a little deeper and rougher than I might have—because by now, of course, I wasn't fucking a tough little stranger in a porn-flick john; I was fucking Ray the way I wanted to once upon a time. The kid was jerking himself off hard and fast, like he had an appointment to get to, and I felt his knees go limp for a second. Then he let out a loud groan. He arched his back, and his come flew all over the stall, hitting the back and side walls and dripping down over the graffiti, melting it. I plunged, fierce and violent, until just before I was about to come. Then I pulled out and gushed like Niagara Falls all over his ass and back, up into his hair. I hadn't had a climax like that in years.

When I got back into the auditorium, I needed a minute for my eyes to adjust to the dark. I stumbled down the aisle until I got to a row I thought was empty. When I finally looked up at the screen, I saw Ray. He was lying on a bed in what looked like a dormitory room. He was wearing nothing but his Jockey shorts and was fondling his equipment under the white cotton. "You ever do it with a guy before?" he said, and an offscreen voice said, "Yeah." Ray peeled off his shorts and opened his legs, exposing his stiff cock and heavy balls and that magical patch of white ass. "Well," he said up there on the torn, stained screen, "then what are you doing way over there?" Then a cute blond guy with a huge cut dick and tight, hairless scrotum walked into the frame. Ray sat up on his bed and opened his mouth like a penitent ready for the Host. As the blond guy approached, he put his dick right up to the hilt into Ray's mouth. Then he turned his hard white ass toward the camera, revealing a neat little tattoo that read: THE END—COME AGAIN.

How To Be A Poet

How to be a hedonist
For Gavin Dillard

Know that it isn't easy.
Give yourself permission
to fail. Most do. It is no
disgrace. Many begin by
finding a lover to
lose themselves in, a body that quivers as
bodies should and
deeper than you've ever
imagined. If you cannot live
for pleasure, live for love or
for the moment. Trace the curves of your
lover's back with cool lips and
hot intentions. Failing that,
live whatever way you can.
Nobody is perfect. Nobody is
keeping track.

Little you have learned will aid you.
"All good things must come to an end"
is *not* a hedonist credo. Neither is
"A stitch in time saves nine."
Neither is
"A penny saved is a penny earned."
Generally speaking, if
your mother learned a thing from
her mother, it will not
help you.
It is better to say
"I'd give up everything for you,"
but it is not best
to believe it.

Michael LASSELL

Reading is irrelevant.
What you need to know is not
in books. You must learn from
trial and error. If you must read books,
do not read anything written by an American
prior to *Tropic of Cancer*.
Do not read poetry by T.S. Eliot or by
Ezra Pound. Do not read
Dante or Goethe or
anything by a Scandinavian, a Lutheran, or
a computer programmer.
Do not read Greek tragedy unless
you think it's funnier than
Roman comedy. Read instead the moods
of your lover's eyes. Try to
outguess them.

Do not think. No matter what.
No matter how much you are moved or
tempted to do so. Unless you are one of the few—
one of the rare few—for whom ideas
are sensual, for whom
concepts slide like heavy cream
around the white porcelain bowl of your brain,
unless abstractions
tickle the inside of your thighs
like a ride downhill taken
as a child. If you must think,
invent new ways to make love
without accoutrements.

If you must think, in spite of all advice
to the contrary, if you must think of
other things than love,
do not
express your thoughts. Thoughts given tongue
can kill. There is no
antidote for an aphrodisiac
more effective than a thought
spoken aloud.

| *The Hard Way* |

If you must speak your thoughts aloud
speak softly and
in metaphor.
Do not say:
"The trade embargo imposed against the
legitimate government of Nicaragua by the
right-wing faction of the Republican Party
causes me as much anxiety as the threat of
nuclear annihilation."
Say, rather:
"The flavor of your skin
gives me reason to live."

No matter what happens, do not
despair. Five senses are not many,
but they are sufficient. One alone is
sufficient if
properly handled. Start
with one. Practice. Become
a gourmet. An aficionado. A
connoisseur. When you have
mastered one, try another. Try them
in concert.
It is not impossible to enjoy all five senses
at once, but it is impudent and
inadvisable. Indulging more than three senses
at any one time is
superfluous. Any fool can see that,
even an old fool with
new tricks.

Do not live in a cold place.
Do not live under martial law
or inhabit any nation ruled by
a zealot.
Do not live in a country at war with
itself or in any territory occupied by
the Soviet Union, and do not dwell in

| Michael LASSELL |

Israel, Jordan, or Lebanon—even if you are
a journalist (and it is not wise to be
a journalist: fact is anathema to hedonism).
There are lamentably few places left
to live. Do not live
in most of the United States. Do not live
near a factory or a retirement
village. Try to live in a Catholic country,
but do not live in the vicinity
of a church, unless it is very old and beautiful
and named for a saint with a past.

Live on a tree-lined street in a city with
parks, views, broad boulevards and
excellent native cuisine.
Live there a long time in love until you take
everything for granted.
Then move, leaving your lover behind because
his skin is beginning to taste
salty.

Take up an occupation that requires little
regimen. Move to a small apartment
by yourself. Drink large quantities of
alcoholic beverages. Lose control. Speak to
strangers in strange bars. Follow them home
by taxi or on foot whether or not you're
invited. Taste their skin.
Lie to them.
Lie to yourself. Dream.
Forget your dreams. Live
for the moment. Think that
the scent on the spring air reminds you of
someone you left behind.

Turn suddenly, without warning, in public at a
voice like his voice. Eat. Drink. Be merry,
for tomorrow you die, and the next day too.

| The Hard Way |

Receive a telegram.
Follow its directions to a graveyard.
Do not ask questions. Ever.
Read the inscription on the headstone.
Say the name aloud without
moving your lips. Listen to
the granite. Touch it with
your tongue. Smell the dead
flowers. Say:
"The taste of your skin
gives me reason to live."
See if you mean it.
Leave in tears.
Develop an irrational appetite for
salt.
Have neurotic dreams. Remember your
dreams.

How to watch your brother die
For Carl Morse

When the call comes, be calm.
Say to your wife, "My brother is dying. I have to fly
to California."
Try not to be shocked that he already looks like
a cadaver.
Say to the young man sitting by your brother's side,
"I'm his brother."
Try not to be shocked when the young man says,
"I'm his lover. Thanks for coming."

Listen to the doctor with a steel face on.
Sign the necessary forms.
Tell the doctor you will take care of everything.
Wonder why doctors are so remote.

Watch the lover's eyes as they stare into
your brother's eyes as they stare into
space.
Wonder what they see there.
Remember the time he was jealous and
opened your eyebrow with a sharp stick.
Forgive him out loud
even if he can't
understand you.
Realize the scar will be
all that's left of him.

Over coffee in the hospital cafeteria
say to the lover, "You're an extremely good-looking
young man."
Hear him say,
"I never thought I was good enough looking to
deserve your brother."

The Hard Way

Watch the tears well up in his eyes. Say,
"I'm sorry. I don't know what it means to be
the lover of another man."
Hear him say,
"It's just like a wife, only the commitment is
deeper because the odds against you are so much
greater."
Say nothing, but
take his hand like a brother's.
Drive to Mexico for unproven drugs that might
help him live longer.
Explain what they are to the border guard.
Fill with rage when he informs you,
"You can't bring those across."
Begin to grow loud.
Feel the lover's hand on your arm
restraining you. See in the guard's eye
how much a man can hate another man.
Say to the lover, "How can you stand it?"
Hear him say, "You get used to it."
Think of one of your children getting used to
another man's hatred.

Call your wife on the telephone. Tell her,
"He hasn't much time.
I'll be home soon." Before you hang up, say,
"How could anyone's commitment be deeper than
a husband and wife?" Hear her say,
"Please. I don't want to know all the details."

When he slips into an irrevocable coma,
hold his lover in your arms while he sobs,
no longer strong. Wonder how much longer
you will be able to be strong.
Feel how it feels to hold a man in your arms
whose arms are used to holding men.
Offer God anything to bring your brother back.
Know you have nothing God could possibly want.

| Michael LASSELL |

Curse God, but do not
abandon Him.

Stare at the face of the funeral director
when he tells you he will not
embalm the body for fear of
contamination. Let him see in your eyes
how much a man can hate another man.

Stand beside a casket covered in flowers,
white flowers. Say,
"Thank you for coming," to each of several hundred men
who file past in tears, some of them
holding hands. Know that your brother's life
was not what you imagined. Overhear two
mourners say, "I wonder who'll be next" and
"I don't care anymore,
as long as it isn't you."

Arrange to take an early flight home.
His lover will drive you to the airport.
When your flight is announced, say,
awkwardly, "If I can do anything, please
let me know." Do not flinch when he says,
"Forgive yourself for not wanting to know him
after he told you. He did."
Stop and let it soak in. Say,
"He forgave me, or he knew himself?"
"Both," the lover will say, not knowing what else
to do. Hold him like a brother while he
kisses you on the cheek. Think that
you haven't been kissed by a man since
your father died. Think,
"This is no moment not to be strong."

Fly first class and drink scotch. Stroke
your split eyebrow with a finger and
think of your brother alive. Smile

The Hard Way

at the memory and think
how your children will feel in your arms,
warm and friendly and without challenge.

How to go to the theater
For Howard Junker

Wait until it is too late to eat and
get to the theater on time, too early to
leave without eating. Be
at a loss.

Be ravenous. Be angry. Be alone.
There will be beggars enough later for sympathy.

The play will have been written by
an avant-garde Austrian with a penchant for long speeches and
spurious Marxist overtones.
(At the intermission, you will be told
he has since left the theater; you are to
nod sagely and say *Ahh!*)

Sit in the seat immediately to the left of
the center aisle in the third row. This
is the perfect seat. Do not move
if requested. You will feel comfortable in
no other chair. Beside you will sit
a man with a shaved head.
"My hands are still chilled from driving," he will say.
You will wonder if he arrived
on a motorcycle or
in a convertible, but you will say nothing.
Focus instead on the young man in the row
in front of you, a Japanese with the forelock of
a cockatoo. He will hope you think he is a
French dissident, but
you are not deceived.

You may covet him if you like. The choice is yours.
It is a matter of preference, or indifference.

| *The Hard Way* |

The play will begin. That
is inevitable.

A large role will be played by an actor you remember from
another play. You remember hoping
you would never have to
see him again. Again your hope proves
bootless.

The room becomes warm and your mind begins to
wander, to stray from the path of
dramatic argument, to lose itself by way of
insulation from the dialectic of
fusty Teutons and their
crumbling ethic.

Think of the following things:

the sharp pain in your left thigh since
a year ago Mother's Day when you
walked your own mother to the
burned-out pier in San Francisco;

the flesh of your right thigh that has
begun to recede, to sink toward the bone like
the earth over underground streams;

the weakness of your right shoulder, no longer
sufficient to hold your arm out from your
body long enough to retune a radio;

the spasms in varying degree that inhabit the
muscles of your tight, tight neck;

the flab of your stomach as it
presses against your trousers; your
sagging breasts.

| Michael LASSELL |

You are thirty-eight, but your body's always been
an enemy.

Fear the worst:
the temporary filling will not stop the abscess.
(Wonder how to pay for root canal with poetry.)

Know that you need serious medical attention.
Know that it is beyond your means.
Think of England and the National Health.
Despise Republicans and your country in general.

Try to get your mind off the pain:

Desire the actor you met last night at the drag bar in
Hollywood;
laugh whenever anyone on stage says anything remotely
amusing;
become mindlessly absorbed in a block of ice melting on
stage,
a mound of dough rising on a white pedestal, overflowing the
pan;
applaud loudly and read the bio of the short actor from
Australia.

When you leave the theater, there will be a traffic jam.
Every street will be crammed with cars,
the Mexicans rolling in on low-riding chassis.
It will look like the evacuation of L.A. before the
bomb or after the earthquake, whichever comes first.

Swear at every driver. Confront racism.

Arrive home fatigued, the knots in your spine throbbing,
promising a long-seated future on wheels of your own.

| *The Hard Way* |

Eat chocolate candies that melt in your mouth as well as
your hands. Stare at a book by
Marguerite Duras. Sit at your desk until dawn.

It will be the ninth anniversary of your last drink,
a gin and tonic in the bar of the Biltmore Hotel, but
you will tell
no one. You will
drive to Little Tokyo and photograph the Nisei parade.
You will applaud Danjuro, the Kabuki star you
saw at UCLA on Wednesday, and you will
weep over internment at Manzanar and the
annihilation of Hiroshima as if you had been there.

You will vow to drive a Honda always. To hate
Harry S. Truman.

You will remember a film in French and a cluster of
children holding origami cranes—symbols of
peace, *mon amour*. You will remember the film and the bodies of
survivors, your own pain, the lawsuit you lost on
Friday, and your lost faith, cold in the ground and
no one to mourn its passing.

It will be an eventful day, not a happy one.
But you will endure.

That very night you will
go to the theater again,
experience yet more pain,
fear again the impending doom,
suffer again the indignity of
flesh, and write another poem.

How to write a poem
For David Trinidad

Make arrangements to have dinner
with a man you hardly know
but whose work you've admired
from afar.
When he arrives at your apartment
show him
around. Exchange
pleasantries. Be embarrassed
as usual
by the mess, the
peeling paint, the kitchen grease,
an excess of
the undusted and
uncared for, unanswered letters
six months old.
Explain the boxes of records and books
piled in every corner:
"My lover is moving out," you will say,
"which is also why I don't have a car,
which is why intimacy's
a bitch on a budget."

When you squat into his Civic
he will ask, "How long were you together?"
"Ten years," you will answer,
"more or less. I cried
most of January, but I'm
pretty much over it now."

Go to dinner at Hampton's on Highland.
Refuse to valet-park.
Sit in the smoking section.
Do not say, "People who smoke
should have their lips cut off

| *The Hard Way* |

with garden shears," which is
how you actually feel.
Say, "I don't mind,"
and wonder why you'd rather risk
lung cancer than
disapproval.

You will share nachos
with sour cream and guacamole
on the side (he hates one, you
the other). Having been so
appetizer honest, you will tell the
stories that make up your lives:

You will tell him about the
erection you got posing nude for
Don Bachardy while Christopher Isherwood sat
looking on,
smiling and nodding,
rocking and dying in Santa Monica.

He will not tell you
how Rachel was killed. You will have to
read that later, between the lines.
You will see in his face
someone you will be missing
somewhere down the line.

Talk about Gavin, Dennis, Rudy—
poets you have loved or read—
Hockney photocollages and
O'Keeffe's *Hundred Flowers*,
thoughts in common,
continents of difference.
You will agree that the older you get
the more reasonable reincarnation seems
as an explanation.

Do not touch at all
all night.

When you get home
walk once through each of the ill-lit
empty rooms, then sit at your desk and
read his tiny books. Dial his number.
Say to the machine: "*Living Doll* made me
laugh, and *November* made me cry, and
I like you a lot."

Then write it all down while you watch
a sentimental movie on HBO, sitting in the
vinyl recliner your lover...your *ex*-lover
gave you for Christmas...six years
ago—or was it in 1602?

Hold back the tears,
then let them come.
After all,
if an act of grieving falls in the woods
and there's no one there to hear,
does it really hurt at all?

When you and the movie are done—
eleven minutes into St. Patrick's Day
by the digital clock on the VCR,
know you have made a friend. Wonder
who will die first.
And wonder again if
when you die
there will be anyone left behind
to mourn.

How to choose life
For Eric Latzky

Put off the decision for as long as you can.
Wait until your body has begun
to decline,
until you are swollen with food swallowed
to keep from gagging on hunger.

Many will have died. You will have made
lists, wept at funerals, made excuses.
You will not be one of the nurturing ones,
not yet.
You will be He Who Mourns.

One will hurt the most.
For three days
you will weep whenever your mind
reads his name aloud like a mother
calling her child to dinner.
For three days you will weep, and your red eyes
will suddenly realize that the weeping has not
begun. It will come in waves like
calendar pages, like autumns dropping
needles into stacks of leaves as
dry and brittle as the skin of
one whose body sang once with life
on mountaintops with eagles in the snow,
in deserts, and in cool dim rooms.

Wait.
Wait.
Do not rush. As rash a decision
as you now might make must not be
hurried,
cannot be made
before its time.

| Michael LASSELL |

The time will be
the Day of All Saints.
You will be paying bills at your desk when
the Santa Ana winds blow open the casement windows
with Mojave howling.
It will be exactly noon on the Elgin
your mother gave your father on their wedding day
the year before Pearl Harbor.

There is nothing to do but laundry,
nothing to do but read the inscription
on your father's watch,
sink into the expression in your dead friend's eyes,
see a film about Nazis and Jews and know
you have decided to live after all.

At midnight you will sit again at your desk.
You will remember younger days when
strangers approached just to touch
your tan, remember the first time you saw the man
you will see again only in photographs.
You will even remember
joy.

No lover will be returning home to your arms
this night. You will go alone
to a too-warm bed
having chosen to dance
in the mouth of death
and will pray for the strength
to dance again
tomorrow.

Part Five

NEW FRONTIERS

PRIDE

PETER was a drunken faggot when I first met him, but so was I, both of us just off booze—and God knows what else we'd tried. We were both looking *up* at "low self-esteem." By the time he died, Peter had chaired a convention for thousands of clean and sober gay men and lesbians at a high-rise hotel in Studio City and had been on the Palm Springs Roundup Committee for years. His big thing was encouraging people to pursue the desires of their own hearts—even if he thought they were nuts. Peter and Julio gave me a pen for the fifth anniversary of my own last drink because I wanted to quit my job at Fox to become a writer, and I did.

Whenever I scribble now, it's Peter's unjudgmental generosity that guides my hand, and what I write is tribute to his tireless endeavors on behalf of others.

RON was a dentist, and something of a leather queen, too. I used to see him in the sling at the 8709, but I tried to be discreet. After all, he was the best dentist I ever had: He winced and said "Sorry!" like he meant it every time he hit a nerve. He couldn't understand why my teeth were covered with green slime when I found my way to his door. I told him I never expected to live long enough to need dentistry. When he found out he was sick, he turned his life over to AIDS education and changing the safety mandates of the California Dental Association.

Whenever I'm called upon to offer solace to a friend, it's Ron's own peerless well of empathy that guides my words.

IRWIN was a strung-out, in-the-gutter junkie from near where I was raised. I met him in L.A. after he'd cleaned up his act at a detox center in the Valley. We made out on Venice Beach on my birthday and made love at Ray's apartment later. I'd never felt more desired—and I needed to feel desired. We pierced our ears the same day—in July of '77—just so no one would have any questions if they saw us walking hand in hand down Hollywood Boulevard. Then he started to use again, and I lost him to death or time, but he left behind an unlocked door and memories of sweet sex in summer.

Whenever I sit on a patch of sand and feel the sun soak into my skin, it's Irwin's undiluted passion that warms me, and his care-filled, caring eyes.

DENNIS was an artist, a Hawaiian with a Japanese name. We were *so* hot for each other, but he was my lover's friend, too, so we kept a coy distance (except, of course, that one time at the baths we never mentioned afterward—it was the merest taste of him). Dennis loved art, men, and all things Asian. He gave his time to inventing logos and colorful schemes for the Asian Pacific Lesbians and Gays group he helped to organize. Under a forest of flags he concocted, he marched in the Pride Parade taller than his five-foot frame, and I miss his enthusiastic mania.

Whenever I hold my breath at the beauty of things—of art or the pigment of skin different from my own—it's Dennis's unbridled delight in life that I remember with a tear.

ED was a publicist for a "major studio"—oh, okay, it was Disney—who didn't want his diagnosis known, but he was slipping away by pounds and then ounces. Ed loved Richard, cooking, talking (particularly about his mother—Oy!), and the entertainment of friends. He made everyone laugh and feel at home on holidays, no matter who or what you were. I won't pretend he had a kind word for everyone, but he had words, and the words he had were funny, direct, and wise.

Whenever I stand at a door and hold it open for a stranger or a friend, it's tea-drinking, hospitable Ed I remember and the importance of safe harbor away from home.

It isn't hard in this time of plague to do it again:

PAUL loved Roger and wrote of his devotion; loved Stephen after and wrote of that, too;

RONNIE learned sign language because both his parents were deaf, so was able to sign for the hearing impaired at AA meetings;

IRA, a cleaned-up high-school drugster, dedicated his first book to absent friends, and hangs their artwork in his living room;

DANIEL, my former student, was an actor/porn star who abandoned centerfold posing to run Shanti and train volunteer buddies for a terminal clientele;

ESSEX gave up two years' work of his own to finish a respected friend's collection of writing by other gay African-Americans.

Or even again:

PASCAL, who tried to get sober again and again, is still on the streets, but he left behind him countless sober souls he helped to recover;

ROBERTO RAMÓN was my first great love. He opened his family's arms for me, and asked me to be a pallbearer at his father's funeral long after we had gone our separate ways, because family's family no matter what; then he got sick and died without ever letting me know;

ISIDRO, the tour guide in Spain, had a wife and a jealous lover he couldn't choose between and would not choose until he knew the honorable thing for them all;

DARRELL is a light-skinned dance-hall hustler who goes to NYU and spends his week nights reading to the AIDS-afflicted blind;

ELI was a technical writer and computer whiz who started to counsel at the gay and lesbian synagogue so teenage Jews need not share his adolescent pain.

These are the men I emulate, who give me strength and inspiration to go on when going on seems impossible. These are the men I march with when I march each June, the ones I have marched with for over twenty years, some standing tall, some fallen and falling, some lost and some who struggle still, against disease—sweet PIERCE; dear ROBERT (whose unrequited love I've carried since my freshman year); Irish IAN, hated by his clan; dancing DAVID, who kissed me while his mother made dinner in the next room; and the talented but closeted EUGENE—or other demons: child-beaten PHILLIP of the dazzling eyes; man-loving single-father ROY; ISAAC of the afternoon massage; boyish DALE, who never ends his search for a father of his own; and ERIC, the outsider, who reached through his marginal existence to pull me out of the abyss of despair when death was overwhelming, and just stood there as a friend—men who overcame and overcome the things society shamed us into being, who became, instead, the men they were and are:
Powerful
Responsible
Imaginative
Devoted
Enlightened...
...Men of PRIDE.

Lovesick

I hate love. Love is a pain in the ass. It takes a lot of time, and too many people have already written about it. But I hate Valentine's Day the most, since it's the public celebration of erotic, romantic love...and I ain't got no honey toward which to let fly my bolt, as they say. If this was Greece in the 5th century B.C., we'd all know that Eros was the god of everything life-affirming, including sex. But also including architecture. (Maybe that's why they call them "groin" vaults.)

But this is the erotophobic USA, where sex is not to be enjoyed, but employed (in the guise of romance) to sell, sell, sell. Here in America, sex (all kinds) is BAD and romance (neutered sex) is GOOD—as long as the romance is in life *exactly* the way it is in prime-time perfume ads. But it isn't. Romance is messy, and so is sex if you're doing it right. So, point number one: Given who we are and when, there are two kinds of love: The kind in which erectile tissue becomes engorged, and the other kind. I have more experience with the latter.

Of the kind of love in which the erogenous zones play only a secondary role, if they are cast in the drama at all, there are also two kinds: the conditional and the unconditional. I have more experience with the former.

LIFE LESSON NO. ONE: LOVE CAN BE CONDITIONAL. So it's Mother's Day the year I am eight years old, and I have selfishly spent my allowance on candy for myself instead of on a Hallmark card for Mrs. Mom. Mrs. Mom refuses to speak to me for the entire day. Mrs. Mom refuses to say why she is not speaking to me. Mrs. Mom *lies* when I ask her what is wrong. "Nothing," she says, and in that word I learn that mothers only love you when you do exactly what it is they want, but they won't tell you what they want, so if you guess wrong...no more love. And this is why, to this day, I am in constant need of therapy, and my mother walks around alive because I don't want to live out my remaining days as a sex slave to a tattooed junkie.

Happily, there were others in my life. There was, for example, Aunt Helen, whose name was really spelled Helene, but if you write that people think it has three syllables, which it does in Polish, but not in Brooklyn, which is where we're from. So Aunt Helen is married to my mother's brother Jack, and she is Outcast City for being...dum-de-*dum*-dum: Catholic! (The horror!) She is also my godmother.

She is also the only human being in my childhood who loves me unconditionally, absolutely, and without limit, and...get this...not *in spite of who I am,* but *because* of who I am. She is a combination Auntie Em and Auntie Mame who smokes and eats bonbons and says "Shit!" when she vacuums. She buys me art stuff instead of chemistry sets and *nothing* shocks her. She is my hero. Naturally, she dies—on the twelfth of February, 1966. I am eighteen and devastated. When I get back to school after the funeral, there's a Valentine's Day card from her in my mailbox and a five dollar bill. "Not feeling too good," it says. "Have a drink on me."

Then there was Ralph, a kid from my church. He was four years older, but we kind of grew up together being shepherds in Christmas pageants and so forth. He was the All-American Boy: state track champ in high school, scholar, cute, popular. You know. You had to love him or kill him. I had an enormous crush on the spectacular hollow he had at the side of his buttocks, where the leg meets the cheek. So naturally I chose him to be the first human being on earth to tell I was gay.

It was summer. Night. Lots of stars. (Think Ron Howard.) We were sitting on the Little League Field, where Ralph had been a star and I had been a washout. But he didn't care. He liked the me about me, and was completely accepting, even though homosexuality was about as alien to his nature as, say, cruelty. We played folk songs together on the guitar. He taught me "Johnny, I Hardly Knew Ye" before he went off to Vietnam, his college education having been paid for by the ROTC. He was shot down and killed while I was living in London learning about "I love you as a friend, but not as a lover." His name is about a third of the way down the flank of the Vietnam Memorial nearest the Potomac. I have a picture of his name on the wall. And one of Ralph and me when we were, what? Eight and twelve. So, I begin to get this message: Love, conditional or not, can hurt. Maybe more than it's worth. This lesson comes in handy later.

I met Kenny Moore in 1976. He was a sunny character who took an instant liking to my lunatic early efforts at sobriety. He's been a Jesus Radio deejay and the owner of a fag dive on Selma called Sewers of Paris. Now he's in real estate. He could be Mr. Right, but not for me. We both like the same kind of men, and we are not it. So we just become complete soulmates. We fought over a man once—Kenny got the man, and his crabs—but it felt so bad we vowed that nothing on earth would ever come between us. It was just like, no matter how depressed we were, just seeing each other would cheer us up.

Life Lesson No. Whatever: Love can have sex or not; love can be conditional or not; love can hurt a whole lot; love can soothe the troubled breast.

Can you guess the ending? Oh, yeah, it's a sad story, *the* sad story of our age. AIDS. He got it because this crackpot New Age preacher in San Francisco told him if his faith in God was strong enough, he didn't need to use condoms. So Kenny wound up dying thinking it was because he didn't believe hard or well enough. He died in October, and I got to see him a few days before, on Columbus Day, a day to mark adventure and exploration. So, he was there on his deathbed in Lake Tahoe, worried sick that I might not be okay about his dying, that his dying might just cause me a weeny spiritual trouble of my own. So up I fly so he can make it be okay in his head that I am okay, so he can die in what peace he can. And he does. In a lovely, cold, dark peace at the edge of a forest he loved.

So, I'm no expert. I loved my Aunt Helen, and Ralph, and Kenny. And there have been others, too. My first real lover, a little Latin spitfire named Roberto. It was a roller coaster, honey, but the love was deep, and the sex was great. He's dead, too. The great love of my life was Ben, *is* Ben, I guess I should say. I don't know if we loved each other unconditionally. But we loved each other a lot. And then we didn't. So we broke up. We reconciled later, but now there's a country between us, so whatever I know about love, I know it's not so easy with the Rocky Mountains in between.

Now, we jump forward a bit. To Christmas, so I'm getting cards from the friends I left in L.A. when I came back home to New York to be depressed with the ocean on the right. One's from my friend Paul. Why be coy? It's Paul Monette. He writes, you know. The card is a couple of kids (art fags will recognize them as Jesus and John from DaVinci's "Virgin on the Rocks" sketch—check out the National Gallery in London). The inscription says: "Earth's the right place for love; I don't know where it's likely to go better." It's from a poem by Robert Frost, a cranky old bastard, according to most biographers, who knew less about love than you might think from his poetry. So, point number... I don't know, I lose count: There are two kinds of love: the kind in poems (which is real mushy a lot of the time), and the real kind, the nitty-gritty, dirty-rotten, people-die-and-leave-you-in-pain kind. Inside, this little seasonal greeting, *cher* Paul (who has buried two lovers) has written: "I officially got diagnosed with AIDS yesterday (cryptococcus), so the walk through the dark wood becomes trickier for '92." And you know, I just couldn't find the poetry or the romance or the spiritual lesson in that sentiment at all.

I'm writing a book about love. It's called *Fragments of Blood*. It's dedicated to Paul, because I guess I kind of love him unconditionally, and for real, even though Paul is a pretty peculiar character sometimes. Since Paul may never see the book in print, I want to send him the dedication by way of a gift for the feast of St. Valentine, patron of putti. It's from the heart, and it's got an arrow through it:

For Paul Monette:

For his talent, intelligence, industry, wit,
and compassion;
his dogged romanticism, consummate hospitality,
and limitless friendship;
for his excellent work;

but mostly

for his glorious and avenging anger.

It's not a Hallmark. But it will serve. It will serve.

A New York State Of Mind

NEW YORK, NEW YORK. The city so nice they named it twice. The Bronx is up, the Battery's down, and so am I so much of the time that "neutral" seems like a manic phase. Although I'm Home Sweet Home after all those years "abroad" on the other side of the country (a continental inconvenience between oceans), I'm still pining away for the L.A. ex I left behind three years ago. And all the *fabulous* gay men who are beating down my double-dead-bolted, reinforced-steel door to become my next ex seem to have forgotten my address and phone number (which is unlisted—talk about your intimacy issues). It's too late now to blame unhappy singlehood on the bossa nova, so blame it on my age. It's a lot in homo years.

"I feel like a carton of milk approaching my expiration date," a soon-to-be forty-six-year-old psychologist friend recently said, having noticed that the MEN SEEKING MEN personals in the *Village Voice* seem to say things like: "No paranoid schizophrenic drug addicts, beached whales, identifiably gay men, New Agers, or decrepit geriatrics over forty-five need apply."

And that's the thanks I get for trucking my then-firm young

butt up the streets of Sixth Avenue (oh, I mean Avenue of the Americas—I'm still not used to that) at the *very first* gay pride parade or for picketing *Boys in the Band* for its shockingly self-loathing portrait of our burgeoning community ca. 1969, or for having survived the plague long enough to become...of a certain age, I believe the diva terminology goes.

Lately I find I rather like *Boys in the Band*. But I'm seriously pissed off that my sweet actor friend Frederick Combs is among the casualties of our age, dear loving lost Frederick, who was actually in *Boys in the Band*, although it was years before I knew either him or its author, Mart Crowley, whom I met when he was producing *Hart to Hart* for Twentieth Century Fox TV, for heaven's sake (although I never did mention to him that I lined up in front of a Times Square theater to protest the film version of his biggest hit—such are the follies of youth).

So, I'm a relentless name-dropping star-fucker. Get used to it. I kiss and tell even if I haven't kissed. That's why they call it writing, and since there were no candy canes in my Christmas stocking to suck on these long winter nights, I need some amusement. Furthermore, since we're being rigorously honest and laying down the ground rules, you may as well know I'm a dysfunctionally self-involved cantankerous grouch, in which I take some perverse satisfaction, although I'm not nearly so expert as my friend, the très, très humorous novelist and gadfly David B. Feinberg, a kvetch extraordinaire with pecs to choke a horse and an even bigger sense of humor. If you read that anyone else is passing himself off as the hunkiest humorist around, he's lying.

And have I mentioned that the late-year air in New York feels like a successful first date? That the complex of sensations while walking across Washington Square Park—the droning bagpipe squad from NYU rehearsing by the playground, the crackle of dried leaves on the paving stones, the tart smoke of burning fireplace wood, the soft "herb and incense" sales patois of the immigrant drug dealers, memories of those who died when an out-of-control car careered into a row of filled benches—is as thrilling and intoxicating to me as was the backroom of the International Stud?

Talk about depressing. The International Stud, famed location of Harvey Fierstein's *Torch Song Trilogy* and my wasted youth, that dank dive in which I fucked my first anonymous stranger, sweat running down the inside of my clothing since I didn't know I could check my winter wrap, is now a Caribbean restaurant swarming with the het'ro-seggshell yuppie scum who inherited all the historic-building Village apartments from dead faggot brothers. Girlfriend, when there are kiddie shops on Greenwich Avenue, Queer Nation is in trouble.

"Is there anything you *do* like?" a sweetly acerbic and unaccountably optimistic former Yalie I worked with recently badgered over a bad deli lunch nibbled absentmindedly while adoring the crotch of our honest-to-God Italian waiter. And you know, I had no problem coming up with an answer. I like New York. And I like sex. At least I used to.

Sex and the City

"Oh, nobody's having sex anymore," a clean and sober *ami du moi* recently exclaimed. And I thought for a moment he might be right, that I would have to rechristen myself a homo-emotional, homo-social, or homo-spiritual—since I was clearly no longer defining myself by my sexual behavior but by my affectional orientation. And *preference,* honey, make no mistake. (Note that I am aware it is dangerous to articulate a preference: Once one utters a desire, much less a need, the combined forces of the universe conspire to see to it that that need, or desire, is never met. That is what is meant by reality.)

Once upon a time, New York was all about sex. It was not only the availability of sex, but its intensity, so palpable it stuck out a clammy hand and grabbed you by any appendage as you walked down the street like a drunk clasping his bony fingers around your ankles. Even the old broads in their mothball-scented minks schlubbing in and out of St. Patrick's Cathedral—and don't get me started on Cardinal John (as in tea-room) O'Connor!—used to ooze sensuality…of a dying-lily kind, to be sure, but something to pin a hard-on on nonetheless. Nowadays, of course, the hand that reaches out is usually attached to one of New York's tens of thousands of homeless men, women, and children, perhaps the saddest facts of urban life in the waning days of the 1990s.

And at least a couple of those guys jiggling coins in blue, white, and gold paper cups from the local Greek coffee shop—ephemera now iconized on T-shirts—are queer brothers, cruising for human contact as well as spare change. Think of them as the archetypes of millennial sexuality. I AM HOMELESS AND I HAVE AIDS say the crudely lettered signs on nonrecyclable shirt cardboard. You'd have to be a New Yorker—or a het'ro-seggshell—to pass them by without letting loose at least a nickel. Even though most of them are probably lying.

But the old-style sexual archetypes are still in evidence, too, from pre-Stonewall Ivy Leaguer and pre-Mattachine Society pansy poofter all the way on up to the latest street-savvy trendoid (think tattoos and a subtle gold nose ring). Men in leather jackets, of course, abound, this being New York, New York. Now, men in leather jackets fall into a few basic categories:

1. Tom of Finland impersonators. I just love it when the *New York Times* runs respectful if arm's-length reviews of Tom of Finland documentaries and Tim Miller performances: so staid, so antiseptic, so silly).

2. Actual real-live S&Mers. There are four of these, and they shop at the Leather Man on Christopher between Bleecker and Hudson, which is where the adorable Michael—he of the sweet smile and subtle nose ring—works (be still my covetous and underused heart).

3. ACT UP babies from the East Village who buy theirs at discount joints on St. Mark's Place and wear them over T-shirts. There are, needless to say, more ACT UP T-shirts in Gotham than actual ACT UP members, but radical chic was, of course, invented here.

4. *Artistes manqués*. If everyone in L.A. is writing a screenplay, then everybody in New York wants "ta be a ahtis," usually a writer or some other genre which is perceived not to require any special talent, training or dedication, and:

5. The rest of us, those who remember New York before SoHo, who cruised the long-gone Howard Johnson's at Sixth and Eighth, who read John Rechy before he became an English teacher and jerked off to *City of Night*.

| *The Hard Way* |

"Do you ride or are you making a fashion statement?" asked the clerk who fitted me for my original Schott (the kind Marlon Brando wore in *The Wild One*) at the corner of Christopher and Bleecker (it's Dutch, you know, the street, or at least its name). Do I ride, indeed! Isn't it obvious?

So if all the homos in New York, as I am assured, are bottoms in search of a top, where are they? I'm all greased up with no one to pole.

And speaking of Christopher Street...

It's always been outré. In fact, the phrase "up the river" originated not from the location of Sing Sing (*way* up the lazy hazy Hudson), but from the location of New York's original prison—when Manhattan (a.k.a. Manatus, now the name of a popular eatery) was still a Dutch-held island with a little fishing village at the end of it. And where was that prison? At Christopher Street, right smack where the piers are now.

There are still some bars on Christopher, the resurrected Stonewall Inn, Boots and Saddles, and Ty's, where once upon a lovely Christmas vacation from graduate school I met a bearded taxi driver from the Lower East Side, who took me home for some of the hottest, highest-spurting sex of my life. Only now I think it was the poet Michael Klein—or maybe it was his twin brother—or maybe I'm completely wrong about everything. God, sex was fun, although the pursuit of sex in New York is pretty exhausting: Bars are open until 4:00 A.M. and club parties start after midnight.

There is still, of course, gobs and oodles of s-e-x in New York City, even the kind you don't have to pay for. In fact, New York reminds me of my favorite childhood book, Dr. Seuss's *Bartholomew and the Oobleck*, a fantasy about a medieval village deluged from the heavens by a thick and gooey green slime. Seems the whole town was up to its ink-outlined noses and pointed turrets in it. Think of it as an allegory.

As in many places, sex took it in the neck with the advent of the AIDS epidemic, and not having sex became somehow politically correct. Ugh! Thank God that's over. The motivation was fear, which was not, to be fair, inappropriate. But ever since the boys in the lab coats decided that it was okay to do just about anything except stick an unrubbered dick up your pumpkin shoot, sex began inching its way back up the charts.

Or as my friend the playwright, novelist, and columnist Paul Rudnick says in his new play, *Jeffrey*, "AIDS is the enemy, not sex."

Somebody say Amen!

Nowadays Ty's and Boots and Saddles are pretty seedy. Gone the glory of bygone days (I used to hate it when my parents said shit like that about World War II). Sometimes on my way to work at the uptown magazine salt mine, I pass by the boys of summers long, long gone scarfing up the Rolling Rock boilermakers for breakfast and I think: There but for the grace of the drug-and-alcohol recovery movement, go I. At night, the tourists hang here.

There are happier bars, to be sure, of the supermarket variety, like The Monster at the corner of Grove Street and Seventh Avenue, a kind of local emporium of homo types. It's got a bar, a piano player, dance floor, and showroom, so it's a lot like San Francisco disco palaces of the '70s, but smaller. Like nouvelle cuisine. It's a fairly eclectic, mostly neighborhood-minded, generally older group than hangs at Uncle Charlie's, the fashion-victim bar for aging teenagers on Greenwich Avenue. Oy! When will video bars ever die? The boys in leather jackets hang at places called the same thing in every city—you know: The Spike, The Eagle, Rawhide, etc. The waterfront bars that proliferated in the '70s are boarded up, but not forgotten.

Of course, the West Village, spiritual home to so many generations of fairies, is not where "it"—whatever "it" is—is happening. It is still happening in the East Village (at Crowbar and Tunnel Bar and Wonder Bar) and in Chelsea, the new gay-rage spot—from Spike and Splash to the bar at upscale restaurant Man Ray, where I finally got actually to meet—and touch—the splendiferous dancer/choreographer Bill T. Jones, who was eating dinner, not slumming, after a performance at the neighboring Joyce Theater. What a beautiful, not to mention apocalyptically talented, doll. This is a star I would like very much to...fornicate with.

(Forgive the dangling preposition. Think of it as an allegory.)

Speaking of Bill T. Jones (and who doesn't?) reminds me...

Dancing is back in style, all kinds and big time, which means, as a corollary, so is dance fashion—costume jewelry and the scantiest of mix-and-match spandex, net and chiffon...and those ubiquitous, but adorable mini-kilts. Yes, I confess, I love 'em. Clubbing is in high gear, and each week the dedicated denizens of the demimonde fan out through the city snatching up *HX* (that's *Homo Xtra*). Folks live by *HX*, which is published by Matthew Bank and Marc Berkley, that dear sweet impresario who invites me to all his parties, to find out what club is happening where and who the DJ is and which Lady This and which Lady That is going to be on the door or hosting the drag contest, yadda-yadda-yadda. And *HX* has discount coupons.

Now, if I have to mention that this twinkled-toed crowd took briefly to sucking on pacifiers (some of them sterling silver), you haven't yet gotten the message that the club scene is for children. Children of all ages, to be sure, but we are in New York still in the throes not only of a tuberculosis epidemic, but the heinous and seemingly immortal Boy Boom.

I am, of course, as days dwindle down, increasingly bitter about this phenomenon, having forgotten to enjoy my own young years. Oops, sorry, fella—you blew it. And I did. But apparently too long ago for anyone still alive to remember.

Actually the thing everybody says about New York—and generalizations, as we know, are useful only as the touchstones for debate—is that everybody is either married or creepy, and that goes for women and men of all stripes. New York still remains the city so crowded you are never alone, and the loneliest place in the world, and that's why people are still taking drugs.

Now, drugs are interesting. Take it from me, I tried my share, but it was, of course, long before the boutique drugs of backroom boy bars. My heyday was not about ecstasy but about laying back. And the drugs the New York puppies are wolfing late into the wee hours strike me as sadly desperate. Sure, joy is hard to come by in the opening rounds of 1993, but surely not impossible. And a lot of these tykes at the sex clubs are standing around watching—just like they used to do at video bars—or showing off (sex as show: exhibitionism and voyeurism. No wonder so many people want to be paid for it these days). Isn't it just a weeny tad jaded to treat a naked Adonis with a hard-on as just the latest throwaway from MTV? Isn't it just the teeniest bit self-defeating for twenty adorable boy-men out looking for love to be shoving dollar bills into the spandex posing strap of the only unavailable man in the room? Okay, so I'm a boring old fart who's been clean and sober since before cocaine was known to be addictive. I'm just not looking for sex as an overpriced substitute for the E channel.

The problem with drugs, of course, is not that they're expensive, dangerous, and ultimately degrading, but that whatever one's justification for taking them, they're all about fear, and fear is death on intimacy.

Buzz Term of the Decade: *Intimacy Issues.*

Of course, New York is a magnet for people who crave anonymity (i.e., people who isolate as a lifestyle), and it's clearly not the best choice of hometown if intimacy is a goal. Which is in part because of the fear. Fears are a big part of the New York charge, and we have lots and lots of them here, and shrinks of all sorts to sort them out.

So many phobias, so little time. (Where else could someone actually *dream* the term "euphoraphobia"—as in, fear of happiness?) In New York you not only have to be afraid of each of eight to ten million people who are never more than a subway ride away, but you have to be afraid of buildings collapsing on your head and of subway trains careering off their tracks and into the rush-hour commuter crowd at Union Square, but you have also to be afraid of rusted fire escapes letting loose from their moorings and spearing you through the cranium and utility pipes that blow up and not only kill whoever's walking above them but shoot billions of gallons of asbestos into the air (about which said utility companies, of course, lie like phone-sex jockeys). And don't forget to be afraid of the critters—rats, mostly, big enough to beat up the average Manx.

So what's to be afraid of?

So, there's AIDS, of course.

A man in some weird state was recently convicted of attempted manslaughter or murder or something because he was HIV-infected and didn't tell his girlfriend. Well, girlfriend, sorry, honey, but the exchange of body fluids is a two-party contract. We are past the stage of blissful ignorance. At this point, there is no excuse not to know and practice safer sex. So if you put yourself at risk, point your stubby, ill-manicured finger in your own direction if the bunny dies, so to speak.

Buzz Term of the Last Decade: *Taking Responsibility for One's Own Actions.* This concept has not yet reached its expiration date and is, consequently, still in effect.

Actually, I'm pretty pissed off about AIDS right now, not just because it knocked off most of my best friends in L.A. before I left, leaving a big hole where my life used to be, but because it's claimed folks I left behind (R.I.P. dear Garys—Essert and Abrahams) and is chipping away at some of my closest friends on both coasts (sweet Yves, be valiant, you angel of the apocalypse; Ramón, will I see you alive again?). And it's a bitch. If AIDS is to be feared, it's not just because it's a life-threatening illness, but because death, whatever it is for those who go through it, is a motherfucker for those who watch.

There was a time when I didn't want to meet anyone new who was HIV-positive. And, oh, little honeys of the nation, I can I hear those tongues wagging.

Sorry, I know it's not PC, but it seems sometimes that there is just so much grief that one body can bear, and this one has borne a shitload more than it cares to. So, naturally, one is afraid of intimacy. The man whose ear you are now nibbling may soon be leaving you behind. And that's selfish, sure, but selfishness is a human trait. Some aspire to overcome it; others revel or drown in it, leaving witnesses behind to console one another. And New York is about nothing if it is not about self-centeredness, the heroic selflessness of some individuals and groups notwithstanding.

This may sound a smidgen pejorative. I admit it. But the essential truth about New York—as opposed to L.A., and I promise not to do a comparison chart—is that New York is all about eccentricity and L.A. is all about conformity. Which is just two different ways of saying everyone wants to belong. In

L.A. it's about having the "right" everything; in New York it's about having everything so "wrong" it's kooky, and hence newsworthy, or at least noteworthy, and that's why it was a New Yorker, Andy Warhol, whom Fran Lebowitz calls the man who made fame famous, who coined the phrase "Everyone is famous for fifteen minutes." But on both coasts it's about trying to belong to a tribe, a bleached-blond, deep-tanned, all-American, bare-chested tribe, or a darkly introverted, smoldering-eyed, heavily ethnic, bare-chested tribe, the kind I prefer.

And endangered tribes tattoo, says my friend the fabulous lesbian novelist Sarah Schulman. She has a tattoo. I have two, the newest one unveiled at the Publishing Triangle's recent Writers Weekend at City University (where homo historian Martin Duberman runs the first graduate center in the country dedicated to gay and lesbian studies). I had hoped, of course, to attract a literate young lad with time on his hands, but it was lesbian poet and educator Cheryl Clarke, with whom I served on a panel on "The New Queer Criticism," who seemed the most intrigued. *C'est la vie. C'est la guerre.* Have you ever noticed, that if you are a gay man looking for love, women come swarming out of the woodwork in the same measure men disappear into it. It's the old "If nobody wants you, neither do I" thing. That "If it's too easy to come by, I really don't want it" thing. Well, you know.

So, a lot of this party-party-party new-tribalism business is fiddling with the Jockey shorts of smooth young bodies while Rome—and other capitals of the world—burns from high fevers and mourning. And who can blame the little stud puppies for claiming and celebrating their bodies? I'm not averse to hedonism. I'd just like to play. Unrequited love is only slightly sadder than unrequited lust. Very little lust, as I remember, was unrequited in the '70s. That was then, and I'm glad I was there with a hard-on, neuroses notwithstanding.

Welcome to the melting pot

So I was sitting in a movie theater with my friend, the writer Eric Latzky, waiting for the screening of a Jeremy Irons film about water in England and Pittsburgh. "So, what would you say is the state of gay life in New York City these days, Eric?" I asked. And what he said, I already knew, which was, "A lot of separate segments that never connect."

"Oh, yes," said I, "that is true, true, true." In fact, if one didn't live in Greenwich Village, as I do, and if one always went to bed before midnight, which I don't, one might never even know that the club-puppy phenomenon—clad these days in Calvin Klein long johns—existed. (Speaking of Calvin Klein, don't you just love Larry Kramer, who lives in the Village and whom I sometimes just meet walking down West 8th Street? Check out his interview in the *Advocate*, where he calls the now-het'ro-seggshelly married Klein a self-hating homo who rips off the community for profit. And don't you just want to slash Marky Mark into sawdust?)

Running into Larry Kramer on the street is just one of the joys of New York, New York. Running into Wendy Wasserstein is another. So is running into Christopher Bram or Felice Picano (not usually together), meeting Michael Cunningham at the theater, hanging out at literary receptions with cute funny boys like the aforementioned David B. Feinberg and his gallows-humor buddies, John Weir and Joe Keenan.

Oh, have I mentioned that I'm a writer and that I surround myself totally with the many, many literary types who inhabit what I call the "quote mode"? If you need friends, write a book. Give readings at gay bookstores. Although you'll be asked to sludge through a lot of bad writing by strangers who think knowing your P.O. Box number gives them some right to your time, attention, and expert advice, you'll meet the best and brightest.

Writers are the easiest of all creative types to meet. And our egos are so totally damaged by being writers in this, our antiliterary American society, that we're eager to be salved by the adoring comments of the adorable public. Wait...is this over the top? Where was I? Oh, yes, diversity and what a good thing it is.

For New York is about nothing if it's not about diversity. There are still old queens here who live in faux Louis Quatorze prewar co-ops. Really. I've heard about them.

There are also preppies and nerds (who communicate via computer module) and swank Upper East Siders who have never

| Michael LASSELL |

been on a subway in their lives and professionals of various stripe who don daily oppressor business drag and truck to midtown luncheries, and every manner of every other manner. And they rarely meet, except at places, perhaps, like Rounds, where the affluent meet the indigent for fun and profit.

Which raises the issue of race and class, not to mention gender. (You didn't think you could slog all the way through this without some politics, did you?)

I'll race ya

Now, L.A. would seem to have the headline lock on racial tension these days, but not so. New York is waiting to blow. And nowhere is this more apparent than in our own negligent queer enclave, Greenwich Village (both the literal and metaphorical).

Once upon a time, in the late '60s and early '70s, gay liberation (including the Gay Liberation Front, founded in 1969 in the wake of the Stonewall Riot—or Uprising—and the soon-thereafter splintered-off Gay Activists Alliance) was the sole power province of middle-class gay white men. Now, middle-class gay white men deny this—or some do—but facts is facts, ma'am. I was there, and I'm telling you that all the disenfranchised groups—women, people of color, the poor, the gender "transgressors" (what Jim Pickett calls the Bad Homosexuals[3])—were subtly and not-so-subtly excluded in the "good" old days. And this should be a matter of great shame to our tribe, but, horrifyingly, despite rainbow coalitions, the gulf seems wider than before.

Part of this comes from Our Bad Times, sure. When the whole world is preaching scarcity, everybody's afraid they're not going to get their slice of the pizza. And, in New York, where the economic recession is deeper than in most places, the pizza (although it is described routinely and accurately as the best on earth) is getting sliced really, really thin.

Christopher Street, where black and Latino gays were made to feel like intruders in the days when the street bustled like a nightly street fair, is now, after dark at least (God, remember

---

[3] Playwright James Carroll Pickett died of AIDS in 1994.

After Dark?), almost exclusively "ethnic." It is a young, mostly poor, Afro-Hispanic crowd, both queer and not (or not sure), and lots of the old white boys don't like this at all. Although I've walked Christopher Street at all hours of the day and night—at times the only Caucasian face in the crowd—I've never once had "an incident." I've been ignored, I've been cruised, and I've been asked for money—both in exchange for sex and for the hell of it—but no one has ever acted out any hostility.

Hostility, however, festers. And what is going on between people of color and the Jewish community in New York—open warfare in some parts of the city, notably in Crown Heights, where a rift between blacks and Hasidic Jews may well unseat gay-positive Mayor David Dinkins—is mirrored in little in the Forest of Hard-on that is queer New York.

This is not to say the white, brown, red, yellow, and black boys are not rubbing their crotches together. We are—just look at the personals in the *Voice* (everybody's favorite place to look for love these days), but whether interracial relationships—sexual or personal—can ever transcend colonialism and sexual mythology is matter for a queer *Jungle Fever,* Spike Lee's lamentably lame look at black and white lovers together. Actually, Marlon Riggs, our community's own African-American filmmaker, has had brighter things to say in both *Tongues Untied*.[4] Right now, it's PC in the color community to look to one's own kind (as the embittered Anita sang to the dewy-eyed Maria in *West Side Story),* and this is an empowering, self-affirming and probably altogether necessary situation. But it's sad to this die-hard activist, in that it speaks of separatism I don't think is cool at all. Or do I?

Fag separatism

"I just think we should all get guns," I have said more than once, and even written, "and go out and kill ten het'ro-seggshells at random, and then we'll be even for their inaction on AIDS." Of course, I sometimes speak in extremes for effect.

Call it, as my dear, dead Clark Henley (he of *The Butch*

---

[4] Marlon Riggs died of AIDS in 1994.

Manual) used to, festive gay exaggeration, or FGE. I think it's a sex-linked trait.

But there I was watching Spike Lee's *Malcolm X*, which everybody seems to have an opinion on—whether they've seen it or not, whether they know anything about Malcolm or not—thinking that maybe, just maybe, we homos ought to just say "Fuck off" to the mainstream and separate. Okay, so Malcolm had a religion around which to organize his separatist movement; and, okay, so he came to reject his own black separatism just before he was iced—probably by some nefarious interventionist secret police arm of the government, but maybe not—and, okay, so most of the "leave me alone to screw in peace" sissies would have nothing to do with it, but I'm beginning to think it may be necessary.

First, I think, when this rage-induced mode comes upon me, after some fresh hell of homophobic expression, let's just separate from the bullshitters and come together as queers. Let's get back into the ghetto—Greenwich Village, the Castro, Montrose, West Hollywood—and oust the interloping opportunist gentrifiers. Then once we're fortified against the barbarians, we'll sit down and work out the caca that's fucking up all our lives: racism, sexism, classicism, ageism, ableism, et al.

But let's find *our* solutions, for ourselves. And fuck the brain-dead 90 percenters, those homophobic het'ro-seggshellers. Who needs 'em? We used to need them for making more of us. Now, thanks to science and a growing number of queer medical professionals, we can make our own babies with sissy sperm and dagger ova. Or am I losing my mind?

I was sitting at a Cuban/Chinese diner on Eighth Avenue with the Haitian-born poet Assoto Saint recently,[5] and when the check arrived the Chinese waiter put it right in front of me. Assoto, who is volatile as well as articulate, was pissed off. I have never noticed, as he has, that whenever a white man and a black man are having dinner together, the check is delivered to the white man. But incidents of racism are not hard to find.

The same thing happened recently when a highly placed lesbian editor invited me to lunch with her in a moderately expensive

---

[5] Assoto Saint (né Yves Labin) died of AIDS in 1994.

but altogether-mismanaged midtown café. The editor requested the check from the waitress, who handed it to me. The editor claimed the check and gave the waitress, a young blonde, her credit card. When she returned, the waitress gave the check and credit card to me for my signature.

So, we might well ask: Has any progress been made at all?
Yes.
No.
I don't know.

Recently I was with a group of ten het'ro-seggshells (it was business), and the subject of the Colorado boycott came up.

"What happened in Colorado?" asked one woman, who apparently had no idea there was anything going on despite being the editor of a major national magazine.

"Colorado just passed a law mandating homophobia," I answered.

To a man, and woman, the other hets screeched: "NO, THEY DIDN'T. THEY JUST PASSED A LAW SAYING GAY PEOPLE COULDN'T BE PROTECTED AS A SPECIAL CLASS."

Now, these happen to be well-informed, decent, gay-friendly type breeders, but the lesson is this: Just as race oppression was practiced by the Asian waiter and sexism by the young blonde waitress, the homophobia of this distinction was lost on the hets. Because gay people are oppressed especially as a special class, denying us protection as a group is morally and ethically tantamount to allowing, thus mandating, further oppression. This is a fact that should not be lost in the debate over the boycott. I am boycotting Colorado. And so are all my friends. Straight people do not get it. And I am inclined to believe, as Malcolm believed of whites, that when push comes inevitably to shove with authorities, when you look around, all the faces you see will be tribesfolk.

There was a related situation in New York. The former chancellor of the New York City school system, Joseph Fernandez, a man dedicated to teaching respect for all people, suspended a local white working-class neighborhood school district for refusing to teach its first-graders from a proscribed "Rainbow Coalition" curriculum. Out in Queens, where white working-class "Christians" routinely beat black youths to death, the objection was to nonjudgmental language about gay men and lesbians. The curriculum was based on the notion that many youngsters in the school system come from gay households. Well, the heteros in Queens (can you believe it?) said that teaching that homosexuals are just like people is "dangerous gay and lesbian propaganda" and thus somehow inherently offensive.

I am not interested in entering a dialogue with these people. I am interested in presenting them with the mutilated bodies of their children.

That is what homophobia has done for me: fed a rage that dulls the moral borders of my own conscience. And so, I say, to the school board in Queens: Watch your backs. We know where you live.

So why stay?

You know, I don't know if I will stay. I love New York, as everyone who knows me knows. I love having been born here. I love having a family that has been from here for generations. I love that my gentle American grandfather was the floorwalker in the men's department at Saks, where I am slowly going bankrupt, and that my German grandfather made pickles in Brooklyn in a building that I pass every time I take a taxi to JFK, and that my great-grandfather Harry Meyers rose to the top of the upholstery business here after emigrating from England to escape anti-Semitism. But New York often feels like a once-legendary relationship gone sour (you know, six months after Happily Ever After: still great when it's great, but the nether regions of the inferno when it's not. In between, there's a lot of dull, aching subway transportation).

Certainly there's no logical reason to stay here. It's outrageously expensive. It's impossible to get anything done. Everybody's deep into a boho depression they're constitutionally committed to. There are so many of us queerlings here that if any of us isn't perfect, we're instantly disposable, like this morning's *Post* after you read Page 6. The weather's extreme, the theater season's been terrible, every uptown avenue is always under construction, and nothing ever gets any better.

But that's why I love it.

| The Hard Way |

New York is a city of moods rather than character. Of rapidly changing moods. And I am a moody person, a product of my hometown. I love the claustrophobic gray clouds that drop rain and snow that obscure the view of New Jersey across the Hudson. I love the bad weather, because I believe, as Shakespeare and the Romantics believed, that the physical world ought to reflect inner turmoil. I love the raw edginess of it. The "so bored I can hardly stay awake" pose of the dance brats, the in-your-face swagger of the hip-hop kids, their pants belted now around their wiggle-bait buttholes and their Tibetan knit caps dripping Goofy dog ears with arrogant insouciance.

I confess I even love the history-blind young activists who actually think my generation was totally apolitical and irrevocably wrongheaded about everything. I love the "sliding scale" of their sexuality (up and down the hetero-homo axis), a vast improvement on the either/or lie of my own generation, which dismissed bisexuality as a politically incorrect cop-out, when in fact it probably more accurately describes the erotic impulse of every human being unfettered by social dictum.

I love that New York is, whatever it is, a town full of survivors. Even the losers are survivors somehow, like the homeless man who stands on the corner where I live and tells jokes while he panhandles. I love that everyone here is engaged in the metaphysical battle with contrary evidence for the meaning of life (for the inkling that life has any meaning at all). Of course the Gay Liberation Front "failed" and spawned the Gay Activists Alliance. Of course ACT UP "failed" and spawned Queer Nation. Because what everyone knows in New York is that New York is not so much a place as a process. Not a place to succeed but to forge one's mettle in the blast furnace of trying to succeed. A laboratory for eventually getting it right for scientists who know that every solution presents a new problem.

Is it exasperating? Yeah.
Is it upbeat, easy, comfortable? No.
And yeah.
I find the reality of New York to be its own reward. Even the saddest day in New York is filled with redemption, with humor, with heads wagging in recognition.

Okay, okay, okay, so I'm feeling good today. I'm full of New York possibilities today. I'm full of the past and present and future of New York all coming together today in a kind of continuum of action.

Of course, I got laid last night.

And nobody died. At least not anybody I know.

Two Poems For New York City

Return to the Naked City

A 707 taking off from LaGuardia:
a DC10 coming in at JFK;

a woman with bad breath pressing up to you
on the uptown bus even though there are seats
enough across the aisle; a woman in red who
throws her cigarette onto the sidewalk (ringed
with lipstick, it rolls north in the wind);

poppies in a crystal vase; a stripper with
a small tattoo at the base of his penis;

a golden retriever who carries a
telephone receiver in its mouth;
a poet whose air conditioner drips
onto the terrace of the poet below;

the soft hand and sad eyes of the faded rock
star, her platinum head turning over her
shoulder in absent greeting (a has-been Venus
in black leather); lightning and thunder;

Greek breakfast, Chinese lunch, Cuban dinner;

Gregory Hines on the street;
Julie Andrews at the theater;
Jessica Tandy in a muddle;

Easter coming and a rainy day so cold, the city so
old it splinters, and you are so relieved to be here
you could weep at the weather, the racket
of jackhammers morning, noon, and sometimes night,
the breakneck pace of people standing stock still;

cherry-blossom pink and the pink of boxed geraniums;
the green of sycamore buds and the green of shutters;
a hustler named Tim
who's an NYU student
in early education;
Manhattan memories;

a plaque with your father's name on the wall
of a church he joined as a boy; the woman you
gave a dollar to who leans in to give you a kiss,
and the kiss itself, and the cheek on your cheek;

the affable cabbie who said he'd take you to
Ghana whenever you're ready; the building where
your mother worked during the war, and her
jubilant smile, her one-armed wave on V-E Day
(your father safe now) surrounded by ticker tape
that drops through the photo in a snowy blur;

a chance encounter with an old acquaintance;
the Village bar where you had your first beer;

the apartment where you learned to play guitar;
haircuts at Vidal Sassoon's, afternoons at MoMA;

the color of light; the patterns of air;

cornhusk angels with tin wings in a Lincoln Center
window; the view from the editor's living room of
the East River, the current racing north, it seems,
against the southbound vessels;

a sense of the future;
the scent of the past;

your grandfather's monogrammed steamer;
your grandmother's dining room table;

your face in the mirror at last;
and the mirror on your wall.

Open windows

The sound of the city in summer is

the satin plaint of the tenor sax that floats from
a Lower Broadway corner to the upper floors; the
infant gurgle of the sax man's half-white son; the
dull indifference of mere coins in a cardboard cup;

the No. 9 train as it rushes into stations;

firecrackers, air horns, helicopters, planes;
generators of carousels at Italian church fairs
and the venomous spit of sausage fat on griddles;

gypsy curses; the high-five slap
of hustlers; Times Square shills;
harpsichords and the hiss of aerosol canisters;

the rhythmic panting of long-haired dogs tied
to fences too hot to touch; the mechanical
clank of slow fans with lazy blades; the dry
crack of ice in tall glasses of foreign tea,
the exotic ting of the ice, and your sigh as
you touch the tumbler to your forehead;

overzealous entreaties that spill onto the
street after last call and closing;

the lupine squeal of truck wheels and children
in fountains; the grinding of trash and the bellow
of the trash collectors; flutes and guitars in
Washington Square, the slap of the geyser on concrete;

the rustle of the ginkgoes as a cold front
rushes to the sea; the plunk-plunk...plunk of
rainwater falling through gutters;

foghorns, church bells, gunshots, taxis;
arguments that escalate to violence; young male
boasting, the laughter of unamused women, radios
blasting the latest rap; breaking crystal,
broken vows; the sshush of razors on rashy skin;

weeknight parties that last too long; the trained
soprano's highest C as it curls down the air shaft
like smoke; bullhorns at rallies, marches, parades;

an insistent green electric blip; the drip of
blood on linoleum tile; an asthmatic catarrh;

finger cymbals; subway Spanish; the meshing
zippers of models dressing; the ball-peen tap
of high-heeled shoes on uncarpeted floors;

the creaking of new leather on new leather;

the ominous drone of a common fly that has
made it in despite your defenses, as you
swat and it spirals, landing in the upraised
hand of your bedside Buddha, the one you bought
in Beijing before the massacre (the sound of
tanks and screaming in the summer madness);

and the silence of memory in the thin, blue night;
the settling of down in your goose-feather pillow;
the click, slight click, of your eyelids as they
open for the last time, then close for the day;

the inverted hook of an unanswered question
intuited through walls.

Near The Fire:
The March On Washington, 1993

Normally speaking, I don't like any situation in which I am not in control. I grow claustrophobic in crowds. Bus travel makes me carsick. Losing sleep turns me into a demon. In fact, I consider myself to be a total hedonist, a self-centered cream puff who doesn't like his feathers ruffled. Yet there I was gleefully shelling out my shekels to take a 3:00 A.M. bus chartered by the Publishing Triangle to schlep from New York City to our nation's capital in order to crawl down Pennsylvania Avenue with a million or so of my closest personal friends.

Trust me, I thought of every possible excuse not to go. I just couldn't stay away. Maybe it's because I've been putting my shanks' mare at the disposal of gay/lesbian rights since the first pride march in 1970. Maybe it's because I'm afraid I'll miss something every time I stay home. Or maybe it's because I have just had enough of the lies those viperous breeder-scum Christians have been spewing about us/me.

Golden Rule for the '90s: Do Unto a Christian, Before He Can Do Unto You—and do it so it lasts an eternity.

So my father called and said, Justin is coming for a visit on Sunday, can you come out? (which was not a political query—he meant *physically*, from Manhattan to Long Island).

Now Justin, who is three going on heartbreaker, is a most popular new baby in our mostly geriatric family, and I love him to distraction. But I had already made the big decision.

"I'm going to Washington," I said.

"Didn't you just get back from Barbados?" Dad asked, suspicious.

"That was business," I said somewhat overdefensively, pulling several layers of sun-murdered skin off my tattooed shoulder.

"Exactly what kind of business are you in?" he asked.

That's when Mom got on the phone.

"What are you protesting this time?" she asked, her voice as cheery as ever.

"It's more of a demonstration *for* a platform of civil rights issues than a protest *against* anything," I said (okay, I'm summarizing).

"Well," she said. "I hope that the demonstration is a success and that you achieve all your goals," she said as if she'd enrolled in the matchbook school of diplomacy.

"What have you done with my real mother?" I asked.

It's not that they haven't had over twenty years to get used to having an out son, I'm just surprised that they did.

So if I'm doing the Washington thing for a *reason*, maybe it's so that the next generation of gay and lesbian puppies can have an easier time of it than I had. And if Justin turns out to be one of the tribe, he'll know that the elders have made a place for him in the hogan as near the fire as he needs to be.

A word about my companion in the adventure. Matt is twenty-four (which is not quite half my age, but he could easily be my sonny Jim). He's from St. Louis and is a graduate student in philosophy. He is about six feet tall and weighs about 160. He has smooth white skin, long dark hair, and eyes the color of forgiveness in Renaissance paintings. We were thrown together in life in one of those mother/daughter kind of relationships so common in twelve-step recovery programs.

The Hard Way

Matt says I've saved his life. If it's true, I was happy to do it. The truth is, he's been saving mine. Anyway, he's smart, sensitive, and companionable. For most of the next twenty-four hours, we hold hands. Although we are not, have not been, and never will be lovers on the romance/sexual axis, I am glad not to be alone in this crowd. I have been too much alone. To quote somebody or other.

Here's one thing I've learned as a long-time homo: You can have sex without love (sometimes even legendary sex), and you can have love without sex. Inter-fagular relationships are as varied as any.

Matt wears dark glasses all day, which means he has to tell me each time he rolls his eyes. Which is not infrequently.

We arrive bleary-eyed at 7:30 A.M. on Sunday. The sky is getting it in mind to turn as blue as Matt's eyes. We head out for downtown, backpacks loaded with a day's provisions.

Birds chirp. Dogs bark. The occasional human being nods good morning. Everything is blooming: cherry, magnolia, dogwood, azalea, tulips. The lilacs are so fragrant, they practically knock you over.

It's spring. With a vengeance. I am being reborn—about as willingly as I was for my weeks-late first nativity.

Occasionally I am a grouch.

By the time we eat breakfast—on a table in front of the Library of Congress—where my books are, yes indeed, catalogued, I say without blushing—the braves of all sexes have begun to assemble on the Mall.

We walk through the grounds of the Capitol. We walk along the Mall to the Washington Monument (it's closed today). We walk to the Lincoln Memorial. We walk to the Vietnam Memorial.

I've been here before, to pay homage to my friend Ralph, whose name is engraved here.

Ralph and I grew up together, although he was four years older. We went to Sunday school together. We were on a basketball team together. Later I got arty. He became a state track champion and all-around charmer. He was also the first heterosexual I ever told I was gay.

| Michael LASSELL |

It was late at night and summer, in 1964 or '65. Ralph was working late at the airport, unloading shit from planes into the tankers that hauled the blue sewage away. I would drink (I was seventeen or so) and wait for him to come home. We'd talk. Just talk. Long talks. The kind men have when they're about to evolve out of boyhood.

"Have you had sex yet?" he asked.

"No," I answered.

"Then how do you know?" he asked.

"I just know," I said. And I did.

"Well," he said. "I don't care. My only advice is, do it with a woman first."

It was advice offered lovingly. I never took it. And I've never regretted it or stopped loving him for the giving of it.

Ralph became a pilot in the U.S. Air Force after a gig in the ROTC at one of the New York state universities. He was shot down and killed while I was taking my senior college year in London and learning at the same time how to be gay with balletic flair.

I've wept at this wall before. It's hard not to. And today, in line with several hundred gay men and lesbians, I begin to feel the weeping coming up on me again like a thunderstorm on the horizon.

Matt feels the first quake, and takes my hand.

It's not just for Ralph that I'm weeping today, of course. It's for all the unnecessary deaths that politics has caused. The deaths of boys in wars, of men in the AIDS wards of America. I'm weeping today for those people whose names are stitched into the quilt laid out on the Mall near the Smithsonian Institute (where my college roommate and I, yes, we really did this, went in and asked the guard where the John Dillinger exhibit was located).

And I wept for those who could not be here today because they are too ill. And for those who could not be here because they cannot come out and who will be taking persons of the opposite sex to Grange meetings in the hate-centered hamlets of the heartland for the rest of their unhappy and pointless lives.

I'm weeping for us all. Matt says nothing, hands me a napkin.

If he is judging, he is not condemning. It's a great deal like having a son. It's a great deal like immortality.

We take our first break at 11:00, sitting in the cool shade of a band shell near what some lesbian "comic" on the loudspeaker refers to as "the biggest dick in the world." Very tasteful.

I am not a fan of (a) humor; (b) loud humor; (c) earnest political rhetoric shouted at me through electronic devices that render the words moot and their cadence horrifying.

"Maybe you just don't like propaganda," Matt says.

We eat apples and talk to Michael, a toddler who has discovered running and disobedience simultaneously. He is eating a cookie. Homos and queers are walking in a steady wave up the hill from the Mall to the beginning of the march site, near the White House.

I came to Washington, D.C., for the first time in 1963, exactly thirty years ago, as a fifteen-year-old delegate to a national convention of the Walther League, a youth group for Missouri Synod Lutherans. I was heterosexual in those days, more or less, and was one of the brain-dead faithless.

Dick Gregory addressed the thousands of us assembled one morning, and I was photographed sharing a hymnal at this event with, in the parlance of the time, a Negro girl. What was for me a completely human and natural moment became an introduction to movement politics when that photo appeared in the *Washington Post*.

Back in 1970, as a fledgling flaming-fag radical, I held a banner that said, "The New Haven Gay Liberation Front Expresses Solidarity with Bobby Seale and the Black Panther Party." I was a graduate student. The other end of the banner was held aloft by a local high-school student. Now, *that* was courageous.

I recognized Jean Genet right away. He'd been an enormous influence on me as a writer—being an out queer and all—and he'd been an organizer of the 1968 general strike in Paris. An undesirable alien, he had snuck into the United States through Canada. Then, at a meeting with the Black Panther Party he convinced its leader, Huey Newton, to issue a statement including gay men and lesbians in the vanguard of the movement for justice.

On July 15, 1984, I marched in a gay and lesbian parade in San

Francisco at the Democratic National Convention. Farmworker/saint Cesar Chavez marched with us to show his support. I was glad my first lover, a sweet, tempestuous Chicano named Roberto, had induced me to join the grape boycott in the early '70s (the 1984 march strode right past the Market Street Safeway that was the first target of our grapeless shopping). Roberto is dead now. And so, alas, is Cesar.

Today Jesse Jackson addresses these uncountable hundreds of thousands of us gathered in this racially divided city, and the head of the NAACP, Benjamin Chavis, offers a trade of support with lesbians and gays in a joint struggle for social justice.

If you stay alive long enough, things sometimes change a little. Maybe. But people you love still die, and you're still stuck with the existential questions, even in the midst of what may be the largest political demonstration in history.

I'll say one thing about Matt. If he gets sick of hearing me rant about my idiotic past, he keeps it to himself.

Matt and I sit in front of the Corcoran Gallery, the BAD art institution that ran scared when Jesse Helms barked at them over the National Endowment for the Arts. Jesse Helms is the devil.

So is Cardinal O'Connor.

Bottom-line realization, April 25, 1993: Religion is the single most evil institution ever conceived by man (and it was, surely, a *man*. Not only does religion cause virtually all dispute, it pits us against each other and brainwashes us with the lie that we cannot come to a spiritual life without the intervention of a special class of god-goons, a.k.a. priests.

I am not cheered by the existence of gay churches. Perhaps some people need to believe in the afterlife most religions offer as a reward for putting up with a lot of priest shit along the way. It's a trade wind that cools the fevered sleep of the guilt-ridden and the anxious.

The way I look at it is this: If there is a God, you can be sure he wouldn't be so cruel as to have created eternity.

Here's who I love in the march: The Gay and Lesbian Youth. With their pimply faces and limitless bravura, they are the future.

Us Stonewall types are dinosaurs to them, and that's as it should be. I nearly shed another tear at the idea these kids have already gotten past the "being queer thing" and can get on about the business of life. God...oops...I mean, Larry Kramer bless them.

We watch the march for hours and finally join in. We don't talk much. I take a few half-hearted pictures. We dish and drool a bit. But the march is SO slow and there are SO MANY people, that we bail and wander over to the Los Angeles contingent, still waiting to step off.

I spot my friend Bill, a lovely man I helped get sober five years ago or more. He throws his arms around me and gives me a great big interracial kiss.

There is nothing more gratifying than having someone you care about show in unfettered, effusive terms that he is delighted to see you.

"You know him," says Bill and points to Art, a lovely man who helped get me sober almost seventeen years ago now.

More hugging and kissing. More introductions.

I am overcome with a feeling that my life as a gay man is beginning to make sense. I am nonetheless extraordinarily fatigued. Perhaps it's because I haven't slept.

At Matt's suggestion, we head away from the crowd and toward the Mall. Destination: The National Gallery of Art.

Here is a thing about crowds (separate from how claustrophobic they make me): No matter what the group is, and no matter how legitimate my participation in it, I invariably come to feel like an outsider.

Now this may be just a personal idiosyncrasy, a kink in the twisted wire of my psyche. But I'm not sure that's the whole of it. I believe it's also a function of internalized homophobia.

It's part of the tragedy of being treated like an outsider on a daily basis. And make no mistake: out or not out, I believe, we homos, queers and fairies deal nonstop with the enormity of the hatred heaped upon us. We leave our homes each morning knowing that we are targets and that the law not only allows us to be targets but delights in our deaths. So three marines beat up a gay man outside a bar and they are ACQUITTED(!) because they have convinced the judge that the THREE MARINES acted out of SELF-DEFENSE when attacked by the ONE gay man.

No wonder the Pentagon doesn't want fags in their army: They're afraid we're going to beat them up.

In the air-conditioned East Building of the always-free National Gallery—the modern I. M. Pei addition Matt loves—we run into Ramón, a New York friend who has AIDS and who has been traveling around Asia for six months.

I've already run into the poet Mark Ameen, novelists John Weir and David Feinberg, and some of the little spider monkeys from the gym. I know there are friends here in the crowd somewhere: Betty Berzon and Richard Rouilard from L.A.; poet Assoto Saint (whose lover died only three weeks ago); the queers I know from D.C.—Andy Mellen and the gang from Lambda Rising, but they're all off in their own widening consciousness.

Are you out there, Essex Hemphill? Eric Guttierez?

It feels like a party here. A powwow. A family reunion. They may all be strangers, but they're much nicer strangers than a lot of my relatives.

In the museum coffee shop, we have six cups of coffee and head for the oldest art we can find.

In 1963 I was overwhelmed by Dalí's rendition of the last supper with its semi-transparent participants giving way to a cloudy sky. I remember having a discussion with a pair of nuns at the time about whether it was sacrilegious or not.

Today Matt and I head for the coolest and quietest corner of the museum. I point out favorite paintings I visit when I'm in town.

This sense of sharing, of passing on the things we love, is another portion of immortality, of continuity. We are revived by the quiet, by that sense of being whole.

By five o'clock, we're done in, and head back down East Capital Avenue toward Robert Kennedy Stadium, where the bus is parked in a sea of similar vehicles.

As the upscale white neighborhood gives way to a less-opulent

African-American neighborhood somewhere beyond the rather embarrassing statue of Lincoln with a slave bowing at his feet, I begin to feel vulnerable. We are not only the sole Caucasians in sight, we are also clearly queer.

The first time we are called faggot, Matt doesn't even hear. It's a young man and woman in a small grocery store we pass. The next time, within sight of the stadium, it's an adult black man improving the world this Sunday afternoon by smoking dope in a car near a basketball court.

"Well," I say, "that was courageous."

"Faggot," the man says again. Apparently my brother in the liberation struggle has not heard the director of the NAACP saying how kindred we are, we faggots and niggers and all.

Was I angry? I was. Was I sad? I was. Was I afraid? No.

And it was not the numbers of us in Washington this day that made me strong. It was the one, the one I have become by being an out gay man going on three decades.

A house divided against itself cannot stand, it is written. But a human being who is wholly him- or herself is undoubtedly a lone sapling that *can* stand, tossed or not, against the general hurricane. It was not *physical* strength I was feeling (although I did feel that), but political strength, the strength of being absolutely content with who I am today, a spiritual strength, I might say, that comes from putting myself in the service of a higher authority.

And this, for me, was the lesson of the March of '93. I am a deeply flawed, often-unhappy human being. But I am not confused about being gay. About being gay, I am quite happy. Now, happiness is a feeling of limitless freedom; and freedom, we know, is powerful. As powerful as any sermon.

"That's amazing," Matt says, noticing the concentric rings of gold, purple and lilac pansies ringing the trees on the plaza of the Capitol Building.

"Yes, it is," I say, and point to the Mall, at the sea of pansies not segregated by color, and not arranged in neat patterns, but ranging freely, hand in hand, across Washington, undoubtedly stronger than ever before.

Amateur Night:
On Masks, Gender, And The Hellacious Halloween Hoedown Of 1970

"You're looking piratical," said a friend recently. I took stock: beard, bandanna, hoop earring, forehead furrow that looks like a cutlass scar...what could have been her clue? Not that it surprises me to be found *in costume flagrante*. It's just that it wasn't Halloween...or October...or any particular special occasion at all. It wasn't even Bruce Weber Look-alike Week. I flipped through the disintegrating card file of my life, back—you guessed it—to childhood, that treasure island of a-moldering psychic doubloons.

You see, back in Suburbia, USA, in the halcyon days of the Korean Conflict and the McCarthy witch-hunts—yes, the original prerevival '50s—"pirate" was my Halloween modus operandi. Each year, Momsy and I would dive into her scarf drawer and pull out something loud and silky to wrap my head in. Dad would bring home an eye patch from God knows where (Heller's Pharmacy, probably). Burnt cork would provide facial hair; lipstick a lovely cheek scar. We'd poke a hole in a faded striped polo shirt and fray the bottoms of my oldest pair of pants, then cinch them with one of those Liz Taylor *Butterfield 8* belts. A café-curtain ring tied around my ear would provide the perfect glitter accessory, and—*voilà!*—a petite and pudgy privateer.

It's hard to say at this point whether my fascination with things buccaneer had anything to do with masculine imagery—popular in the swashbuckling adventure films I favored at the now-defunct Alan Movie Theater on Hillside Avenue (the athletic courage and gymnastic prowess of these chiseled hunks being about as far from my own Crayola crybaby persona as possible), or whether it was a prequeer fascination with that drawer full of scarves and lipstick scars.

Needless to say, Halloween always had its horrors—it was bad enough to be harassed by daylight hooligans whose faces you could see. Masked by dark and cloaked in plastic, they were terrible forces of teenage terrorism. The big kids. The eighth graders! Which of us lil'uns didn't feel like Ichabod Crane pursued by the Headless Horseman of Sleepy Hollow?

By first grade I'd had my first Halloween humiliation when my prefab Frankenstein costume ripped up the seat during recess and I stood against the chain link fence until every other child in the neighborhood had gone back in to Miss Asherman's class in the gray wooden schoolhouse built as temporary structure in 1947 (and which still stands).

There are happy memories, too. There was the year my best friend Michael—diminutive epileptic son of the local Mafioso—arrived in second grade, the only kid in the class with no costume at all. Averting a near psychological disaster, Miss Behrens (who still remembers this) whipped out a few sheets of flexible poster board, an orange marker, and some brass fasteners and turned my now-beaming classmate into Pumpkin Man—a kind of Superhero Squash.

"And what are you doing now?" asked the still *Miss* Behrens when I ran into her last Christmas.

"I'm a writer and editor," I said, "which is what you get for teaching me to read."

And then there was Mrs. Barr, the Witch Woman of Evans Street, who could turn you to stone with her naked glance for so much as having your ball land on her lawn, but who was unaccountably the most generous of all the women in town come

Trick or Treat (for those of us bold enough to ring her doorbell), as if she, too, decided to change character once each year. One day you weren't allowed to play on her street; the next you were invited *inside the house* while she plied you with whole boxes of Cracker Jacks and quarters. Quarters! A week's wages for the those of us on allowance (and the living room a moss-green oasis of chinoiserie in a town of reproduction Early American).

Yes, these were the days before razor blades in apples; before the unaccountable abduction of children by white slavers or parents involved in ugly custody battles; before parents had to guard their children's plastic jack-o'-lanterns from thieving mini-muggers or to test wrappers for insertions of noxious substances from Draino to heroin; before, even, the notion that feeding pounds of sugar to children might not be the very best thing for their health.

I liked dressing up as a kid. I loved the Christmas pageant at church, when I was invariably cast as a shepherd (the spear-carriers of Christian theatricals)—snore. I liked school plays better: the year I wore my mother's Chinese silk pajamas with the red frog closures and the fierce dragon-embroidered jacket for our choir's *Mikado* (I was Koko, the Lord High Executioner). And it was inevitable, I suppose, that my mother's closet started calling my name in soft, alluring tones, and I would stay home from school (where I was as bored as I was frightened) and entertain myself with her jewelry, dresses, makeup—the whole nine yards of an appropriately dressed woman of the '50s (moving into the '60s), crinolines included.

Then there was the scandal (small scale) when I dressed from head to toe, from skin out, in the most elaborate full drag of my young life, and my father came home unexpectedly from work with a colleague. Oops. They never actually *saw* me dressed to the nines, but Dad knew. In my mother's meticulously kept household, there was no moment ever when everything she owned was strewn around the bedroom and bathroom. There was a confrontation, of sorts, which I averted by lying through my clenched unbraced teeth (since boys didn't need to care how they looked), and the matter went uneasily to its well-deserved rest.

I joined the theater group at school and stuck to gender-appropriate attire for most of the rest of my life, although I was invariably in the vanguard of the feminization of the American male—from love beads at the first possible moment in the '60s, to the ruffles and frills of a London year abroad at the height of the Mod thing (not without a certain resemblance to the puffy pirate shirts Douglas Fairbanks wore with such muscular élan), to skirts and nail polish in the early '70s genderfuck days at CalArts. (And can you guess what very, very famous pop-culture icon was right there leading the way, egging me on?) And I did appear onstage in women's clothes, once (bearded and glittered in the style of the Cockettes, the San Francisco theater troupe that gave birth to Sylvester, the disco diva who is spiritual ancestor to RuPaul). But by and large, I was not as an early adult into drag, and I admit that I thought it made me a superior fag.

I am fairly certain that my forays into female attire had nothing to do with wanting to be a woman. It had to do with a rather more desperate notion that I should have been a woman (having been brought up as one), and that notion was a corollary of thinking that my mother and I were a single entity. Some dare call this inappropriate brand of merging incest—well, emotional incest in any case, and at my house we had it in spades. My mother still hasn't begun coping with postpartum depression. And won't.

I had a lover for ten years who celebrated Halloween the way the Windsors celebrate nuptials. He'd prepare for weeks, if not months, conferring with every other hair-burner in L.A., and massing together for sewing bees, the products of which were sequin-encrusted showgirl outfits with headdresses you had to rent an extra room for. I remember feeling like a guest in my own apartment from about mid-August until November, when the hot glue and bugle beads would finally come unstuck from the carpet (just in time for the pine needles of December).

And then there was the clone thing, remember that? You see, I am of the generation that fell between the camp drag eras of Charles Pierce and Lady Bunny. And my coming out was accompanied by the political-rights movement, which tsk-tsked feathers, favoring the butch look most of the boys in denim and leather forgot was a drag all its own, and which, in fact, turned its cowardly back on the noble laddies of the well-dressed night who had in fact turned out the Stonewall Inn that fateful June night of Judy Garland's funeral in 1969.

Having thought of myself as a boy who should have been a girl and having sidled nearly to the line in velvets and flounces of my own design, I swung to the jeans-and-boots thing. But the truth is, I was a kid so adept at changing personalities that Halloween became irrelevant. Alcoholics call New Year's Eve "amateur night." It's what I thought of Halloween. Why get dressed up one day of the year when I was somehow in costume every day of my life, pretending to be a nice middle-class boy in a blazer for my parents, a street radical during the antiwar movement in my pea jacket and rimless glasses, an aspiring artiste at school in bell-bottoms and sensitively blousy shirts? And did I mention that I was at the time an aspiring actress?

It's a truism of theater types, of course, and of primitive societies, which theater troupes frequently resemble, that one puts on a mask and becomes the mask, or at least some creature balanced between mask and wearer. The mask, the costume, gives us permission to be someone else, to behave in an "inappropriate way," to reverse roles, to suspend the rules and upend the status quo, as whole cities did during medieval Fools' Days celebrations (from which modern Halloween customs generally derive). Growing up without a personality, I tried to acquire one with a succession of wardrobes. I went from a Motown-inspired rock 'n' roll preteen (the look, as you know, is back) to Beatles bohemian one Tuesday afternoon. As an adult, I've come to realize that I was motivated by a desperate need to be accepted even before there was a self there to be accepted.

And then there was the Halloween Party of 1970, the last time I have acknowledged the holiday, possibly for all time.

Call it naïveté. Call it folly. Call it…a mistake.

I was living in New Haven with a medical student from Queens and his lover, a graduate student in linguistics from one of those states east and west of states that touch oceans. I had tried to have an affair with the budding Doc, but before I got his holey Jockeys all the way off his hairy legs, the phone rang. It was my girlfriend of the moment wondering why it was that I was in New Haven when I was supposed to be in New York seeing her off on her six-month trip to Europe. Oops. I forgot. My shy physician was dressed before I hung up. But this was in the days when bisexuality was a kind of mask, too, and politically incorrect big time, a kind of failure of nerve to be gay (or lesbian).

I had a lesbian lover at the time, by the way, who also slept with Baby Doc, who also slept with my lesbian lover's lesbian lover, who was also sleeping with the boy I was obsessed with who was living with me (although he wouldn't have sex with me, but he did have sex with the lesbian and the medical student and their shared lesbian lover, and we did a lot of sex in groups and pairs among ourselves and with others, which is why I look back so fondly on the '70s). I took revenge by porking the linguist, who cunningly pretended to be asleep. So that was when we decided to have a Halloween party.

Wouldn't it be wonderful, we reasoned in that way the insane have of sounding rational, to have a party in our swell ghetto digs and invite our friends from the medical, drama, and graduate schools and from our many political activities to meet each other—without, by the way, telling them: (a) the other types would be there, or (b) that the three of us were gay. After all, why should that matter? After all, it was 1970. All of our various friends were going to meet each other and love each other, as we loved each of them, and it was going to be the glorious Flower-Power Fall of festive-leafed New England. A love feast in the north country. Oops again. The best-laid plans were aft agleying before the apartment was dusted.

The night of the party, a Saturday, our first guest arrived. Jay, a political activist who had reverted, as most do, to New York City, had been called Guy when we met him, but abandoned his nickname as a piece of unnecessarily sexist baggage. Having politicized all of us, he decided to wear a dress to our party, although there was, believe me, nothing remotely feminine about this young person. Since the secondhand dress was wool, and wet for some reason, having made the rail trip from the city in a plastic bag, he popped it into the oven to dry it out.

Katrina, a public-health student who lived downstairs, and

who was guarding our neurotic feline, Mishka, popped up with some hors d'oeuvres only to find the oven occupied. The stalwart trio of hosts, having opted not to costume ourselves, were busily spiking the punch with vodka, gin, and rum—all the invisible alcohols (it was a theme), and preparing reefers, as other guests began to arrive. The drama-school students came in costume (Kate and her husband Yanni came as each other) and spoke loudly with large gestures; the medical students came, some directly from the operating room, looked around, and retreated to the far corners to chat judgmentally among themselves; the graduate students wandered around smoking dope and gathering data.

The party remained strained, but civil, more or less, until the real people got there—the folks we had met in our street-duties as blossoming revolutionaries: i.e., drag queens, some of them drag queens of color (and a colorful lot they were, too). This seemed to put the Yalies more on edge than the queer thing...the race and class thing, you know (after all, alma mater had a long, long tradition of secret-society homosex). But it was the alcohol and drugs, I suspect, that really kicked it all over the edge.

I'm not sure who invited the RadicaLesbians of Boston who were in town for some major dance/concert/woman thing. But they were not amused by cher René, a local character of no apparent affiliation who was dressed rather authentically if tweedily, I thought, as Joan Bennett. Words were exchanged between René/Joan and a beefy person with short hair whose name or gender I never really learned. The word *cunt* may have been spoken. Guy, I mean Jay, whose dress had shrunk to a mini in our ancient oven, defended the honor of the ladies of all sexes present by inviting René/Joan to leave, which invitation was declined by the screaming queen of the night (hitting all her high C's, D's, E's and even F-sharps), who took the opportunity to seize the spotlight by kicking in the antique glass-enclosed bookcases.

The RadicaLesbians did what women always did when things got ugly along gender lines in those days: they walked—en masse. It was at this point, I believe, that I tried to get everything back in control. Was it too late? Jay, whose flirtation with the feminine did not preclude him from exercising his rather powerful arms and upper body, had Miss Joan in the air and, before my rather horrified eyes, was tossing him/her down the stairs. Not altogether undeserved, or inappropriate, but Ms. Thing did insist on an ambulance, since he/she was bleeding rather profusely through her shredded hose (from kicking in the glass-fronted bookcases, it turned out when she was delivered to the emergency room of the hospital where my roommate's best friend—and our upstairs neighbor—was on duty). Did I mention that this was in the days that a doctor could lose his license just for being gay? Everybody say oops!

    I was now, inspired by rage and fueled by grass, hash, and the invisible liquors, standing in the middle of the living room (on a carpet I had shampooed with my very own sensitive hands) screaming for everyone to love each other. People were leaving, fast, presumably because the word "police" was being muttered, as were the words "Black Panthers," who were headquartered rather conveniently next door, and there were a lot of white middle-class careers at stake. It was the night I first experienced hysteria—literally—the kind of sobbing that comes from someplace prehistoric and cannot be the least dissuaded by reason and which does not spend itself. Happily, the medical roommie's little black bag was handy, and he dosed me up with Thorazine to get me down to manageable. When no one was left but the black drag queens, the doctor and the linguist retired to their bedroom. One of the generally despised street people held me until I stopped crying while the rest restored the apartment to some kind of dignity. Then they left, too, planting on my sweat-soaked head the gentle kisses of a beloved aunt or godmother.

    I don't exactly remember being the last person awake in the apartment, but there I was. I managed to get myself to the local donut shop for a half dozen or so chocolate-covered munchie-killers, and then back home. Where, I believe, I slept in the living room, certain I was the only human being of any gender to be sleeping alone that night. And did I mention that the following morning, a Sunday, at 9:00 A.M., i.e., three hours later, I had to be at work? Well, I wrote "I quit" on my drafting table, and walked around a dying New Haven on All Soul's Morning until I managed to find a corner of the cemetery to lie down in. I hadn't yet learned about Mexico's Days of the Dead, but when I did, they made all the sense in the world to me.

And although I occasionally find that I have unconsciously dressed myself as a would-be Jean Laffite, that was the last Halloween I ever participated in, or at least got dressed up for. I have lost touch with most all of the people who were at that party; many are now dead, of course, of overdoses, AIDS, or poverty. My fledgling sawbones, a sweet man I wronged much and often, is now a Freudian analyst in New York City. Kate, long divorced from Yanni as well as her second husband, teaches acting brilliantly in Los Angeles.

I last saw Jay/Guy/Jason in San Francisco at a Louise Hay evening I was attending with my two best friends, Clark and Kenny, both of them now dead, and Jason, too, probably, the man whose birthday was the same as mine, who explained to me the relationship between homosexuality, repression, and political action, who showed me the gay section of Jones Beach (to which we would go in matching North African djellabas), and who is a recurring figure in my life, a minor character from one of those multi-volume British novels we always mean to read all the way through, a man who pops up at the oddest moments in ways you'd say were overly ironic or implausibly coincidental if they were fictional.

And so when I stay home on Labor Day, while all of queer New York is at Wigstock, and on Halloween, when all of New York masses in Greenwich Village for the parade (either to dress up or to throw eggs and/or bricks at those who do), I am left with a set of images enjambed against one another like impacted wisdom teeth: a childhood fascination with the accoutrements of femininity; a sense that male attire is somehow drag for me, too (a suit-and-tie oppressor drag); the knowledge that my own masculinity was harder won than my acceptance of my femininity; images of Charles Laughton as Quasimodo dressed up as the King of Fools, *the* character I most identify with in literature; a whiff of seasonal sadness—like the smell of smoke in a chilly wind; the intimation that I have shut myself off from some aspect of being that I truly love, that I can't just let go and join the fun.

But there is healing too, I know it, whistling down the chimney with memories of Guy, and a forgiveness for the ill-informed follies of my own overambitious youth.

    So, who knows? Maybe you'll see me decked out one of these days—a pirate in a hoop skirt, perhaps, with all the various little compartments of my life integrated, like that fucking Halloween party was supposed to be: a harmonious convergence of all the people I cared about—without regard to gender, orientation, race, or class. Or maybe I'm in costume already, whatever I wear, waiting for the real party to begin…the real Feast of All Souls—the Come as You Are Party to which we're all invited, and no one feels a need to be anyone else at all.

Oh, God! Not Again!
Confessions Of A Reluctant Agnostic

Well, here I am, still all warm and toasty from those interminable and inescapable cathode-ray images of our "progay" president kissing the rectal sphincter of the geriatric genocide of a mile-high pope. What better time, I ask you, to think about, to write about...God (asshole spelled backwards), the former organizing principle of the universe—but that was before George Stephanopoulos and Susan Sontag (who, I kid you not, is currently directing *Waiting for Godot* in Sarajevo! Hard to imagine a metaphor for that particular folly more figurative than the thing itself).

Now, this may surprise many of you, but calls out of the blue from editors on the far side of the Rockies are relatively rare in the lives of us New York City poets manqués. Seldom do they begin conversations with questions like: "Do you believe in God?"

"For about four minutes a day," I snap, master of the jaded telephonic retort. Surely our editor must know that anyone who has ever made a living as a full-time freelance writer cannot help but believe in God. But as timing, and divine injustice would have it, the request for a few words on the spiritual come at a funny (not the ha-ha kind) time in my day—halfway between a suicidal morning in the salt mines of Gotham and a second date with a practicing Roman Catholic PWA. Which is to say, right smack dead on the Hiroshima of my crisis in faith. Oh yes, *mes enfants,* these are truly times to try men's souls, the worst of times and the worst of times—not to mention the rediscovery by the world of fashion of tie-dying, peace symbols, and macramé. (I never thought I'd live long enough to be reduxed).

All right, then, a little *histoire*. (I don't, by the way, speak French, but the language sounds so damn snotty that a liberal sprinkling seems apropos.)

So it's 1978, '79, one of those years in there with a lot of sex, a lot of anxiety, and nary a fatal disease on the horizon. I'm driving south on Vermont having just made the two-hour left turn from Hollywood B. It is summer—as always in L.A.—so I am sweating my balls off in my tiny red Civic. The fuel tank, I am aware, is nearly as empty as (a) my pocket and (b) my stomach (which is why the air conditioner is off). Unemployed and deeply depressed about it, I've got enough money to buy (a) lunch, or (b) enough gas to get home to eat it.

Since I am, in these bygone days of tight skin, abdominal muscles, and great resilience in all things, a relatively new member of a certain recovery program that strongly suggests (i.e., *mandates)* belief in some kind of higher power, I reach into the vortex of my seething anger and muster what I can by way of prayer: "All right, you asshole, what now?"

At which point—I kid you not, my little love-puppies—a loaf of bread came flying through the open passenger window of the unapologetically Japanese car.

I was so taken by the Mosaic symbolism (sliced and wrapped American white though it was), that I became addicted to a belief in a supreme being, an organizing principle of existence, a benevolent and protective force. Which is to say, I came to believe in my thirtieth year (after a descent into the Inferno) in God. Everything good that happened in my life, I attributed to the PM (prime mover); I blamed self-will for all that went awry. It was neat and cozy, and many well-meaning fellow travelers praised my spirituality. Say Amen! Say shallow as a b-builder on steroids.

| The Hard Way |

I had been happy in God as a child, too. God, in those days, was long-haired and bearded, bathed invariably in a bastard-amber key light (Hurrell could not have done better), with the terrified and hungry eyes I have since come to associate with unattractive men on the prowl for anonymous nookie. Each Christmas we kiddies-in-shepherd-drag were given a box of imported milk chocolates to enforce our affection for this sentimentalized Bavarian icon of conformist rectitude neutered by two thousand years of human interpretation.

It wasn't until puberty (a nice segue from "neutered," don't you think?) that I paid the slightest attention to the teachings of my fundamentalist Protestant church. Oops! Big mistake. I was going to hell forever for the way I felt about Ralph Manners, Georgie Bowen, and Ray Singer. Happily, I was by now quite happy to go to hell, since it would be free of the likes of Mrs. Rechenberger—chain-smoking, blood-taloned Sunday-school teacher of my increasingly rebellious youth—who donated the rose window in the church renovation and then lobbied for the rest of her justly short, emphysemic life to replace the common Eucharist cup with individual little juice glasses...just in case one of them Negroes should ever join the congregation (about as likely as a camel ever trying to slip through the eye of a needle, camels generally being smarter than tailors, well, you know what I mean). Religion, I came to believe, was a puddle in which the aqueous beetles of humanity frolic. To paraphrase W. C. Fields: No religion for me, boy, Christians fuck in it!

And, I am here to say, I have not yet changed my mind about religion at all. All extant religions of note are the invention of heterosexual men and exist primarily for the same purpose served by all inventions of heterosexual men: so that they may accrue power in the control of others (cf. Colin Powell and the joint chiefs of staphylococcus). Religion is therefore inherently homophobic and therefore bad. All right, I simplify. But you get the gist. If they all love Jesusjesusjesus so much, say I, let them spend their weekends crucifying each other instead of bashing us. (And ditto, by the way, Orthodox fanatics from both east and west banks of the River Jordan.)

But spirituality, of course, is not the same as religion.

Spirituality is the wine; religion, the cup. The cup exists for the sake of the wine; but the wine exists for itself, irrespective of its container—for itself, and to slake thirst. And, God knows (to coin a phrase), we are parched people, we humans. I am so dry on life I would drink arsenic if someone told me it would soothe the savage breast (no, not Brigitte Nielsen in *Red Sonia*—although, oddly enough, Brigitte and I share a birthday with Rembrandt and Linda Ronstadt, thus proving everything relates and astrology holds no answers).

The first time I decided I wanted nothing to do with God, I was in high school. "You don't really believe that Jonah was swallowed by a whale, do you?" mocked my sophisticated classmates. "Actually, it was a big fish," I retorted, but the truth is, I was embarrassed into hating God.

Learn my lesson? Hah! After spending most of the last year desperately (key word!) in love with a young atheist who showed no sign at all of taking comfort from me in lieu of a supreme being, I had to confess (another key word!) that I had spent the year (a) denying the existing of God just because Matt did and (b) pursuing Matt with the fervor of a pilgrim crawling to Mecca over a bed of nails, glass, and hot coals. Have no God? Who needed one? I had Matt. Or didn't have him, actually, but I believed in him, pursued his pleasure, sacrificed myself to him, prayed to him, made him the measure of my existence. I have a habit of deifying inappropriate entities: money, alcohol, sex, and a variety of now-aborted careers. I am a person, *mes amis,* who requires a God even when I do not wish to believe in one. A reluctant agnostic, then, who wishes he could be either a true believer or an atheist. Agnosticism always seems so cravenly wishy-washy, like bisexuality (another former God of mine). He who sits on fence gets sore crotch, said a sweet boy from France recently. His name was Jerome, and he was no saint, though he looked like an angel.

But I have been hating God ever since the long, slow dying began. I watched my friends blister and shrivel like Job, not cursing God but thanking him/her/it/them for countless blessings. "If my faith had been stronger," said the man I loved more than anyone in the world, "I would have been able to be fucked countless times without a condom without getting AIDS." He learned that from a festive fag preacher in San Francisco, who, I hope, will spend eternity breathing the secondhand smoke of the odious Mrs. Rechenberger.

So, I have spent a many, many years, *mes chers*, in a state of perpetual anxiety about the existence of God. And so, here I sit in New York City, forty-six years old, queer and single (I'd avoid that particular parlay, by the way). My life has been devastated by plague, despite my own ludicrous negative HIV status—just because I never had the fortitude to discover anal eroticism back in the resilient days of my manipulative youth. Can we wonder that I find the notion of God a trifle difficult? Can we wonder that I find blind chance a more likely organizing metaphor for who gets blinded in Bosnia and who gets to direct quintessentially existentialist plays by Beckett (I can't go on/I must go on)? Can we wonder, even allowing the existence of God, that God seems either remote, indifferent, or malevolent—hostile rather than beneficent? Fuck God!! Fuck God and Republicans and Christians and popes and presidents and the joint chiefs of staff and cardinals from L.A. and New York—may they all rot in heaven forever with the carnivorous God of their devising!

How is it none of them has suggested that killer floods in the Midwest are God's retribution for homophobia?

Yes, I could build quite a head of atheistic vitriol—if I had not experienced what I somehow intuitively know was…God. In a loaf of bread flying through the window at an opportune moment. (I had done an unaccountable kindness to a delivery-van driver stuck in traffic and the sweet bearded stranger who was driving the truck was thanking me the best way he knew how.)

I have felt this thing called God in the kindness of strangers (a dirt-poor family who stopped to help me change a flat tire who would take nothing for their effort more than the promise that I would someday do the same for someone else). In the eyes of a man who steps into my life for no particular reason on Seventh Avenue South—Valentin, from Nicaragua, for example, who may have been mixing just a little lovely lust in there with his divinity—which is how many primitives discovered God: in tumescence (Higher Power = Huge Penis). I have known God in the selflessness of others, and in courage, both of which attributes I lack in spades.

I have known God in the passion of Martin Luther King, Jr., on the steps of the Lincoln Memorial. In a perfect L.A. day driving down Rodeo Drive from Sunset to Wilshire. In a phone call that comes at the right moment. In the arms of a man who just let me cry. And cry. And cry.

So my crisis in faith is a bit backward. The elect, of course, have faith despite having no experience of God. I lack faith, despite my knowledge that God, or something like God, truly exists "It's just emotion," says Matt, my love, my lost Matt. But it is, if it is nothing more, a very special emotion.

I can remember sitting in that white concrete cathedral on top of that hill in San Francisco (the one that looks like a nun's starched coif). And the sun slipped between the clouds and hit the slivers of windows in the soaring ceiling and danced around the cascading sculpture of metal shards, rippling downward to where I sat, depressed as usual. I felt the presence of God in that moment. I felt forgiveness for my failures (and there have been many). I felt acceptance for everything I was. I felt the peace and serenity I feel in any authentically holy place, from the Muir Woods to the Buddhist temples of China.

I felt, in that one bright, shining San Francisco moment…grace. Which, by no coincidence, turned out to be the name of that sculptural mobile of quivering light.

If it is true that we are all on some path of spiritual quest, then we only need to have faith in walking (or crawling). I do not know if I believe in God, or if God believes in me. But I am a creature who feels the need for God enormously. I am not, in fact, so much on a path in search of God, but on a path to a willingness to have faith despite my skepticism. I am, if you will, moving toward some ineluctable essence of something divine. If I could understand it, or frame it, prove it, explain or even describe it, I suppose, it would not be what I am looking for: an answer beyond any comprehension I have yet experienced.

And where can I look? In those moments of good between people. In love. My dearest Kenny, who died six long, dark years ago, cherished our friendship because we laughed together so much. Because it was a laughter so without anxiety or hysteria. Because the laughter felt so...divine. When I begin to lose track of the path to God, I must remember to start looking where I know he lives if he is anywhere: in the sound of laughter.

Acknowledgments

Part One: The Cradle of Civilization
"Brooklyn/Long Island/Los Angeles/New York" was first published in *Hometowns: Gay Men Write About Where They Belong* (edited by John Preston; New York: Dutton/Plume, 1991).
"Cold heat" was first published in *The Literary Review* (Vol. 30, No. 1, Madison, NJ, Fall 1986).
"Daddy" was first published in *Decade Dance* by Michael Lassell (Alyson Publications, Boston, MA, 1990).
"His mother's incest" was first published in *Central Park* (No. 22, New York: Spring 1993).

Part Two: For Better or Worse
"Willie" was first published in *Men on Men 3* (edited by George Stambolian; New York: Dutton/Plume, 1990).
"Making a mark" was first published in *The James White Review* (Vol. 8, No. 2, Minneapolis, MN, Winter 1991).

Part Three: Our Bodies and Our Blood
"Confessions of a Clothes Whore" was first published in the *L.A. Weekly*, March 23, 1984.
"25 Reasons to Hate Heterosexuals" was first published in the *L.A. Weekly*, November 18, 1983.
"Writ of Habeas Corpus" was first published in the *L.A. Weekly*, July 19, 1985.
"When Death Is Too Much with Us" was fist published in *L.A. Edge*, September 7, 1983, and subsequently in *The Weekly News of Miami* (November 9 and 16, 1983) and *Body Politic* in Toronto (March 1984).
"Heart in San Francisco" was first published in *L.A. Style*, March 1987.
"Saturday night in New York City" was first published in *Queer City* (New York: Portable Lower East Side, January 1992).
"Keepsake" was first published in *Kansas Quarterly* (Vol. 23, Nos. 1–2, Manhattan, KS, Summer 1992).
"Prism" was first published in *ONTHEBUS* (No. 5, Los Angeles, Spring 1990).
"What it means to live alone again" was first published in *City Lights Review* (San Francisco: December 1990).
"Kissing Ramón" was first published in *Poetry New York* (No. 5, New York, Winter 1992); it also appeared in the "Out Auction" catalog of

the Los Angeles Gay and Lesbian Community Services Center (edited by Eric Guttierez, June 1992).

"Shuttle, 9:00 A.M." was first published in *Jugular Defences* (The Oscars Press, London, 1994).

"Andrew, Son of James" was first published in *The James White Review* (Vol. II, No. 4, Minneapolis, MN, Summer 1984), and subsequently in *Poems for Lost and Un-lost Boys* by Michael Lassell (Amelia, Bakersfield, CA: 1985).

"How to visit your ex" was first published in *Poems for Lost and Un-lost Boys*.

"Brady Street, San Francisco" was first published in *Art and Understanding* (No. 1, Albany, NY, Fall 1991).

Part Four: My Life in Art

"Skyfires" was first published in *Indivisible: New Short Fiction by West Coast Gay & Lesbian Writers* (edited by Terry Wolverton and Robert Drake; New York: Dutton/Plume, 1991). Portions were published in *Male Review* in 1985.

"Negative Image" was first published in *Torso* (July 1984), and subsequently appeared in *Flesh and the Word* (edited by John Preston; New York: Dutton/Plume, 1992).

"How to be a hedonist" was first published in *Poems for Lost and Un-lost Boys*.

"How to choose life" was first published in *Decade Dance*.

"How to go to the theater" was first published in *ZYZZYVA* (Vol. 1, No. 4, San Francisco: Winter 1985).

"How to watch your brother die" first appeared in *Poems for Lost and Un-lost Boys*. It subsequently appeared in *Gay and Lesbian Poetry in Our Time*; in *Poets for Life: 76 Poets Respond to AIDS* (edited by Michael Klein; New York: Crown Books, 1989); and in *Decade Dance*, as well as in numerous other anthologies and textbooks.

"How to write a poem" was first published in *Out/Look* magazine (San Francisco: Winter 1992).

Part Five: New Frontiers

"Pride" was first published in *Frontiers* (Los Angeles), June 21, 1991.

"Lovesick" was first published in *Frontiers*, February 14, 1992.

"A New York State of Mind" was first published in *Frontiers*, January 29, 1993.

"Near the Fire: The March on Washington, 1993" was first published in *Frontiers*, May 21, 1993.

"Amateur Night: On Masks, Gender and the Hellacious Halloween

Hoedown of 1970" was first published in *Frontiers*, October 22, 1993. "Oh, God! Not Again! Confessions of a Reluctant Agnostic" was first published in *Frontiers*, September 10, 1993.

"A Simple Matter of Conversion" and "This is the Story of Kay" are excerpted from *Fragments of Blood*, a novel-in-progress.

ALSO AVAILABLE FROM RICHARD KASAK BOOKS for $12.95

THE BEST OF THE BADBOYS

"...*What I like best about* BADBOY *is the fact that it does not neglect the classics....* BADBOY *Books has resurrected writings from the Golden Age of gayrotic fiction (1966-1972), before visual media replaced books in the hands and minds of the masses....*"
—Jesse Monteagudo, *The Community Voice*

A collection of the best of Masquerade Books' phenomenally popular BADBOY line of gay erotic writing. BADBOY's sizable roster includes many names that are legendary in gay circles. Their work has contributed significantly to BADBOY's runaway success, establishing the imprint as a home for not only new but classic writing in the genre. The very best of the leading Badboys is collected here, in this testament to the artistry that has catapulted these "outlaw" authors to best-selling status. **233-7**

EDITED BY AMARANTHA KNIGHT
LOVE BITES

Vampire lovers, hookers, groupies and hustlers of all sexual persuasions are waiting to entice you into their sensuous world. But be prepared! By the end of this book, you will have not only succumbed to their dark and sexy charms, but you will also have joined the swelling ranks of humanity which understand on a very personal level that Love Bites.—from the Introduction by Amarantha Knight, author of *The Darker Passions: Dracula*

A volume of tales dedicated to legend's sexiest demon—the Vampire. Amarantha Knight, herself an author who has delved into vampire lore, has gathered the very best writers in the field to produce a collection of uncommon, and chilling, allure.

Including such names as Ron Dee, Nancy A. Collins, Nancy Kilpatrick, Lois Tilton and David Aaron Clark, Love Bites is not only the finest collection of erotic horror available—but a virtual who's who of promising new talent. **234-5**

GUILLERMO BOSCH
RAIN

"*The intensely sensual descriptions of color and light, the passionate characters, the sensitive experiences of love and pain depicted in Rain moved me a great deal. Rain is really a trip...*"
—Dr. Timothy Leary

"*Rain definitely pays homage to the European tradition of an erotic literature which stimulates intellectual and moral questioning of social, economic and political institutions. Rain is an important book.*" —Robert Sam Anson, author of *Best Intentions*

"*Rain is a vivid novel that transcends its genre. Only Guillermo Bosch could blend the political and erotic with such ease.*"
—David Freeman, author of *A Hollywood Education*

"*This book will sear the flesh off your fingers.*"—Peter Lefcourt, author of *Di and I*

"*It was Bosch's poetic language which first attracted me to Rain, but his unprejudiced mixing of ethnicity, different sexual persuasions and diverse personalities is unique and most refreshing.*" —Meri Nana-Ana Danquah

An adult fairy tale, *Rain* takes place in a time when the mysteries of Eros are played out against a background of uncommon deprivation. The tale begins on the 1,537th day of drought—when one man comes to know the true depths of thirst. In a quest to sate his hunger for some knowledge of the wide world, he is taken through a series of extraordinary, unearthly encounters that promise to change not only his life, but the course of civilization around him. **232-9**

A RICHARD KASAK BOOK   **$12.95**

MICHAEL LASSELL
THE HARD WAY

"*Michael Lassell's poems are worldly in the best way, defining the arc of a world of gay life in our own decade of mounting horror and oppression. With an effortless feel for dark laughter he roams the city, a startling combination of boulevardier and hooker.... Lassell is a master of the necessary word. In an age of tepid and whining verse, his bawdy and bittersweet songs are like a plunge in cold champagne.*"

—Paul Monette

Virtually all of the material in this book was written and published between 1983 and 1993, although it covers all the years I can remember. The focus, of course, is on the post-Stonewall Liberation Years.... I am, like most writers, horrified to read work written as recently as ten days ago, much less ten years ago, but I have bitten the bullet and made few changes, except when some reference is so out of cultural currency as to obscure my own obscure point, or when I can't remember what the hell I meant by something. But what you see here, is pretty much the way it was the first time it appeared in black and white....

—from the Introduction

The first collection of renowned gay writer Michael Lassell's poetry, fiction and essays. Widely anthologized and a staple of gay literary and entertainment publications nationwide, Lassell is regarded as one of the most distinctive and accomplished talents of his generation. As much a chronicle of post-Stonewall gay life as a compendium of a remarkable writer's work, *The Hard Way* is sure to appeal to anyone interested in the state of contemporary writing.   **231-0**

SAMUEL R. DELANY
THE MAD MAN

For his thesis, graduate student John Marr researches the life and work of the brilliant Timothy Hasler: a philosopher whose career was cut tragically short over a decade earlier. Marr encounters numerous obstacles, as other researchers turn up evidence of Hasler's personal life that is deemed simply too unpleasant. On another front, Marr finds himself increasingly drawn toward more shocking, depraved sexual entanglements with the homeless men of his neighborhood, until it begins to seem that Hasler's death might hold some key to his own life as a gay man in the age of AIDS.

This new novel by Samuel R. Delany not only expands the parameters of what he has given us in the past, but fuses together two seemingly disparate genres of writing and comes up with something which is not comparable to any existing text of which I am aware.... What Delany has done here is take the ideas of Marquis de Sade one step further, by filtering extreme and obsessive sexual behavior through the sieve of post-modern experience....

—Lambda Book Report

The latest novel from Hugo- and Nebula-winning science fiction writer and critic Delany... reads like a pornographic reflection of Peter Ackroyd's Chatterton *or A.S. Byatt's* Possession.... *The pornographic element... becomes more than simple shock or titillation, though, as Delany develops an insightful dichotomy between [his protagonist]'s two worlds: the one of cerebral philosophy and dry academia, the other of heedless, 'impersonal' obsessive sexual extremism. When these worlds finally collide ... the novel achieves a surprisingly satisfying resolution....*

—Publishers Weekly
hardcover 193-4/$23.95

A RICHARD KASAK BOOK $12.95

THE MOTION OF LIGHT IN WATER

"A very moving, intensely fascinating literary biography from an extraordinary writer. Thoroughly admirable candor and luminous stylistic precision; the artist as a young man and a memorable picture of an age."
—William Gibson

"A remarkably candid and revealing...study of an extraordinary and extraordinarily appealing human being, and a fascinating...account of the early days of a significant science fiction writer's career."
—Robert Silverberg

The first unexpurgated American edition of award-winning author Samuel R. Delany's riveting autobiography covers the early years of one of science fiction's most important voices. Beginning with his marriage to the young, remarkably gifted poet Marilyn Hacker, Delany paints a vivid and compelling picture of New York's East Village in the early '60s—a time of unprecedented social change and transformation. Startling and revealing, **The Motion of Light in Water** traces the roots of one of America's most innovative writers. **133-0**

KATHLEEN K.

SWEET TALKERS

Kathleen K. is a professional, in the finest sense of the word. She takes her work seriously, always approaching it with diligence, imagination and backbone; an exceptional judge of character, she manages both customers and employees with a flair that has made her business a success. But many people would dismiss Kathleen's achievements, falling as they do, outside mainstream corporate America.

Here, for the first time, is the story behind the provocative advertisements and 970 prefixes. Kathleen K. opens up her diary for a rare peek at the day-to-day life of a phone sex operator—and reveals a number of secrets and surprises. Because far from being a sleazy, underground scam, the service Kathleen provides often speaks to the lives of its customers with a directness and compassion they receive nowhere else. **192-6**

ROBERT PATRICK

TEMPLE SLAVE

...you must read this book. It draws such a tragic, and, in a way, noble portrait of Mr. Buono: It leads the reader, almost against his will, into a deep sympathy with this strange man who tried to comfort, to encourage and to feed both the worthy and the worthless... It is impossible not to mourn for this man—impossible not to praise this book.
—Quentin Crisp

This is nothing less than the secret history of the most theatrical of theaters, the most bohemian of Americans and the most knowing of queens. Patrick writes with a lush and witty abandon, as if this departure from the crafting of plays has energized him. **Temple Slave** is also one of the best ways to learn what it was like to be fabulous, gay, theatrical and loved in a time at once more and less dangerous to gay life than our own.
—Genre

Temple Slave tells the story of the Espresso Buono—the archetypal alternative performance space—and the wildly talented misfits who called it home in the early 60s. The Buono became the birthplace of a new underground theater—and the personal and social consciousness that would lead to Stonewall and the modern gay and lesbian movement. **Temple Slave** is a kaleidoscopic page from gay history—a riotous tour de force peppered with the verbal fireworks and shrewd insight that are the hallmark of Robert Patrick's work. **191-8**

A RICHARD KASAK BOOK   **$12.95**

LUCY TAYLOR
UNNATURAL ACTS
"A topnotch collection..." —Science Fiction Chronicle
The remarkable debut of a provocative writer. *Unnatural Acts* plunges into the dark side of the psyche, past all pleasantries and prohibitions, and brings to life a disturbing vision of erotic horror. Unrelenting angels and hungry gods play with souls and bodies in Taylor's cosmos: where heaven and hell are merely differences of perspective; where redemption and damnation lie behind the same shocking acts.   *181-0*

DAVID MELTZER
THE AGENCY TRILOGY
With the Essex House edition of *The Agency* in 1968, the highly regarded poet David Meltzer took America on a trip into a hell of unbridled sexuality. The story of a supersecret, Orwellian sexual network, *The Agency* explored issues of erotic dominance and submission with an immediacy and frankness previously unheard of in American literature, as well as presented a vision of an America consumed and dehumanized by a lust for power. This landmark novel was followed by **The Agent**, and **How Many Blocks in the Pile?**—taken with **The Agency,** they confirm Meltzer's position as one of America's early masters of the erotic genre.

...*'The Agency' is clearly Meltzer's paradigm of society; a mindless machine of which we are all 'agents' including those whom the machine supposedly serves....*   —Norman Spinrad
216-7

CARO SOLES
MELTDOWN!
An Anthology of Erotic Science Fiction and Dark Fantasy for Gay Men
Editor Caro Soles has put together one of the most explosive, mind-bending collections of gay erotic writing ever published. **Meltdown!** contains the very best examples of this increasingly popular sub-genre: stories meant to shock and delight, to send a shiver down the spine and start a fire down below. An extraordinary volume, **Meltdown!** presents both new voices and provocative pieces by world-famous writers Edmund White and Samuel R. Delany.   *203-5*

BIZARRE SEX
BIZARRE SEX AND OTHER CRIMES OF PASSION
Edited by Stan Tal
Stan Tal, editor of *Bizarre Sex*, Canada's boldest fiction publication, has culled the very best stories that have crossed his desk—and now unleashes them on the reading public in *Bizarre Sex and Other Crimes of Passion.* Over twenty small masterpieces of erotic shock make this one of the year's most unexpectedly alluring anthologies. Including such masters of erotic horror and fantasy as Edward Lee, Lucy Taylor, Nancy Kilpatrick and Caro Soles, *Bizarre Sex and Other Crimes of Passion,* is a treasure-trove of arousing chills.   *213-2*

GAUNTLET
THE BEST OF *GAUNTLET* Edited by Barry Hoffman
No material, no opinion is taboo enough to violate Gauntlet's *purpose of 'exploring the limits of free expression'—airing all views in the name of the First Amendment.*—Associated Press

Dedicated to "exploring the limits of free expression," *Gauntlet* has, with its semi-annual issues, taken on such explosive topics as race, pornography, political correctness, and media manipulation—always publishing the widest possible range of opinions. Only in *Gauntlet* might one expect to encounter Phyllis Schlafley *and* Annie Sprinkle, Stephen King *and* Madonna—often within pages of one another. The very best, most provocative articles have been gathered by editor-in-chief Barry Hoffman, to make *The Best of Gauntlet* a most provocative exploration of American society's limits. *202-7*

A RICHARD KASAK BOOK $12.95

JOHN PRESTON
MY LIFE AS A PORNOGRAPHER
The erotic nonfiction of John Preston. Includes the title essay, given as the John Pearson Perry Lecture at Harvard University, and the legendary "Good-Bye to Sally Gearhart," and many other provocative writings.

...essential and enlightening...His sex-positive stand on safer-sex education as the only truly effective AIDS-prevention strategy will certainly not win him any conservative converts, but AIDS activists will be shouting their assent.... [My Life as a Pornographer] is a bridge from the sexually liberated 1970s to the more cautious 1990s, and Preston has walked much of that way as a standard-bearer to the cause for equal rights.... —Library Journal

Preston's a model essayist; he writes pellucid prose in a voice that, like Samuel Johnson's, combines authority with entertainment.... My Life as a Pornographer...is not pornography, but rather reflections upon the writing and production of it. Preston ranges from really superb journalism of his interviews with denizens of the S/M demi-mond, particularly a superb portrait of a Colt model Preston calls "Joe" to a brilliant analysis of the "theater" of the New York sex club, The Mineshaft.... In a deeply sex-phobic world, Preston has never shied away from a vision of the redemptive potential of the erotic drive. Better than perhaps anyone in our community, Preston knows how physical joy can bridge differences and make us well.
—Lambda Book Report
135-7

HUSTLING:
A Gentleman's Guide to the Fine Art of Homosexual Prostitution
John Preston solicited the advice of "working boys" from across the country in his effort to produce the ultimate guide to the hustler's world. **Hustling** covers every practical aspect of the business, from clientele and payment options to "specialties," sidelines and drawbacks. No stone is left unturned in this guidebook to the ins and outs of this much-mythologized trade. *137-3*

SKIN TWO
THE BEST OF SKIN TWO   Edited by Tim Woodward
For over a decade, *Skin Two* has served as the bible of the international fetish community. A groundbreaking journal from the crossroads of sexuality, fashion, and art, *Skin Two* specializes in provocative, challenging essays by the finest writers working in the "radical sex" scene. Collected here, for the first time, are the articles and interviews that have established the magazine's singular reputation. Including interviews with cult figures Tim Burton, Clive Barker and Jean Paul Gaultier. *130-6*

MICHAEL PERKINS
THE GOOD PARTS: An Uncensored Guide to Literary Sexuality
Michael Perkins, one of America's only serious critics to regularly scrutinize sexual literature, presents an overview of sex a seen in the pages of over 100 major volumes from the past twenty years.

I decided when I wrote my first column in 1968 that I would take the opportunity presented by Screw to chronicle the inevitable and inexorable rise of an unfairly neglected genre of contemporary writing. I wondered if I would remain interested in the subject for very long, and if the field would not eventually diminish so there would be nothing to review.... Every week since then I have published a thousand-word review, and occasionally a longer essay, devoted to discovering and reporting on the manifestations of sexuality in all kinds of fiction, nonfiction, and poetry. In my columns I cast a wide net (a million words so far) over a subject no one else wanted to take a long look at. It has indeed held my interest.   *186-1*

A RICHARD KASAK BOOK $12.95

LARS EIGHNER
THE ELEMENTS OF AROUSAL

Critically acclaimed gay writer Lars Eighner—whose *Travels with Lizbeth* was chosen by the *New York Times Book Review* as one of the year's notable titles—develops a guideline for success with one of publishing's best kept secrets: the novice-friendly field of gay erotic writing.

In *The Elements of Arousal*, Eighner details his craft, providing the reader with sure advice. Eighner's overview of the gay erotic market paints a picture of a diverse array of outlets for a writer's work. Because, after all, writing is what *The Elements of Arousal* is about: the application and honing of the writer's craft, which brought Lars Eighner fame with not only the steamy *Bayou Boy*, but the profoundly illuminating *Travels with Lizbeth*   *230-2*

MARCO VASSI
THE STONED APOCALYPSE

"...Marco Vassi is our champion sexual energist."—VLS

During his lifetime, Marco Vassi was hailed as America's premier erotic writer and most worthy successor to Henry Miller. His work was praised by writers as diverse as Gore Vidal and Norman Mailer, and his reputation was worldwide. *The Stoned Apocalypse* is Vassi's autobiography, financed by the other groundbreaking erotic writing that made him a cult sensation. Chronicling a cross-country trip on America's erotic byways, it offers a rare glimpse of a generation's sexual imagination.   *132-2*

A DRIVING PASSION

"Let me leave you with A Driving Passion. It is, in effect, an introduction and overview of all his other books, and my hope is that it will lead readers to explore the bold literary contribution of Marco Vassi."   —Norman Mailer

While the late Marco Vassi was primarily known and respected as a novelist, he was also an effective and compelling speaker. *A Driving Passion* collects the wit and insight Vassi brought to his infamously revealing lectures, and distills the philosophy—including the concept of Metasex—that made him an underground sensation. An essential volume.   *134-9*

THE EROTIC COMEDIES

A collection of stories from America's premier erotic philosopher. Marco Vassi was a dedicated iconoclast, and *The Erotic Comedies* marked a high point in his literary career. Scathing and humorous, these stories reflect Vassi's belief in the power and primacy of Eros in American life, as well as his commitment to the elimination of personal repression through carnal indulgence. A wry collection for the sexually adventurous.   *136-5*

THE SALINE SOLUTION

During the Sexual Revolution, Marco Vassi established himself as an intrepid explorer of an uncharted sexual landscape. During this time he also distinguished himself as a novelist, producing *The Saline Solution* to great acclaim. With the story of one couple's brief affair and the events that lead them to desperately reassess their lives, Vassi examines the dangers of intimacy in an age of extraordinary freedom. A remarkably clear-eyed look at the growing pains of a generation.   *180-2*

A RICHARD KASAK BOOK $12.95

PAT CALIFIA
SENSUOUS MAGIC

Sensuous Magic *is clear, succinct and engaging even for the reader for whom S/M isn't the sexual behavior of choice.... Califia's prose is soothing, informative and non-judgmental—she both instructs her reader and explores the territory for them.... When she is writing about the dynamics of sex and the technical aspects of it, Califia is the Dr. Ruth of the alternative sexuality set....*

—*Lambda Book Report*

Don't take a dangerous trip into the unknown—buy this book and know where you're going!
—*SKIN TWO*

Finally, a "how to" sex manual that doesn't involve new age mumbo jumbo or "tricks" that require the agility of a Flying Wallenda.... Califia's strength as a writer lies in her ability to relay information without sounding condescending. If you don't understand a word or concept... chances are it's defined in the handy dictionary in the back.... —*Future sex*

Renowned erotic pioneer Pat Califia provides this honest, unpretentious peek behind the mask of dominant/submissive sexuality—an adventurous adult world of pleasure too often obscured by ignorance and fear. Califia demystifies "the scene" for the novice, explaining the terminology and technique behind many misunderstood sexual practices The adventurous (or just plain curious) lover won't want to miss this ultimate "how to" volume. ***131-4***

For a FREE complete catalog write to:
MASQUERADE BOOKS
Dept Z54K
801 Second Avenue
New York, NY 10017
or Fax 212-986-7355

ORDERING IS EASY!

MC/VISA orders can be placed by calling our toll-free number

PHONE 800-458-9640 / FAX 212 986-7355

or mail the coupon below to:

Masquerade Books, Dept. Y54A 801 Second Avenue New York, NY. 10017

QTY.	TITLE	NO.	PRICE
			FREE
			FREE

All transactions are strictly confidential and we never sell, give or trade any customer's name.

Z54A

SUBTOTAL	
POSTAGE & HANDLING	
TOTAL	

Add $1.00 Postage and Handling for the first book and 50¢ for each additional book. Outside the U.S. add $2.00 for the first book, $1.00 for each additional book. New York State residents add 8-1/4% sales tax.

NAME ─────────────────────────────

ADDRESS ──────────────────────────

CITY ─────── STATE ─────── ZIP ───────

TEL. ( ) ────────────────────────

PAYMENT: ❏ CHECK   ❏ MONEY ORDER   ❏ VISA   ❏ MC

CARD NO. ───────────────── EXP. DATE ──────

PLEASE ALLOW 4-6 WEEKS DELIVERY. NO C.O.D. ORDERS. PLEASE MAKE ALL CHECKS PAYABLE TO MASQUERADE BOOKS. PAYABLE IN U.S. CURRENCY ONLY